SORCERER'S
EDGE

THE TETHERED CITADEL BOOK 3

DAVID HAIR

Jo Fletcher

BOOKS

First published in Great Britain in 2022 by

Jo Fletcher Books
an imprint of
Quercus Editions Ltd
Carmelite House
50 Victoria Embankment
London EC4Y 0DZ

An Hachette UK company

A CIP catalogue record for this book is available
from the British Library

TPB ISBN 978 1 52940 2 100

10 9 8 7 6 5 4 3 2 1

Typeset by Jouve (UK), Milton Keynes

Printed and bound in Great Britain by Clays Ltd, Elcograf S.p.A.

Papers used by Jo Fletcher Books are from well-managed
forests and other responsible sources.

SORCERERS
EDGE

This book is dedicated to healthcare workers the world over, and also to Peter and Hazel Wooding, who invited us to their daughter's wedding in Japan, and to their daughter Chloë, who shared her very special traditional Shinto wedding with us; and to Kelton Boyer, who showed us a very different side of Japan.

TABLE OF CONTENTS

PART 3: THE PURITY OF SACRIFICE

What Has Gone Before

The World of Shamaya

Shamaya, a world orbited by planetary rings, is in the grip of an Ice Age caused by misuse of magic. The polar caps have encroached thousands of miles, engulfing huge tracts of land and constricting humanity into a narrower band of life, two thousand miles either side of the equator.

This magical catastrophe occurred five hundred years ago, when the dominant elite, powerful sorcerers known as Aldar, went to war. They may (or may not) have been a different race who ruled over humanity. They wore masks in public, used a destructive magic called *mizra* and lived long lives of decadence and cruelty.

The collapse of Aldar rule coincided with the discovery of a new form of magic called *praxis*. The antithesis of the unpredictable mizra, praxis emphasises discipline. The credit for discovering praxis is given to a woman, Gerda, a messianic figure within the dominant human religion revering the god Deo. Gerda is said to have slain the last Aldar god-king in his palace at Rath Argentium, triggering the Mizra Wars and the onset of the Ice Age.

Recent History 1000-1530ME (Magnian Era)

At the beginning of the Ice Age, millions of people were displaced, crowding into the equatorial continent of Magnia, the largest landmass free of ice. Three centuries of barbarism ensued, until the 1400s saw a renaissance in which the study of science and art was renewed and political institutions took on increasing democratisation. Personal freedoms grew, accompanied by new wonders from telescopes to clocks to gunpowder, through the alliance of education and the praxis.

But from the 1520s, those freedoms collapsed when the giant, backward kingdom of Bolgravia sought dominance. Using assassination, corruption and war, the Bolgravians defeated the Magnian royal house, then conquered their vassal kingdoms. By 1534, the Bolgravian Empire is dominating the Magnian continent, their rule based on fear and exploitation, military might and superior sorcery, thanks to a mineral called *istariol*.

Istariol and Sorcery

Istariol is a naturally occurring substance which, when utilised by a sorcerer, vastly increases their magical output. Any sorcerer can start a fire, but with istariol, that fire can be an inferno; a magical breeze may become a hurricane; a wave can become a flood. Istariol cannot be manufactured and natural reserves are now few; the Bolgravian Empire controls all mining and distribution, although there is a thriving black market.

Both forms of sorcery, praxis and mizra, require a sorcerer to bind with a familiar spirit which channels and enhances magical energy; they bond when the sorcerer first manifests power in their teens, communicating via words, symbols and gestures. Choosing a benign spirit accesses the praxis, but choosing a wild spirit results in mizra, which is illegal. In Magnia, all mizra-witches exist in secret, for fear of execution.

The Events of Spring and Summer, 1534 (as told in Map's Edge)

In Teshveld, at the western edge of the Magnian continent, an imperial party newly returned from the recently discovered land of Verdessa demands aid from a local healer. One of them, a cartomancer (a magical map-maker), is suffering from a mysterious ailment. The Bolgravian lord commanding the mission menaces the healer and his daughter, demanding they save the dying cartomancer or face punishment.

The healer, Raythe Vyre, is an exiled Otravian sorcerer-lord living incognito. Surreptitiously reading the dying man's encrypted journal, he discovers that traces of istariol have been found in Verdessa. He sees this as a chance to restore his fortunes and strike back against the empire. He is unable to save the man, and is facing exposure and death, so Raythe kills the Bolgravians and steals the journal.

Istariol must be mined, so Raythe recruits surreptitiously in Teshveld. Soon after, a caravan of three hundred souls quietly slips out of Teshveld, taking the northeastern Ghost Road. Accompanying Raythe are his daughter Zarelda and some trusted comrades: the Shadran blademaster Jesco Duretto, the Deist priestess Varahana, and the bearskin Vidar Vidarsson, a shapeshifting berserker.

The travellers comprise three factions: a third are Teshveld villagers led by Varahana and the healer Kemara Solus. The trappers and hunters are loosely led by Cal Foaley. The remaining third are the duplicitous Sir Elgus Rhamp's company of mercenaries. Conflicts soon arise, mostly involving Rhamp's men.

Despite Raythe's best efforts, their exodus hasn't gone unnoticed. Toran Zorne, a sorcerer-assassin of the Ramkiseri, the Bolgravian Secret Service, was already on Raythe's trail. He commandeers soldiers and ships and sets off in pursuit, catching the travellers as they cross into Verdessa. As the ships' cannons and marines prepare to annihilate the fugitives, all appears to be lost.

But the day is saved when Kemara reveals an unsuspected power: she is a sorceress, not of the praxis but the illegal and deadly mizra. Linking her magic to Raythe's in a bonding called a meld expands their individual power, and augmented by istariol, they are able to destroy one imperial ship and drive the other away. A meld between opposing forms of magic is supposed to be impossible; it's certainly far deadlier than any bond Raythe has experienced before. To allay fears, Raythe and Kemara keep her mizra secret by pretending she used the praxis.

The expedition follows the trail of the istariol out of Verdessa into the northern ice wastes, following a river that's been frozen for five hundred years. They believe they've eluded the empire, but Toran Zorne is with them, pretending to be a wounded sailor they fished from the sea. He's secretly using praxis to guide the pursuers.

Nevertheless, the travellers manage to stay ahead. They find a vast patch of fertile land deep within the ice wastes: a clear sign that istariol is present. At the heart of this region is an ancient ruined city built on an old hollow mountain – and floating above is the peak with a castle at the summit, broken away from it but tethered to the ground by giant chains. They have discovered Rath Argentium, once the heart of the Aldar civilisation.

But no sooner have they found this legendary place than they're assailed by the pursuing imperial forces. Spotting campfires away to the east, Zarelda goes to investigate with Banno Rhamp, the boy she's in love with – but they're captured by a hitherto unknown tribe of people, the Tangato, a human tribe trapped here for five hundred years and believing themselves the last people alive.

During the imperial attack, Toran Zorne battles Raythe and Kemara, who he believes to be mizra-witches. But Zorne, defeated, falls into a canyon river and is swept away, once again believed dead.

While Raythe leads his people across the ancient bridge into the ruined city, the Bolgravians, out of gunpowder and taken by surprise, are annihilated by the Tangato . . . who then encircle Rath Argentium.

Raythe's expedition has found the istariol, and so much more. But will they ever be able to leave?

The Events of Autumn, 1534 (as told in World's Edge)

Fearing a Tangato attack, Raythe's people have taken refuge in the ruins of Rath Argentium. However, the Tangato are curious and offer a parley, sending a young female sorcerer called Rima to treat with Raythe. They discover a common language, for Gengo, the Tangato ceremonial language, is the root language of Magnian, the language of Raythe's people. Raythe pleads for time, and is given permission to meet the Tangato Queen.

Raythe's daughter Zarelda, and Sir Elgus' son Banno Rhamp, are prisoners of the Tangato. But Zar, a sorcerer like her father, has been claimed by Rima and her master Hetaru for the tribe. Banno, who's in a concussion-induced coma, holds no value for the Tangato, so to save his life, Zar pretends he is her husband.

Raythe meets with the Tangato Queen, a masked woman named Shiazar, and her senior advisors. They reveal that the Tangato, who once served the legendary Aldar, survived the Ice Age because of the soil-warming properties of the istariol in the region, which they call the Fenua Tangato. Startlingly, Shiazar reveals that the Tangato elite, all female, are part-Aldar: they call themselves Yokei. The Queen demands that Raythe's expedition depart, but allows them a month's truce to replenish supplies. As a token of faith, the comatose Banno is returned to Raythe's people for treatment.

Living among the Tangato, Zar makes the startling discovery that the Tangato sorcerers Hetaru and Rima are far stronger magically than even her father. They help her become more powerful by introducing her to maho, a style of sorcery that blends the best of the praxis (controllable and constructive); and the mizra (strong and fast). Rima takes her to Lake Waiotapu, where a giant mechanism of concentric metal circles remains, a sphere-gate built by the old Aldar. There Zar encounters Onkado, a likable young Tangato man from another tribe, and begins to see her captors in a new light.

Raythe's plan is to extract as much istariol as possible from the mines below the city, then lead his people home, and initial searches of the mines are promising. During those explorations, Jesco picks up a ring that subtly alters his personality. However, Raythe's plans are beset by treachery: Elgus Rhamp's lieutenants launch a coup (not supported by Rhamp himself), intending to seize all the istariol, then abandon everyone else and run. On a bloody night, they come within a whisker of succeeding, but are defeated.

Raythe leads further exploration of the mine, but with disappointing results, which makes Varahana, a scholar as well as a priestess, start to think that the istariol is actually in the soil surrounding the city, not beneath it, and thus out of their reach. The Magnian refugees are in despair.

As the truce runs down, fresh crises develop: Kemara and Jesco, guided by the mysterious ring, discover a way up to Shiro Kamigami, the floating citadel, riding a flying stone platform up to the fortress. However, that drains the platform's final energy and it crashes to the ground, trapping the pair above.

Shiazar has called a major gathering of the Tangato, including the warlike Manowai tribe, led by the fierce Ikendo and his son Onkado, who Zar met at Lake Waiotapu. Ikendo challenges Shiazar's leadership, claiming she's betrayed her people by tolerating Raythe's intruders. To her shock, her Yokei sisters uphold the challenge, which means her champions must fight a ritual combat. Rima is unaccountably missing, so Zar takes her place, and Ikendo's champions prevail. Ikendo and Onkado are revealed as part-Aldar, the first males of their kind since the fall of the Aldar. Ikendo takes the throne and condemns Shiazar to death. Zar is also condemned, but is protected by Onkado, who claims her as his bride, while promising her he won't abuse her vulnerable position. She reluctantly agrees, which infuriates Ikendo.

Rima went missing due to a treacherous attack by Ikendo's servants, but Raythe finds and rescues her. Soon after, there is another arrival in the city: Shiazar has escaped and now throws herself on Raythe's mercy. She and Raythe make a new agreement: he will protect her in return for her aid against Ikendo's forces. Shiazar and Rima help Raythe to repair the flying disc, so that he can attempt a rescue of Kemara and Jesco from the citadel above.

Matters come to a head: Ikendo launches an assault upon the city, whilst his Yokei empower the sphere-gate, opening another way up to Shiro Kamigami. From there, Ikendo purposes to reactivate ancient Aldar weaponry and destroy Raythe's people from above. However, Raythe and Shiazar have just ridden the stone disc up to the citadel, where a deadly struggle ensues for its control.

In the city below, Elgus Rhamp commands the defence, unaware that Ikendo's Manowai warriors are slipping into the city from the rear, until Zar, who's seen the troop movements, manages to escape the Tangato camp to bring a warning. Elgus is slain, but Cal Foaley, Vidar and Varahana lead a desperate final defence, praying that Raythe will return and save them.

In the banquet hall of Shiro Kamigami, Kemara and Jesco penetrate a bubble of frozen time, in which the dreaded Aldar prince Tashvariel the Usurper is still alive. Their arrival breaks the spell, bringing the insane Aldar lord into the present. Ikendo and the Yokei are slain by Tashvariel and Jesco and Kemara are at his mercy – until they unite, using Raythe's praxis, Kemara's mizra and Shiazar's maho to slay Tashvariel. In the fight, Kemara loses her mizra familiar, and therefore her magic. Raythe and Shiazar are able to return to the lower city in time to effect a ceasefire and save Raythe's people.

With Ikendo dead, Shiazar takes Onkado prisoner and reclaims the throne. She gives Raythe an ultimatum: he and his people must remain as her subjects. With no choice, Raythe agrees. Hostilities cease and Raythe's people celebrate, although there are mixed feelings about remaining in the Fenua Tangato for ever.

However, their dreams of peace may be short-lived: Toran Zorne, thought to be dead, has returned to Magnia, where he is approaching Luc Mandaryke, Raythe's nemesis. Mandaryke immediately vows to conquer these new lands for the empire – and to kill Raythe.

Prologue

Servant of the Greater Good

From the balcony of his suite in the Mandaryke family mansion on Kalla Vista Heights, Toran Zorne could see the beating heart of Perasdyne, the capital of Otravia, the greatest city of the western empire, its famed oak-lined boulevards gilded by autumn's touch, basking in the afterglow of another prosperous day.

Thriving under imperial rule, Zorne mused, *with dissent silenced, every threat to Order quelled and the Greater Good allowed to prevail.*

It was nearly five years since the Otravian Republic had surrendered to Bolgravia. After initial victories, Otravia fell from within when imperial sympathisers, led by the Mandarykes, seized power. Zorne remembered it well. He'd been assigned to covert operations within the capital, specifically to silence anti-imperial voices. Lists of key Liberali Party supporters supplied by Mandaryke's people enabled his team to reap a deadly harvest, easing the transition to the new Bolgravian-sympathetic rule. In many ways, he'd made Luc Mandaryke the man he was today, including his elevation to Western Governor of the Empire.

But that was the past, and now he wondered if he'd been right to come here. Rath Argentium was a massive prize, so protocol demanded he go straight to the Western Governor, but when it came down to it, Mandaryke wasn't Bolgravian. Should he put ambition ahead of his duty to Bolgravia, he could threaten the imperial throne itself.

'Master Zorne?' a voice called from behind him.

Zorne had already detected the servant's approach, assessed any potential threat and dismissed it. Without turning, he said, 'Yuz?'

'Governor Mandaryke requires you attend his meeting,' the servant said uneasily. He was an older man, one who'd witnessed his nation's 'disgrace', so his loyalty couldn't be taken for granted. Zorne had noted the way his facial features tightened at the sound of his Bolgravian accent.

He hates me, and he may even be a rebel spy.

'What is your name?' he asked, staring at the man.

'Rofort, sir,' he replied, clearly discomforted at the attention.

'Have you served the Governor long?'

'Fifteen years, sir,' Rofort answered, shuffling nervously.

Zorne mused on the different ways he could kill him. *Dagger to the throat, or slam the back of his skull onto one of the balcony spikes . . . or just pitch him head-first over the railing?* Luc Mandaryke wouldn't question it: a Ramkiseri, a Bolgravian Secret Service agent, answered only to the Imperial Throne. Zorne had been a law unto himself for most of his career.

But whatever guilty secret Rofort harbours is likely just some abuse of status, he decided. *And perhaps knowing he's corruptible will be useful one day.*

'I know the way,' he told Rofort. 'Dismissed.'

He waited until the servant was gone, then faced the mirror. An impassive, clean-shaven face with iron-grey eyes framed by cropped brown hair looked back at him. It was an unsettling visage, when he wished it to be, and that suited him far more than being handsome. His tunic was clean, his jacket passable. Deciding he'd suffice, he turned his mind to the meeting ahead: another duel of civility, prestige and innuendo he'd rather avoid, but couldn't. So he reset the little traps that would indicate if anyone entered the room in his absence, then wound his way through the guest wing to the governor's ceremonial hall.

'Under-Komizar Zorne,' the doorman announced as he entered – and the room stopped. The novelty of meeting a known Ramkiseri was rare for most, though all senior officials would – unwittingly – have at least one in their household, monitoring them for the empire.

Just nine people awaited him in the vast space. These people would be his companions on the road ahead, his allies in name, but each one a potential enemy, and not least his host, Governor Luc Mandaryke. The governor, the highest representative of the Bolgravian Empire in Otravia, cut a flamboyant figure, wearing embroidered velvets so intricate that he looked like a walking tapestry. Blond, square-jawed and handsome, he was famed as a gentleman sorcerer and noble, the man all highborn Otravian virgins dreamed of, or so it was said.

Luc's face lit up as he came to greet Zorne, as if he was the missing piece in a puzzle he'd been battling to complete. 'Ah, the man himself! Toran, my friend, come and meet our fellow travellers!'

His wife had followed him: Mirella Mandaryke was an exquisitely beautiful woman, despite being in her thirties and a mother. Her dress was all delicate pastel hues, more like confectionary than cloth, and dripping in jewels. Her honey-blonde hair gleamed. Only her face didn't shine: she wore a sour look as she contemplated Zorne.

Because of me, her husband is whisking her off the edge of the map, rather than leaving her alone here in Perasdyne. Zorne had no sympathy: Mirella had chosen her bed. With Great Houses came great risks, and House Mandaryke was the greatest in Otravia. *And leaving her here would indeed be foolish. She's a serpent.*

Despite his distaste, he went to her first, kissed her reluctant hand, clicked his heels and bowed. 'Milady, you are as fair as sunrise over Reka-Dovoi,' he recited, a line from a Bolgrav poem. Then he faced the adherents Luc had assembled for the mission. 'My Lords.'

'Toran Zorne, you know my father by reputation, I'm sure,' Luc said, introducing a vision of his own future: a stout, balding giant with broken blood vessels in his cheeks and suspicious eyes. 'Premier Rodias Mandaryke, this is Komizar Zorne.'

'Under-Komizar,' Zorne corrected by reflex, noting Luc's wry smile. He suspected the governor deliberately misspoke his rank to amuse himself. 'I am honoured, sir.'

The Premier – officially the ruler of Otravia, as long as he did what the Emperor wanted – puffed up. 'So you're the man who lit this fire? House Mandaryke thanks you, Zorne.'

Touching the premier's hand was a queasy experience, because treachery disgusted Zorne, even when it benefited his Emperor. Traitors to their own country could readily betray another.

We should have beheaded these scum once we seized this country.

But he hid his distaste and feigning camaraderie, turned to the next in line.

'Toran Zorne,' said Luc, 'this is Ferdan Verdelho, Imperial Courser.'

Zorne assessed Verdelho, a dapper man with fashionable moustaches, as dangerous. There was an ages-old rivalry between the Coursers, who were emissaries of the Imperial Court, and the Ramkiseri. Their duties overlapped and they constantly came into conflict, something the Emperor apparently encouraged.

Next were two generals; one in Otravian red and the other in Bolgravian grey. 'This is General Nemath Torland, who will command the Otravian division, and General Romoi Lisenko, who'll lead the imperial division.' It was mandatory that any military operation in a vassal state be at least half Bolgravian.

'Zorne,' said General Torland, who was one of Luc's drinking comrades. He was a tall, elegant-looking man, with a somewhat feminine air that belied his reputation: when Otravia fell he'd been placed in charge of enforcing the imperial Perversion Dictates: exterminating Liberali subcultures – artists, playwrights and musicians who didn't embrace the new regime, homosexuals, immigrants and the disabled, suspected mizra-witches, and anything else he decided might be a threat or liability to society. Torland had earned the nickname 'Torcher' for the number of people who'd been burned in his reign of terror. Zorne had met him before, and knew Torland disliked him. The feeling was mutual.

'Under-Komizar,' Romoi Lisenko greeted him. He had the reputation of being a blusterer with little talent, which fuelled Zorne's fears that the governor was using this expedition to further himself, not the empire.

Zorne kept his face neutral as he bowed. 'Exalted General.'

Luc turned to the sorcerers who would accompany the mission. All Ramkiseri were sorcerers as well as trained assassins, so rival magicians were therefore of prime interest. An army division typically had two or three senior sorcerers attached, plus up to a dozen juniors, who were beneath anyone's notice. The two senior Bolgravian sorcerers were introduced as Tresorov and Drusyn; the elder was a hollow-eyed man with lank silver hair, the junior a skinny youth with uncertain features. Zorne had never heard of them, which was another concern: if the empire valued this mission as they should, they'd have sent better men than these no-names.

Mandaryke is stacking the deck with his own cards.

His unease grew when he turned to the final guest, the Otravian sorcerer. Non-imperial divisions were allowed only one senior sorcerer and despite her youthful looks, she radiated puissance. Her long hair was prematurely grey and her skin's deathly pallor was accentuated by her white clothing. Her violet eyes looked empty.

'This is Lady Teirhinan, of the Imperial Otravian Order of Magic,' Luc Mandaryke told Zorne, his voice solemn. 'We are honoured that the Order saw fit to lend us their best.'

Zorne knew the name, of course. Everyone did. *Teirhinan Deathless.*

Some called her a saint; others thought her mad – but no one said that to her face. He'd heard that she'd killed then resurrected herself, to enhance her power – that wasn't theoretically possible, but in her presence it was hard to deny. 'An honour,' he murmured, recognising a kindred spirit: she was as single-minded as he was.

'Master Zorne,' she replied. Her voice was scratchy, her breath foul. 'Your reputation precedes you.'

Does it? Zorne didn't like having a reputation. Self-effacement was a defining credo of the Ramkiseri.

Luc Mandaryke stepped in. 'Take a glass, my friends. This is a solemn moment. We represent Otravia and Bolgravia, working together to eliminate a dangerous rebel.' He gestured and servants appeared with trays of sparkling wine.

Once they'd finished handing them around and had vanished again, Luc Mandaryke raised his glass. 'Five years ago, when my father and I signed a treaty between Otravia and Bolgravia, there were dissidents who failed to see the wisdom of alliance, preferring to fight on in a vainglorious resistance. Tens of thousands died until we crushed it.'

And thus the victors rewrite history, Zorne mused cynically.

'We have hunted down the ringleaders, and now just one remains at large,' Luc said, 'and now we know where to find him. Let us drink to the imminent death of Raythe Vyre.'

As they drank, Zorne tried to read Mirella's face, but she was inscrutable. She met his gaze coolly, then looked away, leaving him none the wiser.

You were married to Vyre – and you betrayed him for Mandaryke. That makes you Otravia personified.

Ever since Zorne had arrived with his tale of Raythe Vyre, lost peoples and a legendary city surmounted by a floating citadel, utmost secrecy had prevailed. Mandaryke would need an army to seize Rath Argentium, and that required the cooperation of the Bolgravian military – but all Luc had told the imperial court was that Vyre had been found in Verdessa and a military expedition would be required to defeat him.

If we even breathe the words 'istariol' or 'Rath Argentium', every nation will seek to intervene, Luc had told Zorne, which made sense: istariol, the mineral that enhanced sorcery, was the most valuable commodity in existence. But Zorne worried that Mandaryke wanted it all for himself. Every day he wondered if it was time to inform his Ramkiseri masters. Luc had asked him not to, 'friend to friend', and Zorne had so far acquiesced. But Mandaryke was the only non-Bolgravian governor in the empire, an anomaly that had always worried Zorne.

I know they helped us greatly, but we should never have left these traitors in charge. The entire ruling class should have been massacred, starting with him.

Luc lowered his glass and gestured towards the far doors that led to the banquet hall. 'Let us dine, my friends,' he said grandly. 'We have a long journey ahead of us.'

PART ONE

Stranger Here

1

Trust

Trust is hard, Raythe Vyre remembered reading somewhere. No one is self-sufficient, so we must lean on others, placing our lives in their hands. But how well do we know them? Just because we've shared food, laughter or a bed doesn't mean they wish us well. Yet we must trust someone, because solitude is impossible.

Some days Raythe wondered whether he shouldn't try disproving that theory by becoming a hermit, because sometimes the turmoil of daily life didn't seem worth the risk of having another blade – metaphorical or actual – thrust into his back.

My wife left me for my best friend, who betrayed our country and everything I love. I've fought an empire and lost, and even out here, beyond the known world, I've been repeatedly deceived.

He wasn't sure why he was feeling so gloomy, the morning after a miraculous escape from annihilation, but it had been costly. Of the three hundred who'd set out on this mad journey with him, barely two hundred remained. Most of the losses had been men, who'd borne the brunt of the fighting. Many widows had been left with children to feed; he could hear them now, mourning below.

But the real reason for his morose mood, he decided, was that all their tribulations had been for nothing. He'd promised them riches and freedom, but instead they were stranded with nothing to show for all their blood, sweat and belief. Last night, to stop the slaughter, he'd agreed peace terms with Queen Shiazar of the Tangato, and that meant they would join the Tangato nation – and remain here for ever.

I still don't really know how I feel about that . . .

He was profoundly grateful to have survived, and to have found a way to save his people, but it was a high price to pay, giving up on everything they'd come here for. So much for their dreams of istariol and wealth, and returning to their homelands as free people. Now they'd never go home again.

I've failed them, which is pretty much the same as betraying them. And that was why, he reluctantly admitted to himself, he was hiding on the roof of the mansion they'd named Rim House, watching the dawn.

If he looked down, he'd see bodies lying around the grounds and piled up beside the crater rim fence, where the fighting had been fiercest. Instead, he looked up. Silhouetted against the pale glow of the planetary rings was a dark rock hanging in the air, tethered by four massive chains rooted in the lower slopes of the hill upon which Rath Argentium was built. Atop that rock, out of his sight, was the citadel, Shiro Kamigami, where another battle had been fought last night, a sorcerers' duel against the deadliest foe imaginable. The after-images of that insane battle against a mad Aldar lord, in a place where time fluctuated and the past had come to life, still haunted him.

Shiazar, Kemara and I prevailed – but only just. We won the chance to move forward and fight another day. The sun would rise soon: life went on, and his people were his responsibility.

He stood, his joints creaking in the cold, reflecting ruefully that for all he was only in his thirties, he was no longer a young man. He shoved aside that unwelcome thought and gazed out over the ruined city, marvelling anew at the view.

Rath Argentium had been the seat of the Aldar Kings, a city built upon a hill so full of istariol that the peak had broken away and now floated above, leaving a massive crater. The city had been uninhabited for five centuries, but the Aldar had built well, and the place was surprisingly intact.

Beyond the city were plains, forests and hills, rivers and lakes – but for less than a hundred miles in any direction, for this miraculous place, lush and verdant by grace of the istariol in the soil, was deep within the Icewastes; that was how the Tangato had survived the Ice Age that devastated the rest of the planet.

Light footsteps brought him back to the present and he turned, not sure who he was expecting, but still surprised when a dark-skinned woman wearing a flax kilt and bodice and wrapped in a feather cloak appeared. Black hair billowed around her lively, pugnacious face.

'Rima – what is it?' he asked, worried some new emergency had arisen.

The young Tangato grinned at his anxious expression. 'There's no problem. The Queen merely asks that you attend upon her at noon. There's much to arrange.'

'That's the truth,' he sighed. 'We must recover our dead and prepare them for burial, secure food and water and move back into the buildings we've been living in. That's assuming my people don't just shoot me for bargaining away their right to go home. They'll take some convincing.'

'My Queen believes strongly in your ability to talk.'

He snorted at the backhanded compliment. 'How does the Queen fare?'

'She has reclaimed her throne, Ikendo is dead and his son Onkado imprisoned, and all praise her for ending this conflict and asserting authority over your kind. Some are unhappy that she arrived in time to save your people, but most are just pleased to see peace restored.'

'That's nice,' Raythe drawled. 'Is Zar all right?'

When he'd been briefly reunited with his daughter last night, he'd expected her to rejoin him, but she'd chosen to return to the Tangato village where she'd spent months as a prisoner. She'd also announced she was married to Onkado, son of the man who'd usurped Shiazar's throne: a man of *Aldar* blood.

Onkado did it to protect me, but it's not been consummated, she'd reassured him, and rationally, he understood – but he hated his inability to protect her.

'Zarelda is well,' Rima reassured him. 'Midday, just over the bridge, Rangatira Raythe.'

Shiazar had made him rangatira, or chieftain of his 'tribe', the Ngati Magnia in her tongue. He wasn't yet sure if that was a gift or a curse. 'I'll be there,' he told her.

She bobbed her head and was gone, and Raythe turned back to the dawn, to prepare himself for the arguments and anger he'd face today.

'My Queen believes strongly in your ability to talk.'

It was all right for Shiazar: she was Aldar and was revered by her people. Magnians, on the other hand, viewed dissent against authority as their Deo-given right. But that attitude also made them resilient and adaptable, virtues they'd certainly needed on this journey.

Thinking about the Tangato Queen and her Aldar blood was its own maze of miracles. Though Shiazar was the child of an Aldar woman and a Tangato man, being 'part-Aldar' didn't really exist: anyone with Aldar blood was Aldar, a being of innate sorcery, requiring no familiar to use magic. She usually wore a mask, but he'd seen her inhumanly beautiful, timeless face and been entranced. She was a courageous woman, dedicated to all her people, Aldar and Tangato alike. In the short time he'd known her, he'd come to admire her immensely.

The sun broke through the eastern hills; bouncing shards of colour fractured on the unseen ice sheets beyond the rim of the Fenua Tangato, a sight to dazzle even his tired, jaded eyes. Then Magga Kern's roosters crowed and a baby cried in the rooms below, setting off others.

It was time to rejoin his people and face their music.

'Kragga mor, Raythe, could you not have gained us *something*?' shouted Relf Turner.

'Did ye promise them our firstborn while you were at it?' Ardo Myle threw in.

A storm of voices rose, some adding to the condemnation, others backing him, making the Rim House courtyard throb. They'd woken to grief, trauma and empty stomachs, all of which distilled into vocal anger.

He'd explained the terms of his deal with Shiazar the previous evening and they'd accepted it then, for anything was better than death. But now they'd slept on it, of course they had a thousand questions, picking away at details he couldn't even answer –

'Will these barbarians try and kill us the moment we drop our guard?'

'What about our guns? Will we have to give them up?'

'Can't we ever visit Magnia?'

'Can't we even trade?'

'What does being a 'tribe' actually mean?'

'Who owns the land we've been given?'

'What's a kragging *rangatira* anyway? What if we want another leader?'

He was about ready to tell them to *go ahead and restart your kragging war* – but that would do no one any good; this needed to be worked through. 'The Pitlord writes in the margins' went the old saying: you had to get the details right in any contract if you didn't want the knives to come out later.

Thankfully, he had some support.

Vidar Vidarsson, the gruff Norgan ranger, called out, 'You're damned lucky we've got a Raythe to pull our fat from the fire.'

Jesco Duretto told them some of what he'd seen in the citadel above, concluding, 'Without Raythe and Kemara, we were all done.'

Even Kemara, who seldom took Raythe's side, admitted, 'You know what I think of Lord Vyre most times. Well, this time, he got it right – thank Gerda and Deo.'

But it wasn't until Mater Varahana, the shaven-scalped Deist priestess whose flock included most of the caravan, rose to speak that the tide of anger began to ebb. 'Shame on you all,' she started. 'We've been gifted our lives, when we all expected to die. This is the beginning of a process, and after Raythe's meeting with the Queen at noon, we'll know more. And we all know one thing for sure: he'll be fighting our corner – as he's always done.'

That took the wind from the protestors' sails, and though there were still mutterings, most agreed that Raythe had saved them and the rest could follow.

'But we do need those answers,' Gravis Tavernier grumbled. 'We din' come're to found a colony, least of all one we don' even rule. We was always meant to go home.'

'Aye, an' go home rich,' Lynd Borger added.

'So did I,' Raythe admitted. 'I fought the empire for four years before this trek, and I intended to return to that struggle. But sometimes our destinies don't match our dreams. If Deo has denied me my chance at revenge, I'll accept His will, not fight it.'

If you want to win an argument, invoke God, he thought, throwing Varahana a grateful look. *Even better, get a priestess to do it for you.*

With that, the debate more or less fizzled out. Time was passing and there was much to do. They needed to reclaim their homes in the bridge district and start rebuilding their lives, yet again.

As he made for the doors, Raythe glanced at Vidar. The Norgan's attention was entirely on Varahana, watching her with aching eyes. *He's in love.* He'd seen the signs, and heard how in the midst of the battle, the bearskin and the priestess had kissed. When Varahana looked back at Vidar, he knew it was mutual.

Something else we'll have to work out, Raythe worried, as he headed for the bridge.

Cal Foaley, the senior hunter, joined him on the road down. 'Looks like the Tangato are keeping their side of the deal, Raythe. They're recovering bodies but keeping clear of us, for now, at least.'

That was a major concession, as there were many Tangato bodies in the city. Raythe took it as a sign that Shiazar was in control of her people.

'Keep your eyes open. I trust Shiazar, but some might hold a grudge.'

Foaley raised a thumb. 'Already on it, Chief . . . or "Rangatira", if you prefer?'

Raythe snorted humourlessly as they parted, but he was immediately intercepted by Kemara Solus, their healer and mizra-sorceress. 'Lord Vyre,' she greeted him ironically, as she fell into step.

'Thanks for speaking up,' he replied. 'It's appreciated.'

'It's the most I could do,' she answered drily.

Up close, she looked terrible. She was naturally pale, like most red-heads, but today she looked completely wrung out, her eyes bloodshot and her lips cracked. Her thick hair was matted and dirty and she was covered in bruises, cuts and grazes. Yesterday she'd lost more than most: she'd freed her mizra familiar, banishing that dark spirit. She was, right now, a sorceress without magic.

Back in the empire, mizra-witches like her were burned, and even out here, they hadn't dared let anyone else know what she was. But she and Raythe shared a sorcerous meld. That was a rare occurrence, even between praxis-sorcerers – and unprecedented between the different strands of magic. They'd overcome much by working together. He feared what she was, but he needed her.

'We'll get you a new familiar,' he said quietly. 'I mean it. Our meld has saved our lives, and many times over.'

'So you want me restored to being useful,' she harrumphed, difficult as ever.

'I value you, Kemara–'

'How sweet – whereas I regard you as a half-arsed chancer who takes on massive tasks with no real plan or preparation, relying on wits and luck to pull you through.'

Harsh . . .

'No one's perfect.'

'Kragga mor.' She met his gaze. 'Honestly? The mizra was killing me. I don't want it.'

'Fair enough,' he said regretfully, and turned to move on, but she caught his arm.

'I haven't given up entirely. Rima has a form of magic she calls "maho". She says she can teach me, as she did Zarelda.' She sounded unusually hopeful.

'I'm told it nearly killed Zar,' Raythe warned, 'and you're our only fully trained healer and midwife.'

'I won't risk it until we're through this mess,' she assured him, then she gave him a hard look. 'Will you really stop fighting the empire? Or were those just political words?'

Not long ago, he'd have died before giving up, but it felt impossible now. 'I meant it.'

'Look at you, going all "better man" on us,' she snorted, before pointing upwards. 'What about that floating castle? You've seen what's up there: hourglasses that *stop time* . . . and enough istariol to level a mountain. We must have a say about how it's handled.'

She wasn't wrong, although it was uncharacteristically big-picture thinking for Kemara; she usually only fought her own corner. 'Absolutely,' Raythe agreed. 'I've told Queen Shiazar she needs our help with it. She'll keep us involved, I'm sure.'

Kemara raised sceptical eyebrows. 'Your new sweetheart.'

'She is not,' he answered curtly.

'Knew that'd rile you.' Kemara drawled. 'Go on, Lord Vyre, go and play at rangatira – and don't give her an inch.'

When she turned to go, he called, 'Wait – why don't you come with me? You're a sorcerer – a *mahotsu-kai*, as they say here. They'll accept your right to attend. And you're worth listening to – even if you think I don't.'

He doubted she'd ever thought of herself in such a way, despite being part of his leadership group from the first day.

But she shook her head. 'We've got to move the wounded back to the infirmary, and two women are close to labour. I can't waste time jawing with the high and mighty.'

He went to protest, then let her go. *Chances are we would end up arguing in front of the Tangato chiefs, anyway. No one needs that.*

He went to meet the Queen of the Tangato.

Zarelda Vyre was washed and dressed early. Today would be her first time attending upon the Queen. Nerves and the trauma of the previous day had kept her awake most of the night and now she was yawning as she sat at her door, watching the Tangato village come to life.

Her secret wedding to Onkado, her escape and frantic flight to the city still made her head spin. But she knew her warning of the Tangato attack from the rear had saved lives. And she'd survived the fighting – although she'd *hated* having to kill – and now they had a truce. She was still struggling to take it all in.

But her thoughts were mostly of Banno Rhamp, who she'd thought she loved; and Onkado of the Manowai, who'd protected her when no one else could.

She and Onkado hadn't consummated their marriage, so by Magnian law, it could be annulled. *But it wasn't a Magnian marriage*, Zar thought, *so who knows? And if it is annulled, I'll lose my right to plead for his life and Shiazar will be obliged to execute him, to prevent him from becoming a rallying point for another coup.*

It should have been simple: let Onkado die and the problem went away. She could go back to her people and marry Banno, and everyone would think she'd done the right thing.

But in all the chaos, Banno had broken her blind faith in him. The young warrior Hekami had saved her from drowning, but Banno, thinking Hekami was attacking Zar, had killed him. When she'd confronted him, shocked and upset, Banno had struck her.

'He *hit* me,' she whispered aloud. He'd given her a 'tap', he'd said – *like men do to hysterical women.*

She wasn't sure she could ever forgive him for that, so after her father had accepted terms, it'd been easiest to plead tiredness and return to the Hiriwa village, trusting in Shiazar's authority that she'd be safe, and giving her time alone to think things over.

And as for the new treaty and the prospect of staying here for ever? *Back in Magnia, Father and I were fugitives and all we did was run and hide. But here, I'm a mahotsu-kai serving an Aldar Queen!*

And then there was Onkado . . .

She remembered standing with him before Kuia, the Tangato priestess who'd married them, and how his unmasked Aldar face had amazed her, beautiful and eerie as a mountain at dawn, a lord of light and air. And how brave and noble he'd been, and thoughtful.

He could have had anyone, *but he chose to protect me, even though it enraged his father.*

Perhaps it was just chivalry? But what if it was more? Banno was solid, eager and comforting, but utterly earthbound. Onkado's mystery fascinated her. She'd always wanted a life that was more than ordinary, and she firmly believed that had planted the seed of sorcery inside her. *I want to find out more about him.* Admitting that to herself made her gut churn, but it didn't change her mind. She remembered her mother Mirella saying 'we're so alike' – meaning, she was drawn to shiny things and tenacious in pursuing them. She pushed that thought away; she hated thinking about her mother, who was a *Mandaryke* now.

Just then, Rima appeared, calling, 'Are you ready? The Queen's about to leave.'

They pressed noses in greeting and Rima grinned and brushed her fingers over Zar's ridged chin, which bore similar tattoos to her own. 'It's your first time attending her in counsel, so just follow my lead – and stay silent unless you're invited to speak.'

'Will the chiefs accept me?'

'Of course – the Queen commands it. You're one of us now.'

Clearly not everyone thought so, judging by the surly looks she got from the rangatiras and mahotsu-kai of the sub-tribes gathered outside Shiazar's wood-and-bamboo palace. The gaudily coloured royal palanquin awaited, with four bronze-skinned warriors dressed in ceremonial flax kilts waiting to heft it. To Zar's eyes, Tangato culture was a strange mix of almost barbaric simplicity and intricate beauty.

A gong sounded, silk-screen doors opened and the Queen emerged.

Yesterday, Shiazar had descended from Shiro Kamigami holding the head of the usurper Ikendo, with Onkado, his son, kneeling at her feet. She'd been masked, armoured and drenched in blood: a true Goddess of War.

Today, she was clad in beautiful emerald and yellow silks, which, Rima whispered, symbolised peace. Her mask was yellow too, rimmed with leaves of oak and laurel, and her hair was piled up in a delicate tower. She was once again the remote, doll-like figure who ruled with a light – if absolute – touch.

Everyone fell to their knees and pressed their foreheads to the ground, even those chiefs who'd actively supported the usurper. That was expected to be forgotten now.

Zar ran her eye over the rangatiras, wondering what her father would make of them. Sitoko of the Wakatoa tribe, a big man and reputedly cunning. Natomo now led the Hiriwa, his predecessor having died in Ikendo's revolt. He was a silver fox who looked more politician than warrior. The Tanuahi, the second biggest tribe, were led by plump old Monarohi, who stood with Kuia, his tribal sorceress. Behind were Ihanodo of the Puketapu and Ranakodo of the Rotomaho, allied and of an age.

Shiazar walked past the five rangatiras, acknowledging each before halting before a sixth figure, a kneeling woman. 'Anata ha darei?' she asked, in her cool, musical voice.

Who are you? Zar's familiar, Adefar, translated inside her head.

The woman, who looked about Zar's age, raised her head. 'I am Haru. Ikendo was my husband. I surrender myself to your will, Great Queen.'

'Are you with child?' the Queen asked.

'No, Great Queen.'

'Do you have living children? Clearly Onkado is not yours.'

'No. And I knew nothing of Ikendo's true nature,' Haru said meekly.

The Aldar used 'flesh masks' made of real human skin to move incognito among the tribe, Zar knew, but it seemed improbable that this woman hadn't even suspected that her husband and his son weren't human.

Nevertheless, Shiazar chose leniency. 'There will be no retribution. You are an honoured widow, entitled to all that brings. But who now claims leadership of the Manowai, Ikendo's tribe?'

There was a stir among the warriors, then a burly man stepped forward. 'I am Kotabashi, shoganai of the Manowai. As warleader, I submit myself as temporary leader of my tribe, until a new chieftain is appointed. Our mahotsu-kai are also dead, so only I have the experience.'

Zar shuddered, remembering the two Manowai sorcerers who'd tried to murder her; she knew it was mostly by luck she'd managed to kill them instead.

'What of Onkado, son of Ikendo?' Shiazar asked.

'Onkado is a traitor to your rule,' Kotabashi replied warily. 'The penalty for treason is death – yet his *wife* refuses his execution.'

Everyone looked at Zar, who was that wife. The doubtful inflection he'd placed on the word 'wife' was unmistakable. *He's testing the waters,* Zar sensed. Would Shiazar truly execute an Aldar, one of her own kind? Would she punish the Manowai for Ikendo's revolt? Did she even countenance Onkado's marriage?

Why the Tangato had a law allowing a spouse to prevent the execution of their partner, Zar had no idea. Perhaps it came from the early days of the Ice Age, when they could ill afford to lose anyone, even a criminal.

But I bet it suits Shiazar just fine to have the Manowai, the most dissident tribe, shorn of a true voice, she thought. *Even though Kotabashi clearly thinks he should be rangatira now.*

Shiazar considered, then said, 'It's not right that the Manowai do not sit upon my council of chiefs, and Onkado cannot be both rangatira and Yokei. The Manowai have my permission to elect a new rangatira. In the meantime, you may represent the Manowai.'

'I shall serve her Majesty as if I were rangatira of my tribe,' Kotabashi vowed.

'Then come, all. The sun is high and there is much to discuss.'

Zar glanced at Rima, who gave her a firm nod. With Hetaru dead, Rima was now the senior sorceress of her tribe, and that made Zar her second. Here she was, barely sixteen years old, and from another culture, but somehow on the Queen's council. She held her head high and joined Shiazar's entourage like she belonged there.

Conscious of Kotabashi's hostile gaze as she passed, she looked back suddenly and made a hand gesture Rima had showed her: the first two fingers placed to the eyes in a backwards vee: it meant *You're not worthy, so look elsewhere*, more or less. Everyone saw, and Kotabashi went puce, but he dared not retaliate.

Making enemies wherever I go, she grinned inwardly. *I'm a true Vyre.*

Banno sat hunched over the body of his father. They'd found Sir Elgus Rhamp's corpse near the gatehouse, and his remaining mercenaries – just a score left, now – had cleaned him up, combed his hair and beard and laid him in repose. Elgus had led the defence heroically, everyone said; even men who didn't like him praised his spirit in that desperate last hour.

Gerda herself will raise him up, some were saying, although why Deo's maiden would interest herself in a backsliding bully like Elgus, Banno had no idea. And heroic or not, everyone in his company had perished, apart from the twenty-odd married men he had permitted to retreat, under Tom Corday's command. Tom was sensible and competent – not the usual type of man Elgus hired – and he'd been running things since, collecting bodies and preparing them for burial, ensuring any bequests were handled properly.

Banno knew he should be taking charge, showing he could lead, but that would mean opening himself up for challenge and possibly mortal combat. *I don't give a shit about that*, he thought numbly. *I'm glad the old bastard is dead and I don't want the captaincy.* Elgus had been a treacherous thug, not at all what Banno aspired to be. His grief right now was for himself. *I've ruined it with Zar . . . I've ruined everything.*

Why he'd slapped her, he could no longer say. They'd both been overwrought, having barely survived drowning in the river, and she'd been screaming at him about that stupid Tangato, and his hand had just swung. If he could have recalled that blow by cutting off that errant limb, he would have.

I thought that savage was trying to kill her – why can't she understand that? he asked himself for the thousandth time.

Clearly, he needed to talk to her.

Abruptly, he realised that the room has gone silent: the priestess, Mater Varahana, had entered with her shadow, the hulking Norgan bearskin, who was oozing menace.

'Our sympathy for your loss, Banno,' Varahana said gently. 'I'm here to give Gerda's Final Blessing. Have you chosen the grave goods?'

Deo, I've not given it a thought.

'Um . . . his sword is, uh, a family heirloom . . . His Gerda medallion?'

Varahana gave him a kindly smile and made the holy signs over Elgus' body. He'd been killed by enemy sorcerers, who'd broken his neck, but there were no other serious wounds. A gravesite on the other side of the bridge had been chosen, and a mass burial was planned for the next day.

'Are you all right, lad?' the priestess asked softly, for his ears only.

When he nodded bleakly, she patted his arm, then moved on to the next body, Vidar close at her side. The watching mercenaries had shunned her religious services at Elgus' behest, because Varahana supported Raythe Vyre, but soldiers were notoriously superstitious, and by extension, religious. Now everyone had bowed their heads and were mumbling prayers for the fallen.

When they left, everyone turned to face Banno.

The time had come.

I'll stand down – let the company carry on without me. I don't care.

But before he could speak, Tom Corday stepped forward and said, 'So, this was always the Rhamp band, and as far as I can see, it still is. Anyone got words to say on that?'

Banno blinked, then he thought he understood. *Tom had always been Number Two – perhaps he doesn't want to be Captain, even though he's the best soldier left?*

But he wasn't necessarily the best swordsman . . .

Banno held his breath, waiting for the challenges to rain in, for drawn blades and blood.

22

No one said a word for what felt like a month.

Then Tom Corday nodded, as if it was just as he'd thought. 'It's settled. Banno leads. Lad? Who's your lieutenant gonna be?'

Banno swallowed. 'Uh, right . . . You – you, Tom, of course it's you.'

'We'll give your Pa a good send-off, lad. I promise ye that.'

Corday's eyes told Banno who was really in charge.

The next few minutes were surreal as the mercenaries – every of them considerably older than him – filed up to Banno to kiss the hilt of his sword and pledge their loyalty. He kept having flashes of them pulling hidden knives and stabbing him, a waking nightmare he couldn't shake.

Finally it was over and he was left alone with Tom, who asked, 'So, what's on your mind?'

To Banno's surprise, his mouth opened and he just vented, from some deep pit of fear and rage inside him. 'I want to ask Raythe *kragging* Vyre what in the *Pit* he thinks he's doing, bowing and scraping to some Tangato *whore* and selling our lives into slavery when he *promised* me his daughter and said he'd make us all rich. Instead, what've we got? Nothing! Nothing at all, except friends and fathers to bury. I want to take what we were *guaranteed* and get out, whether Lord *bloody* Vyre likes it or nor.'

Abruptly his brain caught up and he slammed him mouth shut. He realised he was shaking, as if he was having a fit.

The grey-flecked sandy-haired veteran shook his head. 'Nay, lad. That's gone. There's no will for that any more. The wild lads who would've backed you on that are all dead. Those left are family men, level-headed enough in their way – like you when you're calm. Think about what you're saying. We're thousands of miles from an empire that has beaten us all down. If we walk back into it with a handful of istariol to peddle, we'll be betrayed to the Bolgies and kragged over in pretty short order. Here, well, we've got a bit of freedom, and we can finally get out of the killing business. Raythe Vyre's a tricky bastard, mark you, but he knows when to accept the hand that's been dealt. You do the same and you'll be fine. Maybe even win your girl back, too.'

Banno thought about that. He was self-aware enough to know that he was no rebel, and no real leader either. But at least Tom hadn't invoked the old codes and claimed the company for himself by the usual means: murder.

'Then what are we now?' He wished his voice didn't sound quite so plaintive.

Tom smiled mildly. 'Lad, the Rhamp mercenary company isn't needed any more. In truth, it's been nothing but a festering sore on this journey. When it's time, we'll disband it.'

Banno swallowed, trying to imagine life outside the trade he'd been born into. They'd rampaged through the western empire, always on the run from someone, leaving a trail of death, violence, theft and abuse. He couldn't think of a single place that would be happy to see them back. And yet, it was all he'd ever known.

'But what will we do?'

'What all people should do: honest work. Me, I always fancied carpentry, and Deo knows there'll plenty of work in these old ruins.'

Banno hung his head, but after a minute, he looked up. 'I like animals.'

Tom smiled. 'We ain't got much in the way of horses left, so we'll be needing to breed more. When it's time, talk to Jed Vine; he's organising the livestock.' He clapped Banno's shoulder, then his eyes shifted to the body of his former commander, laying on the table like a dead king. 'Good luck, Banno. You're the only Rhamp worth a damn.'

With that, Tom left Banno to his vigil, one last night with his father, before he could bury him and hopefully forget the kind of man he'd been.

2

No Easy Answers

Someone had marked out a circle with Shiazar's throne at the southern end, facing the bridge. The Tangato chiefs and their entourages sat on mats around the open space, facing inwards. The introduction of a seventh tribe – the first new one in centuries – had thrown out the symmetry of the traditional seating arrangements, forcing the ritual-obsessed Tangato to devise a new pattern that didn't insult any of the rangatiras by implying demotion. In the end, Raythe was positioned opposite the Queen, which was fine by him – it gave him the best view.

Weirdly, there were big, colourful kites tethered to the ground behind each tribal mat, giant silk contraptions larger than a man. Naturally, he didn't have one. As they arranged themselves, Zar hurried over and pressed noses in the Tangato way. 'Kon'ika, old man.'

'Old?' he snorted. 'What're these kite things?'

'Autumn is the wind festival, Rima says,' Zar replied. 'The kites are sacred.'

'What isn't, here?'

'How is everyone, Dad? About the new treaty, I mean.'

'They're pissed off at me for forfeiting the right to go home, but they're grateful about not being dead. So they both love me and hate me, as usual.'

'You'll win them over. You always do.'

He could see Rima was gesturing madly. 'Go on,' he said. 'Get to work.'

She scuttled back as the Tangato rose and sang a hymn to the Queen, emerging from her palanquin in a spectacular robe of green and yellow silk, with a similarly hued mask.

He couldn't stop thinking about how lovely she was behind it.

Shiazar took her throne, Rima thumped a stave into the ground, and the meeting began. It was conducted in Gengo, the language of ceremony among the Tangato, which was helpful, because Gengo was more or less the same as Raythe's native Magnian.

Firstly, the chieftains stated their names and tribes and pledged to give faithful and true counsel. The main tribe, the Hiriwa, who were roughly four-tenths of the Tangato, always spoke first, then came the Rotomahau, who wore beards, followed by the Tanuahi with blue tattoos, the Manowai with their narrow crests of hair, the red-tattooed Wakatoa and the Puketapu, who had a uniquely geometric tattooing style.

Raythe assessed each in turn, wondering who would emerge as allies and who as enemies. Sitoko of the Wakatoa was brawny but spoke shrewdly; Natomo of the Hiriwa was sleek; Ihanodo of the Puketapu and Sinokodo of the Rotomaho could've been brothers, while old Monarohi of the Tanuahi looked a little vague. The Manowai were represented by their warleader, Kotabashi, who looked ambitious and angry.

And then there was him, newly made rangatira of the 'Ngati Magnia', who numbered only two hundred foreigners. Everyone gazed disapprovingly, but no one challenged his presence – perhaps because he'd been at their Queen's side when she'd returned from the floating citadel with Ikendo's head in her hand.

'My people, let me speak of the situation we are in, and how we will deal with it,' Shiazar began. 'Outsiders have found our lands, and they tell of a greatly altered world beyond the fields of ice: a place where masses dwell, constantly at war, where all things are commodities to be traded by "kings" and "emperors", without consideration of right or wrong.'

It was an ugly summation, ignoring many good things, but Raythe had to admit she wasn't wrong. When everyone looked his way, he said, 'It is so.'

'So miserable is their world that Rangatira Raythe's people fled,' Shiazar continued. 'They arrived here by chance, not knowing we existed.
They came to mine istariol, the use of which we forbid; and brought
pursuit behind them. This triggered turmoil and suffering for us all.'

Again, harsh but true.

'But his Magnia people are not without virtue or value. Moreover, it
is not in the way of our people to kill when restraint will suffice, nor to
face a threat without seeking first to understand and disarm it. I have
fought alongside Rangatira Raythe as hitoshii and he is not lacking in
courage, skill or honour.'

She paused and let that sink in: Aldar sorcerer-warriors once fought
as hitoshii, in pairs or trios, a sacred bond. To invoke this honoured
Raythe greatly – and caused obvious disquiet among the chiefs.

'You all know the terms that he and I have agreed,' Shiazar went on.
'The Magnia tribe are given the bridge district in which to dwell, and
in time, they will have land outside the city to cultivate. They will give
their allegiance to the Tangato throne, and never leave our lands. This,
Raythe Vyre has sworn.'

'Have all his people so agreed?' asked Natomo.

'They have,' Raythe replied. *Kind of . . . mostly.*

'But other outsiders may come,' Shiazar resumed. 'His people fled a
larger tribe: the Bolgravian people, who have huge armies and an
uncontrollable lust for istariol and conquest. We must be prepared, and
in this, Raythe's people have a key role to play. They understand that
world: they have fought in its unending wars and lived in cities that
dwarf even Rath Argentium. They are not harbingers of doom, but a
sign of hope. For this reason, they must not be plagued or shunned,
however much you might blame them for the turmoil visited upon us.'

She fell silent and Raythe watched the chieftains digesting their
Queen's words. He admired her even more, for confronting their fears
head-on and seeking to disarm them.

'What of the "flintlock" that kills from afar?' the Manowai warleader, Kotabashi, demanded. 'We must take them away.'

'We do not steal from our fellow tribes,' Shiazar replied sternly, before turning to Raythe. 'However, I do command that your people create these weapons for the Tangato and teach their use.'

Everyone looked to see his reaction.

His first instinct was to refuse: their exclusive use of flintlocks felt critical to their survival: if the secret of their making was handed over, they risked becoming disposable.

But in reality, we're at the Tangato's mercy regardless. A few guns wouldn't save us.

'As you wish,' he replied, imagining the uproar among his own people. 'But they're not easy to make and it takes time. The powder is simpler, but we will also need lead for the shot.'

'The earth is bountiful,' Rima put in. 'And many hundreds of flint-locks were captured from the Bolgravian force who followed you here.'

He had no idea how many weapons they'd captured. The Bolgies had been taken by surprise; they'd run out of gunpowder and were weak from travel, Raythe knew. 'We will be happy to work with you on mastering those weapons,' he reiterated.

'Thank you,' Shiazar said. 'Let this be a token of faith between us.'

The Tangato leaders bobbed their own heads, and Raythe was struck again by how cowed they were. These were hard issues to deal with, integration of foreigners into what had been a closed society for five hundred years, but they were accepting her words without dissent.

She and I went up to Shiro Kamigami, the floating citadel, a place not just forbidden but dreaded, and came back with the head of her enemy and a new alliance. They're scared of us, however much they might pretend otherwise.

That suited him just fine.

It was to the citadel that Shiazar turned next. 'You all know that Rangatira Raythe and I ascended to the forbidden citadel of Shiro Kamigami above. The Usurper, Ikendo, sought to seize it, to use what powers he could gain there to destroy those who opposed him. We had no choice but to prevent him.'

The circle of Tangato leaned in, listening intently. Shiro Kamigami

28

had loomed over them all their lives, yet no one had been up there in centuries.

'You also know that when our ancestors survived the fall of the Aldar, they forbade the use of istariol,' Shiazar went on, 'for it had become the bane of our Aldar masters, amplifying their powers to the point of self-destruction. But now we know that in Magnia, the Bolgravians use istariol as a weapon. They will rape our land for it, and will destroy us in doing so. They outnumber us, and they have far deadlier weapons. So we have no choice but to embrace that which we fear. Istariol can protect us, not just from the ice, but from such enemies. Each of our mahotsu-kai must become the match of ten enemy sorcerers – for that is how many they may face.'

Most of the assembled mahotsu kai who advised the rangatiras looked wide-eyed at this terrifying vision of the future.

'Does anyone here even know how to use istariol?' one of them asked.

'I do,' Raythe stated. 'I place this skill at my Queen's disposal.'

'You are very free with your promises, Rangatira,' Natomo said sceptically. 'Can we trust them?'

Raythe sensed Shiazar's annoyance, but he was well-used to criticism. 'The road that brought me here has taught me that community makes us stronger. The rebellion I fought in to save my country from the Bolgravians was hopeless, for we were vastly outnumbered. But we took all-comers, no matter their race, religion, nationality or background, accepted their differences and learned from their strengths. By the end, our army had men and women of seventeen different nations and eight religions, and together, we defeated Bolgravian armies twice and thrice our size. We performed miracles.'

'Then how did you come to lose?' Natomo sniffed.

Raythe had to bite his tongue, because the friends he'd lost were still an ache in his heart. 'Because when a five-fold advantage is insufficient, Bolgravia sends tenfold. Sometimes miracles are not enough.'

'Then your gods are weak,' Kotabashi remarked offhandedly.

'Gods don't fight our battles for us,' Raythe answered, temper still in check. *Arsehole.*

Shiazar broke the rising tension by speaking again. 'Ikendo erred in seeing Raythe's people as an enemy. His second mistake was to treat me the same. He concealed his existence for forty years before emerging to usurp the throne – and see what it has cost us: a dozen of my sister Yokei lie dead, and many warriors. For five hundred years we Yokei forbade a male Aldar to be born, because we feared their aggression. The first to appear after all that time vindicated that fear. But he failed, and I still rule.'

Her warning was clear, and the tribal leaders bowed their heads.

Shiazar turned to Raythe again. 'Rangatira Raythe will instruct all of our mahotsu-kai in the use of istariol. There are rooms full of it in Shiro Kamigami – enough that the mining ban can remain in place.'

And once again Raythe found himself agreeing to something that his people would probably baulk at.

In for a copper, in for a crown . . .

Shiazar went on to promise each tribe would have zones of the city, with instruction from Raythe's 'experts' on how to repair the plumbing, drainage and housing. 'We have a short window of time,' Shiazar told them. 'When the world comes knocking, they must find us prepared.'

She was putting up a bold front, but Raythe knew it could take years for the Tangato warriors to be fully equipped with guns and comfortable with using them, let alone resettling rural villagers into a city of stone that had been falling into disrepair for five centuries.

It's the work of a lifetime, but we won't be given that long a reprieve.

At this point, the rangatiras and their advisors began debating which parts of the city they should be allotted, bartering this well against that blockhouse, that square against this watchtower. His own site was agreed and well-established, so Raythe tuned it all out, enjoying the sun and wind for a while.

At least an hour later, he realised that Rima had directed a question at him. 'Rangatira Raythe?'

He blinked and looked up. 'Ah, apologies,' he muttered. 'What was that?'

Rima frowned. 'In your opinion, what should be done about Shiro Kamigami?'

The citadel contained a massive istariol stockpile, and who knew what else. There were the bodies of Ikendo and the Yokei who had followed him, as well as Tashvariel and all his court, mostly cut down by the mad ruler himself in the carnage that had ensued when the Aldar usurper's bubble of frozen time failed.

'It's too dangerous to allow access,' he replied, 'until experienced sorcerers can secure it.'

Shiazar's barely perceptible nod told him he'd said the right thing.

'Rangatira Raythe and I will lead that exploration, as we have been up there. It is a matter of the highest priority.' She looked around the circle. 'Is there anything else?'

Raythe saw a few of the chieftains think better of voicing their thoughts.

'What about Onkado?' he said, when it became evident that no one else would ask.

Neither Shiazar or Zar looked happy to have the matter raised. 'It's under consideration,' the Queen answered. 'He and your daughter are legally married, which cannot be lightly put aside.'

'It's not been consummated—'

'That is of no moment in our culture,' Shiazar replied. 'Marriage is a religious and legal binding – it can be entered into before birth. Physical union does not alter those bindings. A spouse has the legal right to appeal to the throne for the sparing of a condemned partner, commuting even a death penalty to imprisonment.'

'But my daughter—'

'Zarelda chose to appeal and I have upheld that. She is alive thanks to Onkado, and now she repays that debt.'

'But you *could* reject her appeal?'

'I could, but I haven't. We do not take lives lightly here.'

Raythe bit back his retort. There was nothing to be gained by arguing the point here, especially as Zar wasn't helping him out.

With that, the formal meeting ended with a prayer to the Aldar gods. Raythe went to Zar, who had begun reeling in the sacred Hiriwa kite. 'What's the kite actually for?' he asked.

'It's religion, Dad. It's probably placating a wind-god, or symbolising universal harmony, or something like that.'

'Ah. So, are you going to visit your own people?' he added, which was the real thing he wanted to ask. 'Your friends want to see you.'

'Soon,' she muttered, hauling on the rope. 'I need more time to think. Onkado did help me, Dad. I owe him.'

He searched her face and listened to what she wasn't saying. There was an unexpected edge, a hint of curiosities and longings he'd heard in many young people's voice, but not so often in hers.

'What do you think of him?' he asked sharply, thinking, *She's too young*.

'I think he's . . . honourable. He didn't . . . take advantage . . . And he worked with Kuia to help me escape.' She lifted her tattooed chin defiantly. 'I don't know how sincere you are about staying here, Dad, but this is where I belong. Magnia was horrible.'

His heart lurched: he'd always known she missed her mother more than she'd ever admit, just as he did, and until now, she'd always spoken longingly of Otravia. 'Are you sure?'

'Aie. Watashi ha Tangato desu, ima,' she replied. *Yes. I am Tangato, now.*

'What about Banno Rhamp?' he asked.

'I don't know if he's right for me any more.'

Gerda on High, she's sixteen going on sixty! But he tended to think she was right.

'Be careful about Onkado,' he warned. 'We don't know how an Aldar thinks – you might feel indebted to him – and you are right to feel that – but he may see you as nothing but a playing piece in some elaborate game.'

'I'm a Vyre,' she replied, sticking her nose in the air. 'I'm *nobody's* pawn.'

He grinned, wishing she was still young enough to piggyback home. 'Good girl.'

Rima joined them, saying, 'My Queen wishes to return to Shiro Kamigami first thing tomorrow. You are to bring whoever might be of value.'

'Of course – but I'll tell her so myself.' He could see Shiazar was being loaded into her palanquin, but there was another matter he wanted to raise, for her ears alone. Patting Zar on the shoulder, he hurried forward, only to be blocked by a warrior brandishing one of the lethal Tangato spear-clubs.

'He may approach,' the Queen said, as she took her seat.

Raythe hurried forward and knelt, admiring her green and gold mask, which was beautifully intricate and artistic, like a swirl of autumn leaves. But he longed to see her face.

'Thank you, Majesty. There's another matter, which I couldn't raise openly.' He glanced at the four bearers, burly warriors all, and decided none of them could understand his words. The other chiefs and mahotsu-kai were watching curiously, but none approached.

'What matter?'

'A decade ago, the Bolgravian navy found an island kingdom that had been isolated since the Mizra Wars, much like the Tangato. There was a large native population, at least fifty thousand – but in ten years they were all but gone – not by violence, but slain by diseases the Bolgravians were already immune to.'

Shiazar visibly flinched. '*Immune?* How so? By sorcery?'

'No, not magic. Because of the millions of people, new diseases often arise, kill by the thousands and then become a minor irritant, as the survivors are those who are less susceptible. They still carry the disease, but now have an immunity. But those islanders had never met these diseases, so they had no such immunity, no defence.'

Shiazar's voice dropped to a horrified whisper and she leaned away from him. 'You're saying that your people could spread such diseases among my people? *Oya maa!*'

Before she panicked, Raythe put in, 'We have learned how to fight such infections – Kemara, Varahana and her holy sisters know what's needed.

33

I think we can prevent widespread loss of life, but the integration of our people with yours needs to be carefully handled. That's all I'm saying.'

She gave a jerky nod and he wished again he could see her face and read her emotions.

'Thank you,' Shiazar said, finally. 'But isolating your kind from ours carries other perils. We must foster community, least we allow our differences to become irreconcilable.'

'But if sickness comes?'

'Then we will overcome it.'

That felt extraordinarily naïve to him. 'You don't know what it'll be like – I've seen plague-cities and they're a living nightmare.'

'From what you've said, these sicknesses will come regardless, so we can only slow the onset, yes?'

He bit his lip. 'Aye. But the slower the better.'

'But if we keep our peoples apart, the sense that we are each other's enemy will become embedded. That is the greater risk, to my mind. I trust in our ability to fight what sickness may come; but I do not trust the warriors in either community to remain at peace. We must forge friendship, regardless of the risk.'

This wasn't the reaction he'd anticipated. 'What did you have in mind?'

'Among the Tangato, we have many festivals. Autumn is the time for the Matsuri-Tako, the Kite Festival. Do your people fly kites?'

'Of course – well, when we are young.'

'Are you no longer young?'

Taken aback by the warm humour in her voice, he failed to find a comeback before she'd dropped her curtain. The bearers lifted the palanquin and carried her away, leaving him gazing after her with a restless itch in his heart he hadn't felt in years.

Not since Mirella, he realised guiltily. *And if that's not a warning . . .*

He sighed, waved farewell to Zar and Rima, then headed back across the bridge on his own.

34

Theft was almost unknown among the Tangato, according to Rima. Possessions were more or less communal, except for family heirlooms. Their houses didn't even have doors.

So locking someone up wasn't done lightly, and it normally relied not on barriers but honour. Onkado – the son of a usurper, one of the worst crimes – was given a small hut and made to promise not to escape. Because he was both Tangato and Aldar, he wouldn't even try.

But even though Zarelda was legally his wife, her visits to him were disapproved of.

'Forget him,' Rima urged. 'Ask the Queen for an annulment and move on.'

Perhaps that's what I'll do, Zar thought. *But not without understanding it all properly.*

So here she was, with Rima as her chaperone, outside Onkado's stilt-house. The guard looked unhappy, but she and Rima were mahotsu-kai, so he stood aside.

'Are you sure?' Rima asked, yet again. 'You don't have to do this.'

'Yes, I do,' Zar replied. She took a deep breath, then plunged through the bead curtain, Rima close on her heels. Inside the dark room, she could just make out Onkado, sitting cross-legged on a mat before a smouldering fire.

She caught her breath.

There were many legends about the origin of the Aldar, but the Tangato believed they were once human. Certainly his face was almost human; but that *almost* was crucial. It was the differences she saw first. The intricate swirls of delicate tattoos on his cheeks and chin accentuated his narrow features and intense dark eyes; his ears had an elongated aspect, but it was his teeth and jaws that differed most. They were longer, sharper and more powerful, with a touch of the feline: nine parts human and one part cat, perhaps.

And entirely beautiful.

'Onkado?' she said, more breathlessly than intended.

'Zarelda,' he greeted her, and the music of her name on his lips made her shiver. 'Rima. This is unexpected.'

35

She sank to the ground, as Rima had taught her, keeping her knees pressed together demurely in maiden stance until she was resting on her right buttock, thigh and calf. Beside her, Rima sat cross-legged, peering belligerently at him.

When Zar first met him, Onkado's flesh mask had allowed him to pass as human. He'd been friendly, interesting and curious, and she'd liked him. But the second time, she'd been in the Arena, part of the team fighting against him for the Queen, although they hadn't crossed blades themselves. On their third meeting, he'd whisked her to a shrine and married her. They hadn't even kissed, let alone discussed feelings; it had been an act of survival.

This was the fourth time they'd been together, and he took her breath away.

'Are you well?' she asked weakly.

He glanced around the dilapidated hut with understated irony. 'I am fed, rested and left alone, thus far. I am told that I will not face execution, because of you.'

She nodded, but instead of thanking her, she was taken aback when he said, 'You believe you have done me a kindness, I see that. But it's a cruelty.' He sounded defeated. 'In truth, I would rather die than rot my very long life away. I am Aldar, and we are cursed with longevity. Put me aside and permit me a swift, honourable ending.'

Her throat caught. 'But—'

'Zarelda, I ask you this,' Rima interrupted. 'Would you end the suffering of a wounded animal, or watch it die a slow and painful death?'

Tears welled up in Zar's eyes. 'No, this is wrong,' she blurted. 'Surely there must be some other way? Onkado had no choice but to follow his father's lead—'

Rima flared at that. 'Ikendo's men captured me so I couldn't protect the Queen, and Ikendo intended to kill me himself. He forced Shiazar into suicide, and she escaped only by slaying her own sister, who Ikendo had seduced to his cause – and you think that Ikendo's *only son* had no knowledge of this? He is as guilty as his father and I wish he'd shared his father's fate! It sickens me to breathe the same air as him.'

Zar stared, heart thudding because she'd never seen Rima so angry – and because Onkado had bared his leonine teeth, glinting in the gloomy hut. Violence felt just an eye-blink away.

Then he sagged, shaking his head. 'Truly, I *didn't* know all my father's doings. He said he'd do what was *necessary*, so that in my time I could do what was *right*.'

Rima was having none of that. Jabbing her finger at Onkado, she said, 'You probably wed Zar for lust, not to protect her at all! We know what Aldar males were like – they were *monsters* – so don't you pretend you're any better!'

'But I'm not like that,' Onkado protested, plaintive as a teenaged boy.

'We've heard enough – come on, Zar, let's go!" Rima snapped, and when Zar didn't move, she snarled, 'Up! Do you want me to drag you out by the hair?'

The threat roused Zar's temper. '*I've* not heard enough,' she said, but Rima jumped to her feet and grabbed her arm and pulled her up. Her normally cheery face distorted by anger, she shouted, 'He's no different from his father!'

Zar planted her feet. 'How do you know that? I didn't come here to hear you. I want to hear him, but you won't shut up – so how am I supposed to know anything?'

'Oya maa,' Rima exclaimed, throwing up her hands. 'I thought you were smarter than this–'

'What, smart enough to think for myself? Or just smart enough to agree with you all the time?'

And with that Zar stormed out of the room and strode angrily through the village. She broke into a run when she reached the paddy fields, until she found shelter in a copse of trees. Sinking to the ground, she let the floodgates inside her open.

3

Fortress of the Gods

To return to Shiro Kamigami, the fortress in the sky, less than two days after escaping it, was not what Kemara Solus wanted to do, but Raythe Vyre insisted.

'You're our best healer, and you bring a unique perspective,' he told her.

'In other words, I'm your only available mizra-witch – but I have no familiar,' she argued.

'It's your knowledge we need. Shiazar, Rima and I can handle the rest.'

She could have refused, but somehow, that felt like cowardice. So she rose with the sun and checked on her patients; as well as those wounded in the fighting, Meg Tuffey's labour was imminent. Once she was sure that all was well, she clambered through Rath Argentium to find Raythe and Varahana already waiting in the bottom of the crater beside the stone disc that would carry them up to the fortress.

'Thanks for coming,' Raythe called. 'I've been telling Varahana what to expect.'

'And you still want to go?' Kemara stared at the priestess. 'Aren't you supposed to be intelligent?'

'I can't wait,' Varahana replied. 'It's a dream come true.'

Two days ago, Shiro Kamigami had been more like a nightmare: Kemara and Jesco had become stranded up there, and inadvertently freed the insane Aldar lord, Tashvariel the Usurper, who had preserved himself and his court from the passing of time by locking everyone in an infinitesimally slow-moving orgy of pleasure and cruelty. Raythe and Shiazar had repaired the broken disc to come to their rescue, but Ikendo, Onkado and the Yokei had used the Aldar's rainbow bridge – and then the real carnage had unfurled.

'How are you coping?' Varahana asked sympathetically. She knew Kemara had lost her familiar, but she wasn't aware that it had been a mizra spirit.

Good question, Kemara thought. Losing magic was like losing her sense of smell or taste; it had left her feeling horribly vulnerable. And she'd been shocked to discover it hurt her self-esteem too, no longer being *special*. But she'd also lost the lurking menace of the mizra, and the horrible sense of always being on the verge of violence.

'I'm getting by,' she replied. 'Sorcery isn't hugely useful for healing, anyway.'

'What about this "maho" business?' Raythe asked her quietly.

'I've not talked to Rima yet . . .'

'Well, you'll get your chance soon,' he said, gesturing towards the eastern slope at a line of Tangato, all cloaked against the morning cold, making their way towards them. Queen Shiazar had eschewed the palanquin and was walking with Rima and Zarelda.

'Zar looks good in a skirt and bodice,' Kemara remarked, just to annoy Raythe. 'I bet those Tangato men like the look.'

'I'd thank you for not bringing that up.'

'But they're such practical outfits –'

'Then why don't you get one?' Raythe retorted, riled as always by any hint that his daughter might be growing up. 'Mind you, they have no cotton here, so give it a bit and we'll all be dressing like that,' he added slyly.

'Except you lordly types,' Kemara harrumphed. 'You'll be in silks, no doubt.'

'Of course,' he replied, still frowning over his daughter's attire. 'As she should be.'

As the royal party arrived, Kemara, Varahana and Raythe genuflected before their new ruler, then Raythe walked over to his daughter, while the old woman Zar named as Kuia introduced herself to Vara-hana. Kemara was left to fidget awkwardly, wondering what she was doing there, until Rima approached.

She looks like some kind of nature goddess, clad in her flax and feathers, Kemara thought.

'Have you thought about what I said?' Rima asked, speaking stilted Magnian.

'I've thought of nothing else,' Kemara admitted. 'But I need to speak to Zarelda about it.'

'Naturally,' Rima replied. 'There will be danger, but she got through it.'

'But she wasn't using mizra,' Kemara muttered, glancing down at her filthy, threadbare dress. *Vyre's right, we'll all be in flax soon enough.* She examined Rima's clothing: a bodice of plaited flax and a beaded flax skirt, the whole wrapped in a light shingar-hide cloak, with feathers sewn on for warmth. Her legs and arms, shoulders and waist were left bare, but she certainly had the figure for it, Kemara thought enviously.

The Tangato girl noticed her regard and posed. 'I have silk also – everyone has at least one special kimono – but we mahotsu-kai are expected to dress traditionally.'

'You look wonderful,' Kemara sighed, 'but I'd look like a plucked chicken.'

'You are young and well-made,' Rima disagreed generously. 'I am sure your body pleases your handsome man.'

'My handsome–? Oh, you mean Jesco? No, no, he's not my man.'

'Oh – I am sorry, I thought . . .' Rima flicked her gaze up to the citadel.

'I have no man,' Kemara blurted. 'It was just bad luck, Jesco and me getting trapped up there. Nothing improper happened,' she added defensively.

'Next time, maybe,' Rima quipped, winking.

Jesco held no temptations for her, nor she for him, but before she could explain, Raythe waved them over. 'We've decided that to start with, only those of us with some sorcery will go up,' he said. 'And you, Kemara, obviously, and Varahana and Kuia, for their knowledge. Shiazar's warriors, however good their fighting skills, won't understand what we'll be facing, nor how to deal with it.'

Sensible, though neither do we, Kemara thought, but what she said was, 'Six women and one man? That's the kind of balance of power I like.'

The other women grinned and she had the feeling Shiazar was amused too, although her mask hid her reaction.

'Six on one side, me on the other, and we're balanced?' Raythe laughed. 'I must be *really* good.'

'You keep telling yourself that, Dad,' Zarelda retorted, following him onto the disc. Shiazar touched the plinth, the stone quivered beneath their feet and as the watching warriors gazed in awe, it slowly ascended towards the underside of the citadel. As they rose over the rim of the crater, the sun appeared, illuminating them in dazzling light.

'It will be winter soon,' Varahana noted, looking around at the green hills and pine forests, and the glistening of ice on the horizon, on all sides. 'What will happen here?'

'There will be snow soon, but it'll only settle on the heights,' Shiazar answered. 'The rivers don't freeze and the hot pools enable us to bathe. The warm ground protects the crops until spring.'

She and Raythe fell to discussing the seasons, while Zar sidled over to join Kemara and Rima. 'We'll help you gain the maho,' she said earnestly. 'As soon as you wish it.'

'How?' Kemara asked.

'What Rima and Hetaru taught me was that a praxis or mizra familiar is only half what it could be – Adefar was only the praxis side, but when Rima and Hetaru summoned the mizra part, it reformed him.'

'Does this mean that all the praxis sorcerers in Magnia are the same – they have just half their familiar?' Kemara asked doubtfully. 'Surely they'd have noticed?'

Rima chimed in, 'We believe the other bit perishes after a time, when it is abandoned – or that it becomes a wild spirit.'

Kemara thought about her own lost mizra familiar. Buramanaka had been quite a different matter: an Aldar ghost who'd clung to his own corpse for five hundred years before Kemara had disturbed his crypt and he'd entered her. She would never forget his cold fury and hunger for vengeance. He'd been a mizra-sorcerer, a deadly creature – did he have some shadow-half somewhere?

'Why doesn't the whole unsplit familiar appear to us when it's first summoned?' she wondered aloud.

Mater Varahana offered an answer. 'The rituals used to summon a familiar in Magnia force the spirit to split in two, perhaps – Raythe, does that sound possible?'

'Probably,' he responded. 'We actually compel the familiar to "purge itself of darkness and hunger" as part of the calling, so perhaps this forces them to mutate before bonding with us.'

'But why?' Kemara asked, thinking of her first mizra familiar, who'd latched onto her when she was twelve.

'Well, this is just speculation,' Varahana started, 'but if the Aldar began using mizra, the human sorcerers serving them would have mimicked that. After the Mizra Wars, only praxis sorcerers were permitted, so the practice of splitting the familiar became traditional – even though we didn't understand what we were doing.'

'Whereas we Aldar who survived did understand,' Shiazar put in. 'Having seen mizra destroy the world, we ensured the Tangato sorcerers embraced only whole familiars. The maho is less powerful than mizra, but can be used without danger to oneself.'

To Kemara, who had always been terrified of what the mizra could do, the maho sounded much more manageable. 'But Zar started with half a familiar,' she pointed out, 'while I now have none.'

'That should make it easier, because we can start from the beginning,' Rima replied, patting her shoulder. 'It is Rangatira Raythe who will be difficult, being older than you, and having been praxis-only all his life.'

Raythe scowled, which made Kemara smile. *So I might overtake you, Lord Vyre – wouldn't that just piss you off?*

But the explanation did allay some of her fears. *It might be just like starting over*, she hoped, looking at the Tangato sorceress with a rare feeling of kinship. As the only healer in Vyre's caravan, she knew everyone, but she'd always kept them all at arm's length. But there was something about Rima she liked – perhaps her independence and strut.

Just then, they were enveloped in darkness as the platform rose into the shaft driven in to the underside of the floating rock; moments later they emerged into a circular chamber, the disc slotted into the stone rim and this time, when Raythe touched the plinth, metal pincers gripped the disc, locking it in place.

She realised Rima was still watching her, and they shared a tentative smile. Rima had called maho the best of both worlds, which would be a fine thing. New hope kindled inside her as they disembarked, and prepared to re-enter the haunted citadel of Shiro Kamigami.

Even her father was afraid, Zar could tell. Although he and Shiazar had dealt with Tashvariel, no one knew what other horrors might be lurking. Like all the other sorcerers, she was keeping her spirit-fox Adefar close at hand; her father's parrot-familiar Cognatus was on his shoulder, while Rima's lizard, Mokomoko, was perched on her head. Shiazar had no need of a familiar, being an Aldar, but she was also on edge.

Poor Kemara has no one any more, she worried, *but Rima will help her.*

She and Rima had been tiptoeing around the subject of Onkado, just about managing to keep their spat from flaring up again, which felt important right now: with Hetaru dead, Rima was now Shiazar's chief mahotsu-kai, a huge responsibility as the tribe's new leaders, Rangatira Natomo and Shoganai Imbataki, were also inexperienced.

Having to think about politics was a new experience for Zar, but she put all that aside for now, as the wonders of Shiro Kamigami began unfurling before her.

Her father led them up a spiral stair rising higher than any building Zar had ever seen, even in mighty Perasdyne – and these were just the underground levels. First they found dozens of storage rooms filled with Aldar war gear. Although the leather and cloth had perished, the metal was still solid and untarnished. Next were chambers stacked with more than a thousand istariol ingots – more than existed in the whole of Magnia, her father estimated.

They looked at each other in awe.

'Can I ask something?' Kemara said eventually. 'How much danger are we in, right now?'

'Very little,' Varahana replied. 'Istariol is volatile only if exposed to sorcerous energy, in which case it will *implode*, not explode. It's that implosion that feeds the sorcerer energy.'

'So if Lord Vyre had a meltdown and used one of his energy blasts in here . . .?'

'To amplify a spell with istariol, you have to powder or liquefy it, then you ignite it with sorcerous energy and use that to fuel your spell. If I were to amplify a destructive spell aimed at more istariol, it could create a chain-reaction,' Raythe conceded. 'We sorcerers are the danger here.'

'How comforting. Do let me know if you start feeling suicidal, won't you.'

He gave Kemara a terse look. 'I'm fine. How're you?', which shut her up.

Above the istariol storage levels were dormitories intended for the servants: sad little cells, eerie and disquieting. Zar remembered the legend of 'Tashvariel's birds', remembering that the Aldar lords had thrown their human servants off the edge of the rock. Some of the ancient pillows had dried-up envelopes on them, too delicate to touch – farewell notes to loved ones that had never been read.

The next level, just below the surface of the floating rock, contained sealed glass vats of red liquid istariol, with pipes running out into the citadel: the power behind the citadel's most vaunted weapons, Shiazar guessed.

'There are eight metal dragons on the exterior walls which spat fire for miles around, according to legend,' she told them. 'Shiro Kamigami was besieged in the Mizra Wars by Tashvariel's enemies, and eventually the dragons fell silent.'

'Why?' Raythe asked. 'Clearly they didn't run out of istariol.'

Shiazar's masked face turned his way. 'The tales do not say,' she conceded thoughtfully. 'Perhaps they failed in some way?'

They proceeded to the ground floor, a huge, high-ceilinged hall ornately decorated and lined with massive windows. Several bodies lay in the dust, only a few days dead: the Tangato warriors who'd served Ikendo and died here.

'Are you all right?' Rima asked Kemara, who had begun perspiring and breathing fast. She put an arm round her shoulder. 'You're safe with us.'

'I'm fine,' the midwife snapped and strode away, leaving Rima perplexed.

'She's grumpy with everyone,' Zar told her. 'It's nothing personal.'

Kemara struck out across the hall and the rest followed warily, as if tiptoeing into a dragon's lair – apart from Varahana, who was pirouetting like a wide-eyed child.

'Isn't it wonderful?' she exclaimed, beaming.

Zar caught her father looking at her and knew he was thinking it wasn't long ago that she'd have been doing the same. So she stuck her tongue out, to reassure him she wasn't entirely grown-up yet.

Raythe grinned at his daughter, then returned his mind to the dangers at hand. He kept his senses primed as he led them up the main stairs, past the meeting room and guest levels, to the infamous banquet hall, the scene of Tashvariel's time-locked death-orgy. They flinched every time they passed another body; the dead Tangato, Yokei and Aldar guardsmen were still lying where they'd fallen, slain as he and Shiazar had fought their way through.

The banquet hall itself still stank of smoke and death. Amid the burnt remnants of once-rich tapestries and the scorched wreckage of wonderfully carved, lacquered and inlaid furniture were more than sixty charred and dismembered bodies, devastated by the whirling blades and dark energies Tashvariel had unleashed indiscriminately, not caring whether he was cutting down friend or foe.

'Everyone wait outside whilst Raythe and I investigate,' Shiazar said. 'We need to ensure there are no other traps and find the hour-glasses. I do not wish to be trapped in time as these people were.'

Together, the two of them entered the room, stepping over severed limbs and pools of caked blood and guts, seeking the treacherous little artefacts. But they found none, and the time bubbles were gone too, leaving this place once again moving in time with Creation.

'He probably made just enough for what he needed,' Shiazar speculated. 'I can see nothing else that might cause us problems.' She moved to a window, opened it, lifted her mask and breathed in deeply.

For a few seconds, Raythe lost himself in her unearthly beauty, then he composed himself before she noticed him noticing.

'I agree, there's nothing of immediate import left in here,' he said. 'But what about the dragon-cannons – how did they work?'

'It's said that they were controlled from the Serpent Throne, which was in a hidden chamber only the god-king could enter. We need to find it.'

She pulled her mask back into place and they rejoined the rest of their party. While they fanned out to search the lower levels for anything useful or untoward, she and Raythe set to exploring the rest of the upper level. Opposite the banquet hall was a large atrium where giant statues of the gods and goddesses of the Aldar pantheon knelt, as if paying homage to whoever passed. Beyond them were erect sarcophagi of past Aldar rulers. Intricate relief carvings on the lids were painted in such a lifelike manner that eyes seemed to follow them wherever they went. Beyond that lay the royal suite, which was larger than even the grandest houses Raythe had seen. It had been near to the epicentre of the time-lock and looked eerily pristine, as if its owner had just stepped out.

They found no hidden rooms.

Frustrated, they rejoined the others on the ground floor. Shiazar sent them to wait at the platform below, then she and Raythe went to inspect the other known place of danger up here: the sphere-gate that generated and controlled the rainbow bridge.

'In our tongue, it is a tamakado,' she told him as they entered the wilderness that was once formal gardens between the main keep and the outer walls. What had once been an ornamental garden had clearly gone wild, but gradually failed as the good soil was washed away and not replaced. Now it was mostly dead vines and shrubs, with a few tenacious weeds clinging on. Even birds seemed to shun the place, perhaps because of the time distortions.

A tower perched on the southwest side housed a larger-than-man-sized metal hoop tilted to an angle. 'About ten miles away at Lake Waiotapu there's a larger mechanism,' Shiazar told him. 'When activated, a path is created between the two points – the Rainbow Bridge.'

'I'd like to see that other place,' Raythe commented, examining the mechanism. 'If this is how Ikendo reached the citadel two days ago, we should disable it.'

'We're the only ones here – and we don't know how to disable or repair it.'

He *tsked*, then offered a compromise. 'We should study it properly before we try to alter anything. Do any of your Yokei know how?'

'Those who understood it supported Ikendo, and they died with him.'

'Then we'll leave it alone,' Raythe decided, before remembering that he wasn't in charge. He added quickly, 'If that's your will?'

Shiazar tilted her mask up onto her head again and gave him an amused look. 'It is, Rangatira Raythe.'

Dear Gerda, she's beautiful, Raythe thought helplessly. *Utterly glorious.* He turned away before she decided he was staring inappropriately, or worse, that he was an absolute fool. *My position here is fragile*, he reminded himself. *Don't do anything stupid.*

They spent a few minutes peering down – a giddy experience with only a few feet of rock between the walls and the void. There were eight bronze cannons shaped like open-mouthed dragons, set at each primary and secondary compass points, connected to metal tubing that disappeared into the stonework.

'I presume these are linked to the vats of liquid istariol below,' Raythe said. 'Were they effective weapons?'

'They could destroy everything around their impact point for a hundred yards. They were used to level cities, destroy terrestrial armies and sometimes even take down other floating fortresses,' Shiazar replied, her voice hollow. 'According to legend, of course. Perhaps the tales exaggerated.'

'They often do,' he breathed, awestruck. 'But not always.'

'What should we do about this place?' Shiazar asked. 'It's been forbidden since the Mizra Wars.'

'Isn't it yours by birthright?'

She looked up at the largest tower, shaped like a giant statue of an Aldar warrior, wrought of marble and stained by time. 'Perhaps, but it's not a good place. The royal sarcophagi, the kneeling statues, the darkness – I don't like any of it. It speaks to me of madness, of kings who thought themselves gods. And it feels haunted: there's a presence here, something dark and twisted. Do you feel it?'

'It's like the walls have eyes and ears,' he agreed.

'Perhaps we should leave it empty. I would be afraid, dwelling here so far above my people, that I would become deaf to their concerns.'

Any Magnian ruler would just see the grandeur and the power, Raythe mused. 'Majesty, this place is strategically vital if intruders come. You need not dwell here, but you must secure it. I suggest you establish a rotating guard up here – and we'll disable that sphere-gate, once we've worked out how. That's my advice.'

Shiazar stroked an errant lock of hair from her face as she considered his words. 'You know, this place is the heart of our land and I have dreamed all my life of standing here. But now I am, I don't want to return.'

'Imagine waking at dawn and watching the sun rise over the mountains from the windows of the royal suite,' Raythe countered. 'I wager you can see the entire kingdom on a clear day. That would be grand.'

'But to get there, you'd have to walk past those blasphemous statues, and the coffins of every past king,' Shiazar replied. 'I wouldn't want to sleep here alone.' Then, surprisingly, she blushed, reminding him that she'd never married and was still virginal, at least as far as he knew. 'Not that I would be,' she added hurriedly, 'with my sister Yokei to attend me.' She looked around, then announced, 'We will reclaim this, but for ceremonial occasions only. The priests must purify it with incense and tethered kites to ward off evil spirits. It will be a place of sanctuary, but no one will dwell here permanently, not even me. I'm not a goddess, only a Queen.'

Only a Queen. The thought struck Raythe as droll, but it spoke to something he sometimes felt: the isolation of power, and being seen as more than he was. And that led to something he'd been wanting to ask her, but it was a delicate question.

Who and what is an Aldar?

Trying to sneak up on it, he instead said, 'Majesty, I see the reverence and obedience your people show you. It's a hard thing to bear, sometimes. I'm just the nominal leader of a ragtag bunch of fortune-seekers and I feel the pressure of their expectations all the time.'

'But you are a former general and a sorcerer, and from what I understand, you have performed miracles to get here,' she responded, with what sounded like genuine respect. 'You've earned their trust, where I've merely been born with it.'

'Perhaps, but they all overestimate what I can do. It takes me five or six seconds of concentration to summon and ready my familiar so that I can use a spell, and even then a single flintlock or arrow could kill me easily if I can't see the shot coming and prepare. But they all think I'm a miracle-worker.'

'I know how you feel,' the Queen said soberly. 'I can use magic instantly and intuitively, as I don't require a familiar. But truly, we Aldar are only a little stronger than the mahotsu-kai, few of us have trained to use magic in battle – and only I have ever done so. With a sword, I'm even less capable than most of my warriors. Despite this, we are seen as demigods by my people.'

'I've seen you fight,' he reminded her. 'You undervalue yourself.'

'Perhaps, but of my surviving Yokei sisters, only I have had weapons training. For centuries now we've been a repository of tradition and knowledge, but we are all untested. All the great lore of the Aldar of old, like Tashvariel's time spells, is completely lost to us.'

He had suspected as much, and feared it too. *Really, if there's a crisis, there's just Shiazar, Zar and Rima, and maybe Kemara, that I can count on.* It gave him a chill, but he was grateful to know. 'I had hoped for more,' he admitted.

'My people saw the horrors of war and put it aside,' she replied sternly. 'We have lived in peace, apart from a couple of dark periods, ever since: five hundred years of peace, until you came – not that I blame you,' she added. 'But the value of my fellow Yokei and the Tangato mahotsu-kai is not in warfare. We are the glue that holds our people together. That is not without value.'

'I'm sorry if the question gave offence,' he said humbly.

'I'm not offended, but I am troubled,' she replied. 'I fear for our people.'

Then she lowered her mask, the remote Queen again, and led the way back inside.

Raythe followed silently, mulling over what he'd learned. He suspected that no one unsettled her as he did, but that she valued it.

They rejoined the others at the transportation platform and Zar was asked to take the control plinth. It was simple, just a touch of the hand required to move it up or down, but she looked delighted to be given the task, and proud of her prowess.

Quietly, so was Raythe.

As they descended, Varahana approached him. 'Have you raised the matter we discussed?' she asked him.

'About the threat of disease? Yes, I have.'

'What are we going to do about it?'

They both turned to Shiazar. 'My Queen?' Raythe asked.

'Majesty,' Varahana said, 'we need to discuss the possibility that we

50

carry diseases your people are vulnerable to, and that your Tangato may have some common sickness we can't tolerate – although that's less likely, given your small population.'

Shiazar said, 'I have pondered this deeply. The logical extension is that I should ban interaction between our peoples – but that will have two consequences, neither to be desired. We will be denied each other's skills and expertise in opening up the city for my people. And emphasising our differences will prevent friendships from forming.' She looked at Varahana. 'What is the worst scenario?'

'That thousands die,' the priestess replied baldly.

'We number only ten thousand,' Shiazar said, shocked. 'Are you sure about this?'

'Mater Varahana was a scholar before being forced into the priesthood,' Raythe told her. 'She's forgotten more than I've ever known.'

Varahana smiled. 'Oh, surely I've forgotten more than that – but I'm not an expert on *everything*, Raythe. One thing I do recall is that people who contract and recover from most of our more serious diseases rarely catch them again. In fact–'

'How can we use that?' Raythe interrupted, before they got a lecture.

Varahana went on as if he hadn't spoken, 'In fact, the Medicalus Andre Skovoya claims that using the blood of the recovered can convey immunity to the uninfected, but I never heard the details, nor read any verification. Last I heard, he was facing charges for necromancy.'

'That doesn't sound like much of a recommendation,' Raythe said wryly.

'What's a medicalus?' Shiazar asked.

'A praxis-healer,' Raythe replied. 'It's the least developed field of sorcery, unfortunately – a praxis-healer can restore damaged or diseased or poisoned flesh, bones or body fluids to their natural state, but unless you're doing it to yourself, it's hugely exacting, very slow and requires a very particular mind to perform. I can heal myself, but I can barely help anyone else. Kemara's better at it than I, but even so.'

'Andre Skovoya was Bolgravian, and he was trusted by the Emperor,'

Varahana added. 'Well, he was until his enemies had him arrested. A skilled medicalus can do amazing things –'

'Sometimes,' Raythe interrupted. 'If only I was skilled, eh?'

'Maybe I could try,' Zar put in hopefully.

'To do what, exactly?' Raythe enquired.

'Um . . . I . . . someone would need to show me.'

'Who?'

Zar winced and ducked her head. 'Thanks for the offer,' Raythe said, turning back to Shiazar. 'I guess it's another "top priority" matter?'

'We do have a lot of those,' the Queen noted.

As they descended, Raythe went with Varahana to the southern side and peered out, straining his eyes through the haze and ground mist. 'Winter's coming,' he muttered. 'There'll be heavy snows and violent storms in the mountains surrounding this place, extending all the way into Verdessa and the coast of Magnia. Hopefully, that means we've got four or five months to prepare for outsiders.'

Varahana gave him a hopeful look. 'Perhaps no one knows we're here? The Bolgravians who followed us were wiped out.'

'But they probably told someone where they were going,' Raythe replied. 'Do you remember the Ramkiseri agent – Toran Zorne?'

'The so-called "Moss Trimble"? He's dead, isn't he?'

'Well, he went into the river, and he was badly wounded. But his body was never found.'

'It's probably been trapped underground or eaten by fish,' Varahana said soothingly. 'From what you're saying, he was practically dead when he went in, wasn't he?'

'But if he –?'

She squeezed his arm. 'You know what you need? Some loving, to work off all that pent-up worry.'

'Is that your religious advice?'

'It's my friendly advice.'

He glanced sideways at her. 'Is it advice you're taking yourself, Priestess?' He'd noted that since they'd kissed very publicly, she and Vidar had been at pains not to be found together, which made him sad and slightly angry. Forcing celibacy on priestesses was something he'd always thought cruel.

'Certainly not,' Varahana replied. 'I'm still the Voice of Deo in this wilderness and my congregation would feel betrayed if I broke my vows.'

'You never meant to be a priestess,' he reminded her.

'I've grown into it, and someone has to provide the comfort of Deo to our travellers. That someone is me.'

He sighed. 'Very well, I'll back off.'

They shared a look that bore the weight of shared history: they'd met during Colfar's Rebellion, he the general and she the chaplain, and had been through a lot together. They'd even been in love for a time, or something very close to it, though they had never acted on those feelings and eventually, the possibility had faded away. Now it was big-hearted Vidar she longed for, but she was still trapped by her vows.

'Duty must come before love,' Varahana told him. 'Always.'

As he turned away, he caught Shiazar watching, and despite her mask, it was she who looked away first.

The Queen wasted no time with her plans to bring everyone together, inviting Raythe's refugees to the Hiriwa village the next day for their kite festival, the Matsuri-Tako.

That gave Raythe precious little time to sell the idea of the festival to his people, so that night, he found himself standing on a table in the food hall, trying to persuade them it was a good idea.

It wasn't easy: they were nervous of the Tangato – after all, they'd been fighting for their lives only days before.

'Listen,' he shouted over the rising babble, 'can I be clear about something? Our position here is indefensible: if they decide to attack, we're done. But Queen Shiazar believes we can enhance their lives with our knowledge and skills. And they can enhance ours too, because I don't know if you've noticed, but we are on the *bones of our arses*. We have no food reserves, no fields and no seeds even if we did have land. We need the Tangato, and Queen Shiazar is busy making them believe that they need us. So what's *required* is that we all be *friends*. That way, everyone's better off, and no one gets hurt. And you might actually *enjoy* escaping these dismal ruins for some sunshine, fresh food, new songs and dances, kite-flying, and much more. Those people out there are *amazing*, and they want to meet you.'

He was hoarse by the time he'd exhausted his words, argued down the objectors and persuaded a decent minority of his people to accompany him.

'Did you have a stall in the Perasdyne Market before all this?' Jesco chuckled, as Raythe flopped into a chair and grabbed a jug of water to soothe his abused throat.

'Roll up, roll up, get 'em while they're hot!' Vidar guffawed.

'You can't change people overnight, Raythe,' Varahana put in. 'They're grieving over having to remain here, and they're scared of the Tangato. Don't expect miracles.'

'We don't have time for small steps,' Raythe grumbled. 'The door to this land is open now and someone's going to walk through when we least expect it – most likely the Bolgravian Empire. We have to be prepared, and that means coming together.'

Varahana gave him a hard look. 'You didn't mention the risk of sickness once,' she murmured. 'This festival could trigger it.'

'How could I?' he muttered back. 'If I whispered even a word – well, you know no one would go anywhere near them. The Queen's made a decision, and it's my duty to uphold it.'

Her disapproval was tangible. 'Some of our people could die because of that silence – and maybe thousands of theirs.'

'And we could *all* die if we *don't* do this. The risk is there, but it's not certainty. But if I stood up on that table and told them our fears, it'd kill any chance we have of friendly relations with the Tangato stone-cold dead.' He indicated the table. 'Shall I?'

Varahana's usually serene face showed supressed anger and helplessness, then she let out an exasperated breath and said, 'Could we not just wait a few months?'

'For what? We may not have a few months! We have to teach them, trade with them, learn from them – and you know as well as I do that interactions will happen, festival or no festival. Shiazar is acutely aware of the risks because she knows her people will most likely bear the brunt of it. The decision has been made, and now we, as community leaders, must uphold it.'

The priestess sagged. 'Aye, yes, I know. But I don't have to like it, and don't say you weren't warned.' With that, she rose and strode away, causing several people to give Raythe enquiring looks.

He agreed with her, but leaders weren't permitted the luxury of doubt, so he began circulating again, to encourage more people to attend the forthcoming festival.

The day of the Matsuri-Tako dawned, blustery and cold. After breakfast – and more arguing – Raythe set the gatehouse at mid-morning as the rendezvous so they could set off together for the village.

He feared he'd be standing there alone, but he got a pleasant surprise: usually he was dealing with the men, taciturn and pragmatic. He hadn't reckoned on the influence of the children, clamouring about kites and sweets, or the wives, fed up with scratching about for what meagre food they'd managed to hunt or forage. They all wanted to go, and eventually their husbands relented, after badgering Raythe to swear that the Tangato weren't lying in wait to murder them all.

'You need to guarantee it's safe,' Relf Turner kept demanding. 'This is on your head!'

'Nothing in the world is safe, Relf,' Raythe replied. 'But are you better to starve outside your neighbour's gate, or risk going in? That's up to you.'

In the end, more than half of his people followed him over the bridge, including the majority of the women and children – and the

Turners. He also noted that some of the men who'd forbidden their wives from attending had been defied – it looked like he'd managed to further divide his little tribe. If it all went horribly wrong, he would be damned in everyone's eyes.

Shiazar, I really hope you've got your people under control.

They reached the edge of the Hiriwa village an hour later, where they were confronted by a wall of armed warriors.

'Stay calm,' Raythe told his people. 'This is a ritual challenge, and you win their respect by facing it. You're in no danger.'

'Oh, I don't know,' Jesco murmured, gazing admiringly at the ranks of young, muscular, half-naked men and women. He grinned wolfishly. 'My heart might give out.'

Many of the women were also staring avidly, and the children looked awestruck. The Tangato warriors, stripped down to flax kilts, were chanting belligerently while slapping their thighs and chests, their tattooed faces contorted into expressions of fierce aggression, male and female both. Behind them stood the married Tangato women, resplendent in colourful silks, their own children pressed against their skirts, equally amazed by the pale-skinned foreigners.

For their part, the Magnians were dressed in their best – but that didn't mean much any more. After months of travel and danger, their worn-out clothes had been indelibly stained, sometimes with blood. Confronted by the stark barbarity of the Tangato men and the sculpted elegance of the women, Raythe's people looked lost and forlorn.

When the challenge came, many flinched and looked behind them for a way out.

Raythe held his breath as the first chants rang out from the phalanx of warriors just a few feet away. Would the Queen's peace hold? For these warriors weren't just dancing – some had picked out men among the Magnians and were advancing on them, tongues wagging in what looked like mockery, the loud crack of hands on thighs rhythmic as a war drum.

Arm these men with flintlocks, and watch them become the most feared men in the world . . .

Imbataki, the new Hiriwa warleader, a grim-faced man with greying hair and an ugly scar down the left side of his face, led the challenge, eager to show his prowess. He closed in on Raythe like a stalking wolf. Though the challenge was a ritual, it clearly mattered. Imbataki began flashing a narrow, sharp-edged granite club around Raythe's head, whistling faster and closer, goading him to react, before a massive roar culminated in a vicious chop that ended with the weapon at his throat.

'Kon'ika,' the big man growled, pushing his face up to Raythe's . . . and then he withdrew the edged club and pressed his nose to Raythe's. 'Yokosu he Hiriwa-mura.' *Welcome to the Hiriwa village.*

Cognatus, fluttering inside Raythe, supplied the required response. 'Na-mihi, eho.' *Bless you, friend.*

Imbataki's ferocious eyes bored into him a few seconds longer, then his visage split into a massive grin, and he stepped back, allowing Raythe to see that all down the line, the front rank of Tangato had mirrored the warleader's gesture, choosing a man, woman or even a frightened but determined child to greet.

Then the Tangato women came through, holding silk ribbons that they knotted around the necks of the Magnian women before pressing noses; followed by children swarming forward and with exaggerated politeness, offering sweet cakes to their pale-skinned counterparts.

They were led to a shrine, where a giant bamboo and flax effigy was burned while the Tangato sang hymns, which visibly worried the more pious of the Magnians, but the ceremony was fairly brief and they weren't required to join in. And then, almost abruptly, the ritual was over and all formality disintegrated into a tangled mingling, each Tangato female determinedly seizing the arm of a Magnian woman and leading them to where heaps of clothing, crockery and utensils were piled up. Meanwhile the children, chattering like birds, dragged their Magnian counterparts towards a stack of little kites at the edge of the green. The men were more hesitant, feeling each other out with a lot of posturing. There would be trouble later, no doubt; hopefully it wouldn't get bloody. But for now, as kites erupted into the air amidst drums and cymbals, it really was a festival.

'Come, the Queen awaits,' Imbataki boomed, and Raythe followed him, trusting to Jesco, Vidar and Varahana to keep his people civil.

Shiazar was radiant in vivid yellow and orange silk and masked like a parrot. She formally welcomed him, then, indicating a wooden stool, bade him sit beside her.

'It looks good for us to be seen together,' she told him. 'We are a symbol of unity.'

He hesitated. 'You realise that you and I are just as susceptible to infection as anyone else, should we be right about exposure to illnesses.'

'Leaders must share their people's struggles,' she replied. 'Please, let us eat.'

The feast was truly astounding to the Magnians, who had endured so many months of privation. Spit-roasted phorus birds were surrounded by hundreds of smaller avians and interspersed with mostly unknown plants and roots, smoked and steamed and roasted in pit-ovens. Such plenty after so nearly starving reduced many of his Magnians to tears. The food was lightly spiced, in a way that accentuated the natural flavours, and there was even a rice wine as delicate as any grape vintage he'd tasted.

I hope those fools who stayed away hear how good this was, Raythe thought, as he filled his shrunken belly.

After the feast came the kite displays, filling the skies, vividly coloured and incredibly agile. They ranged from brilliantly plumed birds and majestic dragons to floating citadels, many modelled on Shiro Kamigami. It was a glorious spectacle, especially as the day warmed and the sun lit the scene. As well as races, there were battles too, with cleverly bladed kites trying to down their opponents through skilful flying. It might have been a religiously inspired festival, but the point was clearly about the kites.

When he wasn't helping Shiazar to adjudicate, Raythe was able to chat to Zarelda.

'Banno didn't come,' she noted sadly. 'Why not?'

It was a good question, but in truth, he hadn't noticed Banno's absence. 'He might be on guard duty,' he replied, though anyone who wanted to attend could easily have swapped duties. 'But is it truly him you want here, or Onkado?'

She took a deep breath. 'Onkado stood up to his father for me, even though he owed me nothing . . .' She swallowed. 'But . . . but I can't even breathe when I see him. *He's an Aldar.* I'm just me.'

'You're never "just" anything, Daughter.' He glanced at the Queen and murmured, 'They do take one's breath away, don't they?'

She gave him a suspicious look. 'Don't even *think* about it, Dad.'

He winked slyly. 'So you don't think the Queen and I–?'

'Yuck! No way! She's *way* above you.'

'Whereas you and Onkado . . .?'

'This is not a joking matter, Dad!'

'That's a shame. Let me know when it is. I've got a wealth of material lined up.'

'Krag off,' she snorted, then she leaned in and kissed his cheek. 'I'll tell Shiazar about you and Mother. That'll make sure nothing happens, ever. Now, I want to go and fly a kite.'

She stood, pulled Rima along with her and scurried off, while Raythe scanned the crowd. His friends were circulating, trying to ensure the inevitable flashpoints were short-lived. Despite the growing inebriation, thanks to the potent rice wine, the peace was holding.

By sundown, Raythe was leading his people home. Many of the younger children were asleep in their mothers' arms and the men were laden down with bundles of food and goods for their homes. The day had undoubtedly been a huge success, and a giant step towards some kind of unity between his people and the Tangato.

But at what price? he wondered. *What toll will Deo's dark angels exact for our happiness?*

He didn't have to wait long to find out.

The day after the festival, Raythe and Rima led a group of volunteers to clear the bodies from the floating citadel, while the best engineers and carpenters joined Tangato work-gangs in the city. Masked, grey-haired Yokei acted as translators as they laboured together to unblock drains and sewers and determine which houses were safe for the Tangato to move into.

For two weeks, all went well, then Kemara and Varahana, just returned from a visit to the Hiriwa village, summoned Raythe to the infirmary.

'A Tangato woman has contracted the feminine strain of grefilia from Semus Rygor, one of the Rhamp mercenaries,' she told them. 'Apparently she's a bit of a wild child and wanted to try out a Magnian man. Cock-rot is easily treated – but she's started bleeding internally, and so have four of the Tangato in Relf Turner's sewage-clearing operation. I can't identify this particular blood-flux.' She looked up at Raythe and Varahana with haunted eyes. 'And Semus caught something in return: some sort of breathing infection which is flooding his lungs. His mates may have caught it from him.'

Raythe caught his breath. 'You're saying that not only have we unleashed sickness among the Tangato, but they've got one we're not immune to as well?'

'Sometimes Deo's plan is unknowable,' Varahana sighed. 'Ready or not, the outbreak we feared has begun.'

4

Bound for Glory

Winter had struck the western edge of the empire, and so had the Mandaryke expeditionary forces. Both left scars. Vicious storms swept the coast, wrecking trees and buildings, and bottling up the fishing and trading fleets, while rivers overflowed then froze.

In Sommaport, the soldiers from Luc Mandaryke's Bolgravian and Otravian divisions settled into a brutal regimen of drinking, brawling and whoring. Violence stalked the streets as Bolgravian greycoats and Otravian redjacks settled old scores and created new ones. No local was safe and theft and vandalism were endemic.

The local governor complained to Luc, who ignored him and spent his nights plotting and partying in the commandeered imperial bastion. Young women of all stations were plucked from the streets, dressed in velvet gowns, plied with drink and opium, used and then discarded. Every entertainment was available, from cock- and dog-fighting to boxing and wrestling, to stage plays that were little more than live sex displays; anything to ward off the crushing boredom of an army doing nothing. The haphazard crackdowns on discipline were completely ineffective.

It's worse than the Pit, Toran Zorne decided. *At least the Pitlords only punish the guilty.* Here, everyone suffered, even if only, like him, by having to tolerate the pernicious evil and decadence of their associates. They were all trapped until the weather broke and they could sail.

He spent his nights reading from the *Book of Deo*, not because he was religious, but because it was the only book he could find. Meanwhile, the usual command-room rivalries festered. Ferdan Verdelho, the Imperial

Courser, was seeking to oust Zorne, merely for being a Ramkiseri. The generals – the Otravian Torland and the Bolgravian Lisenko – were at each other's throats; while Tresorov and Drusyn, the senior military sorcerers, were so frightened of Teirhinan Deathless that they were secretly trying to prove that she was a mizra-witch.

As the resident assassin, he was unsurprised to be approached for use of his professional skills; but the person who approached him was unexpected. He was in a secluded courtyard of the governor's residence on a rain-swept afternoon, honing his knife-fighting technique, when he became aware of a shadowy figure in a grey hooded mantle. He paused, assessing the threat.

'Good afternoon, Master Zorne,' a woman called. 'Please, come with me.'

The voice belonged to Mirella Mandaryke.

Curious, he sheathed his dagger and followed her down a sheltered walkway to the back of the chapel, and in through the vestry door. The candlelit church was an austere place with grey stone walls and leaking windows.

Mirella knelt at the railing before the altar, and indicated that Zorne should join her. He glanced behind him and saw two guardsmen at the front doors, while another pair now blocked the vestry door.

As he knelt, she murmured, 'You move well. I like watching men fence, if they're good.'

He was tense and uncomfortable at being alone with a woman – it was the sort of situation that could easily be used against him, and Mirella reeked of deviousness. *Is she flirting?* he wondered queasily. Her husband was rumoured to use other women, and the soldiers were not above speculating whether Mirella had needs that weren't being met.

He had no idea how to answer her, so he didn't.

'My husband has a problem,' she continued. 'He hopes you can solve it.'

His skin prickled. 'What sort of problem?'

'Do we speak in utter confidence, Master Ramkiseri?' Mirella pressed.

'Of course,' he said stonily.

'Very well. We are all aware that our mission *must* remain utterly confidential if we are to avoid an insane gold rush – but someone has been passing messages to the imperial court and as a result, the Emperor's Secretariat has demanded information.'

Does she think I'm the traitor? he wondered, conscious of the watching men. 'I haven't informed my commanders, as the Governor requested,' he said evenly. 'I am not your leak.'

'I believe you. We think it's the Imperial Courser – we can't prove it, but we can't tolerate it, either.'

Zorne had no qualms about dealing with Ferdan Verdelho. The list of grievances between Coursers and Ramkiseri was of long standing and extensive, and the man was clearly plotting against him. But whatever his personal inclination, there was a question of protocol. 'I am not an assassin for hire, Milady. I am Ramkiseri. I require an imperial death warrant.'

At that, Mirella pulled back her cowl, revealing her face. Up close, her skin betrayed faint traces of ageing; she was over thirty, after all. But she was undeniably beautiful. And what she said next took his breath away.

'Belyi-Lisitza, sem-losem-pyat,' she murmured – *White Vixen 785* – while pulling out a tarnished silver coin, a Bolgravian kopek.

Combined, her words and the coin comprised a code, a protocol for senior Ramkiseri to approach one another. The colour white indicated her rank: she was a Komizar, higher than his own position.

'*Milady?*'

'You require more?' she asked. 'Must I sing "Great of Heart" in Berentic for you?'

He bit his lip, thinking hard. Such codes were unique and verifiable, based on birthdate and age and an old folkloric cycle of animal totems, so that a person's personal identifier changed each year. He knew her birthdate, and the code was correct to that date.

'I am just . . .' *Stunned? Shocked?* '. . . taken aback by this revelation,' he confessed. 'Is Milord Luc also –?'

'No. Luc's party were pro-Otravian independence until I left Vyre for him.'

'But you and Raythe Vyre were married . . .'

'Who do you think provided the names of the Liberali Party's inner circle for your assassins? See, I knew who you were, even then.'

He took another stunned moment to realise that this woman had been a shadowy presence in his life for the last five years without him ever realising. 'Did Vyre come to suspect you?' he asked. 'Is that why you left him?'

'No. I needed to be free of him before the hammer fell. I was already Luc's lover,' she added smugly, as if adultery were an accomplishment. 'I had been for years.'

Zorne inhaled, let the rearranged facts of his world settle inside him, then asked, 'Milady, have you advised our superiors of this mission's true purpose?'

'No,' she said firmly. 'In this, Luc is right: any such word would result in a chaotic power-grab. The Emperor is not without rivals, and some factions have deep roots in our order. And there are external enemies: if the Shadran kings learned of this, their powerful navy would enable them to move before us. The empire is not yet invincible this far west and must tread carefully. We must seize these new lands without any-one realising – and so this mission must indeed remain secret.'

Uncomfortably, that made sense. Shadra was still the primary sea power of the western oceans, which was why they remained uncon-quered. 'Then how may I serve you, Komizar?'

Mirella smiled approvingly. 'Ferdan Verdelho must die, sometime before we sail – but not too soon, lest it leaves time enough for him to be replaced. Can you accomplish this?'

Despite lingering doubts, he touched his heart. *When in doubt*, his masters had always said, *trust in hierarchy. Those above you see the bigger picture, and that vantage makes what appears mysterious to you explicable to them. Trust the hierarchy.*

'Yes, Milady. When would you like him to die?'

'We expect the weather to break in a month or so, enabling us to sail for Verdessa on a late autumnal southerly. If Verdelho were to die in – well, let's say three weeks – that would be ideal.'

He nodded in acquiescence, anticipating the feel of driving his dagger into Ferdan Verdelho's chest.

I don't kill for pleasure, but I do enjoy it.

'Now,' Mirella said, 'what reward do you seek for this service?'

He was genuinely puzzled. 'Madam, I require no reward. I do my duty.'

And the task is its own reward.

'You're an unusual man, Master Zorne. I pray you're never given my name as a target.'

'So long as you never transgress against the Empire, that will never happen,' he told her. It was as clear a warning as he could give. Though she *might well* be his senior, coins and codes were tradable assets in this world, and this privileged woman might yet be a fraud. Part of him hoped she was.

For three weeks, Zorne stalked his prey.

This was no easy task, even for him. Ferdan Verdelho was based in the local Coursers' Stables, a small fortress. There was a stable in every major town, enabling the Coursers to make their legendary breakneck journeys across the empire, ensuring that information always reached those in power ahead of their enemies. The Coursers were, like the Ramkiseri, sorcerers as well as fighting men; the differences lay in their training. A Ramkiseri was trained in infiltration and murder; a Courser learned how to survive in any conditions.

Outwardly, Verdelho didn't look dangerous, but he moved with economy and speed and his fashionable outfits concealed a lean, muscular body with strong shoulders. He trained each morning with two of the Stables guardsmen and, armed or unarmed, he would batter them both, separately or at once. Verdelho was able to fight equally well with either hand, and he knew how to take a blow.

Verdelho was clearly under no illusion as to his personal safety: he never over-indulged in drink or drugs, invariably leaving Mandaryke's banquets early and sober. He abstained from prostitutes, and he travelled everywhere with his own personal guards. He varied his routines and stayed clear of the docklands and slums. Being a sorcerer, if anything did happen, his familiar would provide him with added resilience, so unless killed instantly, he could survive much.

He needs to die instantly, then I must banish his familiar, Zorne thought as he slipped away from his observation post, a grain silo overlooking the stables. Days were passing swiftly now. The coast was still racked by gales and rain, but the storm cycle would break soon.

'It'll be clear next week, with a strong southerly wind,' the Governor told them one evening in that relatively sober hour before dinner. 'We must prepare to move.'

Mirella looked pointedly at Zorne as Luc spoke. The message was clear. *Act now.*

The chance came, quite unexpectedly, the very next day.

That was a *very* bad thing. Because Zorne didn't do the unplanned.

But whilst he was spying from the church bell-tower, which also overlooked the stables, he saw a feminine figure in a grey mantle slip into the postern gate and he realised that the game was shifting under his feet.

Mirella's visiting Verdelho . . . Why?

It didn't surprise him, but it made him ill to see treachery unfold. She was inside for thirty minutes, and when she left, by the same entrance, he was waiting. As she took a back street, where snow was piled up over frozen rubbish, he padded in her wake, wondering . . .

He soon realised that she was heading right towards the grain silo he'd used for observation, and that increased his unease. His instincts said *run*, but he couldn't, not without learning what she was up to.

A minute after she entered the old granary, he followed, dagger in hand. Light streaked in from the high windows, illuminating the woman in the middle of the empty silo.

Before he could decide whether to speak or strike, a sorcerer's conjured light flared above, flintlock hammers clicked in the rafters and two men entered behind him. A quick glance round told him they were armoured, with swords drawn.

'Expecting someone, Master Zorne?' Ferdan Verdelho called. He swung down athletically, like a gymnast, landing perfectly a few yards away, his sword drawn.

Zorne felt positively lumpen by comparison, but he backed towards the woman in grey and placed his dagger against her jugular.

'Move, and she dies,' he warned the Courser, as the soldiers closed in.

Then the lady's hood fell and he realised what he should have sensed already: she *wasn't* Mirella Mandaryke. He was momentarily stunned, because he wasn't that stupid. He'd seen the woman move and a thousand subliminal signals had confirmed for him, even with her face hidden, that she was Mirella.

'Who are you?' he hissed at the mousy-haired, snub-nosed creature with bad teeth.

'That's your only question?' Ferdan Verdelho snorted. 'Gerda's Teats, I can think of a hundred – a *thousand* – better ones! She's just a cheap whore, dolled up to lure you out. Did you really think I hadn't seen you? Go ahead, do your worst to her,' he invited sarcastically, before telling his men, 'Kill him.'

Zorne shifted his grip, purposing to twist her around in front of him as a shield. But as he did, her face flared and changed and a spark blossomed in her right hand, then billowed. His world turned brilliant orange, and heat and flame devoured it.

For hours, Zorne floated in the void, a *nothingness* that didn't surprise him at all, because he'd always known that there was nothing, before or after life. The world was an accident, there were no gods, no Paradise nor Pit. Nothing but the *emptiness* . . .

. . . then suddenly, he woke, and realised that only moments had passed. He was lying on the floor of the silo, or what was left of it, for the walls had been blasted away and the roof was gone, leaving just the frame, which was beginning to burn. The latent heat was enough to sear his eyeballs.

But he was lying within a translucent bubble of light beneath a kneeling woman, her face cowled again. Charred bodies surrounded them: Verdelho and his comrades, rendered completely unidentifiable.

Two spirits clung to the woman: a dove, perched on her right shoulder, and a bat on her left. *Two familiars? Is that even possible?* Then he blinked, and they were gone, leaving him wondering if he had imagined it.

The woman lowered her hood and looked down at him.

Teirhinan Deathless.

'What . . .?' he croaked. 'How−?'

'Lady Mandaryke was concerned that Verdelho had discerned her purpose and asked me to intercede,' the Otravian sorceress told him, her cold reek filling his nostrils. 'I went to the Courser, offering to lure you into a trap. He took the bait.'

He stared up at her, knowing she could snuff him out as easily as she'd destroyed Verdelho. *She summoned a warding that protected us from that explosion. That takes strength beyond what I even thought possible . . .*

'Why are you here?' he dared to ask.

'Duty,' she replied, which cut directly to his core.

Either she is the other half of my soul − or she knows exactly how to intrigue me.

She rose from the smouldering ground, flicked her grey curls from her face, replaced her cowl and looked down at him. 'Shall we go and report? Lord Mandaryke needs to know what transpired here.'

Zorne stood, as a thought struck him. *Duty to whom?*

But he dared not ask, afraid to know whether she was now his staunchest ally, or his deadliest enemy.

5

Unseen Killer

The first day of the outbreak, there were five grefilia cases: the Tangato girl, who'd developed horrible genital pustules, and a pair of Tangato warriors who'd lain with one of Gravis Tavernier's inn-girls, then passed the disease on to their wives. But cock-rot was treatable and of less concern than the other two diseases now spreading fast.

Kemara, shuttling between the two camps, couldn't even identify, much less cure, the new conditions. Semus and a handful of his mates had the choking fever, and between them, they'd infected two widows and three children, while nine Tangato warriors were down with the bloody flux. None of her usual treatments were working.

On the third day, the numbers of both flux and choking victims, which now included Relf Turner and his family, doubled, and then doubled again each following day. Kemara and the Tangato priest-healers had started isolating the victims, but it was quickly apparent that they were already too late.

On the sixth day, Relf's eldest son died, and the distraught engineer almost stopped fighting himself. During the night, Varahana's nuns drained his lungs five times before he rallied – but by then, dozens more were showing symptoms, with phlegm forming so fast in the lungs that it was suffocating them. If the patients couldn't cough, retching it up, every few minutes, they had no chance. Falling asleep could be fatal.

I'm going to catch this too, Kemara though numbly, as she and the five Sisters of Gerda moved from victim to victim, faces and names blurring as they filled steam baths to loosen the mucus before using hollowed-out green bamboo tubes to draw the noxious substance from the lungs.

They lost Sister Flodda on the eighth day, struck down despite her god's protection.

For the Tangato, it was even worse. The healers had no idea how to fight the horrific blood-flux which was overwhelming the villagers, though they tried all their normal remedies, from pine-resin incense to fish-oil lotions. Even the Yokei couldn't arrest or even affect the invisible ailment: the victims were bleeding internally, and bed-rest was only slowing it.

'We're none of us fully trained physicians,' Raythe reminded Kemara, when she came raging to him in her despair. 'We can only do our best.'

'Our best isn't kragging good enough!' she shrieked, stomping out. 'It never is.'

Time passed in a slowly unfolding nightmare. The joy of the Matsuri-Tako vanished completely; instead that magical day now felt like a truly dreadful mistake. After two weeks, there were hundreds sick; after three, more than a thousand were infected and they'd buried two hundred Tangato and twenty Magnians.

By the fourth week, half of the mahotsu-kai and one of the Yokei were dead, and three other Yokei had come down with the disease. The invisible foe was beyond them all.

Praying didn't work, and in any case, congregating only spread the disease. The tribes isolated themselves from each other, some driving out the affected, like culling a herd, but the damage was already done.

There was a little light in the darkness: many people were somehow pulling through, and Varahana worked late into the night, every night, trying to work out why they'd survived – but without any equipment to examine them properly, nothing helpful was gained.

'Is there any way I can help?' Raythe asked her, after another long and fruitless day. The priestess had retreated with her supplies of powders and tinctures to her workshop to brood alone, but she smiled when she looked up and saw him.

She ran her hand over her downy scalp, which she'd neglected to shave in the tumult of the past few weeks. 'Well, do you remember I told you about the Bolgravian Medicalus—?'

'The one facing necromancy charges?'

'Aye, him.' She rolled her eyes. 'Remember who's in power in Bolgravia: racist bigots who believe that only priests should be permitted to heal – and that, through prayer alone. They're anti-scholarship, anti-medicine, anti-everything. Anyway, he's a genius. The thing is, he was advocating injecting dead disease cells into a person to trigger resistance.'

Raythe pulled a face. *Dead disease cells? Did it work?*'

'The Church made sure no one was ever permitted to try it. But I made notes, and the compounds he believed could be used to provide a base elixir are easily obtained, even out here.' She tapped the notebook in front of her. 'If I could be given access to the bodies of the dead, maybe I could work something out . . .?'

Raythe winced. There were strong Deist traditions about burials: most people believed they'd be reborn in Paradise in their earthly bodies, and therefore the Church condemned any kind of posthumous dissection.

'Didn't Sister Emaria die a day ago?' Raythe asked. 'You could sanction that yourself, couldn't you?'

'I'd require the consent of the other Sisters,' Varahana replied. 'Not legally, but morally.'

'Give it a try. They all respect you.'

'I will.' She smiled sadly. 'There's an ancient philosopher, Emmeus Aurenius, who said that life is eternal: he postulated that when we die, every single cell in our bodies will be broken down and turned into something else. We are made of matter that has existed since the dawn of time, and we'll last – in some form or other – for ever.'

'Hmm. Profound but useless,' Raythe pointed out. 'Like most philosophy.'

'Peasant.'

'That's me.' He patted her arm. 'I'll talk to Shiazar about getting access to a Tangato body so that we can examine the blood-flux. And if you do need help with a Magnian body with the lung disease, let me know.'

'Thanks, Raythe. I'll sort some notes for you to take to your meeting with the Queen and her people tomorrow so you can persuade the chiefs.'

'Sorry to load more on you,' he said, impulsively giving her a hug – just as Vidar Vidarsson loomed large in the doorway.

'Not interrupting, I hope?' the big bearskin rumbled. He carefully put down the bowls of steaming broth he was carrying.

'Varahana and I? We're a story that never began,' Raythe told him. He jabbed a finger skywards. 'Your competition is up there – and he's a lot better-looking than me.'

'Do you think?' Varahana said lightly. 'I've always pictured Deo as rather grim and dull.'

Vidar pulled up a stool. 'I had a crush on a statue of Gerda when I was nine,' he chuckled. 'Used to imagine her coming to life and playing chase-the-chicken with me.'

'Better than fantasising about milkmaids, I guess,' Raythe chuckled.

'That came later.'

As he closed the door, Raythe saw Varahana and Vidar, sitting opposite each other, wearing identical expressions of bliss and torture. *The agony of requited but forbidden love.* He got part-way through a prayer for them before remembering that Deo was the problem, not the solution.

But he had other matters on his plate right now. Tomorrow he would have to attend Shiazar's council. The way things were going, he feared the goodwill between his people and hers was evaporating fast.

If this gets much worse, they're likely to turn against us – and then what will we do?

'We're being overwhelmed,' Raythe admitted to Shiazar. 'We're doing all we can, but it's just not enough.' He looked around at Shiazar's council, held on the hill overlooking the village: just Natomo, the Hiriwa rangatira, Rima and Zar, and a token guard. The other chieftains had returned to their tribes, to keep the peace and contain the disease.

'Ikendo spoke truly, that these invaders would be the death of us,' said Natomo, voicing the common view. Rather than blame their Queen, the Tangato tribesmen held the Magnians fully accountable – the fact that Raythe's people were also affected was eliciting no sympathy at all. Raythe's people were now guarding the disease-ridden bridge district like a rampart.

'Hindsight is little better than blindness,' Rima rebuked Natomo. She'd been a constant supporter of Shiazar's decision. 'Is there progress in finding a cure?'

'Varahana has some leads, but we lack proper equipment,' Raythe reported. 'She can't perform miracles.'

The masked Queen said nothing, but Raythe sensed her composure was fragile.

'So you have no answers?' Natomo pressed. 'You've learned *nothing* of how to cure this?'

'We've learned some of what *doesn't* work!' Raythe retorted, 'such as chanting and drums and the other superstitious rubbish your priests use. At least our remedies are prolonging life.'

'Better to be at peace with the gods when dying than incurring their wrath while delaying the inevitable.'

'Peace, Rangatira Natomo,' Shiazar commanded, and the chieftain lapsed into seething silence. 'Rangatira Raythe,' she went on, 'is there any way we can help Priestess Varahana?'

He chose his words equally carefully. 'There is a theory – from a very great healer – that the blood of someone who has survived a sickness can be used to – um . . . pre-cure – no, let's say *protect* those yet to fall sick. Varahana is investigating that. It may help if we were permitted to examine the bodies of the dead.'

'What?' Natomo exclaimed. 'That is blasphemous – a dead body is sacred!'

'If we could examine just a few of the bodies, we could learn so much,' Raythe pleaded, fixing his eyes on the Queen. 'Please, Majesty: once life is gone, truly, a body is just a body. Whether you believe that we all have souls, or that when life ends there is nothing, the flesh itself is an empty vessel.'

'*Blasphemy*,' Natomo spat, jabbing a finger at Raythe. 'The gods will strike you down.'

Raythe was conscious that even Rima and Zar were looking appalled. He'd been terrified that his daughter would quickly fall sick, but when they both remained unaffected, he started to wonder if the post-battle plagues they had suffered from had perhaps built up some sort of resistance. He still wished this was something they could both walk away from.

But we can't. We're committed to this place and these people.

Finally, Shiazar spoke. 'I cannot ask my people to transgress against the gods.'

Natomo bared his teeth triumphantly.

'But I can give you access to the body of Yokei Jatana, who died a day ago, provided it is returned intact, with all incisions closed,' she went on. 'And I will address our people, advising them of this research, and inviting them to do the same, for the good of us all.'

Raythe felt a surge of gratitude. 'Thank you, Majesty.' He ignored Natomo, who was still scowling, and told them, 'This will give us real heart in the struggle. It may save us all.'

Shiazar was as good as her word: the wrapped-up body of Jatana of the Yokei was delivered on a stretcher borne by four warriors, with Rima escorting them. Raythe ignored his jittery guards and met them at the gatehouse to escort the Tangato party to Varahana's workroom. The warriors left quickly, but Rima remained, ostensibly to ensure that the dead woman was properly respected. Raythe guessed she was curious to see Varahana in action.

Kemara joined them to add her own practical experience to Varahana's theoretical knowledge. Raythe had been worried she might object to the Tangato girl's presence, but though she raised her eyebrows, she pressed noses with Rima warmly enough.

Pleasantries completed, Varahana and Kemara went to work, while Sister Marta ensured they received everything they needed and Vidar kept the curious away. Varahana, faced with the body of an Aldar woman, was clearly in scholar's heaven. She treated it with reverence, but couldn't help exclaiming in wonder at each feature that differed from humankind. 'It's like she's a different species,' she kept muttering.

For Rima, watching a body being opened up was a new thing, and it proved to be an ordeal, for all she had a strong stomach, as Varahana and Kemara took samples from Jatana's stomach, intestines, glands, kidneys and bowels before examining them minutely.

By sunset, they were all exhausted, but Varahana thought she'd identified the blood disease besetting the Tangato. 'It's an intense variant of Mersham's Flux, named after a general whose army contracted it in Shadra. It's a vicious thing: the pancreas produces fluids to fight it, but when attacked, the infection dissolves into an acid that eats the walls of the lower intestine, causing bleeding and worse.'

'How do we fight it?'

'I don't know,' Varahana said wearily. 'The original outbreak killed tens of thousands before it weakened enough to become just a nasty bowel irritation. It's never really been cured.'

They all groaned.

'So has this been for nothing?' Rima asked, her voice cracking.

'It's too soon to say that,' Kemara answered, swaying a little. 'We know what it is now, so maybe we can . . .'

Her voice trailed off, and suddenly Raythe realised Kemara had gone deathly pale. She'd been working day and night for weeks now, and she was wheezing – which was one of the early symptoms of the choking disease. Right now she was peering around blearily, her eyes unfocused, and Rima, who was closest to her, grabbed her arms.

'You're *so* beautiful,' Kemara slurred. 'I could *kiss* you . . .'

'Is she drunk?' Rima blurted, tightening her grip on the healer's biceps and holding her away. Then she looked aghast. 'No, I think she's—'

'Kemara—' Raythe started, as she folded and fell sideways, partially supported by Rima, with bile pouring from her mouth.

A moment later there was a foul stench and the back of her skirt went dark red.

'Oya!' Rima shrieked, looking round for aid. 'Help her!'

Raythe dashed in, grabbed for Kemara's pulse and put his cheek to her mouth. 'She's breathing,' he reported, tipping her onto her side so she wouldn't choke. 'How did she get so sick so fast?'

'She hid it,' Varahana answered, hurrying in. 'She said she was fine.'

'I can believe that,' Raythe grumbled. 'Stubborn cow!'

'We need to drain her lungs, right now,' Varahana said.

They used the hollowed bamboo tubes to draw out the fluids, but Kemara continued to bleed from her nethers. 'She's got both conditions,' Varahana noted. 'That's very bad. We've not seen that before . . .'

'How can that be?'

'Who knows? She's been overexposed to them both, after all . . .'

'We have to save her,' Rima blurted. 'There's a place, a sacred place—'

'No,' Raythe snapped, 'no superstitious bullshit—'

'You know *nothing!*' Rima fired back. 'It's the place I've been wanting to take her, to introduce her to the maho. The Kaiju is there – it can save her.'

'The what?'

'The Kaiju: the guardian spirit of the Fenua Tangato.' Rima's voice was getting shriller.

'There's no such thing—'

She gripped his arm. 'She's dying! We *must* try!'

He turned to Varahana. 'What do you think?'

'There's nothing I can do for her but slow her death,' Varahana admitted wretchedly.

Raythe grimaced, then looked at Rima. 'All right. We're in your hands.'

Kemara's awareness returned slowly. First, she felt the dreadful choking sensation of a clogged-up chest, then the queasy feeling of having soiled herself. Her guts felt dreadful, like they were slowly dissolving, her body was icy-cold, though she was sweating. Jolting had woken her, although it took her some time to work out that she was wrapped in blankets and being pulled on a wheeled stretcher. The air was biting, numbing her fingers and cheeks.

After a while she realised the strange shape beside her was a woman, riding a phorus bird.

'Rima?' she croaked.

'Aie,' the Tangato girl answered. 'I'm here. Stay strong.'

'Wh–?'

She heard Raythe's voice and blearily recognised that he was riding the horse that was pulling her stretcher along. 'Hold on,' he called. 'It's not far.'

That meant nothing to her, but she was too exhausted to care, drifting back into a reverie as the daylight faded. Her lungs were bags of sludge, and coughing up the lumps of mucus took all her strength. *I'm dying*, she decided dreamily. *We're on the way to the graveyard.*

As the sun set, the sorcerous light Raythe conjured to show the way revealed ice-encrusted pines. Kemara became fixated by the dance of snowflakes swirling about them, so mesmerised she forgot to breathe, until Raythe stopped and forced a tube down her tortured throat.

'Come on!' he growled, his face swimming before hers as he tried to drain her lungs. 'I thought you had the guts for this!'

Krag you, Lord High-and-Mighty Vyre! She hawked and spat. *I'll show you!*

They went on into the darkness, and now she felt another presence, a pale wraith flitting among the frosted trees: Ionia, her mentor in the mizra. She recalled their last night together, and the ugly spat they'd parted on. *You're a parasite*, Ionia had shrieked. *Why did I let you get your claws into me?*

It's you who ruined me, Kemara had howled back. *You made me into a monster like you!*

Minutes later, when witch-hunters had burst into the inn, Kemara got out, Ionia didn't. The next and last time she saw her, Ionia was tied to a stake, her dress afire and her face contorted in an agonised scream.

But right now, it was as if that had never happened. Ionia was gazing at her from the trees, calling her home. *I've missed you*, she whispered. *I'm so glad you've come back to me.*

'How much further?' Raythe gasped. The air was thick with snow now, and the pines so weighed down that branches were regularly breaking, the deafening *cracks* setting his horse and Rima's phorus bird to skittering. Going on took a real act of will, but they couldn't travel faster for fear of tipping the stretcher.

'We're nearly there,' Rima said at last. 'It's just through these trees.'

Both she and Raythe were uneasy, feeling that tingling of senses that warned of hostile spirits.

'*Lumis amplius*,' he told Cognatus, and the familiar brightened his light globe, forcing the shadows away.

They had entered a corridor of ancient trees with large faces carved onto the trunks, six on either side. He identified Kagemori and Kiiyan, Ankazo the Jade Emperor, Shinija-Kyu the Dragon-King and the other Aldar gods, with old shells for eyes and white stones for teeth, all stained with dark resin.

'Which one's the Kaiju?' he asked Rima.

'None of them: these are the gods. The Kaiju is a spirit, and she is vast as the land.'

'She?'

'She or He; that is meaningless. The Kaiju is all things, a spirit of land and water, forest and sky; a tanefa, a dragon, gifted to us by the gods. Sometimes it manifests as a giant beast, bigger than a mountain; other times as a river in flood, or a storm front, or a comet. It is the spirit of the land, its protector and guardian.'

It might sound like superstition to Raythe, but he was learning that things were different here. 'Why should such a being be here, but nowhere else in the world?'

Rima gave him a superior look. 'We of the Tangato are at one with the land – your kind are not. Now be silent.' She raised her voice and started chanting a prayer.

'I asked the Kaiju to permit us here,' she explained once she'd finished, as they broke through the trees and reached a stream with mist hovering over the water.

'What now?' Raythe asked, as they came to a halt.

'The far side is a sacred island,' Rima told him. 'I must take Kemara there. You should wait here: only mahotsu-kai are safe on the island.'

'I'm not here to be safe,' he growled. 'You'll need my help.'

Rima scowled, then shrugged. 'It's your life.'

They dismounted and unstrapped Kemara, and he lifted her as gently as he could, wincing at her hacking cough.

'Come,' Rima ordered, and she waded into the stream, still chanting her prayer.

Raythe followed, his boots filling with frigid water as the icy water reached his thighs. Rima's feather cloak and beaded skirt spread around her as she went in over her waist, then he was up to his hips and struggling to keep Kemara dry. But that was as deep as it got, and soon they were struggling onto a pebbled shore, staring into an interior thick with tangled willows.

Rima led him through the trees to a gigantic rock. 'This is Atama-Ryu, the Dragon Head.'

How the weathered, mossy rock got its name was easy to see: it was clearly shaped like a reptile's skull, and the 'mouth' was a shallow cave. It was there that Rima bade him place Kemara, on the cold pebbled surface.

'We need a fire,' she said, 'but use fallen dead branches only.' She bent over Kemara, stroking her forehead, and he heard her whisper, 'We're here, Kemara. Be strong.'

Raythe went to find wood, leaving Rima pulling out pouches of powders and herbs. As he worked, he puzzled over the riddle of the Kaiju. *What is it? And why is it here, but such things are unknown in Magnia?* As he pondered, various facts, rumours and legends began to take shape in his mind.

Then Rima called for help, and he returned to help clear Kemara's lungs again as the fight for her life began in earnest.

Mokomoko, Rima's lizard familiar, was not happy. The little islet was a powerful place, one a mahotsu-kai came to only at great need, and Rima had been here just once before, when Hetaru had deemed her ready to be introduced to the Kaiju. It was her intention to bring Zar, once she too was ready.

This is Rima, my Daughter-in-Wisdom, Hetaru had told the listening darkness, that night. *Hearken to her, and withhold thy wrath.*

It was that wrath that Rima feared right now: Raythe's praxis was an unsettling presence and she could feel the Kaiju was hostile to him, as well as to Kemara's mizra taint. But she had to try.

'I, Rima, apprentice of Hetaru, bring you Kemara, my Sister-in-Wisdom,' she called over the fire. 'I am your servant, Great One. Hear my prayers.'

She sensed the darkness hearkening, but Kemara's shallow breath reeked of death; her pale skin was so waxy that her veins looked like macabre tattoos. Shielding her from Raythe's sight, she peeled away Kemara's sweaty, bloodstained clothing, wrinkling her nose at the stench. Only then could she see the healer was too skinny, hollowed out by days of labour and sickness.

It's too late, she found herself thinking, then chastised herself, for they'd barely begun.

She dusted the fire with a mixture of the dried herbs, inhaling the narcotic aroma, then called to the watching night, 'Great Kaiju, hear your servant. Come unto this woman and bless her,' she beseeched, as the rich herbal scent filled the cave. 'Grant her your blessing, Great Spirit.'

She felt the air throb in response. *Yes, the Kaiju is coming*, she exulted. *She'll save her—*

But a cold gust blew across the clearing, like a slap on her skin, and the mist coalesced around a shadowy figure flowing through the willows, full of indistinct menace.

'What in the Pit—?' Raythe began, rising to his feet.

'Mokomoko,' Rima called out loud in alarm, '*kaneska alla maho! Kore wa basho—*'

But before she could finish, something unseen smashed both Raythe and her aside. What felt like a massive fist to the chest battered her across the clearing, while Raythe cracked his head into the Dragon Head rock and went limp.

Winded and dazed, Rima watched helplessly as a burning woman formed in the cave mouth, her flesh like smouldering coal, flames licking her dress. With a hungry sigh, she reached for Kemara—

Kemara dreamed of being cradled in a smoky cavern, where strong fumes made her senses swirl. A voice she knew was chanting something, and a vast shape was forming in the clouds above. Fear rose inside her at its sheer scale, but she clung to that familiar voice and its fierce vitality.

But then another presence slithered in. *She can't have you*, it whispered. *You're mine.*

Kemara writhed, tried to crawl away, but she fetched up against rock and her eyes flipped open. The dark shape looming over her was indistinct amidst the smoke, but still chillingly familiar.

'Kemara,' it rasped, and her blood went cold.

'*Ionia?*' she croaked.

Fear lent her clarity. This was a potent place, a place of the spirits – and Ionia had found her. *They burned her, and in so doing, turned her into a mizra spirit* . . . Her former mentor and lover loomed over her in horrifying clarity, burning still as if on the pyre, flesh blistering and hair ablaze.

Kemara, she breathed, *come – we'll be together for ever.*

If she opened herself up, she'd have Ionia lodged inside her and she'd regain the mizra. All her rage would again manifest itself in blood and power, and she could smash aside enemies and force the world to take notice. And she had never forgotten Ionia's hands in the night, the taste of her mouth and the comfort of having someone to share the darkness.

As Ionia reached out, Kemara found no way to resist . . .

'No!' Rima shrieked, scrabbling towards the mouth of the Dragon Head, where the burning woman now crouched over an unresisting Kemara. '*Kaiju, watashi iru!*' she howled. *Kaiju, enter me!*

Even as she launched herself at Kemara, the Kaiju slammed into her body. It was like having molten rock poured down her throat and being immolated from inside out. She saw her veins go vivid, flaming beneath her own skin as she staggered, then surged towards the burning spectre.

The wraith sensed her coming and turned an instant before they collided. Rolling over and over across the stony clearing, they savaged each other in a desperate battle to survive and conquer.

It was the shrieking that drew Raythe from the darkness. His skull was throbbing and he could feel blood matting his hair – and Cognatus was wailing at him to wake up, *wake up!*

He wiped the trickling blood from his eyes and in the shadow of the Dragon Head rock he saw two shapes wrapped round each other, pulling and tearing at each other: two women, their skin burning like embers, wrestling for ascendancy, hands and nails ripping at throats and faces. Caught up in their frenzy, he couldn't identify either, but he found his sword hilt and staggered to his feet.

One of them must be Rima . . .

Just as he reached them, one of them rolled atop the other, shrieking in triumph as a dagger of molten rock formed in her free hand. The woman beneath caught the wrist an instant before it fell and they howled in each other's faces, as Raythe stumbled closer, aiming a blow at the one on top's back . . .

. . . just as they rolled and his plunging steel took the other woman in the side instead. He wrenched it free in horror as she convulsed, and the woman with the lava-stone dagger plunged it into the stricken woman's throat, cleaved through sinew and lodged it in her spinal cord. She collapsed, then burst into flames as the woman on top scrabbled backwards . . .

. . . and became Rima, her skin cooling to glowing bronze, lacerated by dozens of gashes and cuts, her chest heaving and her eyes like saucers.

The flaming woman howled '*KEMARA—!*' and collapsed into burning bones.

Rima looked up at Raythe, panting. 'How did you tell us apart?'

'Uh . . . easy . . .' he managed. 'Never in doubt.'

For a moment the whole islet was silent.

Then it shook, and the Dragon Head rock *moved*.

Kemara felt like a puppet with no strings, utterly spent and horrified at her own fatal inertia, but capable only of gazing on helpless as her fate was decided. But when Ionia shrieked and collapsed in flames, she felt overwhelming relief – and guilt for all but surrendering to the darkness.

Then came the realisation that this was no victory: nothing else had changed. The diseases inside her were still ripping her apart.

I'm still dying.

As if in answer to that thought, the ground shuddered beneath her.

Are the Deists right? Is there really a Pit below, where sinners burn for ever?

She saw Rima's face swell up in horror, and she shrieked, 'Kaiju, afina kei!' *Guardian Spirit, help her!*

'Kragga mor!' Raythe shouted. 'What's happening?'

Kemara wailed as the ground inside the cave tilted and slid into a sinkhole of falling debris. Rima and Raythe lunged for her, but something thick and wet wrapped round her midriff like a tentacle – or a *tongue*. She went to scream . . .

. . . but instead of emitting any sound, she lost complete control, gushing thick mucus in a surge that almost choked her, and in the same moment, purged her bowels in a bloody rush. Then that thick cord pulled her down and the darkness swallowed her, body and soul.

'KEMARA!' Rima threw herself at the sinkhole as Kemara vanished. Raythe tried to help, shovelling stones from the pit as it filled. She caught a glimpse of a flailing hand and lunged, but grasped only stones – then the hole began to flood with groundwater. They glimpsed something glowing and each lunged, coming up with a fistful of jagged stone, then rolled free before they too were swallowed up by the rapidly filling hole. Above them, the dragon-head stone loomed with menace.

'KEMARA!' Rima wailed again. 'KEMARA!'

But there was no sign of the woman, and they had no choice but to back out.

Frenzy gave way to exhaustion and they collapsed to the ground, winded and in shock.

She's gone . . .

For a time, Rima couldn't think beyond that.

But as rational thought returned, she found a straw of hope. *The mizra spirit who came was destroyed . . . and the Kaiju did answer my call. Earth is Her element . . . so perhaps She claimed Kemara?'*

She tried to recapture her link to the Kaiju, but it was gone. She realised she was still holding whatever it was she had grabbed and opened her fingers to reveal a lump of yellowish crystal.

She turned to Raythe to see he was also holding one, though his was dark red.

'What was that thing?' he asked, his voice sounding a little dazed.

How are you so blind? she wondered. 'It was the Kaiju.'

'Aye, I got that – but *what* is it?' he persisted. 'A giant spirit, a thousand times more potent than any familiar, tied to the only place I know of that still contains massive reserves of istariol . . .'

'Istariol is the gift of the Kaiju,' Rima replied, unable to follow his train of thought. She found her battered feather cloak among the debris and wrapped it around her for warmth. 'How do we bring Kemara back?'

Raythe was lost in his own train of thought. 'If Varahana's theory is right, istariol consumes water, and grows . . .' His eyes lit up in wonder. *'But could istariol be* sentient *as well?'*

'What is that word? Mokomoko does not know it.'

'Sentient? It means something that has the ability to sense and feel – not necessarily able to reason or remember, but able to feel pain, pleasure and maybe even emotions.'

'Meaning?' she replied, none the wiser.

'I think your legends have it the wrong way round,' Raythe said. 'Istariol isn't a gift of the Kaiju – in fact, it *is* the Kaiju. Throughout the world, istariol has been treated as an inert mineral, because we praxis-using Magnians couldn't perceive it like you do. But people like you, who have the maho – you can actually *communicate* with it.'

'I still don't understand,' Rima muttered, too overwhelmed with fear for Kemara to focus properly. 'The Kaiju is our sacred protector, not a lump of rock.'

'I think it can be both,' Raythe insisted. 'The istariol has veins throughout the Fenua Tangato: that's a massive field of energy. In Magnia we couldn't sense it, so we mined it. Here, you worship it. It's like a god you've created.'

She shook her head. 'Gods make people, not the other way round.'

He waved that away absently. 'But why did it take Kemara? Can you ask it?'

'I've tried.'

'Try again.'

85

His insistence was annoying – she could understand why Kemara didn't like him – but she put that aside, bowed her head and *reached* . . .

It was hard, but finally, she sensed *something*. It was akin to a giant spiderweb, or maybe tree roots, or even veins, as Raythe had suggested. But there was nothing 'sentient' about it.

No, wait – what's that? It was like a node in the web of energy, a knot or a cocoon, such as a spider might wrap its prey in until they were ready to feed, or even a pouch to protect their eggs . . .

Is Kemara in there?

If so, then she was going to be consumed – or transfigured. Both options were horrifying, but she had no idea which was more likely.

Trust in the Kaiju, she told herself firmly. *Trust in the gods.*

It was a hope to cling to.

She looked at Raythe. 'I believe the Kaiju has her. There is hope she may be given back.'

Although not much . . .

The Magnian lord scowled. Looking unusually helpless, he admitted, 'Then we've done all we can here.' He held up the red crystal. 'What about these?'

She invoked Mokomoko and examined her own yellowish crystal curiously – and her maho-senses flinched at the noisome *wrongness* radiating from it. That scared her – but then she realised what she held. 'These are crystallised fluids from Kemara's body. This one is the lung disease.' She held out her hand for Raythe's deep red crystal. 'And this is the blood-flux disease. But I don't know what to do with them.'

'Varahana will,' Raythe replied, with a hard smile.

They rose shakily, bringing them face to face, suddenly close and intimate. They'd been through something profound, she knew: they'd fought side by side, overcome a deadly thing and experienced the miraculous. She sensed a sudden heat in him, an awareness of her body and a hunger for life and living.

'May I tell you something?' she said earnestly, as he shaped himself as if to kiss her.

'Aye,' he said throatily, restraining himself.

'My preference is for women,' she said firmly, and stepped away.

'*Oh*,' he said, blinking in surprise.

'In our society, it is known that sometimes we love those of the same gender. It's rare, and it isn't approved of, but it's not blasphemous. The Yokei made us accept this. It's still not easy for those of us made this way, because motherhood and marriage are highly prized. But we are tolerated, and I am mahotsu-kai, which helps.'

Raythe looked away, clearly uncomfortable, then he sighed. 'Well, I can only say that every man alive is in mourning. And, um . . . when Kemara tried to kiss you last night . . . that wasn't drunkenness or fever. The only person she's ever spoken of as being close to was a woman named Ionia.' He gestured at the pile of smouldering bones. 'That was her. She was a mizra-witch.'

'May the gods give her peace,' Rima intoned. Then she added, wistfully, 'I don't know whether Kemara and I might be friends . . . for now it's enough if we can get her back alive.'

'Then I hope your Kiiyan is merciful,' Raythe said, invoking one of the Aldar gods, presumably out of politeness. 'We could really use some mercy.'

Despite their exhaustion, the crystals offered possibilities they needed to explore, so they readied themselves wearily for the return journey. Raythe packed up the stretcher and mounted his horse while Rima summoned her bird.

They set out for home, desperately hoping they now had the means to battle the unfolding catastrophe.

6

This is How I Learn

By midday, Raythe and Rima were only three miles south of the ravine that encircled Rath Argentium, horse and phorus bird, or kikihana, as Rima called it, keeping pace despite very different gaits.

When they came across a solitary Tangato stilt hut in a small glade. Rima called a greeting – at which a boy emerged, his face streaked with mud and tears. She gave a sharp cry, dismounted and hurried towards the child.

'Stay back,' Raythe called, as he too dismounted. 'His parents may have the sickness.'

'We have to start somewhere,' she answered, sweeping the boy up. 'Here, take him.'

Raythe took the boy gingerly, holding on tight as he tried to wriggle free, while Rima entered the hut. Then she poked her head out, her face stricken. 'They're dying in here!'

The cooking pit outside the hut had gone out, and that spoke volumes: keeping the home fire alight was a ritual in most cultures. Raythe peered in and saw Rima hunched over a tangle of bodies. The small hut stank of vomit and excrement. 'How bad is it?'

'There are three of them. The little girl is gone. Her parents live – just.'

He bit his lip. 'It's only one family. Your whole tribe is waiting–'

'You think I know what I'm doing?' she snapped. 'This is how I learn!'

Although they had the crystals, they didn't know what to do with them, but Rima was right: this gave them a chance to experiment without a thousand people hanging over them, waiting to celebrate or condemn.

'Where do you want them?' he asked.

'Outside. It is *vile* in here.'

He edged in and pulled out the dead girl, her cold corpse piteously wasted, and laid her under a tree, then helped Rima move the living. The family were Rotomahau, Rima said, pointing to the man's beard and distinctive tattoos. The hut was old and dilapidated; he guessed that the family had fled the city, found this place and stopped when the sickness took them.

While Rima lit the fire, he rigged up a lean-to beside the cooking-pit, then got water for Rima to feed to the unconscious adults.

'Best we start,' she said, her voice shaking, and took the red crystal from Raythe. The temperature was dropping rapidly and the skies threatened more snow.

When she engaged her maho, the crystal began to glow, like sunlight through red glass. 'Aka nua,' she breathed, her eyes lighting up as well. 'I can see ... ah ... Kiiyan have mercy!' Her voice was filled with awe. 'When I hold this and examine him, I see ... Look, I can *see* something, like spiky seeds, spreading everywhere ...'

Breakthrough ...

Raythe cast his mind back to old medical lessons and conversations with Varahana. 'Those seeds are disease cells – can you see what they are doing?'

Rima groaned. 'How do I tell?'

He had no idea. He grimaced, 'Just watch – and let's hope you'll see.'

Rima hissed in frustration, but it wasn't long before she exclaimed, 'At'a! I see it! The spiked ones keep bursting, and this creates more. It's *horrible.*'

'Can you see the body's response?'

'What response?' she demanded. 'How?'

He gave her agonised look. 'I don't know ... I can't see what you do.' Then he gathered himself. 'Listen, maybe I *can* do this ... let me try, anyway.'

He called in Cognatus, then laid a hand on the fist-sized scarlet crystal she held and sent his own awareness into it. He touched Rima's mind and realised that Zar was right, the maho was much stronger than his praxis. But he reached out as if she were Kemara and they were trying to activate a meld.

It didn't entirely work – there was no synergy between them, no amplifying of strength – but he was able to forge a weak link and see the flow of the cells in the man's gut and the way the disease seemed to reproduce . . .

. . . then he went deeper, and she followed him through. 'Aie, I see now,' she murmured. 'Through you, I see . . .'

She placed the crystal on the man's belly, muttering instructions to Mokomoko. Raythe tried to contain his hopes. *No Magnian praxis-mage could do this*, he reflected. *There's no blame if she can't.*

Oblivious to his doubts, Rima set to work . . . but in minutes, the man was dead. 'I tried to kill the disease, but whatever I attacked split even faster,' she groaned. 'I can't do this.'

Raythe gripped her shoulder. 'There's no time to grieve. Try again!'

She took the rebuke better than he would have. With a sob, she shuffled over to the mother and this time they worked together, with him the guide and her the strength. Finally, he truly *saw*. 'There!' he exclaimed. 'Look – we don't attack it, we *smother* it . . . See *this* type of cell? It's produced by the body in response, it latches onto the disease cell and suffocates it. We need more of *that* . . .'

The young boy, who'd been watching uncomprehendingly, crawled in between them and hugged Rima's leg, watching his comatose mother with big, moist eyes.

'Eh, poia,' Rima said at last, her face lifting. 'She lives! Now for this boy.'

Raythe looked at her in concern. She looked shattered. 'Are you sure?'

'Aie, it's not a problem, now I know what to do. Learning it was hard, but the act is simple. Come on, let's do it.'

A few minutes later, the boy's illness was neutralised too. He was left sleeping beside her mother, while Rima and Raythe were reeling, but it had been worth it.

For the blood-flux, at least, they had a cure.

Both were exhausted, the afternoon had fled and neither wanted to leave the mother and son alone, so they made camp for the night, fretting at the lost time, but grateful for the chance to recover.

Next morning Raythe unpacked the stretcher and loaded up the woman, then settled the boy before him in the saddle. As they rode north, the floating citadel loomed before them, lit by the rising sun.

'It's not so hard,' Rima enthused, despite her visible tiredness. 'I could do ten, maybe twenty a day.'

'That's not fast enough,' Raythe replied. 'At that pace, the disease will outrun us. We need to teach others – and hope Varahana can make an elixir that grants immunity. And there's still the lung disease to work on.'

Rima was clearly burning to return to her village to treat her own people, even though she was out on her feet. 'But the time we waste on teaching—'

'Will be repaid many times over,' he interrupted. 'We have to spread the load, so that the cure reaches every tribe swiftly. And we need to see if we can break up the crystals without losing their efficacy. We've made a big step, but we haven't completed the journey.'

She sagged a little, then lifted her chin, her pugnacious face shining. 'What next, then?'

'Let's go to Varahana's workshop and work on the lung disease. Then you can train your fellow mahotsu-kai, while I work to cure my people.'

She frowned, then agreed, 'Aie, that is fair.'

Cal Foaley, captaining the guard that morning, met them anxiously at the bridge into Rath Argentium. 'Raythe, what's happening? Where's Kemara?'

'No time, Cal – Kemara's still out there, but we've got to see Varahana.

Can you give this woman and her boy some food and drink, then bring them to the infirmary? Don't worry about the sickness, though,' he added, meeting the hunter's gaze meaningfully. 'They had the blood-flux, but it's been cured.'

Foaley's eyes lit up. 'Truly? You're a kragging miracle man, Raythe.'

'She's the miracle,' Raythe said, smiling at Rima. 'It was Rima's work. Pass the word, will you? Together, we can cure this.'

The news spread quickly: by the time they'd reached the infirmary, an anxious crowd was gathering outside. 'Kemara's still out there, seeking more answers,' he told them. Four more of his people were dead, and many more were on the downwards slope.

They met Varahana in the workshop. The body of Yokei Jatana had been returned to the Tangato, but Sister Emaria's corpse, now sewn up, was still lying in state. Jesco and Vidar had moved in to protect Varahana and the Sisters of Gerda, after word of the desecrations had got around and emotions were running high.

But by mid-afternoon, they had a possible cure for the lung-clotting disease too. Gravis Tavernier, currently the worst case, was chosen as their test subject.

'This is different to the stomach disease,' Raythe told Varahana, after two hours labouring with Rima over the innkeeper. 'The invader cells trigger a reaction, causing fluids and mucus to flood the lungs.'

'How do we fight that?' Rima asked.

Varahana perked up. 'This must be a variant of tubertysis . . . I should have known . . . There's no known treatment, but there *must* be a way – illnesses that kill their hosts die out. Successful diseases don't kill; they become harmless.'

Rima looked up, her expression puzzled. 'So what do we do?'

Varahana creased her brow, then began thinking aloud. 'We need to work on suppressing the gland that's responding to the invading cells: the one that's producing the fluids and mucus.'

Rima didn't know the vocabulary of medicine, and Raythe knew only a little, but with Varahana's guidance they were able to work it out. It was exacting work for the partnership, with Raythe's praxis providing the precision, while Rima's maho was the muscle.

Late that afternoon, Zarelda arrived, bearing clay pots filled with the minerals, herbs and extracts Varahana needed for her elixirs, then she joined the efforts, providing fresh energy just when they needed it.

Gravis' breathing sounded stronger and his lungs finally stopped filling up, just as the sun set. Even after Raythe and Rima had relinquished control of his body, he slept on, stable at last. He was, it appeared, cured.

It had been a long day.

Afterwards, they all sat in silence, giving solemn thanks to all the cosmic forces that had come together to allow them this victory. Eventually Varahana roused and began making notes, jotting away furiously with increasing urgency. 'This will be remembered by the ages,' she crowed.

'Well, we do have a path forward,' Raythe agreed. 'We have a method, but it requires both Rima and me; and maybe Zar, if she can be taught it. We'll use the crystals to treat active cases here and in the village. Varahana will work on elixirs for both conditions, so we can protect those who haven't yet caught the disease. We'll give priority to the blood-flux, because there are so many more suffering, and I suspect most of we Magnians have been exposed to the – what did you call it? tubertysis? – already.'

Varahana looked up from her notes. 'Yes, that's reasonable. And politically, it's much better if we're all seen working together.'

Raythe grinned. 'You've been following me around too long, Vara. You're starting to think like me.'

Varahana pulled a look of mock-disgust. 'Now you've made me hate myself.' But her eyes were shining as she contemplated a future that didn't include widespread disease and death.

Zarelda was often proud of her father, but mostly she hid that pride – she didn't want it to go to his head, or use it as emotional leverage to make her do as she was told – but today she didn't need to.

He, Rima and Varahana had come to the Hiriwa village and given Queen Shiazar an elixir that stopped the blood-flux – then they'd set straight to work curing the worst cases, training the other mahotsu-kai as they did. A lot of people recovered quite quickly, although they remained weak, but not all: there were still deaths, still funeral pyres burning constantly outside the village, still priests praying as they poured the ashes of the dead into the ravine, giving back to the land.

But the change was palpable: every day saw fewer cases and brought victory closer.

Zar was proud of herself, too, working alongside her father to wipe out the lung-clogging disease among the Magnians. There were losses and tears as day and night blurred into one long smear of time when she had to be reminded or even forced to wash, eat or sleep. She was drained to the core, feeling like she was ageing years to every day. But she got through, and so did their people.

A week later, Queen Shiazar presided over a thanksgiving ceremony. Rima, one of their own, was singled out for the greatest honour, but Varahana and her father were also honoured. Zar knew it was her father who had once again brought them all together, bridging the gap between the Tangato and the Magnians.

Sometimes leadership is about standing at the forefront; other times it's about arranging for others to shine, she realised. *My father does both . . . as does the Queen.*

Shiazar, resplendent in brilliant yellow and wearing the mask of Kii-yan, Mother of Mercy, led the celebration, and after bestowing precious jade carvings on the three adults, she called, 'Zarelda Vyre, come forth.'

She was presented with a beautiful carving of a stylised fox, and then stood with her father, Rima and Varahana to be presented to the massed Hiriwa. For a moment there was uncertainty – there was still ill-feeling towards the foreigners who had brought the diseases here – but they'd all seen the interlopers working nonstop to save Tangato lives, and the majority slapped their thighs in the tribal gesture of approval.

Then as quickly as a cork coming out of a bottle, the formality was abandoned. The children led the way, swarming forward boisterously, then the adults joined them in acclaiming the heroes of the day. Everyone was swept up in the throng, while the masked Queen sat watching like a gorgeous statue, forgotten for once in her life. Lurking near her was a dour-faced Natomo, who clearly hadn't forgiven Raythe for being right.

Well, krag him, anyway, Zar thought.

'I love you,' she shouted in her father's ear. 'You're the best.'

'Well done, you. I'm so proud.' He admired her new jade, and showed his – a pendant shaped as a bird, in honour of his familiar.

'I wish Mother could see us,' she blurted, then caught herself. 'It'd really piss her off.'

He'd flinched at her initial words, but now he chuckled. 'Aye, wouldn't it just?' He ruffled her hair – getting longer, but still short for a girl – and looked emotional for a second, then masked it. 'You go and have fun. I've got to meet with Shiazar and her advisors to work out the next steps.'

With a wave – and a surreptitious wipe of his eye – he sauntered off towards the royal pavilion.

Rima was still surrounded by well-wishers, so Zar drifted to the edge of the crowd. The Tangato were used to her by now, and once she'd acknowledged their congratulations they respectfully left her alone. As the village settled down for the evening's celebratory feast, she started wondering what life would throw at them all next.

What about Onkado? she wondered suddenly. Once the disease had been dealt with, the Queen would be able to turn her attention to his trial. *Am I right to protect him when he wants to die?*

She'd thought about him whenever she had a free moment – sometimes about the wretched situation he was in; other times about arguments she might use to try to free him. Sometimes she couldn't stop herself remembering how beautiful he was, and how much she longed to know all about him.

And sometimes she worried that he'd find a way to take his own life.

Her skin prickled. *Dear Gerda, what if he's killing himself right now, while everyone's distracted?*

She hurried through the almost deserted stilt-houses and meticulous gardens to Onkado's hut. The guard stared as she approached. 'Lady Mahotsu-kai?' he said anxiously.

'I need to see my husband,' she told him, darting past. Inside, the small fire smouldered, but Onkado's blanket was empty. Her eyes immediately shot up to the rafters, dreading to see him hanging there, but instead she found him sitting cross-legged in the far corner.

'Zarelda?' he said softly, the music in his voice making her shiver. 'What is it?'

She clutched her breast, startled, then relieved. 'Nothing, I just . . . I worried . . .'

'I am well,' he told her calmly, rising and gliding towards her, his Aldar features catching the light in a breath-taking way. 'No one comes here to infect me with foreign sicknesses – until today.'

'Oh, I – I mean . . .'

He stared, his eyes narrowing as if he had caught her thoughts. 'Zarelda, it is beneath my honour to take my own life, even in these dire straits. I will abide by the decision of the Queen, should you allow this trial to proceed.' He indicated the carved poumahi centre-pole supporting the hut's roof, decorated with the faces of the gods. 'Under their eyes, I must keep my honour. But I pray that you change your mind.'

She swallowed at this stark reminder of how strongly he felt. 'I couldn't live with myself if I allowed you to die,' she said hoarsely.

'Then you think of yourself, not me.'

'No! When I agreed to marry you, I had no hope at all, for myself or my people. But that decision enabled me to survive and now I'm helping our people and yours. Maybe that was Fate? Perhaps there's a purpose to you living, too? If you give up, you'll never find it.'

'I am a threat to the Queen, and a blasphemy to the Tangato tradition of forbidding male Aldar. That hasn't changed.'

'If you're trying to tell me you still want to bring down Queen Shiazar, I don't believe you. And if you think she wants you dead, you're wrong. She's a better person than that.'

'This isn't about "better" or "good". It's about stability of rule and law. *No male Aldar are permitted.* She's not going to go against that, "better person" or not.'

'I think you're wrong,' she maintained.

His face became intent, then softened and he got up and stood in front of her. 'You have a new taonga,' he said wonderingly. The word meant "treasure", she knew.

She stroked the jade fox proudly. 'It was given to me today, for fighting the disease.' She lifted her head proudly. 'We've beaten it, you know. We've found a cure, and a way to protect people.'

His reached out and touched the green stone pendant, an intimacy that made her skin tingle. 'Tell me how you earned this,' he said gently. 'Please. I have tea.'

Suddenly, he was once more the curious young man she'd first met, before she'd even known who or what he was. They sat on either side of his little fire and drank tea while she told him everything she could. It was a long story, interrupted by his perceptive questions, and time blurred past.

'Even Father is proud,' she concluded. 'This is the best day of my life.'

His expression became sad. 'Then you should not waste it on me.'

She swallowed, because in the flickering fire, his alien Aldar face looked impossibly beautiful, unbearably tragic. 'It's not a waste,' she blurted. 'You're my husband.'

His expression softened, and she found herself sinking into his eyes – until the intimacy scared her, and she felt utterly unworthy. 'I – um, I should go,' she stammered, rising quickly. 'I'll come again,' she added, backing away.

His face fell and she felt a surge of pity, that such a proud and wonderful creature was so reduced that all he had to look forward to were visits from someone as lowly as her.

But when she was back in her own hut, remembering his face in the firelight, how easy conversing had been, and the *frisson* of wanting that kept stealing over her, she was glad that she had gone to see him.

You coward, she scolded herself. *You didn't have to run.*

Then she remembered the other reason she'd held back. Tomorrow, she was riding south with a group of Tangato and Magnians, to take her turn patrolling the glacier – and Banno was one of the group.

How she was going to deal with that, she had no idea.

But just how natural or awkward it feels might tell me everything I need to know . . .

What does Zar think of me? Banno Rhamp wondered. It wasn't an easy question, especially when she was riding only a few yards away, making it hard for him to breathe. But she'd ignored him all day, though she'd been talking freely to the other riders. The twelve-man patrol was led by Cal Foaley, whose dour presence and legendary hunting skills were enough to keep them all in line. They were heading to the glacier pass to take over from the team watching the gateway into the Fenua Tangato.

During the sickness crisis, he and Tom Corday had formally disbanded the mercenary company, and Banno had felt a burden lift as a result. He'd been enjoying helping Jed Vine with the remaining livestock, even though his Pa would have said the work was menial. And he'd picked out a little cottage in the ruins and was steadily working on it, patching the stonework and cleaning it up. *Ready for a wife*, he kept telling himself – and certainly some of the farmers' young daughters seemed to think so, bringing him gifts of flowers and dried scented herbs and the like to 'brighten things up'. They were all sweet girls, but not one of them meant a thing to him.

There's only Zar.

Finally, towards the end of the drizzly morning's ride, he saw she was alone and trotted up alongside her. 'Ah, good morning, Zar,' he said tentatively.

'What's good about it?' She had a preoccupied look on her face.

'Not much, I s'pose. I'd rather be at home . . . I'm doin' up a cottage in the Bridge district. The roof's a mess, but I'm getting there.' He found himself prattling on about repairing ceiling beams and foraging for roof tiles from other ruins, and then about his work with the few remaining horses and cattle, chattering nonstop to cover her silence, pretending they were actually talking. 'So, what about you?' he concluded lamely, having failed to elicit more than a few grunts. 'You live in some kind of stilt-house, right?'

'They're called "farai",' she said absently. 'Banno, right now, my left eye is seeing through Adefar's eyes, and he's half a mile away. It's kind of hard to concentrate. Let's talk tonight.'

They didn't, though, because Cal Foaley put them on separate watches.

Zar shared a tent with Kinatia Hampden, the only other girl with the patrol, leaving Banno to exchange mindless chat with Roe Mallinkin, a Teshveld grain farmer who was incapable of much more than muttered comments about weather.

And it rained, just to emphasise the misery of it all.

But the next day they reached the glacier and settled in under Foaley's stern eye.

'The empire will come like thieves in the night,' the hunter told them. 'If it happens during our time here, it's up to us to provide a warning, so let's treat this vigil with the respect it deserves.' He set the watches and assigned tasks before vanishing to seek fresh provender for the two weeks they would be stationed there.

The next day, when the Tangato arrived, Zar went off with the masked Yokei to spend the day together, doing whatever sorceresses did.

Banno, ignored, settled in for the long haul, because clearly that was what it would be before Zar looked at him again.

7

Escape

Three nights in his own bed was a rare luxury for Raythe: three sleeps that were a headlong plummet into oblivion, gone in an eye-blink, but somehow aeons long. His days were exhausting, filled with logistics, mostly concerning the brewing, storing and distributing of Varahana's elixirs. It also meant very heated arguments with certain people who passionately believed that taking *anything* from a dead body was the worst kind of blasphemy and so refused the elixir. Ironically, now that the crisis was under control, many people felt aggrieved about the measures taken to save their lives.

You don't get to be a hero for long, he mused. *Gratitude is fleeting, blame is eternal.*

On the fourth morning, washing at the communal bathing troughs, he found himself fielding dozens of questions from fellow bathers unhappy that he was about to go 'gallivanting off' to help cure the Tangato.

'Why can't they look after they'selves?' was the complaint he heard again and again.

'It's the price we pay for peace,' he repeated wearily. 'The Hiriwa are mostly cured, but the other tribes still need help. If we do our bit, they'll start appreciating us. Anyway, I'll only be gone a week.'

Then he hurriedly loaded his saddlebags and mounted up, as Vidar and Jesco arrived, breath steaming in the frozen air.

'Morning, lads. All set?'

'We're ready,' Vidar grunted. 'The road awaits.'

'Oh yes,' Jesco added, with exaggerated enthusiasm. 'The old crew, back together and ready to hit the taverns and fleshpots of the Fenua Tangato, the land where every sin is on offer.' Then he buried his head in his hand theatrically and wailed, 'Gerda's Tits, I miss Shadra!'

'Aye, we all miss reeling around rotten drunk, getting into fights – oh, and the pox,' Raythe snorted.

'I'm with Raythe,' Vidar chipped in. 'Give me a farm, a well-brewed beer and a good woman and I'm happy.'

'You have none of those things,' Jesco noted.

'True,' Vidar admitted. 'Instead I have you two. The gods hate me.'

'With reason,' Jesco agreed. 'Tell me, are you a bear who takes human form, or the other way round?'

'Amusing as you think you both are,' Raythe interjected, 'the Queen is waiting. Let's move.'

They crossed the bridge and followed the clifftop path along the ravine, past the confluence where the rivers met and disappeared underground, before emerging a few miles to the south and flowing south all the way to the glacier pass. If they followed that glacier, they'd end up in Verdessa.

A path I'll likely never take again, Raythe reflected. But he was in no mood for regrets, instead turning his mind to the days to come. 'The Tanuahi know we're coming,' he said, 'and we'll have Yokei and mahotsu-kai with us to smooth the waters. And once we've healed a few, they'll be grateful.'

'I'm looking forward to *lots* of gratitude.' Jesco grinned. 'Ideally, expressed with food, drink and hot, sweaty love.'

The sun was low and bright in their eyes as they left the ravine and headed for the Hiriwa village. They arrived to find half the tribe waiting and went through the increasingly familiar ritual greetings. The Queen, masked and glittering in gold silks, was attended by two Yokei, Rangatira Natomo and a crowd of warriors.

'Good morning, Rangatira Raythe,' Shiazar greeted him warmly.

'And to you, my Queen,' he replied, dropping to one knee.

She invited him to join her and as he sat cross-legged before her, the two Yokei unfurled large, gaudy parasols and began a strange slow dance around them, while musicians struck up hand drums and stringed instruments with a high, quivery tone.

'This gives us a little privacy to talk,' Shiazar explained. 'Yokei Ana-muri and Yokei Kesa will accompany you to smooth the way. But there'll be no problems. The Tanuahi are eager to finally banish this disease.'

'That's a relief,' Raythe replied. 'I'm fond of my head and where it sits on my shoulders.'

'No one will displace it, I'm sure.'

He wished he could see her expression; he was picturing a sly smile. 'We should be back in six to eight days, Majesty. We'll have this defeated soon, and your plans to resettle the city can resume.'

'I eagerly await that day,' she replied, then she dropped her voice. 'Another contentious issue will soon arise. In the past, we Yokei num-bered more than thirty, but Ikendo's coup resulted in the death of all but a dozen, and disease has taken more. Those remaining are old and infertile, apart from me – and Onkado, a forbidden male. Therefore, it is now imperative that I birth a child – several, in fact – which was not supposed to happen until the end of my reign. And Onkado will be permitted to breed.'

Raythe grimaced. 'Are you saying Zarelda must–?'

'No – no, I am not. But their marriage creates a problem, as a married man is supposed to be faithful to his wife,' Shiazar replied. 'I have not objected to Zarelda's actions, for I wish to preserve Onkado's bloodline, but their marriage does complicate matters.'

'I suppose it does.' Raythe sighed. 'But surely it's not insurmountable.'

'If there is one thing you have taught me, it is that any maze can be navigated, if one is open-minded. In the meantime, though, I will trans-fer Onkado to the citadel. His presence unsettles my people . . . as does the fact that Zarelda has visited him twice.'

Raythe felt himself colour. 'Oh? Then that's an excellent idea. Move him today.'

Shiazar's eyes flickered in amusement. 'An Aldar and a sorceress is a potent mix: he and Zarelda would produce fine children.' Then she gestured apologetically. 'I am teasing. But in my case, it is traditional that a contest be held for the right to lie with the outgoing Queen. I will soon announce such an event, to determine with whom I breed, even though I will continue to rule.'

Raythe stared, his face going hot. 'As, er, outsiders, I presume I am not, er . . .'

'You should not presume anything,' Shiazar replied. 'You're a rangatira, proven in battle, in council, even in battling dread diseases. Your people are now mine, and your status gives you the right to compete.'

'What sort of competition?' he asked, his heart thumping.

She met his gaze. 'One in which men with martial prowess and intellect have the advantage – and use of magic is permitted. I imagine you will be a strong contender.'

Does she actually want me to win?

Her voice fell again. 'No reigning Queen has been required to bear a child for generations, for there was no need. But these are extraordinary times, in which *unprecedented alliances* are required to secure our future.'

It was as clear a message as he could imagine. *She does want me to compete . . . The Aldar Queen, the most glorious creature on this world, wants me to win her . . .*

'I'll be there,' he said, somewhat dazed, the added, 'Nothing could keep me away.'

'Good,' she murmured warmly. She signed to the dancing Yokei, who fell still. Despite their masks, he sensed disquiet, as if they knew what was being discussed and strongly disapproved.

'Safe travels, Rangatira Raythe,' Shiazar said. 'Report to me directly upon your return.'

It was the end of another long day in Mater Varahana's workshop and Rima was surrounded by newly fired pots, made from the clay dredged from the riverbanks, and vats of elixirs, four different types. Two were living fluids; the priestess had worked out a way to capture and breed the minute cells that fought the active diseases. Two more held the liquid she'd created from the dead to protect people from getting infected. Rima had spent endless hours using her fragment of the disease crystals and now she felt like she was drowning; she dreamed of swimming in seas of giant blobs that ate spiked balls and things like tadpoles, and chased her remorselessly.

That was when she wasn't dreaming of Kemara, suffocating under the earth while worms ate her alive.

Varahana yawned. 'Are you all right?'

They were the last left, as usual. Raythe Vyre had taken a supply of the elixir southeast into Tanuahi tribal lands the previous day, and newly trained mahotsu-kai were travelling to the other tribes, but Varahana needed her here to ensure the efficacy of the new batches of elixirs. It was draining, but vital.

'Of course.' Rima studied her face. 'But you look sad.'

'I'm just tired. Thank you for everything, Rima. I don't know what we'd have done without you.'

'Any mahotsu-kai would have done just as well.' Then she winked. 'Well, maybe not.'

'Aye,' Varahana laughed. 'If we took you back to Magnia, I have no doubt you'd turn the place on its head.' She reached out and stroked Rima's thick black hair. 'My hair is brown, but it curls like yours.'

'I'm sure it's pretty,' Rima told her. The priestess was a striking woman, despite her shaven skull, crow's feet and lined brow. 'Why aren't you and Vidar married?' she asked.

Varahana flinched. 'Because it's forbidden. A priestess must be chaste: Canon law requires it.'

'Cannon law?' Rima asked, struggling with the translation. 'This is a matter of war?'

'Canon – religious law. We are supposed to be so devoted to Deo that we don't require earthly love.'

'That's ridiculous!'

Varahana pulled a noncommittal face. 'Not really. As well as the rituals of the Church, our primary role is to help people in all the ways that rulers and governments and judges can't, won't or don't. They enforce and punish; our role is prevent people going wrong in the first place, by listening to them, finding solutions or just picking them up again after they've fallen or failed. I save marriages, I show children how to forgive their parents and vice versa, I help neighbours resolve disputes and comfort the grieving so they can endure. There's really no time to be a lover or a mother.'

Rima reflected on her own society; it certainly didn't function that way. The Yokei did those things, not the priests, who could marry and whose lives were ordinary, with a little ritual and worship on the side. She could see what Varahana meant . . . and also a weakness in the system. 'So, who looks after you?'

'Well, that's a problem,' Varahana admitted. 'But my sisters and I support each other. The nuns are very understanding.'

From what I've seen, they don't understand you at all, Rima thought. But it wasn't right to burden her with her outsider's views. 'We should rest,' she said. 'People need us, too.' She thought again of Kemara and blinked back tears. *Kiiyan, bring her back to us.*

Varahana took her hand. 'She'll make it, somehow. She's tough as old boots, that one.'

Rima gave her a sharp look. 'Are you sure you're not a sorceress?'

'If only. But I can read people, and I can see you are missing her. Do you want to talk about it?'

Rima studied her face and decided she looked a little too evangelistic. 'No. But I would ask you to pray for her.'

She made her escape, wishing it wasn't so late and she could sleep in the village tonight. Instead, she headed for the room she'd been given.

At the window, staring up at the rings, she whispered, 'Shinija-Kyu, Dragon-King of the Heavens, please find her, and guide her home.'

But Kemara had vanished more than a week ago, and hope was

fading. There were tales of great mahotsu-kai meeting the Kaiju who'd returned, but not in living memory. Logic said that Kemara was gone.

Life.

All-devouring, ever-changing, eternally renewing life.

Pitiless, remorseless life.

Swallowing, dissolving, breaking down all it can seize, taking and changing and mingling. Feeding. Mutating. Moisture and nutrients, sustenance ... extracted, consumed and broken down further, then drawn up to form new configurations. Billions of links constantly altering. Every living thing made of tinier things, caught up in their own existence, unconscious of the greater whole, in which death was just an exchange of energy and form, a sacrifice to ongoing existence. A linked dream.

The Dreamer stirs, at the edge of waking. A vast thing, like a tangled vine spreading everywhere, above and below the surface, constantly renewing, devouring all in its path. Few things could rouse it from the eternal feast of consuming and becoming. But at times it hears names, or eats something that is more substantial than its usual fare, something that gives it gifts of visions and dreams. Those are the meals it craves, giving it entrée to a world it cannot quite reach – to sights beyond seeing, sounds beyond hearing, a wondrous life of light and colour and taste and meaning that it longs to join. It draws in all that it can with its slow, atrophied limbs, and dreams its stolen dreams, and longs to leave the void.

Such a thing has just occurred – a new feast enabling it to vicariously experience these new sensations. It plunges in, seeking a way through to the other side ... to life itself.

PART TWO
Imperium

1

Beneath the Surface

Rodonoi was the newest outpost of the empire, a wood and stone fort on a bleak bluff, above a harbour clogged with ice and scoured by freezing winds. It was a place to huddle by a fire and pray for summer, normally housing just a few hundred men, but now row upon row of tents spilled out over the plains, crusted in ice and wreathed in shreds of cooking smoke, where Luc Mandaryke's army fought a losing battle against frostbite and pneumonia.

Teirhinan's mastery of weather-magic had given Mandaryke and his regiments passage along the coast to Verdessa, but such magic had a price: a more-than-equal and opposite reaction that would ravage western Magnia for weeks, wrecking settlements and fishing fleets and costing untold lives. But Mandaryke didn't care, and neither did Toran Zorne. Disorder might irk him, but this mission mattered more than a few thousand nobodies.

His concern was how Mandaryke handled the intricacies of command, now that they'd left Magnia behind. Out here, the two generals were the only people capable of holding the empire's one non-Bolgravian governor in check. But Nemath Torland had no desire to do so, and the Bolgravian commander, Romoi Lisenko, was a fool. Since the death of the Courser Ferdan Verdelho, Zorne had become more involved in Mandaryke's decision-making, but that meant he had to endure the eternal wrangling. At nights he shivered in his tiny cell, dispirited by the lack of patriotism and idealism.

Thank Deo Komizar Mirella is here, Zorne sighed. *Only she and I are truly working on behalf of the Emperor.*

That morning, dressed in every item of clothing he possessed, he was trying to eat a poorly made omelette in the fort's canteen when General Lisenko joined him.

Puffing out his cheeks and grumbling under his breath, the general muttered, 'Ah, Zorne. Cold as the arse of the Pit Lord, eh?' He didn't seem to expect a reply, instead concentrating on gobbling his breakfast and slurping mulled wine, his broken-veined face lighting up as the alcohol hit. 'You know that prick Torland has been given the southern slopes,' he added after a while. 'Arse-licker. My men are dying out on the plains while his have a nice sheltered spot on the sunny side.'

It was true that Mandaryke had given the Bolgravians the worst camp, but that was entirely Lisenko's fault. He'd been ranting on about his men's superiority, which gave Torland a fine excuse to argue that such *experienced* campaigners were surely better able to survive the rigours of the plains.

Lisenko's going to get his division killed, Zorne worried. The man hadn't even worked out that Verdelho's death wasn't a tragic accident – but there was no point telling him so. He only listened to flattery.

Thankfully, an aide interrupted, asking them both to attend upon Lord Mandaryke.

Rodonoi Keep was plain and comfortless; even the suite Luc had commandeered from the garrison commander was small and plain, just an office, a sitting room and a bedroom. Zorne was shown in, passing Nemath Torland's consort, a gawky young woman with a ramrod-straight back and shimmering black hair. Something about her struck Zorne as unusual, but he couldn't quite put his finger on what it might be.

The guards showed them into the office, where the governor was already drinking with Torland. Teirhinan was also present, brooding in a corner.

'Ah, Zorne, just the man,' Luc greeted him, before giving Lisenko a laconic salute. 'General, pour yourself a glass. We need to discuss our next steps.'

'About time,' Lisenko observed. 'Where is the rebel army and this man Vyre?'

'There's a fair bit more to it than just catching up with Raythe,' Luc drawled. 'Master Zorne, the floor is yours.'

The two generals turned their suspicious eyes Zorne's way and he began by stating, 'The rebel fugitive, Raythe Vyre, is not in Verdessa.'

Lisenko scowled and went to interrupt, but Luc silenced him with a peremptory gesture.

'Vyre found a way into the Icewastes,' Zorne continued, and described the route up the glacier. 'It's perilous, but it can be traversed, at least in late summer. About sixty miles in, there comes a point where the glacier brushes the edge of an expanse of ice-free lands.'

'Ice-free?' Lisenko exclaimed. 'How can—? *Oh* . . .' His piggish eyes narrowed. '*Istariol.*'

'Indeed,' Luc replied. 'And much more.'

Nemath Torland already knew, Zorne could see; naturally, Luc would have told him first – and Teirhinan as well, judging from her calm equanimity. This performance was for Lisenko's benefit.

'Istariol is imperial business,' Lisenko stated, quite correctly.

'And as Western Governor, I represent the Emperor,' Luc replied smoothly.

'Does the Emperor know?'

'He's been kept informed,' Luc lied glibly. 'To avoid some kind of chaotic gold rush, we have agreed to maintain strict secrecy over this element of our mission.'

Lisenko grimaced, but wisely offered no objections. 'And that's where Vyre fled to?'

'Indeed,' Zorne answered. 'But it's not uninhabited. There are people living there, dark-skinned savages, several thousand at the least, survivors from the Mizra Wars.'

'Holy Gerda!' Lisenko breathed. 'That's incredible.'

'It's the least amazing thing about it,' Luc replied. 'Tell them what else, Zorne.'

'I trailed Vyre to the heart of this new land,' Zorne said. 'There I found a place that can only be the lost city of Rath Argentium.'

This time everyone in the room except for Luc and Zorne gaped. Lisenko was speechless, his face puce. Even Teirhinan's ghostly eyes bulged.

'Gerda's Teats!' Torland swore. 'Are you sure?'

'I saw a great city built on the slopes of a cratered mountain, with a floating citadel chained in place above. A ravine encircles it, and there is a great bridge across, just as the histories tell. Yes, I am sure.'

'Deo have mercy,' Lisenko croaked.

'So now you see what's at stake,' Luc told them. 'It is imperative that the empire takes control of this place. Zorne has witnessed Raythe Vyre using mizra-sorcery, and we know he still has contact with criminals and rebels in Otravia. Imagine the havoc he could cause if he were able to supply the empire's enemies with istariol.'

The generals both paled.

'It is worse even than that,' Teirhinan put in. 'There are old legends of floating Aldar castles being able to move, fighting battles in the skies. If Vyre has control of that citadel, he could destroy our cities with impunity.'

'*Kragga mor,*' Torland gulped.

'I thought those stories were just fairy tales?' Luc asked, shaken from his smugness.

'No, they were very real,' Teirhinan answered. 'The fortress of Rath Argentium – Shiro Kamigami, it was named – was the last one left: eternal and victorious.'

Mandaryke could use that to dethrone my Emperor, Zorne realised, feeling suddenly unsteady. *Am I aiding the destruction of my own people?*

It took a minute for Luc to regain his composure, then he moved to take control of the meeting again. 'So if we can manage ten miles a day up that glacier, we can be at the southern edge of these lost lands in what? Eight to ten days?' he said, turning to Zorne. 'Does that sound reasonable?'

Zorne cleared his head and calculated. 'Longer, Milord. I traversed it in summer, but it's winter now. Halve your rate of travel, and allow for storms and avalanches. It'll be hard, and probably costly.'

At last the generals found their tongues, offering their estimates and suggestions, then Luc held up a hand to stop them and turned to Teirhinan. She was powerful enough to be able to utilise all three fields of sorcery, but her specialty was mundius, magic concerning the environment. 'At this time of year,' she said, 'we will be facing deadly blizzards as we advance north.'

'Can you create a pause, as you did at sea?' Luc asked.

'In theory,' she conceded, 'but in practice, I would need clear skies to swap in for the storms I drive away, and there's no good weather near us for me to work with.'

Mandaryke sighed. 'Then we must march when nature permits. The real question is whether we must wait three months for spring, or if we should try to advance between the storm fronts.'

Torland looked worried. 'That surely risks our entire army.'

'No one travels in the mountains in winter,' Lisenko agreed.

'But we can't afford to give Vyre the time to activate the Shiro Kamigami fortress,' Luc countered.

'He may have already,' Teirhinan put in.

'Then the longer we give him, the greater the probability,' Luc argued. 'We can't afford to wait for spring.'

Especially as the Coursers will catch up with us then, with questions about Ferdan Verdelho's death and what we're really doing out here, Zorne mused. *He can't afford that.*

'I vote we chance it,' Torland said, his voice aching with greed.

Lisenko disagreed. 'We can't survive a storm on the glacier – such storms can suck a man into the sky, or freeze him on the spot. We could all die in one night.'

The room fell silent again.

Then the door opened and Mirella Mandaryke entered. She was clad in red velvet, with sable cuffs and collar. Her blonde hair was piled artfully on her head and she walked with deliberate grace. No doubt she'd been listening at the door. She had the skinny, black-haired girl with her, Nemath's woman, who hurried to her patron's side, flouncing prettily.

Zorne took the opportunity to study the girl again, and finally realised what was amiss. *She's a boy . . .*

She – *he* – was almost perfectly disguised, but when one knew what to look for, it was clear. Which meant that Torland had burned thousands of homosexuals in Otravia, whilst being one himself. The irony was striking, and the fact that Mandaryke continued to patronise the man was even more surprising. But then, the elite always had made their own rules.

The 'girl' looked Zorne's way and lifted her goblet. 'I'm Sonata,' she announced melodically.

'Milady, I am your servant,' Zorne responded, as manners required. *At home, I'd deal with your perversion, but here, I must pretend I'm blind.*

'Darling, have we made progress?' Mirella asked Luc. 'Surely we can find a way to achieve something Raythe Vyre has already managed?'

'By chance or design, he timed his expedition more fortuitously,' Luc replied. 'But we will find a way.' He turned to Teirhinan. 'I have istariol, a whole thimble-weight, if that would help?'

A thimble-weight, about a sixth of an ingot, was worth a fortune. Teirhinan's corpselike face lit up, insofar as it could. 'It widens my options, certainly. But any weather-sorcery carries risks. The backlash could bury the region in ice. Is it worth the risk?'

Luc *tsked*, scanning their faces. 'Any suggestions? *Anyone?*'

Nothing came to mind; Zorne's problem-solving abilities were more usually concerned with how to intersect his blade with someone's throat.

But Mirella leaned back languidly, and said, 'There is one route that would be immune to weather. Is it possible to tunnel *under* the glacier's ice?'

They looked at each other, as if wondering how they could have missed such a thought, and then as one, they turned to Teirhinan Deathless.

Her grey, girlish face remained impassive, but after a moment she said, 'It would not be a fast option, but yes, I could melt a tunnel using the istariol you've offered, Milord.'

'I say,' Torland breathed, '*well done*, Lady Mirella!'

Luc grinned. 'I knew there'd be a way. My darling, you're a treasure!'

Mirella smiled like a cat, drinking in their admiration, and Zorne found himself unwillingly fascinated, knowing that every step they took was bringing her closer to confrontation with her first husband.

Vyre still loved her, he remembered. *And Luc glories in her.* There was something about her that made powerful men vie for her attention. *But they don't share the bond that she and I have: we're Ramkiseri.*

Regardless, he would have no trouble keeping his emotions clear.

My only love is for the Empire.

A week later, Mandaryke's two divisions arrived at a place that made Rodonoi look like a beach in Shadra: an unnamed lake, at the foot of the mountains that protected Verdessa from the Icewastes. The landscape was frozen, windswept and lifeless. The soldiers were utterly miserable, and every day required harsh examples to be made of grumblers before they all deserted or mutinied. A dozen or more died of exposure every night, as the ice found every chink in the flimsy tents. No amount of canvas could keep out the cold.

Initially, Zorne shared a tent with Luchanon, one of Mandaryke's aides. The man snored and chewed tobacco, but he shared his brandy, which made him just about bearable. But next day, he joined Teirhinan and the Bolgravian military sorcerers, led by Tresorov and Drusyn, in working on the tunnel. Armed with the istariol, they went to the base of the glacier, which was around a hundred and fifty feet deep, and began to carve a tunnel, roughly ten feet high and wide. It was an exacting task, for an unskilled sorcerer could easily trigger a fatal flash-flood – and if they were too timid, it would be slower than waiting for spring.

But Teirhinan Deathless was neither incompetent nor fearful. Drawing gradually on the istariol, she unleashed a beam of energy in controlled bursts, carving the initial tunnel as melted ice poured past her. The sorcerers followed close behind, dealing with the scalding water and steam she generated, striving to prevent a collapse. It was eerie work, working knee-deep in water under conjured light globes, totally encased in the ice.

Zorne found watching Teirhinan work an uneasy experience: there was a strangeness to her magical aura he'd never seen before. He knew better than to ask her about it, but he badly wanted to know.

Nevertheless, they quickly settled into an effective team: while Teirhinan concentrated on the main tunnel, Zorne worked on polishing and reinforcing and Tresorov and Drusyn cut drainage channels for the water and ventilation shafts to get rid of the steam before it led to a widespread melt. The junior Bolgravian sorcerers then refroze the walls to reinforce them.

On the first day, they went only two miles. On the second they managed four, and six the next. At night, Zorne shared camp with Teirhinan, while Tresorov and Drusyn dropped back, out of sight and earshot.

'Don't they like us?' Teirhinan mused aloud, as she and Zorne prepared a meal.

'They want to be alone.' That the two Bolgravian men were lovers was an open secret, but as with Sonata, Zorne was compelled to ignore their perversity. It was aggravating.

'Ick,' Teirhinan giggled. 'Men with men. How revolting.'

Sharing a camp with the wraithlike young woman was uncomfortable: she smelled bad, and radiated quite as much cold as the ice. And she was a child too, despite her grey hair, and immature in many ways. But Zorne had never seen such concentrated spell-casting, even allowing for the istariol: she was definitely the most powerful sorcerer he'd ever encountered, and remembering his vision of the two familiars when she'd saved his life in Sommaport, he became increasingly curious about her.

Twenty miles in, they reached the section of glacier that Raythe Vyre had collapsed with Kemara. They had to endure two miles above the ice, moving in between snow storms, before clambering up an old waterfall to where the icepack resumed.

That evening, he left the camp, feigning an errand, then crept back, reasoning that she was so exhausted, she'd be unlikely to notice his intrusion. He came to within fifty or sixty feet of her, his familiar, Ruscht, on his shoulder in white stoat form, peering around in quiet distress.

Only a sorcerer could see another practitioner's familiar, and only then if it was outside their body, in between spells. He'd come upon Teirhinan at just such a moment – and there, on her right shoulder, was a dove-familiar . . . and another shape, a red-eyed crow, hunched on her left shoulder.

Two familiars . . . How is that possible? Then he realised that the second familiar was a mizra-spirit.

He made the mistake of reacting, just the tiniest intake of breath – and instantly she turned her deathly eyes on him.

'Zorne,' she called, in a playful voice. 'Do I have to kill you, too?'

He made no attempt to ward or reach for a weapon, knowing either would be futile, instead saying, 'I've never heard of such a thing.'

'That's because it's unique,' she boasted. 'But illegal, of course. By rights, I should be burned alive.' She advanced on him, moving gracelessly. 'I died achieving it, and resurrected myself. There's a cost to that, which I pay gladly.'

Abruptly she was standing before him, and he realised that he'd not even thought to move a muscle, he was so ensorcelled.

Her dead eyes held him utterly motionless.

'Do not permit a mizra-witch to live,' she quoted. 'Your duty is clear: to condemn and execute. So I ask again: do I have to kill you, Master Ramkiseri?'

He would have no chance against her; he knew that. Somehow she'd already frozen his limbs and all but shut down his mind. She was playing with him.

But perhaps she didn't *want* to kill him?

He chose to hope that was so, as he framed his answer to what he hoped wasn't a rhetorical question. 'I am Ramkiseri, sworn to serve the Empire. That is my only consideration. Right or wrong, good or evil, praxis or mizra; my only consideration is whether an action will serve the Empire. This is not unreasoned: my belief is that only through the uniformity of empire do we as humankind progress and master our world. Therefore, if you serve the Empire, I have no reason to divulge your secret and every reason to help you keep it. But if you do not serve the Empire, it is my duty to destroy you.'

Her eyes lit, violet and uncanny. 'You say this, even though I could carve your heart from your chest right now and you would be entirely unable to resist?'

'Even so. I cannot be other than what I am.'

Her fingernails pressed to his left breast, teasing the death blow . . .

Then she broke into a sharp, bell-like laugh and kissed his cheek in a sisterly way. 'You are a joy, Toran Zorne. Purity of purpose is so hard to find.' She gave him a strangely affecting look, at once lonely and hopeful. 'It is the same purity that enabled me to master my unique brand of sorcery – with which I serve the Empire.'

He didn't react when he felt the shackles dissolve, even though a lightning blow could have taken her head from her shoulders. But the mission needed her.

But he'd lied: his Empire banned the mizra, and sooner or later, laws must be obeyed. At some point, when their mission was complete, she would have to die.

2

On Patrol

Zarelda found herself holding her breath as she took her first step off the rocks and onto the surface of the glacier. It wasn't that she feared falling through, but because of the memories it brought back of their trek to reach Rath Argentium – tramping for days up this glacier, terrified of avalanches sweeping down to bury them, or the surface fracturing and swallowing them, or storms blasting in to turn them all to blocks of ice.

Such a storm was imminent, if the swirling black clouds in the east were anything to judge by, so they'd moved their tents to behind a low ridge half a mile away. They'd been here four days and the twelve Magnians and twelve Tanuahi tribesmen were developing a working relationship, sharing the watch, as well as the hunting and foraging, cooking and campsite duties. That day Foaley wanted another look at the glacier before the storm, so he'd brought Zar, a Tanuahi called Wiramoto and, to her annoyance, Banno, who'd spent the whole time looking at her with puppy eyes.

It was only midmorning, but it felt like dusk. They were all wrapped in cloaks and shivering in the westerly that was blasting down the glacier and freezing any inch of uncovered skin. From their position, they could look north across the frozen lake, but the far shore was lost in the mists and low cloud. To the east, upstream from the glacier, the ribbon of ice vanished into the snowy heights; to the west it descended in a slow arc, turning southwest and then south, Verdessa was just fifty or sixty miles away, but it felt like another world.

'Just a few days' walk and you're in Verdessa,' Foaley commented wistfully, as if he'd read Zar's thoughts.

'Tempted?' She thought that even though the Fenua Tangato was almost two thousand square miles of wilderness, it probably felt like a prison to a hunter like him.

He looked at her soberly, then shook his head. 'It's irrelevant. Our place is here.' He glanced up at the western peaks, where the winds were streaking dusty snow sideways across the sky. 'Here comes that storm.'

In moments, visibility collapsed and all colour had drained away, leaving just grey murk and swirling eddies of snow.

'This is pointless,' Foaley shouted, shielding his eyes. 'Let's go back.'

Zar was happy to go, but just as she turned, she felt . . . *something* . . . the resonance of discharged energy, mild but steady, the distance unknowable.

'Wait!' she shouted, tuning her mind.

But it remained elusive, and then she realised that no one had realised she'd stopped. Everyone else had vanished into the growing blizzard. She went after them, wading into the wind, which was all but lifting her from her feet. Then Banno appeared, grabbing her arm and anchoring her, and although it felt like an intrusion, she had no choice but to huddle into him as they battled on through the battering gusts until they managed to get off the glacier and stumble down the rough scree.

'Are you all right?' Banno asked earnestly.

'I'm fine!' she answered. 'I thought . . . uh . . . I don't know.' She pulled herself free and stomped on, irritated to have needed his help. They caught up to Foaley as they reached the camp and she pulled him aside.

'I sensed something, back on the glacier,' she told the hunter. 'I can't swear it, but it felt like another sorcerer was nearby.'

It would have been easy for him to brush her off, but Cal Foaley was a wary old wolf. 'How close does something like that need to be to sense it, lass?'

'It's hard to say. It's like an echo that only the brain can hear. But it felt close.'

'Are there any other Tangato sorcerers nearby? There are two tribes who live near here, yes?'

'They're both at least twenty miles away, so unless they've also sent people here, no. The mountains can bounce the echo around, though,' she added uncertainly.

'I'm told they do patrol here,' Foaley said. 'Best case, it's them. Worst case . . .' He pulled a face. 'Imperial . . .'

'My father would assume worst case, straight off. It usually is with him.'

'Aye, that man is a lightning rod, an' that's truth,' Foaley chuckled, but his face sobered quickly. 'Lass, we should speak to the Yokei – Hepata, that's her name, right? Will she know what to do?'

It was surreal to Zar, to have an experienced man like Foaley asking her advice about a Yokei who was decades older than her. But his concern was genuine, and so was her worry, remembering what Rima had told her about the Yokei as a whole.

'She's lived her life in peace, and has no martial training. Her expertise is in root crops.'

Foaley frowned, then sighed. 'Let's go and talk to her.'

They went to see the diminutive mask-clad Hepata, who, despite being Aldar, was reminiscent of an elderly auntie, exceedingly polite, her voice creaking with age and anxiety. She asked some obvious questions whilst peering at the glacier. The storm was really building now; going back up there would be foolish, but that left them blind.

'No one can move up there now,' the masked woman decided. 'We will return and listen to the spirits as soon as the storm subsides.'

With that she bustled back to her own people, offering no further advice.

She might be Aldar, but she's old and inexperienced and out of her depth, Zar thought, sorry for her, but scared of all the weight that placed on her own shoulders.

Foaley gave Zar a worried look. 'I don't like it. We'll double the watch, with eyes on that glacier, from the nearest vantage.' He gathered the

Magnians and gave his orders. 'Two sentries, one from each party, four-hour shifts,' he said tersely. 'Banno, make up the roster.' Then he pulled Zar aside again, asking, 'Can you communicate with your father?'

She shook her head. 'No, sorcery doesn't work that way. But he should be with the Tanuahi tribe right now – they're only about twenty miles away.'

'That's a comfort,' Foaley said, then he gave her a sharp look. 'Are you all right having Banno here?'

'It's okay,' she mumbled, not meaning it. 'Were you ever married?' she asked, to change the subject, then she saw him wince and stammered, 'Sorry, none of my business.'

He gave her a measuring look, then to her surprise, he answered, 'When the Bolgies conquered Pelaria, "hunting" became "poaching". But we still had to live. Teghan and I lived in the forest and thought ourselves safe. But one day I came home and found the Governor's foresters had her standing on a stool under the oak, with a noose round her neck. They told me they'd kick the stool away if I didn't surrender. They'd already used her.' His voice went husky. 'Scum of the earth.'

Zar flinched. 'What did you do?'

'I started shooting, trying to take them all down,' Foaley said, blinking fast. 'But one kicked the stool as he died, and her neck broke when she fell. I still wonder if I could've done something different . . .'

'I'm so sorry . . .' Zar patted his arm awkwardly.

'She was an innocent – no education, but a wide-eyed love of being alive, like a child. What they did, she'd never have got past. I still see her face . . .' Then Foaley's face closed up again. 'That's enough memories, lass. Go and get some rest.'

By midday the storm was in a lull, and when the watch changed, Zar took her turn on a ridge that gave a good vantage of the glacier. She was not best pleased, because Banno had assigned himself too, along with a pair of taciturn Tangato warriors. But she'd told Banno he would have a chance to repair things, so she kept civil.

After some desultory small-talk, he blurted, 'What must I do to win you back?'

It was a more direct approach than she wanted, but she answered, 'That's the wrong question. You don't "win" me, because it's not a competition. If women only wanted the handsomest men or the strongest warriors, then only the strong and handsome would ever marry.'

'What do you want?' he insisted. 'Whatever it is, I can be that person for you.'

'Can you? But what if it bends you so out of shape that you're no longer yourself?' She *tsked* impatiently, then told him the conclusion she'd come to about all this. 'I don't see love as a battle. It's an alignment of emotions. It's either there or its not, and if it doesn't come naturally, it's not something you can force.'

His face fell, then became bitter. 'And are things "natural" with you and Onkado?'

'None of your business,' she snapped back. 'Look, I've barely seen him, and I'm in no hurry to resolve anything.' She returned her gaze to the distant point where the glacier met the frozen lake, half a mile away. 'Right now, I need to concentrate on what's out there.'

It was a relief to give something other than him her attention, listening with her sorcerer's senses and wondering what it was she was hearing.

The weather had deteriorated, the skies were buried in cloud and mist swirled about the glacial pass. But when she opened her mind, she could just about sense that faint magical *thrum*. The distance was still impossible to pin down – and then it stopped, and once again, she began to doubt herself.

Did I just imagine it? she wondered.

But there was nothing to see, for the storm was washing over them, soaking them and destroying all visibility. They huddled miserably under their cloaks for several hours, even the hardy Tangato. The magical humming had stopped entirely now.

Finally the rain lifted, the murk dissipated, and they regained sight of the glacier pass. Banno raised the spyglass to survey it . . . and swore violently. Zar followed his gaze and saw two distant figures standing on the glacier, half a mile away, dark silhouettes against the mist. Her heart thudded. The Tangato shared an anxious look.

'Who are they?' she whispered, as if afraid they could hear her. 'Another tribe's patrol, surely?'

'I don't know,' Banno muttered. Then he yelped and jerked himself flat. 'Oh, Deo!' He gave her an ashen look. 'One was a woman in a pale dress, like a Ferrean washer-wraith. *She looked right at me.*'

She grabbed his arm, motioning to the Tangato men to stay low. 'Stay down. I'll fetch Foaley and Hepata.'

Toran Zorne stood in the lee of the cliffs with Teirhinan Deathless, staring out at the stark, sullen landscape to the north – the frozen lake and bleak, lifeless hills, streaked with snow. Behind them, the freshly bored tunnel emerged from the glacier. The Bolgravian sorcerers were already passing signals down the tunnel, and the advance guard, who'd been brought forward in anticipation of breakthrough, would soon arrive. Meanwhile, the sorcerers could finally breathe fresh air, although they were in the eye of a storm and would need to seek shelter again soon.

Just then, the first soldiers emerged from the tunnel. To Zorne's surprise, they were led by Luc Mandaryke himself, in full military regalia, clearly consumed with impatience. He strode up eagerly, flanked by a quartet of aides.

'Congratulations, Lady Teirhinan, and to you too, Master Zorne,' he said briskly. 'Yours has been an incredible effort: truly the stuff of legends.' He saluted them, then gazed hungrily over the scene. '*Miraculous.* How far is it from here to Rath Argentium, Master Zorne?'

'Forty to fifty miles, Milord. On a clear day, the floating city may be visible, but the haze here is constant.'

'Unsurprising, given we're surrounded by ice. It's amazing that it's not entirely underwater.' Luc shook his head in theatrical incredulity.

'A river that becomes a glacier – mind-boggling. This is a great moment, a fresh glory to the name of Mandaryke. And the Empire, of course. We've discovered a whole new land!'

Well, Vyre beat you to it, and the natives were already here . . . but well done, Milord, Zorne thought, with sour amusement. *I daresay we'll be naming it after you.*

Luc basked in the moment, then turned to his aides. 'My personal guard are on the way: two hundred of my best men. The key for now is to remain undetected until we can bring the entire army through. Send scouts out immediately: we must sweep the surrounding area meticulously: no one who sees us can be permitted to escape. I want Vyre to have no inkling that we're here.'

He clapped Zorne's shoulder heartily before swaggering off to see to his own comfort.

It was early afternoon, but the storm would soon be returning with renewed intensity. Right now, all Zorne wanted to do was rest, but he took a moment to reflect. Four months after he'd fled this place, he'd returned with enough men to destroy Raythe Vyre . . . and Kemara Solus.

He turned to Teirhinan. 'When I escaped here, I was fortunate to survive. One of the travellers, Kemara Solus, is also a mizra-witch; she and Vyre forged a meld, making them almost your match.'

Teirhinan's hackles rose. 'I am peerless, Toran Zorne. But I thank you for the warning. The mizra is powerful offensively, but poor defensively; the praxis is the opposite. I have the advantage of both armouries.'

'Is it something one may learn?' he asked hesitantly, knowing that most sorcerers were loath to pass on any advantage they'd found, but compelled to ask because knowledge was a sorcerer's edge.

She preened unconsciously. 'I was a prodigy, Toran, and had the theory worked out before I even became a sorcerer. You get only the one chance, in the hour your first familiar arrives, and only I knew to take that chance. No one taught me. I could teach a thousand young potential sorcerers the theory, and one thousand would die trying. I am a freak.'

It was there in her voice again: loneliness, but pride, too. Enough pride to engender a fall.

It is good to know her weakness.

Then she stiffened and murmured, 'We're being watched.'

'We saw people on the glacier,' Zar reported to Cal Foaley and Yokei Hepata. 'A woman and a man.'

In the short dash back to the concealed campsite, the sun had been swallowed by more cloud and the light, which dropped early on these northern winter days, was fading fast. They huddled together outside Hepata's tent, talking in quiet voices, so as not to alarm those with them.

'Are you sure, child?' Hepata replied. She wore a stern copper mask and was clad in grey robes over spidery black leather armour, with a long curved blade sheathed at her side, but her long hair was streaked with grey and she moved with the stiffness of age. 'Might it not be our own foragers?'

'Everyone's back in,' Foaley replied, 'and I trust Zarelda not to baulk at phantoms.'

'But visibility is poor,' Hepata objected. 'How can we be sure?'

'I know what we saw,' Zar replied tersely. 'My father would say, "Imagine the worst and act on it".'

'I'm in charge here,' Hepata replied sharply.

'No one is suggesting otherwise,' Foaley said. 'But I agree with Zar. Given what's at stake, I believe we should be on high alert. We should send riders out.'

The Yokei's uncertainty was clear, despite being masked. 'Night is coming,' she muttered. 'Can your horse-creatures make such a journey?'

'It'd be perilous, for man and rider both,' Foaley admitted. 'But if there really are people out there, they may be the scouts for an imperial force. Early warning of them will save lives – and if it's a false alarm, where's the harm?'

'Except the panic and loss of faith in the throne it would cause,' Hepata answered. 'It's better to be certain.' She folded her hands into her lap. 'Even if there are people out there, they can do nothing at night. We will look again in the morning, and act accordingly then.'

Zar tried one last time. 'Please, Yokei Hepata, might at least one rider be sent to the Tanuahi? Just to put them on alert – they are closest, and Father is there, administering the healing elixirs and spells.'

The Aldar woman's knuckles whitened, but with a hiss of frustration, she relented. 'One rider . . . but neither of you. I need you both here.'

'Guy Jagisson's the best horseman here,' Foaley said. 'I'll send him.'

With that decided, Zar went to pull Jagisson away from the fire and brief him. Jagisson was a cocky, confident former mercenary; he'd stayed on the right side of all the recent ructions and was now emerging as decent young man. He wasn't happy at the prospect of an evening ride in this weather, but he respected Foaley and was anxious to be seen playing his part.

The rest of the patrol, Magnian and Tangato alike, realising something was up, were watching apprehensively as Foaley and Zar saw Guy off.

'Don't build it up to be more than it is,' Foaley told Jagisson as he saddled his horse. 'Tell Raythe we've spotted two unidentified people at the glacier pass, and that Zar sensed sorcery. We'll know more in the morning.'

Jagisson set his jaw when sorcery was mentioned, assured them he'd ride like the wind, then mounted up and nudged his reluctant mount into motion. In a few moments he was lost in the murk. Foaley turned to the rest. 'All right, we're on high alert for the night. Zar, get back to Banno up on the ridge. I'll join you soon. Everyone else, keep your fires low and your guns primed.'

Zar took an extra cloak and called up Adefar. Averting her eyes from the fires, she conjured night-sight and slipped back towards the ridge, returning to where she'd left Banno, huddled between two boulders with the two Tangato nearby. They reported no further sightings. She reported her conversation with Hepata, first in the Reo tongue, with Adefar's help, for the warriors; then in Magnian for Banno.

'Foaley should be in charge,' he grumbled. 'These Yokei know nothing about war.'

Zar was inclined to agree. 'We'll be relieved in about two hours,' she murmured. 'Now, quiet. I have to concentrate.' With that, she pointed towards the glacier and told Adefar, '*Veni*,' – go there.

A familiar couldn't travel more than a few hundred yards from their sorcerer, and their perceptions weren't human senses, making them ineffective long-range scouts, but they could still be useful. Adefar preferred fox shape, and it was in that guise that he padded away, unseen to any without magical senses. Through him, she felt his thought patterns, although she couldn't see more than snatches of what he saw. There was little light, as the rings were just a pallid arc behind the clouds. Her primary impressions were of the cold. She guided Adefar as best she could, concentrating hard.

Then Banno shook her shoulder and she bounced back to her own body, gasping as she realised he'd put his hand over her mouth and was pressed against her, holding her down. She almost panicked ... but then she heard footfalls, just a few yards away.

She felt her eyes bulge, pulled Banno's hand away and sucked in a breath, then peered round the boulder. Something foul-smelling tainted the air, like a long dead bird or rat. Then more footfalls sounded and a wave of soldiers – a score or more – crunched past them, heading towards their camp.

A few seconds later, the sounds were gone, and Zar faced Banno. 'We have to warn them,' he whispered fearfully.

But then they had to huddle low again, as another rank of men tramped past. *They'll be almost on top of our camp, and there's been no noise,* she fretted. *They'll be caught unawares . . .*

Banno grabbed her shoulder, his expression a kind of resigned hopelessness, and he mumbled, 'I will prove myself to you.' Then he rolled away, snatched up his flintlock and pulled the hammer back, sighting along the barrel.

'Banno –' she blurted, suddenly realising his intent.

He fired a shot down the rearward slope, into the back of the rank of men that had passed. Someone howled in pain and the night burst into life.

Banno spun and hissed, 'Run, Zar, *run!*'

Instantly, voices rapped out orders – *in Magnian, with Otravian accents* – and she realised that to stay here was to die. So she darted over the ridge and went west, expecting Banno to follow . . .

. . . but he went east.

Then more shots rang out, and all she could do was run on.

It wasn't a rational decision, just a visceral, impulsive reaction to Zar's indifference – that, and the overwhelming need to do something. Banno fired his warning shot, then ran – impulsively going the opposite way to Zar, to draw off pursuit so she'd escape. He ran low along the ridgeline as torches suddenly flared in the gully below, where a line of red-coated soldiers were strung out. Some saw him and shots rang out, but most of the soldiers just pushed onwards, towards the camp. He was heartened to see no one going after Zar.

He pounded down a slope, then headed upwards, seeing the silhouette of mountain peaks rising through the heavy mist ahead of him. He imagined himself hiding up there until all was quiet, then striking out for safety, but as he reached a ridge and reeled on the edge of a precipice over a ravine with water snarling below, more shots cracked, lead pinged around him and something hit him in the back.

His legs went numb and he pitched onto his face, cracking his nose on the rock and reeling from the pain. He clawed at the earth, trying to pull himself along until feeling returned, but when he twisted at the waist to look back, he could see torch-bearing soldiers were coming at him, bayonets fixed.

One saw him and shouted, '*There he is! Take him alive!*'

Banno looked up at the skies and saw the clouds forming Zar's face. *Escape them*, he wished. *Be happy.*

Then he rolled, and pitched himself over the cliff into darkness.

Cal Foaley had organised the watch shifts, snatched a bite of food and was about to go and join Zar and Banno on watch. There'd be no sleep for him, not knowing that danger might be creeping closer.

He was a few hundred yards out of the camp, still distant from the ridge, when a shot rang out. Behind he heard startled yelps from his men – then more shots were fired on the ridge above and torches flared.

Hide, his hunter's instincts said. *Wait this out.*

He'd done it before – after Teghan's death he'd spent his life hiding; from soldiers, from officials, from anyone who might have cared for or even loved him. Perpetually alone, he'd instinctively gravitated towards the edges of the known. Then he'd fallen in with Raythe Vyre and found something worth chancing his arm for. Greed was never the driver: he knew that treasure hunts were illusions; no one ever got rich. But belonging to this ramshackle community and having responsibility thrust on him had awakened him, somehow.

The best year of my life since Teghan died, he thought now. *Worth the effort, and worth fighting for.*

So instead of running, he withdrew to the centre of the camp to take charge. His Magnians were frantically pulling on boots, and readying bows or flintlocks. Beyond them, he saw the Tangato huddled around the Yokei. Hepata was masked and looked forbidding, but she was wavering uncertainly.

She might be an Aldar sorceress, but she's no warrior.

'Lady, *go!*' Foaley called to her. 'Warn your people!'

He didn't wait to see how she reacted, but went storming on, barking orders. 'Everyone, pull out – get to the horses! Leave this shit behind – we don't need it! *Get out of here!*'

'But what about the sentries?' Fossy Vardoe called, peering into the dark.

'They're on their own,' Foaley roared. *'Go! Go—!'* But he ran on to the southwest edge of the camp because he'd learned from Raythe Vyre that that's what real leaders did – they hung on till the last second to learn all they could.

Most of his men had begun running, but a few came with him, flint-locks primed.

Then a spectral shape flitted from the pines, a woman in a nimbus of pale violet light, so pale she looked like she'd just been exhumed, her fingers scratching at the world as she advanced, babbling a torrent of words. Around her, the air seemed to billow and warp.

As one, all those with Foaley fired, sending five lead balls into the woman, making her stagger. Foaley, expecting shielding spells, didn't bother, but the sorceress clearly regarded such things as beneath her, for the balls blasted five little holes in her flesh – but there was no blood, and she didn't fall.

Then she shrieked a spell and livid purple light crackled from her hands. Foaley tried to hurl himself aside, but they were all caught in a web that gripped him and sent energy dancing through them all, mak-ing limbs spasm and their skin blister and burn.

He went down with the rest, his gun discharging as he dropped it, blasting impotently into the air as he thudded to the frozen ground, dazzled by a spear of light that lanced him through the chest.

A moment later . . . or an aeon . . . someone was kneeling over him.

It was Teghan, and she was smiling.

He smiled too, and faded into her arms.

Toran Zorne seldom felt like a passenger in a fight, but right now he did. Teirhinan Deathless had bade him stay behind her as she entered the camp, despite him imploring her to wait until they could ascertain what they faced. Her blood was up and it hadn't been worth his life to try arguing.

The result had been both terrifying and irksome.

In a series of complex gestures and spells he couldn't even decipher, she slaughtered anyone who stood up to her – six of Vyre's Magnians and eight of the brown-skinned savages went down. He saw her take wounds that should have been fatal, but all she'd done was stumble for a moment before going on. By the time he reached her, the slaughter was done.

Can she even be killed? he'd wondered, greatly disquieted.

But she'd also kragged this up completely, because several had escaped, and his frantic pursuit had caught only two of the dark-skinned natives.

When he returned to the destroyed camp, he found Teirhinan kneeling over a delirious survivor: a pretty, dark-haired girl. The sorceress had her temples clamped in her hand and faint haze of indigo light was streaming from the girl's eyes and into Teirhinan's. She broke the spell to look up and saw Zorne's face. 'Some of the natives you spoke of were here – and a masked woman. But they fled on foot.'

Zorne looked down at the captured girl – barely sixteen, he guessed, and so terrified she'd soiled herself: *Kinatia Hampden*, he remembered, an athletic girl with a wild streak. Her face was slack now, though, her eyes glazed. There were frost burns where Teirhinan held her. He felt a strange emotion he took a moment to identify: *Pity*. Surprised and a little ashamed, he asked, 'What've you learned?'

Teirhinan returned her gaze to the captive girl. 'This one was part of a patrol, stationed here in case of intruders. And I've learned all sorts as well, about who's in charge and so on. But she's not one to pay attention to the important things, so I rather think she's expended her usefulness.'

With that, she casually waved a hand, and murmured, *'Calvaria ruptura.'*

The girl's skull collapsed inwards with a sickening crunch and she went limp.

'Who led them?' he asked, masking his unease.

'Someone called Foaley.' She pointed offhandedly to a pile of smouldering bodies at the edge of the clearing. 'One of those.'

Zorne remembered the tough, capable hunter, one of Vyre's

lieutenants. *She dealt with him and a dozen others effortlessly.* 'It would've been good to interrogate him,' he noted.

Teirhinan stood and in a peevish voice asked, 'Was that a criticism, Toran?'

'No,' he said quickly. 'Were there any sorcerers here?'

Teirhinan rose, a pleased smile on her face. 'Yes, a sorceress, with a fox familiar,' she said airily. 'I glimpsed the little beastie as we approached. It fled that way.'

She pointed westwards, towards the frozen lake.

Zarelda Vyre, Zorne thought, his skin prickling as he remembered a pretty, pugnacious face. *Mirella's daughter.* It felt like Fate.

This has gone well, Raythe thought, yawning and stretching. The tribesmen had been wary but welcoming, thanks to the local Yokei, and any lingering hostility had been erased when the first batch of cured disease victims had emerged from the makeshift infirmary into a dull day that have must looked miraculously beautiful to them.

After that, Raythe spent another two days labouring alongside the Tanuahi's mahotsu-kai to cure the rest, and they'd done well, using their maho as Rima did, supporting and guiding him. Then they'd distributed elixirs to those as yet untouched, to prevent them from catching the sickness.

Now there was nothing the Tanuahi wouldn't do to help.

At this evening's feast of thanksgiving, Monarohi, the rangatira of the Tanuahi, a plump, dignified old man with thinning white hair, embraced Raythe yet again. In halting Reo, the Tangato tongue, he repeated, 'Blessings be on you!' and 'All praise, all praise!', over and over, tears streaming down his blue-tattooed face. He engulfed Raythe in a bear-hug, then looked him in the eye and in Gengo-Magnian, said, 'I don't understand why the gods permit these plagues, but your people and ours have worked together to cure it, and that is good. Perhaps that is why the gods saw fit to inflict it upon us.'

Raythe felt a pang of guilty irony, knowing all too well the choices he and Shiazar had made that had led to this point. *Would you be so grateful if you knew that we'd predicted this outbreak and chose to forge ahead with contact anyway?*

But Shiazar had feared isolation more, and the threat of xenophobic violence. It still wasn't clear if she'd made the right choice, for many had died – but now trust was being forged from the shared suffering.

'We do the best we can,' Raythe said awkwardly. He was more than a little drunk on the Tangato rice wine, a pleasant glow he'd not felt in months, but he'd stayed the right side of sober, so as not to lose his dignity.

Better a jester than a fool, his old tutors used to tell him, although they probably hadn't had any fun in years.

Monarohi bowed his head. 'As you say. But your best is very fine indeed.'

Raythe looked round the joyous meeting hall: it was a good start to the 'tour'. His plan now was to circle down to the southern glacier to check in on Zar, Foaley and the squad, then to head for the Rotomahau and Manowai lands before returning to Rath Argentium. The other tribes were being tended by the mahotsu-kai that Rima had trained. For now, though, it was time for bed.

But as Monarohi escorted him to the doors, they were intercepted by Yokei Oziniya, dressed tonight in a yellow and green kimono and a bird mask. With her was a lanky, bearded Norgan, Guy Jagisson, who'd been one of Rhamp's mercenaries. He was streaming with perspiration, and looked relieved to see a familiar face.

'Lor' Raythe,' he called, panting. 'Got news.'

'This boy rode from the southern glacier,' Oziniya reported. 'He is one of the patrol there.'

'Aye, I know,' Raythe said anxiously. 'My daughter is with them.' *With Foaley and Banno.* 'What's happened?' He looked around to find Vidar and Jesco, and saw they were already making their way towards him.

Jagisson edged closer, dropping his voice so only those close by could hear. 'Zar and Banno saw strangers on the glacier. Foaley said it might be nothing, just some strays, but he sent me here to warn you.' Then he dropped his voice. 'Zar sensed sorcery.'

Deo on High, Raythe thought, his heart beginning to hammer. *We've not even dealt with the sicknesses properly yet – we're not ready for another crisis.*

While Jagisson filled in what little he knew, Raythe gazed southwest, calculating odds and distances. *I have a horse, and so do Vidar and Jesco, so we can get there in a few hours . . .*

'Sometimes flocks of kikihana birds get up on the glacier,' Monarohi put in. 'It is not unknown for a hunter to see them up there and think they are people.'

'I hear you, but we need to check it,' Raythe said. 'I'll go myself, right now.'

'In the dark?' Oziniya asked. 'Is that wise?'

'What's foolish is to sleep while enemies stalk you,' Raythe answered, turning back to Jagisson. 'Guy, well done, but you need rest. I'll take Jesco and Vidar. You can rejoin the patrol tomorrow.'

'I'm grateful – but you'll need a guide and I know the way,' Jagisson said gamely. 'I'll come with you.'

Raythe studied him up, then shook his head. 'No, we'll manage. but you'll lame your horse if you go any further tonight.' He turned to Monarohi. 'I'm sorry, but my daughter's down there.'

'Then you should go,' Monarohi agreed. 'Your work here is done, and done well. Best you investigate this, for your peace of mind, even if it is only kikihana birds on the ice.'

Oziniya added, 'Aie, find the truth, Rangatira Raythe. Send word as soon as possible.'

'A messenger must be sent to the Queen,' Raythe replied. 'Tell her what I'm doing, and to put her people on high alert.'

'We will send bird-riders immediately.'

Raythe, Jesco and Vidar ran for the guest house to pack their gear and were already saddling up as the Tanuahi began to gather: word had spread and the happy faces had turned anxious again.

Monarohi embraced Raythe before he mounted, and pressed noses with Jesco and Vidar. 'Fare you well, Rangatira Raythe,' he said loudly, his calm demeanour allaying some of the fear among the gathered tribespeople. 'Send word swiftly.'

A wide path formed through the crowd. Digging in their heels, the three of them went thundering down the corridor between the upturned faces, bursting into the open as the clouds shredded and ring-light lit the night. Without a word, they headed southwest.

3

Dangerous Prey

It can't be much further, Raythe Vyre told himself as he pushed his horse onwards. The night had been a real test of patience, for it had been impossible to ride as hard and fast as he wanted. It wasn't just the darkness and the unknown terrain, but intermittent squalls alternately froze and soaked them to the skin. The need to go carefully was a real trial when he couldn't stop himself picturing all the things that could be going wrong.

But at last dawn was approaching, the cloud was lifting and they were able to push on faster. They crested a rise, nearing the frozen lake that marked the southern borders of the Fenua Tangato, and caught glimpses of the mountains through the clouds and mist. Then the clouds tore open and the ringlight beamed through, a glorious arc of light basting the landscape in silver.

'We're getting close,' Raythe commented, reining in and pointing towards the mountains ahead. 'The glacier pass is in that cleft, and there's the Ginoshi River, that flows south from the city. Foaley's camped just to the east of the cleft.'

'We need to find them fast, but from now on, we should stay off open ground,' Jesco said. 'We don't know what we're riding into, and a surprise shot will put anyone in the grave, sorcerers and bearskins included.'

'I hear you,' Raythe said, peering south. 'It's just a few more miles. Let's go.'

Weariness forgotten, they nudged their mounts into motion again and thundered down the slope and across the tundra towards the foot of the frozen lake. Behind them, the eastern sky grew steadily lighter, streaked an ominous red.

For a few miles, Zarelda's flight was headlong, her vision blurred by tears and her senses pulsating from the fear of pursuit. But the flurry of shots she'd heard as she fled had died out and as the storm in the glacier faltered and the skies cleared, her thoughts turned to survival.

It's begun, she thought fearfully. *Those were Otravian redjacks.*

That these men were her countrymen gave her no comfort: Otravia was ruled by the empire, and any military expedition was dominated by Bolgravians. There was no doubt in her mind that the empire was here. They'd all known it was probably inevitable, but they'd all hoped it wouldn't happen.

But it has, and now I have to find a way to warn our people.

To do that, she needed landmarks. The most reliable path north was the Ginoshi River, so she headed northwest until she struck the frozen lake, intending to follow the river upstream to Rath Argentium. She was fit and determined, but it was fifty miles – it would be a hard few days.

I'll do it, she resolved. *I must.*

What she dared not think about was what might have happened to Foaley and Kinatia and the rest. She hoped they'd had enough warning to get clear – and that thought led directly back to Banno and his warning shot.

That was true heroism, she thought dazedly. *But would he have done it if I'd been kinder?*

She remembered the hopelessness in his voice. 'I will prove myself to you.' She would remember those words on her deathbed. *You did prove yourself*, she told the sky, hoping against hope he'd somehow escaped, but feeling in the pit of her stomach that he was dead.

Make his sacrifice worthwhile, she told herself. *I have to make sure his warning shot is heard throughout the Fenua Tangato.*

It was still an hour or two until dawn, but Luc Mandaryke had been awake all night.

He'd been irked that Teirhinan Deathless and Toran Zorne had led a sortie against the sentry post, forcing his guardsmen to follow them in; now he was awaiting their report.

In the meantime, he'd sent word through the tunnel beneath the glacier, urging all units to push onwards without rest. Now he paced the glacier pass, staring down at the glistening frozen land as his mind whirled.

If the alarm's raised, we'll need to move quickly. We're spread across dozens of miles in a tunnel of ice: if we faced a real enemy and they found out, we'd be annihilated.

The first through would be Bolgravian cavalry, the finest riders in the world; they'd be there within the hour. *I'll send them out to screen us and get the lie of the land.*

'Milord?'

He jumped as Zorne and Teirhinan appeared behind him. *Kragging ghosts,* he thought. 'Can't you two wear bells or something?'

The sorceress giggled, but the assassin just looked puzzled.

'What happened out there?' Luc asked. 'I heard gunfire.'

'There was a patrol, which we ambushed. At least one escaped.'

Luc ground his teeth. 'How?'

Zorne hesitated, then said, 'Lady Teirhinan went ahead of the rest of us. She killed a dozen, but the rest got away. I ran down two, but there were at least half a dozen more.'

Teirhinan pouted. 'It wasn't my fault. Some idiot fired their gun before I reached the camp.'

Luc swallowed his annoyance; unfortunately these were the only two people in his service he couldn't afford to lose his temper with. His own sorcerous powers were respectable – he'd graduated with a first at the Arcanum – but they were specialists who'd been honing their skills while he'd been tied up with the demands of politics and a more sedentary life for almost five years. Like all skills, battle-magic atrophied without practice.

'Done is done,' he said. 'I have the Bolgrav cavalry coming through next. They can hunt them down.'

'Those I pursued were natives. They fled northeast,' Zorne reported.

'And the other was a sorceress,' Teirhinan put in, her voice turning malicious. She took professional jealousy to deadly levels. 'I sensed her familiar as we moved in, but diverting to deal with it wasn't possible.'

Zorne coughed. 'It was a fox familiar. Zarelda Vyre has such a spirit companion.'

Luc stiffened. '*Zarelda Vyre?* Holy Deo, *she's* here?' He turned away, thinking hard, then spun back. 'Leave the pursuit of the natives – the cavalry can deal with them. I want you two to bring that girl back – *alive*, do you hear me? That is your only priority now, is that understood?'

The two sorcerers looked at each other, blinking. Neither looked pleased to be assigned to the mission together, and it was no surprise when Teirhinan said, 'I can find her familiar, but I would rather work alone.'

'Alone, together, I don't give a shit,' Luc snapped. 'Just find her and bring her to me. He stared at them both. '*Unharmed,*' he repeated firmly.

Within ten minutes, the pair had packed and saddled their horses. Zorne requested a squad of cavalry and Luc assigned some of his personal guard, with instructions to keep him posted.

'I'll send more men as they arrive,' he promised. 'Remember: *alive and unharmed.*'

Teirhinan pulled a face, but Zorne saluted obediently – then they led the cavalrymen out of the pass and went pounding north across the plains, under the silver light of the rings.

The wind was moaning across the frozen lake, making the branches of the dead trees along the shore hiss. Raythe and Vidar were walking their horses close to the waterline where the woods were thickest. Just a hundred yards inland, occasionally glimpsed through the trees, they'd seen and heard Bolgravian horsemen: the empire was here. He badly wanted to flee, to get back and give warning, but he couldn't.

I have to find Zar first . . .

He'd sent Jesco north to warn the Tangato and his Magnians, but his daughter's life was at stake here and that was the most he could do. With Vidar's bearskin senses and his own sorcery, he prayed they'd have a chance to find her – but so far he hadn't been able to penetrate Zar's veils, leaving him as blind as any ordinary man.

Vidar had found footprints in the mud beside a stream feeding the frozen lake, then caught her scent, but he'd soon lost it again, dissipated by the frost. Dawn was fast approaching and they'd had to hide as a group of riders passed by on the plains, heading north.

The Bolgravs must have set out in winter, Raythe thought, amazed they'd take such a risk – although he knew well the desperate greed that istariol could engender. *If they know about the istariol, and to follow the glacier to here, then Toran Zorne must've survived.*

Vidar growled a warning and they huddled deeper in the thicket, holding fast to their frightened horses as brash Bolgravian voices called and another unit of cavalry rode by. Cognatus fluttered inside him like a caged bird, sensing his distress.

'We've got to push to push on,' he muttered to Vidar, the moment the riders had vanished. 'We need visual contact.'

'Sure, but these woods are filling up, Raythe. It's just a matter of time before we're seen.'

'I know.' *But she's my daughter.* 'Come on, she was heading north . . . She'll be following the river – let's do the same and hope we stumble across her.'

*

The thud of hooves gave Zar a few seconds' warning, enabling her to hit the ground, then crawl to the nearest rise. She watched grey-clad horsemen ride by just yards away, scanning the trees. She buried her head, desperately hoping they hadn't seen the steam of her breath.

She'd been creeping along the edge of the dead forest, in just deep enough to avoid seeking eyes, but near enough to see the plains. There were groups of riders all over the open ground. The lifeless, mist-filled woods were the only cover available.

In a few days, nowhere will be safe.

She edged away and made for the lake, her heart thudding in terror of discovery as a pair of nesting birds shrilled a warning. But no one came; hopefully, the sounds of this land were a mystery to her hunters. When she reached the shoreline, she was confronted by an expanse of mist-wreathed ice. Dawn was coming and there was no cover out there, leaving her no choice but to follow the shore northwards.

Sunrise found her crunching through ice-crusted pebbles until she reached a shallow river flowing in from the northeast, a braided rope of connected rivulets, knee-deep and barely ten yards wide, that had carved a channel through the woods, more than hundred yards of open ground. There were more dead trees on the other side, though, and no one was in sight.

Do I cross? she wondered. *It'll take me two or three minutes, and I'll be in plain sight if anyone comes . . .* The sky was lightening fast now, an ominous red dawn promising a bloody day.

She decided that she had no choice.

But she didn't move immediately, instead calling in Adefar, linking to his senses before sending him upstream to sniff for signs of the riders. In those vital minutes the daylight bloomed over the land, but it did give her comfort that she was alone.

I'll do it, she resolved, summoning her familiar back. *Let's go . . . now.*

She rose to her feet and advanced into the strip of open ground, all her senses straining.

*

Raythe and Vidar had reached the lake, following the north side of a broad strip of shingle that paved the path of a braided river through the woods, to the lake shore. But there was still no sign of Zar's passing.

Perhaps we've got ahead of her? It wasn't entirely unlikely, for the trees closest to the lakeshore were almost impenetrable; he and Vidar had been ghosting through easier paths nearer the edge of the woods, dodging increasing numbers of patrolling Bolgrav riders. 'Any luck?' he asked.

Vidar was wearing his unsettling half-human aspect: shaggier, with an animal muzzle and his features distorted, but still human enough to speak and comprehend. He sniffed the ground, tossed his head in frustration and growled, 'Nothing.'

Raythe bit his lip, thinking hard, then decided. 'Let's try pushing south along the shore. I reckon we've got ahead of her.'

'Back south, towards the Bolgies? You sure?'

Am I sure? No . . . but I must find her.

'Come on,' he urged.

Ten minutes later, they were near the edge of the frozen lake, its gleaming expanse shrouded in fog, and confronting a wide river bed, a slash of shingle and driftwood carving a path through the woods, a place where bad timing could see them caught in the open.

He prepared to send Cognatus out, to see if the familiar could sense any close pursuers; when Vidar grabbed Raythe's shoulder and pointed. Across the strip of open ground, a silhouette had emerged from the trees, a slender figure with a shock of short blonde hair.

Raythe's heart thudded. 'It's Zar!'

Vidar growled anxiously and went to rise.

'Wait,' Raythe warned, pulling him back down. 'Let her come to us – the more of us out there, the easier we are to spot.'

Despite that, it was all he could do to stop himself running to meet her. But he held back as his daughter crept unknowingly towards them, staying low, moving from driftwood pile to boulder, making good use of the scanty cover as she forged a path, wading across the widest streams and jumping the narrow ones. After a minute she was less than a hundred yards away, and Raythe's grip on Vidar's arm tightened.

'Gerda be with her,' Raythe muttered, in a rare moment of piety.

Moments later, horses neighed and hooves thudded as a dozen riders cantered round the nearest inland bend, just two hundred yards away. Zar tried to hide, but a bugle rang out and the riders spurred their mounts to a gallop.

'Gerda, you bitch,' Raythe swore, scrambling back to his horse as Vidar began to hyperventilate. 'No, Vidar, stay with me,' Raythe shouted, swinging into the saddle. '*Cognatus, praesemino cito!*'

Vidar seized a tree trunk, fighting for control as Cognatus bloomed inside Raythe and he shouted, '*Zar! To me!*'

He spurred his horse out into the open and saw as Zar, crouched beside a log, recognised him and her face shone with hope.

But the riders responded too, roaring in triumph and kicking up spray as they stormed through the shallow water.

'To me, to me!' Raythe shouted, and Zar leaped to her feet and sprinted. He reined in, whipped out his pistol, already loaded, checked the priming, then aimed as the distances shrank. Bolgravian pistols cracked at the edge of good shooting range, sending lead balls zipping about erratically, kicking up water and stones. Raythe took the time to aim, then shot the lead rider, striking his torso and hurling him from the saddle.

'*Cognatus,*' he shouted, '*impetus . . . opperio . . .*'

He'd hoped to slow them, but they only came on faster. Zar, trying to outrun them, was tripping over the stones – and moments later, the first four cavalrymen were on them, bursting into the space between Raythe and his daughter. Two peeled off, coming for him, while two headed for her. He conjured a shield an instant before lead slammed into the invisible barrier, but undeterred, they drew sabres and charged.

The other two closed in on Zar, who whirled and also began to conjure . . .

Raythe drew his falchion, a slashing weapon that suited fighting on horseback, and closed with the first man, smashing blades together as their mounts jostled each other.

The second rider tried to flank him, but Vidar, now in full beast form, slammed into the rider, bearing down man and mount. Teeth and claws crunched into the horse's throat and the man Raythe was facing, unnerved, flinched and missed his parry. The falchion hacked into his side and he too went down.

But the next group, five men shrieking Krodeshi war-cries, was almost on them . . . and Cognatus was now ready. '*Impetus nunc!*' Raythe shouted, pointing.

A wave of force burst from his hands, battering the oncoming horsemen, making the horses stagger. One stumbled over a piece of driftwood and went down, leg bones shattering as the rider went flying, while the other four clung on, fighting for control.

But the pair chasing Zar were on her, and Raythe was too late to help.

Zar had only ever slain two people, the Manowai sorcerers who'd tried to murder her when Ikendo seized the throne. She'd been stalked, then, and terror and fury had coalesced inside her, carrying her through those bloody moments. But these men were strangers to her and her only thought was to escape, not kill.

She linked to Adefar anew and lifted her hands as the Bolgravians – Krodeshi steppes-men with dark faces, narrow eyes and shaggy whiskers, bore down on her.

'*Adefar, suishin suru tella ishi!*'

Force belled out, lifting the river stones at her feet and sending them smashing into horses and men, making the animals rear in fright. Pistols cracked in reflex, but the shots went wide. Beyond them, she glimpsed the men facing her father and Vidar go down. Hope flared – until bugles sounded upstream. More riders were coming, too many to count or deal with, but her blood was up now and she hurled another wave of stones at the dazed riders facing her, making them recoil in alarm, then sprinted toward her father.

The next few seconds were bloody work as Raythe and Vidar cut down the Bolgravian horsemen Zar had battered half-senseless, then he hauled his daughter up behind him, feeling incredible relief. A full squad was closing in from upstream, too many to take on, the woods were too thick for galloping, leaving just one escape route: the frozen lake.

'Vidar,' he shouted, 'follow, follow!'

Although the bearskin was caught up in his battle-fury, Vidar was a veteran, better able than most to rule his urges. But there was no way the Norgan's horse would bear him in that state, and no certainty he'd heed his call, so all Raythe could do was go. He spurred towards the icy expanse, hoping Vidar would follow.

In moments, with Zar shouting encouragement, Vidar drew along-side, running on all fours, his loose furs and robes in rags around his bulky, bear-like form.

Bugles blared again and the distant horsemen surged after them.

Ordinary sorcerers could veil themselves and a few others provided they stayed close. Toran Zorne could hide anyone within two dozen yards, more than most.

But Teirhinan Deathless had veiled the whole company of Imperial Guard that Luc Mandaryke had assigned them, and she'd also latched onto Zarelda Vyre's familiar from a few miles away. It wasn't precise – the girl was shielding too, with surprising strength and proficiency – but they knew roughly where she was, and luck provided the rest. When Krodeshi outriders spotted her, the bugles rang out and they all con-verged on the girl, arriving at a wide, stony riverbed running through the dead wood to the frozen lake. Some kind of skirmish was already unfolding ahead, but it was too distant to assess it. Then a beast roared and he suddenly remembered the bearskin, Vidarsson.

Who exactly have we found? he wondered.

Teirhinan rode gracelessly beside him, her grey hair streaming out .
'The girl is here . . . and another sorcerer,' she shouted, her deathly face
gleefully alive.

Raythe Vyre . . . or Kemara Solus? Zorne thought. *Or both . . .* he thought
anxiously, remembering their deadly meld.

'Signal to Lord Mandaryke,' he shouted back to the bugler, then he
gave mind to his own preparations. '*Praesemino, Ruscht,*' he called, and
his familiar streamed into him, expanding his senses – and yes, there
was Raythe Vyre, his daughter mounted behind him, and the bearskin
Vidar Vidarsson, scrabbling along the riverbed beside them.

'Onward!' he shouted. 'Take them alive!'

It wasn't a plan so much as a prayer. Raythe rode hard towards the frozen lake, Zar clinging to his back and Vidar barrelling alongside. When
they reached the river mouth where the chilly water pooled, they
veered north to where the ice was closest. He was scared the ice wouldn't
take their weight, but had no time to test it.

Behind them, the leading group of horsemen were closing in. They
were Imperial Guard, but not Bolgravian, and led by a dour-faced man
with a bowl haircut.

Toran Zorne . . .

He reached for his pistol, but remembering it was spent, instead
urged his horse through the cold water and up onto the sheet ice, which
did take their weight. Vidar followed, giving a startled yelp as he
skidded.

Raythe turned his horse to face the nearest pursuers hitting the
shore just a few dozen yards away. '*Cognatus, ignus! Abeo . . . nunc!*' he
shouted, sending a fireball at the riders, scattering them. '*Habere scutum, nunc!*' he added, and shields flared around them an instant before
pistols cracked among the riders.

No spell was entirely foolproof against a concentrated barrage of
musketry: despite the shield, a ball punched through, and to his horror

his mount's legs wobbled badly. It lurched, and he and Zar pitched themselves free, landing hard on the ice as the horse, hit in the neck, crashed down.

Damn you, Deo – now how do we get away?

He blasted the gunmen with fire and they drew off, but the next group, which included Zorne and a grey-haired waif, reined in at the edge of his range.

Then a bannerman caught his eye and he recognised the flag: scarlet and blue chequers surmounted by a white lion. House Mandaryke.

Luc Mandaryke's guard stormed into the river delta, closing in on their prey, shouting triumphantly as they ploughed through Toran Zorne's outriders. Luc was among them, caught up in the thunderous chaos of the charge. Just staying mounted was a feat, but he'd seen their quarry and scented blood.

Raythe! Deo be damned, it's bloody Raythe!

Instantly, he changed his plans, shouting, 'Pull out, pull out!' and hauling on his reins.

Somehow, his trumpeted voice was heard and heeded, and his guards – young Otravian nobles, known as elans for their reckless daring, veered left and right and pulled up on the edge of the narrow strip of water. Just three people faced them, forty to fifty yards away on the edge of the frozen lake. One was a bearskin, who didn't interest him; his eyes were fixed on Raythe Vyre and his daughter. Raythe had sorcerous energy playing about his hands – and so did Zarelda.

Splendid! Now I don't have to hunt them down.

'Ho, Raythe, well met!' he boomed. 'Are you surprised to see me?'

'Not really,' his enemy called back. 'I've had your stink in my nostrils for hours.'

Clearly, Vyre hadn't changed. 'You're looking tired, Raythe – and old.'

'Whereas you look like you've been eating lard for the past five years,' Raythe drawled. 'The fat of the land goes straight to your belly, eh.'

Behind the renegade lord, Zarelda was glaring at him. Her face was more freckled than it had been when he last saw her, and her once-long blonde hair had been cropped. She even had some kind of dark markings on her chin, which he couldn't identify. Clearly she'd been running completely wild.

We'll soon fix that.

He waved in the nearest officer. 'I want the girl alive and unharmed. The rest are optional. Prepare to attack.'

The man saluted, heartened by his master's confidence, and barked at the riders to form up in readiness for the attack.

'You've nowhere to go, Raythe,' Luc called. 'This land belongs to me now.' Then he remembered that stickler, Zorne, so qualified his words. 'And to the Emperor, may Deo bless him. Surrender, and we can make this a peaceful transition.'

'I don't think so,' Raythe called back. 'This place is a death-trap, Luc. You should leave while you can.'

A bluff, and not a very good one . . . unless he really has activated that fortress . . .

That gave him a slight pause, but really, he doubted Vyre would be out here if that were the case. Regardless, what better time was there to kill him than now?

'Take the girl alive,' he repeated, then he raised his double-barrelled pistol. 'Mirella's here,' he called, as he took aim. 'I'll show her your corpse before we bury it.'

Mirella's here.

The words were a physical blow, even after five years. But Raythe didn't let the flash of a beautiful face surmounted by honey-gold ringlets distract him. 'Zar, ready a heat-shield spell – you'll know when.'

Vidar growled unhappily, but Zar readied herself, her face determined.

Then Luc Mandaryke took aim, the hammers clicked and Raythe shouted, *'Nunc!'*

His shields flashed into place just as the twin lead balls blasted into

149

them, flattening in a burst of sparks just a yard in front of him. Behind the billowing translucent shields, the cavalrymen roared and the horses neighed as they splashed into the water.

He ignited the pinch of istariol dust in his fist and drawing on the burst of energy, shouted, *'Aquæ arderent, amplius!'*

As he did, Zar shouted, *'Adefar, scutum calor!'* and a heat-shield materialised, just in time to protect them from his spell's backwash.

Scarlet light flashed as the istariol was consumed, then that force was unleashed into the water before him as raw heat. What should have been a minor spell turned the delta pool into a boiling cauldron.

The river mouth seethed as dozens of horses shrieked and crashed down, those behind plunging unwittingly into the tangle, crushing limbs and skulls. Those caught directly in the super-hot steam and boiling water screamed horrendously. As the ice began to crack, Raythe moved Zar and Vidar back until they vanished in the massive billowing cloud. He could hear Luc's voice roaring above the clamour, summoning wind and trying to temper the hot water, but unless he had istariol on him, he was whistling in the wind.

We have no horse, so I'll have to draw Luc off . . .

'Go,' he told Vidar, 'fast as you can – I'll meet you at the sphere-gate!'

Zar looked aghast, but Vidar, his bestial face softening, growled something and she clambered onto his back.

'Trust me,' Raythe told her. 'I'll be there!'

She touched her heart, then Vidar turned and went pounding away across the ice.

Raythe turned, pulling out another pinch of istariol, and readied his next spell.

Until the moment when the water began bubbling and his whole front line was boiled alive, Luc had truly forgotten what it was like to take on Raythe Vyre.

Luc knew himself to be bigger, stronger, richer, better-looking, better-connected and just kragging *superior* in every way to his 'best friend' – but Raythe had *always* had a way of punching above his weight, and below the belt, too, something that had completely slipped Luc's mind in the wake of all his successes.

Watching the shoreline boiling, breaking the cream of his charging cavalry, he recalled exactly what a *damnable bastard* Raythe Vyre really was.

He tried to blast the steam away, but his counter-spells wouldn't bite. He couldn't think why until he sniffed and smelled the electric, acrid tang of istariol. *Of course kragging Raythe's got istariol: that's why we're all bloody well here!*

'Go round,' he roared, but amidst the chaos his was just another voice, drowned out by the shrieking of the dying men and beasts and the yapping of frightened officers. Anyone not caught up in the immediate carnage had retreated and he found himself standing alone, staring at fifty or sixty men and as many horses, dead, dying or unconscious, or howling their agony to the skies. 'Kragga mor,' he blurted, utterly aghast.

Then his temper rose and he turned on his aides . . . but they were edging away as a white horse trotted up: Teirhinan Deathless in her pale robes, violet eyes drinking in the chaos.

'Do you require aid, Milord?'

It was typical of a specialist sorcerer, to hover at the back of a fight until they could work out who and what they faced, but it still rankled to have her lording it like this.

'Aye,' he snarled. 'Bring me Zarelda Vyre . . . *alive and unharmed* – as I ordered you before, damn it! *Go!*'

'It is good as done,' she told him.

Then she murmured in her horse's ear and it trotted forward, right to the edge of the boiling water. Her voice rose, twin shadows of light and darkness flashed round her and he felt cold radiate, a merciless counter spell that *refroze* the water, indiscriminate of the living and the dead. He was conscious of the cavalrymen watching, gazing in horror as their stricken comrades were entombed in ice.

The steam cloud dissipated, and Raythe and his group were revealed . . .

. . . as gone.

Everyone fell silent, just staring at the white expanse, and for a moment Luc had to fight not to laugh, or rip someone's head off, because this was *so-very-Raythe*. The card up the sleeve. The trick of the eye. The back window left open. The knife to the back. No wonder Colfar's Rebellion had taken so long to crush.

But I always win in the end, he reminded himself. *Who got Mirella? Who got the power, and whose family ended up on the gallows?*

'Find them!' he roared at Teirhinan, then at his aides. 'Find them and bring them to me!'

The aides scattered, but the pale sorceress murmured, 'I'll find the girl. But I need something from you.'

The one thing Raythe had always been good at was improvising. As the enemy counter-spell flowed over the water and froze it again, he realised what to do.

Istariol and ice, that's all I need.

He spread his arms and murmured instructions to Cognatus, while pointing and making a lifting gesture that pulled ice up from the frozen sheet. Even as the steam cloud began to fail, his simple spell built a wide wall, just a few inches thick and roughly his height, shielding himself from sight. Thanks to the istariol, it took shape in seconds, creating an opaque barrier that would blend with the mist and the ice sheet: a trick of the eye, so that anyone looking from the river mouth would see nothing but an empty expanse of ice.

When he looked over his shoulder, he could see Vidar and Zarelda barrelling towards the middle of the lake, where the mist was deepest. Inside a minute they'd be invisible even without the conjured barrier.

On the shore, he could hear Luc Mandaryke raging, blasting out orders and threats.

He's not changed at all, he thought, smiling thinly. Then he turned and ran, parallel to the thin ice wall, towards the northern shore and the trees.

It took a full three minutes to realise that somehow, Raythe had erected a screen of ice for a few hundred yards in either direction, because even Teirhinan hesitated to advance when a sorcerer like Raythe, wielding istariol, was in play. Finally, she nudged her ghostly pale horse forward – and then peals of laughter rang out as she broke a hole in the barrier.

If he'd dared, Luc would have shot her for laughing. *Kragga mor,* he thought, humiliated and furious, as he joined the pale witch. *I will make you all pay.*

'Where've they gone?' he demanded.

She sniffed the air. 'The girl has gone that way,' she said, eyes glinting. She pointed out across the lake, towards the west. 'She's with the bearskin.'

'And Raythe?'

She shrugged. 'He's veiled to me, but he's not with the girl and her beast, so search nearby.'

Then she murmured a spell and a pair of spikes burst through her boots at the ankle, bone spurs that she gouged into her horse's white flanks, drawing blood. The horse shrieked, reared up, hooves flailing, then thundered away across the ice in pursuit of the bearskin.

Luc stared after her, envious of her power, but still filled with loathing. Anyone of superior skill in any field raised his hackles; and any woman who showed no desire for him was likewise an insult to his sensibilities. Not that he wanted Teirhinan, but he expected all womankind to worship him as was his due.

Once she's done all I need of her, she'll have to go. Someone of her power is always a threat, and the risk that she'll try to seize control is unacceptable. Another job for Toran Zorne.

He turned as the Ramkiseri approached, and snapped, 'Find Raythe. I want his head.'

*

153

After an hour of running over the pitted ice, even Vidar was flagging. Zarelda could hear his heaving breath; his fur was wet and matted and steam gusted from his nostrils, mingling with the swirling fog. The lack of visibility was a mercy as it hid their passage, but she worried they might be going astray.

'You can slow down,' she panted in the bearskin's ear, 'maybe rest for a bit?'

Vidar heeded her and slowed to a trot, for which she was grateful as his spine wasn't really shaped for a rider, not like a horse's. She felt battered and she was exhausted, but she didn't feel unsafe, even with Vidar in beast form. Despite his giant, shaggy, wolf-cum-bear shape, there was intelligence in his eyes. She'd heard that bearskins gained more control as they aged – at least, those who survived. Vidar, who must be in his forties, was obviously such a one.

After walking for another hour, they reached the western shore. Vidar sniffed the air, then made a throaty, satisfied sound and Zar, exhaling and shaking some of the tension from her shoulders, dared to hope that maybe – just maybe – they'd escaped.

Then Vidar pricked up his ears and a moment later she heard it too: the sound of a single horse, its hooves crunching on the ice behind them.

Father? She hoped. *Perhaps he's stolen a horse . . .*

She slid painfully from Vidar's back, wincing at her battered thigh muscles, and turned to face the sound.

Moments later, a white horse rode out of the fog, laden with tack and saddle-bags, but with no one riding. Zarelda glanced at Vidar, who was sniffing the air suspiciously. She did the same, but all she could smell was the loamy rot of the dead forest. 'What's it doing here?' she wondered. 'Do you think it's one of the Bolgravian cavalry horses?'

Vidar responded with a throaty cough, and then his body went through a smooth but clearly painful transformation, bones and sinews popping as he contorted, knee joints reversing even as his face and skin shed fur. His clothes had been ripped to shreds by the first transformation, so he was completely naked.

Zar coloured and looked away. 'Sorry, I've got no spare clothing,' she mumbled, then she called Adefar to her. There was something about this lone horse that didn't feel right, even though there was no sign of danger. 'Be careful,' she called. 'We should just leave it alone.'

Shaking his head, Vidar strode out with no apparent concern for his nudity. The horse didn't like the bearskin, that was clear, but he managed to snag its reins and spoke soothingly, then he called, 'Someone's spurred it so hard they've broken the skin. I've no time for someone who mistreats their horse.' He shrugged. 'Still, it'll help us travel faster.'

'Maybe,' Zar said, thinking, *This is all wrong . . .*

'C'mon, meet your new mistress,' Vidar told it, pulling on the reins. Then he looked past Zar and went still.

Zar looked over her shoulder – and she too went rigid.

The palest woman she'd ever seen was standing amidst the dead trees. If she'd been lying in a coffin, no one would have believed her still alive.

'Yes,' the woman snickered, 'meet your new mistress.'

With Adefar already bubbling inside her, Zar reacted instantly. *'Adefar, ignus nunc!'*

The torrent of fire she unleashed should have engulfed and torched the woman, but she advanced unharmed through the flames behind an opaque disc of air, although her hem did begin smouldering.

'Submergo quod flamma,' she retorted, a praxis spell that undid Zar's fires, then she shrieked, *'Cuzka kazei!'* – words Zar recognised as mizra – and a narrow blast of wind ripped at her.

Reflexes honed by so many practise duels with Rima enabled Zar to shout, *'Avertat ventum–'* and Adefar swept the counterattack aside. By now she could sense two balls of indistinct light, one light and the other dark, in the grey-haired woman's aura.

Praxis and *mizra – how?*

A second later, Vidar came thundering up, roaring and bear-shaped again, hurtling towards the woman like a runaway wagon, trying to close the gap before she could react. Zar sought to time her attack simultaneously, shrieking, '*Impetum cum vestibulum—*' and conjuring crackling energy at the woman as Vidar left.

But the enemy sorceress was somehow babbling two streams of words at once, as if she had two tongues; even as she conjured force and hurled Vidar aside, she unleashed a snake of black smoke at Zar. In mid-air, it became an *actual* snake the size of a Shadran python: it clamped onto her right bicep and punched its teeth into her arm as she shouted in terror.

She slammed her fist down on the python's gauzy head, making the phantasmal creature disintegrate ... but it was too late. Darkness rippled beneath her skin and a numb lethargy began to throb through her limbs. She reeled, struggling just to stay upright.

'Submit, girl,' the woman rasped. 'Let me take you to your mother.'

No, I'm not going back ... to that ... bitch ...

Zar's legs tangled and she fell. She could see Vidar fighting his way back to his feet to try to help her, but with a careless swatting gesture, he was slapped away into the trees. He landed with a crash, and next moment the pallid sorceress was looming over Zar, a blaze of darkness ripped across her senses and the world winked out—

Vidar got his legs under him, despite an attack that would have left others broken and unconscious. He knew he couldn't take many more blows like that, though.

Zar was down and the sorceress was sending a pulse of force through the girl that made her jolt, then go limp. Then she looked at Vidar, her violet eyes alight with glee, and chirruped, 'Now you.'

Raythe charged me with Zar's life ... He gathered his strength to spring ...

But as he leapt, the sorceress shrieked out her spells and slammed her fists together, discharging a blast of kinetic energy that shattered a tree ... right behind where he would have been, had he actually attacked her.

Vidar had never been stupid, and as a veteran soldier and bearskin, he'd learned something of when to fight and when to run. So he feinted his attack, then flung himself sideways, out of the path of the blast he was expecting – and ran like a terrified rabbit, swerving violently as the woman screeched her spells, one after another, with no let-up in power or ferocity. Bursts of fire scorched the air – behind his right shoulder, then his left, then just short of him . . .

. . . and finally, he was away, pelting along the shoreline until he was swallowed up by the mists.

The spells might have stopped, but he didn't, his flight impelled by fear and fury in equal measure, until he'd put miles between him and the wraith-woman. As the night deepened, he slowed his gait to a miles-eating trot, heading for Raythe's rendezvous at the sphere-gate, hoping his friend would make it too.

Frigid air warred with the warmth of a fire a few feet away; Zar's face was burning hot, but her back was frozen, despite the blankets she was wrapped in. She kept her eyes shut, listening hard for clues as to where she was, and what she faced.

The grey-haired witch, who looked strangely young *and* old, was the last thing she remembered – her, and a phantom serpent. She could still feel the punctures on her arm and her head was fuzzy, but she couldn't detect any lasting harm.

She used both praxis and mizra – that should be impossible.

She was afraid the witch was somewhere near, but the sounds around her were a familiar blend of the homely and the military: distant bugles, tramping men, the clank of wood and metal, the neighing horses and the bark of male voices, combined with the gentler sounds of women chatting or humming and the crackling of burning wood. Rich perfume scented the air and someone was scratching a pen over paper.

Her stomach growled – and a young woman with a meek voice said, 'Milady, the coffee is ready.'

The waft of the fresh hot coffee filled the tent, deeply enticing, and in any case, Zar badly needed to pee, so she opened her eyes and rolled over to face the middle of the tent.

A skinny girl in a maid's smock squeaked, 'Milady!'

'Zaza!' – the pet name Zar had always despised – Mirella Mandaryke exclaimed. 'Thank Gerda, we have you back.' She dropped her writing and came to her, arms outspread.

Zar had no wish to held by *her*. 'Stay away,' she snapped, pushing aside her mother's arms and scrabbling backwards on the mattress. Glaring around, she asked, 'Where am I? Where's Dad?'

Her mother looked like an older version of Zar herself, with all the freckles and imperfections removed. Her impeccably painted face was framed by golden ringlets; she wore a blue velvet gown glittering with gems. Her face flashed with momentary hurt, but she cupped Zar's chin and frowned, running a finger over the tattoos. 'What are these hideous marks? I'll have them seared off once we're back in civilisation.'

Zar squirmed and yanked her face from her mother's cold fingers. 'You'll leave them alone. They're a mark of honour,' she snarled, then she called, '*Adefar, animus.*'

Predictably, nothing happened.

Imprisoning a sorcerer's familiar in an artefact was how the Tangato stopped a sorcerer accessing their magic, but in Magnia they used spells. She presumed that was what had been done to her.

That won't stop me getting out of here, she vowed to herself.

'What are you doing here?' she demanded, glaring at her mother.

'I came for you,' Mirella declared. 'When I was told you'd been located at last, I couldn't stay away.' She turned to her maid and said, 'Edisha, get food for my daughter.'

The maid hurried out, leaving Zar alone with her mother.

So many emotions were tumbling through her mind: Mirella been a difficult, peripheral presence in her early years, leaving the real parenting to her nanny and a succession of tutors. Then she'd left, taking Zar to House Mandaryke, which had felt like a prison. She'd hated her mother ever since.

'How did you find us?' she demanded.

'Through a man called Zorne.'

'A murdering Ramkiseri. How appropriate.'

'It takes courage to infiltrate an enemy camp. Zorne is singular, but I can forgive anyone able to reunite me with my daughter. Five years – that's how long Raythe stole from us. *He's* the real criminal.'

'The best four years of my life. At least I had one parent–'

Mirella caught her hands. Her face looked deadly serious. 'My poor girl: Raythe is not your father.'

Of all the things her mother might have said, that was the last thing Zar expected. '*What?*' She searched that beautiful face for tell-tales signs of a lie. 'That's not possible.'

'But true, nevertheless,' Mirella replied.

It can't be – Raythe Vyre is my father. 'I was born a year after you married Dad.'

'I was already having an affair with Luc,' Mirella replied, with a weird kind of malicious pride. 'And I hardly saw Raythe at all. The month you were conceived, he was with the army. I was barely able to pass you off as his.'

It was like taking a sucker-punch to the belly. Zar doubled over as a sea of memories rose: everything she and Raythe – *my father* – had shared, all her life, but especially these past five years. There had been dangers, yes, but also the homely pleasures of life together, the conversations and lessons, all the little domestic trials they'd faced together.

'You're lying,' she insisted. 'I'm a Vyre.'

'My dear, you are a Mandaryke.'

Zar's temper flared and she threw caution to the winds. 'You know what? I don't kragging care if it's true. Raythe Vyre is my father, because he's fought for me and cared for me and taught me how to fight and ride and swim and everything else that matters, while the *shithead* you left us for was busy beheading his own people. So you're an adulteress and I'm a bastard. Thanks so much. What a kragging great start in life.'

Mirella reared back like a Shadran hooded viper and snapped, 'You are *not* a bastard, Zarelda – not since I married Luc. But we've never been able to tell you the truth because *that man* stole you. But everything is legal and attested now: you are a Mandaryke, one of the ruling house of Otravia.'

'No, I'm not. I'm a Vyre!'

'Don't be stupid,' Mirella hissed. 'There are no Vyres any more, except one sad renegade who can't accept that his time is gone. You should hate him for dragging you through wars and plagues and Deo knows what else, following that fool Colfar and all his bloodthirsty cronies. The heartless bastard.'

'He had a heart – I know that, because *you* broke it!'

Mirella gave her the look of someone who really couldn't be bothered wasting breath explaining obvious things to her lessers. She stood and called, 'Edisha, I want this urchin made worthy of my husband.' She faced Zar again. 'If you disgrace yourself when you're presented to him, you'll feel his anger.'

There was a note in her voice that was unexpected – clearly Luc wasn't someone even she dared to piss off.

That's just too bad, Zar thought defiantly. *I'll be damned before I call him Father.*

4

Flight

*I am the Aldar Queen. We have ruled the Fenua Tangato for five centuries and it
will not end now.*

The mantra played in Shiazar's mind as the world she knew fell
apart.

The Hiriwa tribal village was in uproar. The outsiders, the Bolgravians that Raythe Vyre so dreaded, had invaded, months ahead of their
worst estimate. Now she had only a few minutes before she must act.
She had been dressed and made ready: she was clad in a blue over-robe,
for calmness, but beneath it she already wore her elaborate leather
armour, black and polished and close-fitting, reminiscent of a spider's
long, thin limbs. Her mask, a gold sun, invoked divine protection.

She turned to those she'd summoned: Rangatira Natomo, his usual
equanimity all awry; Rima, brave but so young; Kitali, the only one of
her Yokei sisters present, a fragile old woman learned in cooking and
embroidery but not in fighting, and Imbataki, the most inexperienced
of her warleaders.

She gestured irritably as they knelt, impatient with tradition and
protocol today, with so many feathers in the wind. 'Rise, rise,' she
instructed. 'We have warning of invasion and our people must march.
We will fall back into the wildest parts of the Fenua Tangato. Leave
behind everything that is not required for life in the wilds. Imbataki,
send runners to every tribe: we will muster at the hill-fort of the Puketapu tribe. Natomo, I commend the Hiriwa into your hands, and the life
of Yokei Kitali. We must be gone within the hour.'

Natomo gulped. 'You do not accompany us, my Queen?'

She jabbed a finger skywards. 'I must protect Shiro Kamigami, the citadel of my ancestors.'

'But my Queen—'

'Our people will die if they stay, Natomo. Go now. Yokei Kitali will guide you.'

She embraced Kitali, struggling not to cry, then the rangatira and his shoganai bowed and followed the Yokei out.

Shiazar turned to Rima. 'I need your help. We must recover istariol from the citadel and transport it north, to share with your brother and sister mahotsu-kai. May it give you the strength to find victory.' She belted her twinned scabbards to her back, the long-handled karnas sword and the seppun dagger, then picked up a demonic red mask, for war. 'We will make them bleed for coming here,' she muttered.

She didn't put the mask on, just hooked it to her belt, then donned a flesh-mask, the visage of a young Tangato woman she used so she could move anonymously among the tribe at need.

Rima gasped when she saw it. 'I've seen that face – and I wondered who you were, but everyone I asked just said you were from the countryside.'

'I'm amazed you didn't guess,' Shiazar replied, as she wrapped her helmet and personal effects in her cloak.

She led the way out of the royal farai's back door, straight into the bustle and confusion of the evacuation. Everyone was caught up in their own crises, loading precious possessions and vital supplies, so no one noticed them as they slipped away.

At the edge of the village, they summoned kikihana birds and rode for Rath Argentium, five miles away. The cold, blustery wind made it an uncomfortable ride. At the great bridge, Shiazar replaced the flesh-mask with the demonic one. They rode across as the Magnian guards saw them and rang the alarm bell.

They were met at the gatehouse by Jesco Duretto, who'd ridden north to bring the warning. 'Majesty?' he called in greeting.

'We go to Shiro Kamigami,' she called. 'Please grant us passage.'

Jesco bowed formally to her and ushered her through.

In the big square behind the gatehouse, she found the white-skinned Magnians were in as much confusion as her own people, fussing over carts and baggage as they prepared to flee.

Jesco glanced up at the citadel, floating above the city in defiance of gravity and reason. 'Can you hold it against the empire, do you think?'

The castle's ancient weaponry system was still a mystery to be unravelled, but if she could prevent the invaders from seizing it, even if it meant finding a way to destroy it, that would still be a victory.

'We will prevent the imperial men from taking it,' she replied. 'Are your people ready to leave? The invaders may only be hours away.'

'Some have already gone – the hunters, mostly. That leaves about a hundred and fifty villagers and farmers. Varahana's got them packing, but we'll need a guide.'

'Rima will guide you,' Shiazar told him. 'Take nothing unnecessary. Our people will shelter you.'

With Jesco waving them off, Shiazar and Rima sent their birds careering around the edge of the square and up towards the crater rim, where they reined in and gazed back south.

Shiazar caught her breath: a column of riders was already streaming across the plains towards the ravine, like an arrow flying straight for them. The enemy advance guard was almost here.

Shiazar turned to Rima. 'Forget the istariol – Kitali is moving the ingots we've already brought down. Go to Varahana, show her the northern way out of the city. Make for the Puketapu village.'

'I can't let you go up there alone,' Rima protested.

'I won't be alone – Onkado is up there,' Shiazar replied. 'Regardless, this is my destiny. Go and find yours.' When the girl still hesitated, she said firmly, 'Rima, with all my love, I *command* you to go.'

Rima visibly swallowed, then bobbed her head obediently, turned her bird and sent it back down the path to where the Magnians were preparing to leave.

Suddenly alone, Shiazar felt an awful sense of doom, but she guided her own kikihana down into the crater to the floating platform await-ing her at the bottom. She dismissed her bird, wondering if she would ever see it again, then stepped onto the stone disc and awakened the control plinth with a touch. Moments later, she was rising up towards the citadel.

My ancestral home . . . and perhaps my tomb.

The tiny Magnian community was in a state of shock. Mater Varahana, in charge of the evacuation, found herself reliving a similar trauma: the Bolgravian invasion which had driven them out of their ancestral homes. They'd all lost loved ones and been forced to abandon virtually every-thing they owned. Afterwards, they'd felt the oppression of extra taxes and having goods and possessions commandeered without recompense, and many had seen women of their family abused – or been that woman – the prey of swaggering conquerors who saw them as plunder.

But there was no panic, even though this trek had no known destin-ation. Jesco, who owned only his weapons and fiddle, took charge of the fighting men, while Varahana organised the rest, trying to quell her fears for the two men she cared about most in this world. Vidar Vidars-son and Raythe Vyre were somewhere out there. She couldn't help looking up every minute, praying they'd come galloping in ahead of the storm.

We came through so many trials and travails – and for what? she won-dered. But despair was the threshold of death and she thrust it aside. *Vidar and Raythe are alive*, she insisted. *They'll find us.*

She was helping the remaining Sisters of Gerda to load up a hand-cart with the religious paraphernalia and their few personal goods – a change of clothing, a flint and a pot – when Jesco came bustling up.

'The Queen just passed through,' he told her. 'She and Rima are heading for the citadel. They mean to prevent it being occupied.'

'Makes sense,' Varahana commented. 'Did she say where we should go?'

'She says Rima will return to guide us; we're to await her in the square.'

'Any sign of Raythe or Vidar?'

Jesco patted her shoulder. 'They'll come back. Those two don't know how to die.'

'I know,' she said, although more in hope than belief. 'Come on, then, let's make sure everyone's ready to go.'

They'd barely begun to assemble when a phorus bird with Rima on its back pelted into the square from upslope. Everyone hushed, as the Tangato sorceress shouted in her archaic Magnian, 'You must all leave now. From the rim, the invaders are in sight.'

Her words created near pandemonium as families sought each other in a panic, shrilling names and running around madly, until Varahana used her most strident sermon voice.

'Follow Rima!' she shouted. 'She knows the way to go – *stay together!*'

Rima's bird shrieked at the clamour, but the Tangato girl had it under control. 'This way!' she shouted, pointing towards the road round the inside of the walls.

'This way! This way!' Varahana echoed, and at last everyone began to comply. Varahana went to join them – then a horrible idea stopped her in her tracks.

Deo and Gerda, does this impulse come from you? she wondered. *Or from the Pitlord?*

Jesco grabbed her arm. 'Vara?' he asked. 'What are you waiting for?'

She couldn't answer at first, because her thought was calling into question *everything* she believed in. She was struck immobile, agonising over an action that would stretch her moral fibre to the core.

Then she cursed, told Jesco *'Come!'* and ran for the infirmary. It had already been cleared, but there were four particular containers she'd kept hidden. She grabbed two, had Jesco gather the other pair, then hurried back to the square.

'What're you doing?' Jesco demanded.

'What do you think?' she replied, deeply ashamed of her decision. 'Empty them, one in each well – *go!*' She hurried to the nearest, ripping at the wax seal, gagging at the dreadful odour assaulting her senses – but she tipped the stinking contents into the water, then hurried to the next, while Jesco did the gatehouse well and the rainwater tank beside the infirmary. By then, everyone else was gone, scrambling after Rima as she led them north.

'Was that what I think it was?' Jesco asked as he mounted his horse, then pulled her up behind him.

'Aye,' she said, in a hollow voice. 'I've just condemned thousands of men to an awful death.'

'Vara, you made the right choice. Deo understands.'

Does He? she wondered. *Or am I destined for the Pit?*

But the choice was made.

As they climbed towards the rim, she glanced back and saw the distant columns of horsemen on the plains. The orderliness of the lines proclaimed them as imperial Bolgravian cavalry, the most feared horsemen in the world.

We'll never escape them, she thought despairingly. *But we have to try.*

After all the rushing, the immense quiet of Shiro Kamigami, hanging a thousand yards above the city, felt surreal. Silence ruled, from the lowest point where the platform docked, all the way up the vast circular stairwell to the castle proper.

Provisioning wasn't an issue – stores of food had been brought up in the preceding weeks, in anticipation of just such a situation. The kitchens were functional and the water tanks were full from the winter's rain. *I can last here for months*, Shiazar mused. *But if these invaders are as resourceful as Raythe, they may well find a way up. Somehow, I have to make sure they can't.*

The transporting disc was secured, so they couldn't use that. The other way up was the sphere-gate, the Aldar artefact that linked this fortress to the old royal lake-house on the banks of Waiotapu, the Sacred Lake. With that in mind, she walked from the ground floor into the gardens, which were overgrown with vines and bushes. As part of the kite festival, Matsuri-Tako, her priests had placed dozens of gaudy giant box-kites for the spiritual cleansing of the citadel. Two had crashed and a few more had been ripped away by the wind, but most still fluttered in the breeze, bringing this dead place to life.

She walked to the outer walls, to a particular tower with an open-sided cupola. Inside was the mechanism that linked the citadel to the sphere-gate, miles away at Lake Waiotapu. The three runes carved on the stone control plinth marked activation, deactivation, and a lock, preventing its use.

If I destroy this thing, we'll never be able to replace it, she thought. *And so far, only my people know of it.* Keeping her options open felt wise, so in the end she just activated the locking rune.

That done, she walked around the battlements to the southeast watchtower, which afforded views over the city and as far as the Hiriwa village. To her horror, black smoke was billowing up from the village, the only home she'd ever known. Whether her own people or the invaders had torched it, she didn't know, and in truth, it didn't matter. This was what war did.

Blinking away tears, she turned her gaze on the plains below, where columns of mounted men were already passing over the bridge and into Rath Argentium: an invading ant horde storming a rival nest. There was no sign of resistance. It would have been futile, anyway.

If we'd been able to activate the weapons of this citadel, we could have fought, she reflected bitterly. But even Raythe Vyre had failed to find the control chamber, and in any case, it was likely that the whole gargantuan system that connected the eight dragon-cannons to the vats of liquid istariol had broken down, a victim of time.

As she turned away, something caught her eye: a glint of light on the hill across from the ravine. A Magnian spyglass, perhaps. She unhooked the scarlet daemon mask from her belt and placed it over her face, then glared back.

This is mine, she told that distant gaze. *It will never be yours.*

Luc Mandaryke stood at the summit of a hill at the northern end of a low range. Beside him was a strangely carved wooden arch, primitive and barbaric, but across the ravine lay Rath Argentium, a city built on the lower slopes of a mountain, with the peak broken off and floating a thousand yards above, tethered by four massive chains. He could even see the castle atop the rock, a sight to stir the soul.

What a day, he thought. *And what a vista.*

He focused his spyglass on that miraculous place, taking in the delicate towers and weathered stonework, including a relief sculpture of a warrior carved into the main tower, like a giant sentinel.

Imagine the treasures within.

Then he caught his breath.

There was a cloaked figure on the outer walls, too tiny to register in any great detail, but they wore a blue robe, with a scarlet mask over their face, and they were looking right at him. For an eerie moment, he felt like they could converse – but then they vanished from the walls and he let out his breath.

There are people up there – in the citadel of the Aldar Kings.

He felt a chill, remembering what Teirhinan Deathless had said about the fortress and its weaponry. Were they even now readying those weapons to destroy his forces?

Forcibly calming his nerves, he waved forward a waiting aide. 'Maveros, report.'

Jiani Maveros strode forward, saluted and launched into his report. 'General Lisenko's cavalry have entered the city and found it deserted. It looks like only a small district was being used – possibly by Vyre's people. They've fled – it looks like they somehow crossed the river to the north. The General has ordered his scouts to find them.'

'Too damned slow,' Luc commented. 'Who burned the village?'

'One of Lisenko's units got out of hand, Milord.'

'Damn those Bolgies. What of the natives?'

'Gone, sir. We shot a few and captured one, though.' Maveros waved to a pair of soldiers, who dragged up a naked corpse with dark brown skin and black curly hair. He had a savage aspect. Curiously, much of his body, including his face, was heavily tattooed. 'They can run like devils, Milord.'

'Was he armed?'

Maveros clicked fingers and a curious wooden spear was brought forth. It looked more ceremonial than martial, despite being sticky with blood. 'He used this like a club, holding it two-handed near the point. He broke one soldier's skull, then stabbed another with the spear-end. Primitives, sir. We captured a young woman – she fought like a rabid bitch. Oh, and some of the men claim to have seen a masked sorceress, but she escaped.'

Luc looked at him sharply, remembering the red-masked figure he'd glimpsed through his spyglass. 'A masked sorceress? They have the praxis?'

Maveros looked troubled. 'We don't know for sure. It may be mizra.'

'So the bulk of these people have fled, and they may have sorcerers. We must be vigilant, Maveros.' He dropped his voice. 'What news of the hunt for Raythe Vyre?'

'Nothing, sir. But a despatch from General Torland reports that Lady Teirhinan returned this morning with a prisoner, who's been delivered to your wife.'

Zarelda, Luc thought. *Excellent. Mirella will be delighted.* 'Where is General Torland's army now?' Lisenko's cavalry had advanced at full pelt, leaving Torland's red-coated Otravian infantry division far behind.

'Still emerging from the glacier tunnels. They'll be three or four days away, at least.'

'Very well, Maveros. Send word to Lisenko to secure the city. Put them in the district Vyre's people settled: it'll have water and maybe other amenities. Let's make this place ours.' He reflected that with Mirella still days away, the coming night presented an opportunity for some amusements. 'Find me somewhere to sleep tonight, then bring the woman we captured. I want to see what she's made of.'

Maveros saluted and hurried away, and Luc returned his gaze to that impossible castle in the skies, thinking of that red-masked figure on the battlements and wondering who they were. *One of these masked sorceresses, perhaps?* Then his heart thudded as another possibility leaped to mind. *An Aldar? Could it be?*

More likely it was these natives, aping their betters in some twisted homage to the past. But the thought tantalised him as he stared at the citadel again, wondering how to get up there.

5

Trapped in the Sky

Nemath Torland knew that he occupied a strange niche in the world. A child of the landed nobility, his ascent in the ranks had nothing to do with talent and everything to do with his friendship with Luc Mandaryke. When they'd met at the Academy, he'd known immediately that Luc would end up rising to the top, so he'd set about undermining his relationship with Raythe Vyre, all the while making himself indispensable.

That he was addicted to the bodies of other men was an unspoken fact they no longer discussed. Luc knew what 'Sonata' was, but he let her pass without so much as a glance.

Making me murder the Otravian tinderstick community was my punishment for being one myself, he mused often, then shrugged the thought away. Whatever he was, Luc valued him. He was well-connected, and utterly trustworthy, which was beyond price in this backstabbing world, so Luc protected him. All rumours about his 'weakness' were suppressed; there was an invisible wall around Sonata and anyone who voiced suspicions was silenced.

Bringing his lover on this trek had been a risk, but Torland couldn't bear the alternative. Watching Sonata move was its own reward. In public, *she* was all grace and poise, with an exaggerated, ironic manner that drove him crazy – and in private, *he* was wickedly inventive, his body both sheath and sword.

'Well, look who we've found,' Sonata trilled now, as a cluster of brightly caparisoned horses appeared on the road ahead. Two blonde women had half a dozen of the Governor's Imperial Guard protecting them. They all looked bedraggled, soaked by the incessant drizzle that had blighted the journey north.

'Indeed,' Nemath replied. 'The beauteous Mirella and her tomboy daughter. How amusing.' He focused on the daughter. She might look ungainly in a dress, but that shock of blonde hair was appealingly boyish. 'I rather wonder if that wild child is a kindred spirit? What do you think?'

'I think she's *revolting*, darling,' Sonata giggled. 'The opposite of everything I find attractive. No decorum, no femininity, not to mention the wrong genitalia. And feral, to boot. What's to like?'

'She must be driving dear Mirella to tears.'

'I do hope so. What's the little bitch's name again?'

'Zarelda – old Magnian for "Warrior Woman",' Nemath said. 'Clear proof that a man needs to name his children carefully if he wants them to turn out well.' They shared an amused look, then called greetings as the women jingled up.

Mirella greeted them warmly enough; she knew all about them, of course. 'General Torland, lovely to see you. We were wondering if we were lost. This rain and mist makes everywhere so confusing.' She pointed almost due west. 'Is north that way?'

'Just a few degrees off, Milady,' he laughed. 'Please, ride with us, and we'll set you on the right path. He peered at the sullen-looking Zarelda. 'How are you settling in?'

'Krag off, you pompous fraud,' the girl growled. 'Better still, go burn yourself.'

Charming.

'Winners drink wine; losers just whine,' Sonata snickered. 'You've none of your mother's grace.'

Zarelda faced Sonata and bared her teeth. 'You think you're safe? See what happens when he gets bored.'

'Only the boring get bored,' Sonata smirked. 'Tell me, is Jesco Duretto among your rabble? I could retire on the bounty for him.'

'Jesco will gut you both,' the girl fired back.

Nemath felt his eyes narrow; Duretto was famed as a swordsman, someone he'd resolved to personally destroy for eluding him so long.

'I think not, my dear,' he replied, keeping his voice even for Mirella's sake. 'We'll bring the Shadran pervert to justice in due course. I swear it upon my blade.'

'He's twice the man you are—'

'Is he just? On what basis?'

Zarelda spat at the ground. 'Because he hasn't slaughtered his own kind for a so-called "crime" that he commits himself every day, you stinking hypocrite.'

'Keep a civil tongue, Zarelda,' Mirella snapped.

'Oh, it's nothing,' Nemath shrugged. 'My dear girl, have you ever wondered why Jesco Duretto and Raythe Vyre are such good friends? Perhaps we'll burn them together, to ensure that's how they're remembered.'

The girl's whole body tensed. She clenched her fists and took a step forward.

'Go on, girl,' he offered, pitching his voice to goad her. 'Let's see if you've got a *man's* sword-hand.'

Mirella stepped in front of her daughter. 'Stop this, Zarelda. You're making a fool of yourself. I'm so sorry, General. She's still enthralled by her abductor.'

'It's not uncommon,' Nemath conceded. 'No offence is taken.' He faced the girl's hostile gaze with deliberate contempt. 'I do hope you can knock her rough edges off, or no man will ever look at her.'

Mirella gazed skywards. 'Don't even start.' She took his arm and drew him aside, dropping her voice. 'Nemath, is all well? I've heard that Raythe has been seen, but he escaped – is this so?'

'You know as much as I,' Torland replied. He could not quite fathom what Raythe Vyre was to her any more. She'd cuckolded him, then divorced him and married Luc. But whenever Vyre's name came up, there was something in her eyes he couldn't read.

He was a fool and a failure, he thought. *But perhaps she really did love him at first?*

'What's being done to find him?' she asked, her face inscrutable.

'Lady Teirhinan is hunting him,' Torland reported. It was a relief to have that chilling bitch absent.

'Then he's as good as dead. Thank you, Nemath. I'm sure we can find our way from here. Don't let us slow you down.'

Her eyes were saying, *My foolish daughter is too embarrassing for company.*

'You'll tame Zarelda,' he murmured. 'As you did Luc.'

'He's hardly tamed,' she tittered, but she looked pleased. 'I miss Otravia, Nemath. The sooner we can return home, the better. Then I can repair the damage that brute has done to my daughter.'

He was more than happy to let her Ladyship and her mad daughter go on, even if goading Zarelda had been amusing. So he bowed flamboyantly and saw them on their way before joining Sonata. Stroking her hip, he murmured, 'Tonight, I'm going to make you scream.'

'Promises, promises,' Sonata snickered, before leaning forward and kissing him, playing the loyal and passionate *lady*-consort to its limits. They shared a hazy, pillow-eyed sigh, then she said, 'Promise me one thing, darling. Try to take Jesco Duretto alive. I want to be the one who sets the fire alight at his feet.'

'Did he hurt you once?' he wondered, thinking that only love engendered such hate.

'Worse,' Sonata hissed. 'He outshone me, darling. Some things just can't be borne.'

Shiazar spent the afternoon going floor to floor in the citadel, familiarising herself with the layout and hoping to chance upon some miracle of Aldar sorcery that might change her fate, but all she found were swords with rotting hilt clasps and piles of deadly istariol ingots.

If there's no other recourse, I'll use it to destroy this entire citadel. The invaders must never have this place. But then she wondered just how large a blast all that istariol might cause. *Kiiyan on High, such an explosion might destroy every trace of life in this valley. It could turn the Fenua Tangato into a wasteland.*

With that awful thought whirling in her head, she sought the royal chapel and knelt before the twelve gods, praying for guidance. But as always, the only answer they gave was their silence.

Finally, with absolutely nothing resolved, she went to the kitchens, a giant space behind the dining hall, full of broken ovens, rusted pots and utensils, shattered crockery and the grime of centuries. But her people had cleaned one stove, enabling her to prepare a meal. She found some roots and greens, mixed a spicy sauce and simmered them together for a bit. When it was ready, she carried two full bowls to the guest level, to the only occupied room.

Shiazar pressed her eye to the spy-hole in the door, confirmed that the tiny atrium was empty, then unlocked it and entered. She placed one bowl on the little table, rang the bell, then briskly exited, locking the door behind her. Then she put her eye to the spyhole in time to see a young Aldar male in a simple smock and leggings pick up the bowl. She bit her lip, then called, 'Onkado!'

He stiffened, his handsome, aquiline face wary. 'Aie?'

He's the only son of our now-dead Archivist. I could truly use his knowledge, although I doubt he'll want to help – I took his father's head as a trophy and charged him with treason. He'd be dead now, if not for Zarelda Vyre's intervention. He must hate me.

'This is Shiazar,' she called through the door. 'We must talk.'

He bowed his head. 'As you will.'

'Go into your rooms and await me. I think I need not remind you that I have my powers, and you do not. Any unpleasantness would be foolish and unnecessary.'

He picked up the bowl and backed away. 'Aie, Majesty.'

He returned to his room as she entered, fully shielded and ready to fight, but he had retreated to the far wall and was showing no sign of rebellion. He ate a mouthful, winced and said, 'Your Majesty has a new cook.'

'Your Majesty cooked it herself. I'm the only one up here, apart from you.' She sat on the only stool, pulled her own eating sticks from her belt and took a morsel herself.

It's not that bad.

For a time, they ate in silence, then Onkado asked, 'Why are you here?'

She studied him: despite his predicament, his eyes were lively, and the guards reported that he and Zarelda Vyre remained amicable. That spoke well of him. She wasn't sure what she hoped to achieve here, but she felt trapped in a nightmare and if nothing else, she needed someone to talk to.

'A dreadful thing has happened,' she told him. 'Our world is ending. The outsider empire has found us already. They've seized the city. Our people have fled, but someone had to come here and protect it.'

Onkado's face turned ashen. 'How many of the enemy have come?'

'We don't know. Lots, and all mounted on horses.'

'Are they "Magnian" or "Bolgravian"? I am told the two breeds hate each other.'

'I don't know.'

'Did everyone escape the city and the village?'

'I don't know. I'm sorry.' Shiazar felt her voice quaver.

'Who leads our people in the north?'

'I don't know.' Shiazar's voice cracked. 'I had to come here, but now I'm cut off. The tribes are supposed to muster at the Puketapu village, but who will lead them? Only Raythe Vyre knows how to fight these people, and he's likely dead.'

She hung her head, struggling to control her emotions.

'You care for him,' Onkado commented, his voice neutral.

'I do not,' she snapped.

Onkado wasn't fooled. 'I feel affection for his daughter,' he claimed. 'You and I are alike in this. Perhaps the exoticism draws us? I even admire her courage in speaking for me, though I asked her to let me die.'

Shiazar's ears pricked at this admission. 'Do you still wish to die?'

'No,' Onkado replied. 'My land has been invaded. I wish to fight.' He dropped to both knees, hands clasped. 'Free me, Majesty. Let me help you.'

She wished she was wearing a mask, to better conceal her inner turmoil. Ikendo had almost ended her, and Onkado had been at his father's side throughout. Surely he still harboured desires of revenge? Or perhaps he wanted to escape. But he could also be genuine. He'd claimed to have been a reluctant partner in some of his father's actions, and his bond with Zarelda Vyre gave that credence. And the gods knew, she needed help if this vigil was to be anything more than a meaningless gesture.

'What reward do you expect for such service?' she asked.

'None,' he said firmly. 'I just want to help.'

If he was lying, he hid it well. And except for half a dozen old and infertile Yokei, they were the last Aldar. That placed an additional weight on them both.

She stood. 'You will sleep in here, each night: locked in. I won't unbind your magic. You are forbidden weapons, and to leave this fortress, or go anywhere in it without my express command. No task will be beneath your dignity, not even the most menial. Accept those terms and I will return at dawn and release you.'

Onkado pressed his face to the floor. 'You have my word, my fealty and loyalty, unto death and beyond. Let all the gods bear witness, all the ancestors and spirits. I am yours to command.'

It was as solemn and binding an oath as anyone could ask. She acknowledged it with an inclination of the head, and the traditional response: 'The gods hear.'

As she left, her heart beat a little faster. It felt momentous, a profound relief, to have even one ally in this chilling place. But she still locked his door.

Luc Mandaryke walked slowly around the prisoner, bound to a wooden chair that looked like it'd been constructed from the timbers of a wagon. He ignored the stench of fresh blood and voided bowels. The captive's torso was bare and covered in burns. Toran Zorne, who'd inflicted the torture, watched with blank indifference.

The man's name was Gravis Tavernier. He'd been captured north of the city, laden with possessions he'd been too foolish to abandon, unable to keep up with the rest of Vyre's people. He wasn't senior in Raythe's counsel, but he was certainly a gossip, gushing out words as swiftly as blood. Over the past hour, Luc had heard his tale: of Raythe Vyre selling a dream of wealth and freedom and how that led to a trek across the continent and into the Icewastes. He dropped infamous names like Jesco Duretto, Vidar Vidarsson and the heretical priestess Varahana. The bounties posted for those three alone would make this trip worthwhile.

But far more interesting was what Gravis had revealed about the natives. For five hundred years they'd dwelt here, unknown by the rest of the world. There were roughly ten thousand of these savages, ruled by a Queen named Shiazar, who was an actual *Aldar*.

'Let's talk about the mines,' Luc said, resuming his interrogation. 'You say they've been mined out, but clearly there's istariol present or the ice would have reclaimed this place. Where is it?'

'I don't know,' Gravis moaned.

'Answer Milord's question,' Zorne said, with toneless menace.

'Please, the mines are empty. Varahana reckoned the istariol is in the countryside.'

Luc scowled. His expedition weren't equipped for full-scale mining – not even exploratory work – and neither, it appeared, were the Tangato, who were sitting on a treasure hoard but apparently didn't care.

Once we've subjugated them, we'll force them to do the digging.

'How do we get up to the citadel?'

'There's a flying platform what goes up and down,' Gravis sobbed. 'And, and . . . during the battle with the darkies, one lot used this beam of light, from away southwest of here.'

Luc had never heard of such a thing. He glanced at Zorne. 'Any ideas?'

The Ramkiseri shook his head. 'An Aldar device?'

'We must presume so.' Luc considered Gravis and whether they were done with him. But that last snippet had earned him a reprieve. *There might be more to learn from him.* 'Lock him up again,' he told Zorne. 'Then investigate this beam of light. Make it your priority.'

Zorne bowed, and Luc left the room, took a solid lungful of clean air to wash away the stench, and headed for his new suite – recently vacated by Raythe Vyre himself.

He found Maveros in the conference room below, updating a map from the scouts' reports. 'What's the situation, Jiani?' he asked. 'Have Torland and Lisenko reported in?'

Maveros saluted. 'General Torland says the advance guard of his division will arrive the day after tomorrow, with your wife and daughter. They report no sign of the natives.'

'Looks like they've retreated north,' Luc noted. 'Good – we'll hem them in. What of Lisenko?'

'He's securing the city, establishing barracks and stabling and fortifying the bridge area. He reports that the rest of the city hasn't been lived in for centuries.'

'Curious,' Luc commented. 'Clearly the natives are degenerate, if they haven't the wit to choose a stone city over a wooden village. What provisions have we captured?'

'A lot of trinkets and some cloth, exotic enough but of little value. The food stores were emptied, but they were probably low anyway, given the season.'

He had expected that and had had the forethought to bring enough dry provender to see them through the winter, hauled painstakingly through the tunnels on the backs of mules. In spring, he had no doubt the natives' crops would begin to yield. There would be a monotonous diet for a time, but little actual privation.

'Send out foragers and hunters. Let's see what the land has to offer.' He joined Maveros at the map, thinking about what Gravis Tavernier had said. 'What lies southwest of here?'

Maveros peered at the handwritten notes taken by the officers in charge of the scouts. 'No one's gone that way yet, sir, but we passed forested hills in that direction on our way north, about twelve miles away.'

'Tell Zorne to explore those hills. Give him as many men as he wants.'

The aide saluted and left, and Luc spent a few minutes examining the updated map, then a yawn caught him off-guard. It was late and they'd had a long day full of discoveries. Time to reward himself with the native girl they'd captured.

The stairs to the quarters Raythe Vyre had recently vacated led to a small but homely lounge, crudely furnished. From there he entered the sleeping chamber . . . and reeled back at the appalling stench.

Backing out carefully, in case of danger, he summoned his familiar and conjured light, then swore. The girl he'd been expecting to amuse himself with was gone, leaving the manacles hanging empty on their wall hooks – and brown smears of shit had been daubed on the wall, forming symbols he couldn't decipher. The bedsheets were wet with urine and similarly smeared. The window hung open.

For a moment, he rocked on his heels in fury, then he called for the guards. 'Get this cleaned up,' he snarled. 'Do it yourselves – and be glad I don't flog you.'

It was another hour before he got to sleep in a spare room, and the stink from the opposite room never quite went away. It was not a good night, and someone was going to pay.

6

Deathless

For two full days, Varahana walked with her people, battling to keep the straggling column together and their spirits up. They'd had to abandon the carts and wagons on the first day because the forest paths Rima led them down were impossible for wheeled conveyances, so now all anyone had were packs and bags. Hers were stuffed with healing powders and herbs. Every morning and night she led prayers for her flock, to keep spirits up – including her own. There was still no word of Raythe or Vidar, which was sapping her resolve.

Another two days and we'll reach the Puketapu village, Rima had told them that morning. All through the day, the frost never melted, and that evening as they made camp, swirls of snow laced the air. This camp was the first they'd shared with Tangato refugees, Hiriwa and Tanuahi tribespeople travelling together, small children riding on the shoulders of their parents, old folk hobbling along as best they could. There'd been no fighting, but they'd glimpsed enemy scouts far across the plains. It looked like the invaders were proceeding with caution.

Varahana had barely put her backpack down when a horseman came galloping in. Rawleston Sorly, a Pelarian hunter, had gone south to scout the enemy – a risky business. The Tangato eyed him warily, but when Varahana went to meet him, they parted respectfully: in their eyes she was a mahotsu-kai, thanks to her role in fighting the sicknesses.

'Rawleston,' she called. 'Over here!'

Sorly's face lit up as he dismounted and he threw his arms round her in relief. He was one of her congregation, a strong but unorthodox Deist who equated faith with luck, but he was a good man. 'Mater, praise be,' he boomed. 'When I saw the Imperial Orb over the gatehouse, I feared the worst.'

'Did you find Raythe?' she demanded, as Jesco joined them.

'No sign of him, nor Vidar either, I'm sorry. But I did see the enemy banners.' He dropped his voice. 'It's kragging *Luc Mandaryke* what's leading 'em, Mater.'

'Gerda on high,' she blurted. 'Are you sure?'

'I know the heraldry, ma'am. Spent two years with Colfar's folk, in the scouts.' He clapped his spyglass. 'Even laid eyes on the prick, but the range was too great for a shot.'

Luc Mandaryke, here? Varahana winced. *Poor Raythe . . .*

'Did he bring his whore wife?' Jesco growled.

Rawleston shrugged. 'Didna see 'er, but would you let 'er out of y'sight?'

'Raythe and Vidar must've run smack into them . . . and Zarelda too. Dear Gerda, what a mess.'

They fell silent, pondering the vagaries of Fate. Then the hunter asked, 'So Mater, what's the plan?'

'We're making for the Puketapu village, northeast of here, to muster for battle,' Jesco said. 'We've got powder and shot, and the Tangato know the land. This isn't over.'

'Who's in charge?'

'Good question. I guess we'll find out when we get there.'

'Lord Raythe'll be back with us soon,' Rawleston said, in a reverent voice. 'He'll think of somethin', I don't doubt. Pulled our fat from the fire many a time, he 'as.'

I suppose to some, Raythe really is a miracle worker, Varahana realised. *He'd hate that.*

Right now, she'd have given anything to see his crooked smile – and to see Vidar striding towards her, solid as the hills. But wishes were for children. So she thanked Rawleston and Jesco, then began her rounds, going from campfire to campfire, ensuring everyone knew where to find water and had enough to eat.

It was midnight before she lay down on the frozen ground, and she was too exhausted to worry or fret, or even feel the snowflakes as they settled on her blanket and bare scalp.

Rima gazed into the embers of her little fire and fed it a few more twigs to give her a few moments more of heat and light. She'd been riding for days; her thighs and joints ached and her eyelids were heavy. The camp was spread through the trees, everyone huddled up against the frigid wind. Snowflakes danced in the firelight, and the planetary rings were lost behind dense clouds, making the dark outside her little circle deeper.

When a silhouette appeared at the edge of her camp, she thought for a moment that some forest haunt had risen to assail her. But then Kuia's kindly face appeared, her wrinkles and tattoos making her face look like bark, like an ancient forest goddess. 'Child,' she called, 'can't you sleep?'

Rima patted the ground beside her. 'Sometimes you go past tiredness. And you?'

'Old women don't need so much sleep,' Kuia replied, settling beside her and offering a flask of rice wine. They shared sips, then the priestess asked, 'Do you still hope for the return of the red woman?'

Rima flinched, and shook her head. 'There's been no sign.'

They'd had opportunity to speak about Kemara's disappearance, and Kuia, who might not be a mahotsu-kai, but was very knowledgeable, had agreed that perhaps the Guardian Spirit had taken the Magnian woman and might yet return her. But it'd been too long, and hope was hard to sustain.

'Do you know the place called "Te Kopu"?'

'The Womb?' Rima clarified. 'I've heard of it.'

'Hetaru intended to take you there,' Kuia said. 'It's near here, a very potent place. If you wish to speak to the Kaiju, you should go there.'

'But the Queen charged me with guiding these Magnians.'

'Others can do that,' Kuia answered. 'But only a mahotsu-kai can speak to the Guardian Spirit.' She opened a pouch and produced the blood-red crystal they'd used to battle against the blood-flux disease. 'This was drawn from your friend Kemara's body. Use it to call to her, at the heart of Te Kopu. Bring her home.'

Rima's heart thudded as she thought that through. 'You think it will work?'

'It might, child. There are no guarantees. But don't you think it worthwhile?'

Rima considered, then said, 'I will do so. But only once I have delivered these people to safety. The Queen herself set me the task. Afterwards, I shall seek it out.'

What are we, but the sum of our memories . . .?

That question came to the Dreamer as it floated in the void, moving on unseen currents in patterns it couldn't perceive, intact but perpetually fraying. It manifest as a memory, but one that belonged to someone else, a hectoring voice on a dirty street corner, a ragged grey-haired man ranting to himself as people scurried by, ignoring him.

. . . But then, what of our instincts and urges? Where do they come from? Where do they begin and our memories end? Is there such a thing as inherited memories?

The Dreamer pondered uneasily, unused to such existential matters, threatened by such notions but unable to let them be. But it couldn't leave the question of memory behind; not when it had uncovered a bundle of new ones from the sacrifice. At random, another recollection flooded the Dreamer's awareness . . .

Instantly it was hurled into an experience so vivid it became real: watching a woman burn in a city square, screaming silently as *she* cowered into *her* heavy hooded cloak, hemmed in by a seething crowd screaming hatred at the *witch*, wishing her suffering to intensify. The agony the observer felt was surely as great as the pain of burning.

Such pain, the Dreamer thought. *How does she stand it?*

But then it was thrown back into another time and place, in which the observer and that same woman were naked and touching, kissing and bathing in a warm pleasure radiating from their loins . . .

How strange, the Dreamer thought. *What purpose can such a thing serve . . . ?*

'Why are you?' it asked the memory. 'What are you for?'

No one answered. But the rememberer hearkened . . . *She* was listening.

Toran Zorne pushed his extendable spyglass closed and returned it to its leather case, made a few marks on the map he was sketching, then nudged his horse into motion again. Intriguingly, the plain he and his men had been crossing was about to give way to a rugged pine forest, the sort of terrain where much could be concealed. They'd found a stream emerging from the woods, a meandering trickle that flowed back towards Rath Argentium and the ravine.

Hopefully, that which we seek is in here. The sooner it's found, the better.

The task was probably important: to find the source of this beam of light that permitted access to the citadel. But where he really needed to be was right beside Luc Mandaryke, in case the man's loyalty to the empire should waver.

But an order was an order, and he'd been given two dozen mounted scouts to carry it out. They were with him now, watching him with hawkish eyes, patient and predatory. The best imperial scouts weren't actually Bolgravs at all, but Krodesh nomads, expert riders and hunters. Military discipline ill-suited them, but in the field they were hard, resourceful fighting men, for all they looked like a rabble.

They thought he was a pudding-faced zuké, that was clear, even though he was half-Krodeshi himself. To be Ramkiseri was to be hated. 'Listen in, you men,' he said their native tongue. 'We follow this stream into the woods. Keep your eyes open, and stick together.'

'What exactly do we seek?' one growled.

'You'll know when you see it,' he replied. 'Volsheb, znayesh?'

They all spat: a ritual response to any mention of "volsheb" – sorcery. 'Mizra?' one asked.

'Yuz, a'mizra.' Zorne gazed around the circle of unwashed, shaggy men, seeking dissent or disbelief, but they remained inscrutable. 'Gerda zashichit nas,' he added, though assuring them of Gerda's protection was worthless; these men were pagans at heart.

They didn't salute – it wasn't in their nature – but they obeyed, flanking him as they entered the trees, the best trackers leading the way. They soon reported hoofprints, a single horse. 'It's one of ours,' they told him. 'You can tell from the way it is shod.'

Why would a single rider come here alone? he wondered. 'Follow the tracks.'

Intriguingly, the path beside the stream became an ancient road, overgrown but clear. The bush grew denser, the air colder, and as they passed, the birds fell silent and watchful. Sunset was imminent, but he was loathe to let this go.

We're close, he thought. *I can feel it.* He sent half his men ahead, with instructions to take the obvious path at speed and run down any enemy they found, while he followed more carefully with the remaining dozen, in case their quarry had turned aside. *One way or the other, we'll have you*, he told that elusive presence, one that he was increasingly sure had a familiar name: *Raythe Vyre.*

This is it, Raythe realised, as he reined in his stolen Krodeshi stallion. It grumbled placidly and bent to graze while he surveyed the scene. He'd emerged from the thicket to find an imposing set of ancient ruins, mostly swallowed up by the tangled undergrowth. Moving through it, he'd come to a cutting that led to this place, where a giant construction of interlocking metal rings stood on a cracked, overgrown stone platform, enclosed on three sides by jagged cliffs and the fourth by a deep emerald lake.

The night after escaping the frozen lake, he'd come across an encamped imperial patrol, ensorcelled the sentry and stolen a horse. After that, he was able to pick a winding route through the trees, dodging patrols thanks to Cognatus' unseen presence, flitting a few hundred yards ahead of him to warn of danger. A full day and night's ride and here he was, in the dense forested hills around the sacred lake called Waiotapu.

He'd named it as the rendezvous point with Zar and Vidar, even though he'd never been here before, because it lay on the way back to Rath Argentium. But now it felt like an auspicious choice, because he'd been meaning to come here anyway.

An Aldar sphere-gate, he marvelled, gazing up at the mechanism in awe. *A link to the tethered citadel.*

He'd been told what to expect: the ruins behind him were the Aldar King's Summer Palace, abandoned for centuries. Because the sorcerer-kings ruled the world, riding twelve miles from the city to get here was beneath their dignity, so they'd constructed this gate. When activated, it created a path of energy across the sky, linking it to a tower on the floating citadel; it could propel those using it between the two locations in about ten minutes.

There was a temptation to activate it: but the beam of light it generated would bring Luc's entire army here, perhaps before it became fully usable. *What would be the point, anyway? I'd just end up trapped in the sky.*

But he was curious about how the mechanism worked, so he walked around it and identified the controlling plinth, a stone slab about hip-high with three runes carved into it, almost identical to the one that controlled the platform to the floating castle above Rath Argentium.

That one must activate the connection . . . and that one must deactivate . . . What's the third one for? The rune denoted sound . . . *Communication? Useless – there's no one up there.*

But then he wondered whether, in a crisis like this, the Queen might send someone up there, if only to prevent the invaders from getting access.

Might she even go up there herself?

With that, his hand hovered over the runes, as if it had a mind of its own.

He was well aware that he should leave well enough alone, just wait for Zar and Vidar to arrive. *But what if they don't make it? How long do I wait here?*

Impulse took over. He touched the third sigil, and felt it pulse with energy.

For Shiazar, the day had passed with an eerie sense of unreality.

Her life until now had left her no time to be alone. Her childhood had been brief and fleeting; her education had been enshrined at the centre of her existence as she learned their history and its consequences, how the community worked and what it meant to be Aldar and to rule. Even before she was elected Queen by her fellow Aldar, she'd been resolving disputes, solving problems and intervening in the daily crises of their precarious society. So to now have nothing to adjudicate was very disorienting.

Her response was to busy herself, at first with the necessities of life – washing in the cold bathing pool outside, preparing meals for herself and Onkado. Freeing him felt like a plunge into dangerous waters, but his behaviour had been exemplary, completing every task she'd set him, then repeating, 'Command me, my Queen.'

She set him to work cleaning and refurbishing one of the ovens, not because she needed another, but as a test of his obedience and diligence. She stayed close, working through a bank of cupboards, identifying bowls and utensils that remained usable, then washing them. She'd been spared of labour all her life, so she found such tasks both demeaning and curiously rewarding. Her only physical activities before had been fencing and sorcery, but she found manual work to be surprisingly fulfilling.

Mid-morning, she began making bread, working from memory, and baked it in Onkado's newly readied oven for lunch. It came out passably well, she decided.

'What should I do next?' the young Aldar asked, after they'd eaten.

'Refill the water containers and see what can be harvested from the gardens,' she replied distractedly, her mind far away, wondering how her people fared. 'Go over the old storerooms again and see what can be salvaged. Report back here before dusk – you must learn to prepare a meal.'

Onkado bowed expressionlessly and left. Immediately she breathed easier. There was something about his hawk-like face that unsettled her, though he was handsome and well-made.

But does he think of me as an enemy? Does he believe he should be the ruler here?

Time would tell. In the meantime, she would trust, but stay alert. With that in mind, she resumed her inspection of the castle, finally examining the place she'd been avoiding, the royal suite. Climbing the main stairs to the top, she walked past the giant kneeling god-statues and the royal sarcophagi to the place where her royal predecessors had slept. It had been out of bounds to the work-parties she'd sent up here since reclaiming the citadel, but the time spells that had been in effect up here had left it disturbingly lacking in dust or decay. She went through drawers and cupboards of beautiful clothing, jewellery and footwear, before staring at the bed, wondering at the Aldar men and women, royalty all, who had lain on it.

Despite being Queen, she had no desire to lie down here at night. The room felt full of watching ghosts.

Besides the sleeping quarters, she found a bathing room and giant wardrobes, filled with old robes in ancient styles heavy with filigree and brocade, and a wall of masks, beautiful and chilling to behold.

'Majesty?' Onkado called, from the central stairs.

She startled at the unexpected voice. 'Onkado? What are you doing here?'

'Majesty, the tower outside has come to life. There is a light shining in it.'

The tamakado? 'By the gods,' she exclaimed. 'Show me!'

They hurried down through the castle to the great hall and into the gardens, where the giant box-kites soared on a stiff southwesterly wind. Worryingly, the cupola of the southeast tower was limned with light.

'What does it mean?'

'Majesty, my grandmother Jinkatia was the Archivist, and she taught me about these devices. Because the castle controls the pathway, it can be set to forbid anyone using the gate at the lake without permission.'

'I know this,' Shiazar told him. 'It is set to forbid.'

'Yes, Majesty,' Onkado replied. 'I'm not sure, but I believe someone at Lake Waiotapu is requesting that you open the gate and allow them up here.'

'Then it must be an enemy . . .' Then she wondered if perhaps it might be a friend. 'Can we just ignore it?'

'No, Majesty. Grandmother told me that each request must be actively forbidden within fifteen minutes, or the gate will open regardless – I think to prevent a situation where the tamakado sphere-gate couldn't be used to reach the castle if it was empty. In the past, a gatekeeper was stationed in the tower to monitor all requests.'

'We must forbid it,' she exclaimed, scampering along the walkway, Onkado following. 'The enemy have overrun the south – it's probably one of their sorcerers.'

They reached the cupola and saw that the metal ring was pulsing a faint light and there was a strange rhythmic sound, like someone breathing heavily. Then she realised that that was *exactly* the sound, coupled with something that might have been wind in treetops.

I can hear whoever's at the other end, beside Lake Waiotapu – right now! And maybe they can hear us?

She put her finger to her lips, then whispered to Onkado, 'How do we close it?'

He showed her the third icon etched on the plinth. 'Majesty, all you need do is touch this symbol to renew your forbidding. My mother told me that the protocols were this: from the lake, permission must be gained, but if it isn't forbidden inside fifteen minutes, the gate could be opened from the lake side.'

Fifteen minutes . . . 'How long since you first saw it come to life?' she whispered.

He hung his head, not quite meeting her eye. 'Majesty, I was fortunate enough to see it come to life and came straight to you.'

Fortunate indeed, she thought dourly. *Were you out here contemplating using it to escape?* But she'd sent him out here and he'd come to her, when perhaps he could have escaped already. *Trust*, she reminded herself.

'Then we only have a minute or two.' She reached for the symbol . . . but hoping against hope and seeing nothing to lose, first she asked, 'Who's there?'

'Who's there?'

After touching the third rune-symbol on the control plinth, Raythe had been watching and waiting, though all that had happened was that the symbol had lit up and he'd heard a strange set of sounds, like wind flapping laundry and whistling through eaves . . .

Then he guessed that this was Shiro Kamigami and he tuned in with all his senses. But fruitless minutes passed – until he heard footsteps on stone, and muttered words.

Someone's there, he realised. He held his breath, wondering whether to speak . . . then heard the Queen's voice ask, 'Who's there?'

He clenched his fist in triumph and relief. 'Shiazar?' he blurted. 'It's Raythe Vyre!'

'*Raythe*,' her voice came. '*Atua nua la!*'

'It's me,' he told her, throat constricting. 'We ran into invaders, so I sent Jesco to warn–'

'He arrived,' Shiazar cut in. 'I sent my people north, then came here to safeguard the citadel–'

'Who's with you?'

'It's just me – and Onkado – we've locked down the platform. This gate is now the only way in or out ...' Her voice trailed off, then she admitted, 'I don't know what to do.'

He did now. 'Open the path, and come down, Majesty. Your people will need your leadership in the north. We'll go there together.'

'But someone must hold the citadel against the invaders.'

'Leave that to Onkado,' Raythe interrupted. The young Aldar male was still a vexing presence for him. He looked away, gazing across the small lake and thinking furiously ...

Movement caught his eye: a handful of distant shapes had appeared around the shore, just a few hundred yards away. 'Majesty, someone's coming,' he exclaimed, 'How long does it take to activate this gate?'

'Sire, when my father and grandmother were last there, they fully charged it,' came Onkado's voice. 'That took all night, but it should now be able to be opened in five to ten minutes.'

They'll see it activate and reach me before that, Raythe calculated. *And they'll certainly find it regardless.* 'Majesty, I'll have to deal with them. There's no choice.'

'Do we activate the gate first?' Shiazar asked intently.

He bit his lip. If the gate came to life, it'd bring the enemy faster ... But if he could hold off their first rush, he might yet escape through it. The other option was to try and escape on foot, but that would mean abandoning the gate to their enemies.

He decided. 'Activate the gate, Majesty – but keep this voice-link open. If it's not me who climbs up, shut it down as fast as you can, then keep it locked.'

He heard her sharp intake of breathe, then she murmured, 'Kagemori be with you, Raythe Vyre.'

The God of War, he thought. *Aye, I could use his help.*

Surprise was one of the greatest tactical advantages in military conflict, but it came with an insidious price: to kill someone who doesn't know you're there can feel *exactly* like murder, a feeling that could hound you to your grave.

Raythe knew the feeling well, having engineered many an ambush in his time. He'd gone through the guilt, the rationalisation and the self-recriminations, and got to a point where it was just another mechanism in the machine of death: a trigger one pulled, an arrow loosed, a tactic that worked.

So he crouched behind his fallen log, Cognatus ready inside him and his loaded pistol to hand. Behind him, the sphere-gate was humming into life, the big metal rings slowly – and for now, at least, silently – starting to turn.

Then voices raised in wonder echoed along the short defile. Orange torchlight flickered and hooves thumped dully. He heard muttered words in a Krodeshi dialect moments before the first riders emerged, smallish men with weathered brown faces and lank black hair, steppesmen drafted into the imperial military. They rode as if they and their steeds were one being, but their eyes were entirely on the giant mechanism before them.

Each fight is potentially your last, Raythe reminded himself. *Every enemy can be lethal.*

Then he told Cognatus to trigger the spells they'd prepared, even as he fired his pistol and the lead Krodeshi clutched his side, his horse reared and the others flailed for weapons, barking in surprise.

Raythe rose, energy blasting from both hands into the next pair of riders. Caught in the beams, they convulsed in the crackling energy as their horses bolted, colliding with those behind and creating a tangle of men and animals in the narrow defile.

Perfect . . . Raythe stepped forward, lead shot pinging off his shields, and blazed fire into the defile, torching as many men as he could reach and trying to ignore the screaming, terrified horses trying to flee.

'*Cognatus, plus amplius!*' Raythe commanded, and the familiar gave him even more power. This time, wielding two narrow beams, he carved down one man while using the other to send a horse crashing down onto its own rider.

The remaining half a dozen men at the rear had wrenched free their sabres and were hollering war cries, but the dead bodies, stricken horses and injured men prevented a rush. The Krodeshi were in disarray, but that wouldn't last: four of them had already dismounted and were making for the edges of the defile, striving to reach him as he hurriedly reloaded his pistol and reset his shields . . .

Four against one . . . I can do this—

Then a bestial roar filled the defile and something large and shaggy reared up behind the startled riders. The rearmost Krodeshi spun – too late – and was brutally hurled aside. The other men tried to shoot, but the beast – surely Vidar? – was already cutting a swathe through them, giving time for Raythe to shoot the nearest man while Vidar effortlessly tore apart the last two.

Then the Norgan, shedding his rage, embraced Raythe, making throaty sounds in the absence of words. 'Well, a real-life bear-hug,' Raythe chuckled, weak-limbed with relief. 'Your timing is exceptional.'

Behind them, the sphere-gates throbbed louder, lighting the area with a pearly glow. The metal rings blurred into near-invisibility and a beam of pale light shot across the sky.

'Just a few minutes and we can use it,' he told Vidar. 'Watch the defile. There may be more of them.'

The glow coming through the cutting from beyond the ruined palace was tantalising to Toran Zorne – but the tangle of bodies leading to it was a stark warning.

His lead scouts, riding several hundred yards ahead, had clearly pressed on when they saw the mechanism, he guessed, and had fallen into a trap. Now they were all dead, and only two horses had escaped the carnage in the cutting. He'd heard the bestial roar too, so he could guess who he was facing: Raythe Vyre and Vidar Vidarsson, sorcerer and bearskin, probably armed with istariol. And perhaps that murderous mizra-witch Kemara Solus was with them too.

I have a dozen riders left, but we can't just gallop through . . .

The clearing beyond was now bathed in soft luminescence, with a beam of pale light lancing the sky towards Rath Argentium. He thought back to the interminable lectures on ancient Aldar artefacts he'd had to endure, and realised that he was looking at a sphere-gate. *Vyre's trying to escape using it.* If he was to act, it had to be now. Finding alternative approaches wasn't an option, and nor was waiting.

'Dismount,' he ordered his nervous riders. He couldn't see his enemies but he didn't doubt they were there, waiting to cut down the next attackers as they had his scouts. The air was quivering, waves of sound that made his eardrums pulse uncomfortably, and that spear of light was growing stronger.

I won't be first.

'Form up,' he told the Krodeshi, although they didn't fight well in such circumstances – they were scouts and skirmishers, not frontline troopers – so this could go very badly.

Everyone knew that the best way to deal with a sorcerer was to cut him down before he'd gathered his full strength, for although deadly, sorcery was slow. This, together with a bloody-minded desire for revenge, gave the Krodeshi the impetus to shriek their nomad war-cries and swarm forward, pistols poised and sabres waving, when he ordered the advance.

But Zorne, knowing that Vyre had had time to prepare himself, followed at a more circumspect pace, wards set, content to let his men draw Vyre's sting before coming in for the kill. He was still well behind his Krodeshi when they reached the middle of the defile – which was suddenly lit by a great blaze of fire and light. *Istariol!* he thought, as a bright crimson flash split the air, but even as he was congratulating himself on his forethought, he had to dive backwards as a hideous *crack* reverberated all around and a moment later, the walls on either side of the defile collapsed, the solid rock sheering off as if sliced diagonally by giant knives, crushing everything in that narrow space beneath a double rock slide.

Zorne staggered back as falling rocks shattered, sending razor-sharp splinters whistling round him. Then he stared, truly aghast.

Of all his men, only one was visible, the rearmost man. His hips and legs were entombed, but he reached his arms towards Zorne as if to a saviour . . . and expired as Zorne backed away.

He bumped into a tree trunk behind him and cowered, dreadfully afraid. Truly, istariol made mortals into monsters. Shapes moved in the now blocked cleft, then the bearskin, Vidarsson, climbed onto the rockfall, peered through and called over his shoulder, 'I think that was all of them.'

Zorne's flintlock was to hand, but the last thing he wanted now was to draw attention to himself, especially as the weapon was too inaccurate to be sure of his shot. So he stayed hidden until Vidarsson vanished.

He was wondering what to do next when a blast of foul air washed through the clearing and he peered out to see a pale woman on a pale horse – Death in some mythologies – ride into view. She dismounted, climbed effortlessly onto the rockfall and vanished into the cutting.

Seeing Teirhinan Deathless in all her dark power, he had no desire to alert her to his presence. He didn't overly care who triumphed in this battle. *No matter who dies, she or Vyre, my empire wins . . .*

Raythe gazed up at the sphere-gate, wondering how to tell if it was ready. But the noise was too loud now to communicate with Shiazar and Onkado, so he'd have to take his chance. He was painfully aware that the apparent sphere was an optical illusion, created by the metal arcs whirling round so fast they were invisible to the naked eye.

Won't anyone who tries to enter be cut in half? he wondered uneasily.

'How does it work?' Vidar asked.

'Ask me later,' Raythe answered, conscious that the magical energies were intensifying, like a dynamo which produced lightning, the sort they'd experimented with at the Academy in Perasdyne. Experimentally, he drew on the energy it generated, and found it akin to using a grain or two of istariol. *Interesting . . .*

But then Vidar growled, and he turned to see a wraithlike young woman had emerged from the darkness and was gliding over the rockfall.

'Yield,' the woman rasped, then more whimsically, she added, 'or don't, and we can play.'

Raythe aimed his borrowed pistol and fired, the lead ball slamming into the woman. But though she jolted, no blood came and she cackled, 'Try harder.'

Vidar growled and advanced on her, transforming as he went, but she just giggled, 'You again?' and gestured. Vidar was caught by a wall of force and dashed away, hurled almost into the lake. Then she turned on Raythe, conjuring violet energy whilst licking her lips.

He fumbled for the istariol pouch, but his fingers came back with only a dusting of red powder. '*Cognatus, ignis nunc,*' Raythe shouted and gambled. He reached for power from the sphere-gate and sent a livid blast of flames at the shadowy sorceress – and it worked: she ignited, shrieking in agony and reeling backwards. Seeing a chance to finish this, he drew more power and wrenching out his sword, shouted, '*Vidar! To me!*'

Vidar rose, roaring as his beast-form engulfed him anew, and swarmed towards the burning witch fighting to quell the fire engulfing her. But now Raythe could see her body was regenerating even as it burned, and when she lashed out at him, her arm became a bone-like scythe, forcing him to parry, steel on bone.

'I am Deathless,' she shrieked, before gabbling in two languages at once, '*Praesemino kanesk'alla projice mizra, eum ibi nunc, yurei wo shibaru!*'

Two things happened at once: she reached through his shielding as if it wasn't there and slammed him onto his back beneath the sphere-gate, while grabbing Cognatus and pulling the parrot-familiar, flapping and shrieking, out of him.

Dazed, his vision swimming, he shouted for his familiar, 'Cog – nat–'

'*Yurei – kaisaru!*' she cackled, and Cognatus flew apart, taking with him Raythe's access to sorcery. Then she growled and pulled his own sword from his hand to hers. 'Move, and I skewer you,' she smirked, stalking forward with a strange marionette's gait. 'You disappoint me, Lord Vyre. I was led to expect more. But then, your daughter was nothing much. She's with her mother now, and she doesn't think of you at all.'

His chest and throat tightened and for a moment he couldn't breathe. The desire to lash out was immense, but he also knew he was out of his depth, over-matched in a way he'd not been for a long time. To fight would be to lose.

But as his father used to say, not all fights are won by the strongest. Sometimes it just took courage and wit. So he drew his dagger, shouted *'Behind you!'* and threw.

'Fool,' she sneered, her gaze not wavering from his face. She smashed the dagger aside with a contemptuous gesture, then began babbling in her double-tongue . . .

You really should have looked back.

A heartbeat later, a shaggy beast hit her from behind, a slavering wall of claws and teeth that smashed her to the ground and *ripped*, talons plunging into her back, gripping the spine and pulling, a hideous wet rending that tore her head, neck and backbone from her torso and hurled it away in a spray of black blood and the stench of rotting flesh. Then Vidar's hind foot slammed down on the skull and crushed it as he roared to the heavens.

Raythe recovered his weapons then backed away, his heart thudding. *You don't get to walk away from many of those edge-of-the-precipice moments*, he thought. *I'm using my chances up.*

Vidar roared out a final victory howl, then forcibly calmed himself enough to regain a little humanity. 'Who in the Pit was she?' he panted.

The sorcerer community wasn't that large. *I think I know who you were*, he thought, examining the ruined body. *I can see why they called you 'Deathless'.*

'She used both praxis and mizra,' he noted. 'That's supposed to be impossible.'

Vidar grunted, such nuances beyond him. 'Evidently not.'

Raythe called for Cognatus, scared he mightn't appear, but after an anxious wait, the little parrot came arrowing in, slammed into his chest and vanished, squeaking with relief.

Yes, me too, Raythe replied. *But we're okay now.*

He faced the body again. 'Let's burn her.'

It was a truth of sorcery that fire cleansed all. There had been necromancers in the past who'd clung on to life like cockroaches, but burning the body was sovereign. No one came back from that.

While the gate whirred towards readiness, Vidar, naked again but apparently immune to the cold, found Raythe's cloak and knotted it around his waist, then collected enough dead wood to build a pyre.

When Raythe and Cognatus lit the fire, the witch ignited as if made of tinder and oil, her long grey hair going up like a torch as she collapsed into ash and ruin.

And that's that, Raythe thought, thankfully. 'Thank you, friend Vidar. I owe you.'

'You certainly do,' the bearskin snorted. 'Dragging me halfway round the world for krag-all while making me take on a series of magical maniacs? You owe me big.'

'You make it look easy,' Raythe chuckled. 'I distract 'em, you hit 'em. Teamwork, that's our advantage.'

While the sorceress burned, the beam of light emanating from the gate continued to brighten. Relieved – and a little surprised – to be alive, they walked to the gate, wondering again how to enter it–

–until something moved behind them, Raythe glanced back and reeled, gasping, 'No . . . that's *impossible!*'

What rose from the pyre was not flesh and bone, but ash and tree roots, beetles and worms, sticks and soil and charred flesh, that came together in a pulp around the crushed head and burnt spine. At the core of it was a lump of stone – a calcified heart.

But it was much more than that, because somehow it was *still* Teirhinan Deathless.

It wasn't wielding both praxis and mizra sorcery that had rendered her deathless; that had come afterwards, once the potential she'd given herself was fully realised. By having both extremes of sorcery at her fingertips, otherwise closed doors could be opened.

Through one of those portals, she'd thrust her essence, her awareness, her identity – her 'soul', in Deist terms – placing it into her own mummified heart, which she'd turned to stone. That was what kept her essence intact, no matter what happened to her body. She had paid a hideous price, for instead of being inside her body, she used it like a puppeteer. She had delayed reactions to certain situations, her gait was awkward and she'd lost most physical desires. Food, drink, sexual pleasure, pain: all normal wants and needs had faded to numbness, leaving a void inside. She'd never experienced empathy, love or lust, a loss she was only just beginning to realise.

But it had also made her indestructible, so she soon forgot what she'd lost. *I'm the most pure kind of sane there is*, she constantly told herself, *for I am free of human frailty.*

But rebuilding herself from the ash and the ruin that Vyre and the beast-man had made of her was still dreadful, for she had to pour her essence back into what was left of her charred bones, sucking in whatever she could find to rebuild herself, an act of creative destruction, a primal scream of death and rebirth.

But now she was back: with one hand she slashed and across the yards, the bearskin went flying yet again, this time crashing down with a massive splash in the shallows of the lake. Her other hand reached for Raythe Vyre, to pull him to her and *rip him apart.*

Kragga mor . . . For a moment Raythe was paralysed in shock.

She was beheaded and burned – she couldn't survive that!

But he was at the very foot of the whirling sphere-gate and had linked to it during the fighting. Even as Vidar was hurled aside, he was drawing on its power . . .

Then she made a *grasping* gesture and before he could even reach for his sword, he found himself yanked towards her as if on a string—

—until the current of energy from the gate reversed polarity and ripped him away from her and up into the gate-path. He landed on the curved floor inside the tunnel of light while outside, the undead sorceress shrieked in fury.

Inside the beam, the path, lit by a shifting rainbow glow, felt as solid as stone, rippling as it gripped his physical form and *pulled*. He resisted instinctively – Vidar was back there – then the sorceress appeared at the mouth of the tunnel. To stand his ground now would be suicide.

She really is Deathless.

So he spun, shouted to warn Shiazar, and ran like all the beasts of the Pit were behind him.

7

Kite

Running the path of light was one of the strangest things Raythe had ever done, but with his senses overloaded by the throbbing air and shimmering tunnel, he couldn't spare thought or breath to enjoy the wonder of it. Instead, he concentrated on drawing power from Cognatus to put *everything* he had into the act of movement.

'*Plus amplius, Cognatus!*' he shouted when he could spare the air, begging for more strength, more speed, more *everything*. '*Ego postulo magis!*' *I need more!*

Cognatus, also drawing from the gate itself, gave him *everything*. Raythe had never travelled faster. Fists and knees pounding, sprinting like an athlete at the Royal Games, lungs and muscles burning, he shot across the sky – but still the dark thing behind him was gaining on him.

Then a ring marking the far end of the path of light appeared, and though he felt like his heart was about to explode and his legs melt beneath him, he made one last momentous push for safety.

Still it wasn't enough.

Instinct warned him of the witch looming up behind.

His shields repelled the blow and he spun, slamming a burst of energy into her face, sending her reeling back. But he'd learned his lesson: this was not the time to stay and fight. The ring of light, the end of his path, was so near . . .

He turned back and pounded on, shouting to Shiazar.

But Teirhinan Deathless was screaming in rage as she renewed her furious pursuit . . .

It was going to be a matter of a split-second.

Shiazar, gazing down the dizzying tube of light, heard Raythe shouting – but there was a shape behind him, clearly an enemy. *'Run!'* she shouted, doubting he'd hear, and in any case, he didn't need her to tell him that. Behind her, Onkado waited beside the control plinth, his hands hovering over the icons, ready to disable the gate the instant she gave the order.

'Not yet,' she told him. 'Wait . . .'

She saw fire burst, and a shriek echoed, full of almost palpable malice and rage.

'Raythe!' she shouted, gripping the ring's edge and willing him on as both shapes streaked towards her, closing the distance impossibly fast. *'Run! Run!'*

Onkado called to her, hands poised, 'Majesty? When?'

She began counting down: *'San . . . ni . . .'*

Shiazar's voice, and a jolt of pure terror that he was leading this monster straight to the Queen, gave Raythe the spur he needed. *'Cognatus, magis, magis!'* he roared, blindly blazing energy behind him as he forced his legs to move faster and faster. He dared not look back, but he didn't need to: he could feel Teirhinan surging up, right behind him . . .

. . . then he hurtled through the ring, bursting past Shiazar's silk-clad form and clipping the top of a low railing, then space yawned before him and he went off the edge of the cupola. He flailed and twisted and smashed into a cushion of tangled vines, fifteen feet below, his half-formed shields keeping him intact, though they couldn't prevent him having his breath knocked out.

For the next few seconds, all he could do was gasp for shreds of blessed air, while waiting for Teirhinan to blast through and slaughter them all.

Raythe shot past Shiazar, who shrieked, *'Ichi – ima!'* at Onkado.

Momentum took Raythe straight off the edge of the cupola. Limbs flailing, he vanished – but she had no time to worry about him. While Shiazar's sight was filled by the howling shadow that was tearing towards her, Onkado, bellowing wordlessly, slammed his hand onto the panel—

Then the tunnel winked out with a resounding boom and the demon plummeted from sight, its screech becoming a wail that echoed over the city – then went silent.

'*Kiiyan, thank you!*' Shiazar gasped. '*Thank you forever.*'

Then she turned and ran to the rail, her heart in her mouth. Onkado joined her as she peered down into the ruined garden – and saw Raythe Vyre, clothing torn and scorched, caught up in tangled vines, his face purple from exertion as he fought for breath.

Then his lungs finally filled, and even as he convulsed, his eyes sought hers.

'Y-you-Your Majesty,' he stammered, clutching at his chest as if fighting a heart attack.

She pulled down her mask, unwilling to let either man realise just how much her heart was leaping to see him here. She clung to a column, panting as if she too had run all the way from Lake Waiotapu.

'Majesty?' Onkado asked anxiously.

'I'm fine,' she managed. *Dear gods, I thank you with all my being.* 'We were in time.'

She called down to Raythe, 'There are stairs to the battlements in the corner of the garden. We will join you on the wall.' She turned to Onkado and bowed. 'Thank you. You did well.'

He was young enough that his pride showed.

They took the walkway while Raythe struggled to his feet, disentangled himself from the vines and clambered to the corner where he found the stone staircase rising to the top of the inner wall.

Shiazar's heart pounded and she found herself overcome with relief and joy to see that careworn, determined, lived-in face. It took such strength not to fly to him and clasp him to her, like the moment they'd shared after slaying Tashvariel – was that really only a month or two ago?

But Onkado was here, and she was Queen. Discipline held.

'Rangatira Raythe,' she managed in a neutral tone, 'it is *so good* to see you.'

Raythe was still panting, his skin and clothes were soaked in sweat and he looked ready to collapse, but he had mettle, she knew.

'They've got my daughter,' he panted, in an anguished voice. 'She boasted of it, when she attacked me. And Luc Mandaryke, the man who stole my wife, leads them . . . *They've got Zarelda.*'

She did go to him then – his pain required it. She hugged him and placed her head against his shoulder, though he was hot and sodden to the touch and his heart was hammering like a smithy. 'I'm so sorry,' she told him. 'We'll get her back.'

'Vidar might be dead, too,' he croaked. 'But there is still hope . . . bearskins aren't like ordinary men . . .' He looked up at the kites, as if he might see answers in the patterns they were weaving in the sky. 'There's still *hope*, Majesty.'

'Aie,' she said, tears in her eyes, and a lump jammed up her throat. 'Hope.'

Only then did Raythe notice Onkado, and his reaction was plain to Shiazar: the shock first of seeing an unmasked male Aldar, followed by the realisation that this was his daughter's husband.

'You . . .' Raythe breathed, then he said, 'My thanks.'

Onkado knelt to them both, while Shiazar wondered what she could say. *They've both lost Zarelda and they both care for her,* she thought. *But this is the first time they've met.* She held her breath, waiting to see how they reacted to each other.

Then came a sound that made the matter irrelevant.

With a crunch, a bone-coloured hand raked the top of the outer wall, and then another, and the pale witch appeared. Her body was horribly misshapen, with exaggerated claws and teeth, and extra pairs of half-formed arms emerging from her ribcage, so that she resembled a skeletal beetle as she crawled onto the parapet.

'*What is she?*' Shiazar heard herself whisper.

Raythe went pale. 'We've already beheaded and burned her. I don't know what else to try.'

Onkado rose, and before the still-dazed Raythe could react, wrenched Raythe's sword from his scabbard. 'Go, Majesty. Lord Vyre has knowledge, and you are our Queen. Between you, you can find a way. Let me purchase you the time to do so.'

Shiazar hadn't taken her eyes off the corpselike demon-woman, but she reached over her shoulder and drew her own curved blade. 'This is Shiro Kamigami, the last refuge of our people. This is where we stand and fight.'

Raythe straightened. 'No, Majesty, this isn't a fight we can win.'

Fatalism gripped her. 'Then we lose it, and die with honour.'

Raythe knew many men who could honestly say they'd never run from a fight. They were all dead, though; mostly cut down by the Bolgravians' rolling volleys on the fields of western Otravia and Pelaria. They were heroes, all of them, men who'd died with their honour intact but still ended up as corpses, nothing more than blood and bone fertiliser for the fields.

With little hope of not ending up like those old comrades, especially without his trusty falchion, he backed away, calling the exhausted Cognatus to him and racking his brain for some answer to what was now the most important question in his life: how to kill the Deathless witch.

But nothing came as Shiazar and Onkado went to meet the multi-limbed, grey-skinned sorceress. She seemed to be sucking in energy and matter, inflating herself to twice human size as she stormed to meet them. She had no weapons, but her multiple hands became huge spurred and jagged bone talons and her skin some kind of carapace. By the time she reached the two Aldar, she looked like a giant insect created by a mad taxidermist from dead reptile parts.

Raythe conjured fire and tried to blast it at her to distract her as Shiazar slashed at her hands and Onkado tried to crash a blow through her left leg. Steel, augmented by sorcerous energy, crunched through bone and broke it, the giant sorceress reeled and for an instant Raythe saw a path to victory.

Bring her down, throw her off the walls, and she's someone else's problem . . .

Then Teirhinan shrieked and even as the shattered limbs reformed, she exploded into a blur of whirling limbs. Onkado caught a sideways blow across the chest and was almost smashed from the walkway, only his maho keeping him alive as he twisted gravity and replanted his feet, while Shiazar launched herself into the air in a graceful arc that carried her between two vicious swipes. She landed and struck again, crashing a blow into Teirhinan's ribs. When Raythe's third fire-blast finally ignited the witch's hair, he blazed light at her eyes, seeking to blind her, looking for any kind of edge that would give them a respite. But the spell died stillborn, for she was sucking in all the energy in the air around them – then she reached out with a suddenly expanding claw that grabbed Onkado and smashed him like a doll against a wall which broke at impact, leaving him sprawling limply, the sword in his hand dropping behind him.

Then she waded toward Shiazar and Raythe.

The Queen, shrieking an Aldar war-cry, interposed herself between them, while Raythe leaped for his lost blade, shouting, '*Cognatus, afferte meum gladius!*'

The familiar responded, the sword spun through the air toward him, he caught it and turned in time to see Shiazar perform a miraculous backflip, evading the three slashing claws trying to disembowel her. He swung and lopped off two of the limbs, but Teirhinan's response was a blast of black light from her mouth. The Queen just managed to evade that deadly beam, which shattered stone behind her.

The sorceress paused, and new limbs wriggled out of her torso like worms emerging from rotten meat. 'This is fun,' she cackled. 'I can go all day, how about you?'

Raythe looked at Shiazar, who was panting and drenched in sweat, and knew neither of them had much left.

Onkado groaned, but as he tried to stand, Teirhinan scuttled toward him. He heaved himself to his feet and looked back at Shiazar, his face hopeless. 'Majesty,' he panted, 'please, go. Please, live.'

Raythe grabbed the Queen's arm, his eyes fixed on the young man. The two Aldar had, for self-proclaimed amateurs, fought with stunning speed and skill, but they'd achieved precisely nothing, and now they were exhausted, drained and no closer to finding a winning stratagem.

If he'd thought the three of them together might be able to deal with Teirhinan, he'd have tried it, but the waves of dark energy radiating from her were undiminished. It was time to accept they didn't stand a chance against her.

Shiazar made a sobbing sound, then threw her blade to Onkado.

Despite being almost out on his feet, he caught it and kissed the hilt. 'Lord Vyre, please, tell Zar that my regard is real,' he called, then he turned and faced the slowly advancing Teirhinan.

Raythe took Shiazar's arm, and trying to place himself between her and danger, hissed, 'Majesty, please, *go*.'

They backed up, then turned to run, but they were still halfway from the main doors leading into the Great Hall when Teirhinan reached Onkado. The young Aldar slammed energy at her, but she seemed to *devour* it – then her flailing insectoid limbs scythed through Onkado's shields before she hurled his limp body from the walkway into the ruined garden below.

She didn't go after him but instead, rampaged after Raythe and Shiazar, conjuring violet energy into a crackling ball as she came on in a deadly, flailing rush . . .

She's too fast for us – we'll never both make it. All he could do was give Shiazar a chance on her own.

'Go on!' he cried out, planting his feet and preparing to die for his Queen. 'Make for the disc!'

She responded by seizing his hand – and clamping it around a rope.

It took him an instant to realise it was one of those tethering the dozen or so kites decorating the walkway. She gripped it too, her hand just above his – then she whipped out her long curved dagger and slashed downwards with all her strength.

Realising the danger of escape, Teirhinan, shrieking, unleashed a ball of energy, which she hurled at them in a crackling mess of forces–

–just as Raythe dropped his falchion, clamped his other hand onto the rope and wrapped his legs around Shiazar's waist – even as she lost her own grip on the rope. She managed to grab his belt as she started sliding down his body.

The winds were pulling the freed kite away into the skies, while Cognatus lent his power to help him support the jarring weight of two bodies, which was almost dislocating his shoulders. Tendons and ligaments shrieked and popped as he howled at the pain.

Teirhinan's spell exploded just beneath them, burning the ropes attached to every other kite, so that they all came loose in a cloud, the wind sucking them up and away from the floating citadel. The sorceress shrieked in rage, carving the air with bursts of energy, but they'd been borne swiftly out of range.

'Climb up me,' Raythe shouted to Shiazar. 'I can't hold us both!' When he glanced down, he saw her mask had been ripped away. Her beautiful face was naked and terrified, but she roared like a lioness, loosened one arm and threw it up, gripped his shoulder and anchored herself so she could haul herself up, all the while he held on for dear life, imploring Cognatus for just a bit more strength.

Her other hand came up, she knotted them together behind his neck and hoisted herself a bit further up his chest. For all too brief a moment she was face to face with him – then she stunned him with a kiss, assailing him with spice and adrenalin, but it was all too quickly over, for she was already planting her feet on his thighs and pushing off again, her silk-clad body brushing past his face, until she stood on his shoulders, reached up and moving hand over hand, climbed the rope about a dozen feet.

'Now you!' she called down. 'There are knots up here – they're much easier to grip.'

Still dazed by the taste of her, Raythe followed her lead, his shifting weight making the dangling rope shift and spin, but he reached the knots that bound the decorative ribbons to the main rope, where it was easier to find a perch. His fingers and arms were burning by the time he reached a spot just below the Queen. The climb, the fights at the lake and in the gardens, the sprint up the tunnel of light, and then this – he felt utterly wrung out.

'Are you all right?' he called, once he could breathe again.

'We lost,' she answered, her voice despairing. 'We've lost Onkado and Shiro Kamigami and everything in it!'

'It's my fault,' he groaned. 'I led her to the citadel – I'm sorry, I should have stayed away from the gate –'

'No, Raythe,' Shiazar answered, 'you are not to blame. Sometimes we are overmatched, as I have been. I have failed my people, and now we are doomed.'

'No,' he said firmly, 'it's *not* over.' His innate defiance rose, just as it had when the Mandarykes executed his parents, and again when Colfar's valiant rebellion collapsed. 'I've lost my country, my family and everyone who ever put faith in me. But no defeat is truly final unless you let it be.'

He was looking up at her and their eyes met, an intense exchange of energy and emotion, a wordless outpouring of the soul – and then they looked away, retreating into themselves while they worked on recovering their physical and emotional strength.

For a long while they clung on in silence, until Raythe sensed a grim resolve settling on Shiazar, armouring her face as well as any of her masks. It was a look he'd seen on many a comrade's face after a defeat: the look of someone who'd somewhere found the fortitude to fight on.

You're stronger than you know, he thought. *A worthy Queen.*

The twilight sky was bitterly cold and the wind gusty, but the box-kite held its altitude as it was propelled towards the northeast. The clouds had parted somewhat, allowing the planetary rings to light the landscape. They were sailing over hills, roughly tracing a river's path towards the Puketapu tribal lands. Rath Argentium was a dark smear behind them, the floating citadel silhouetted against the darkening sky.

Raythe tried to work out exactly where they were: currently near the edge of the Fenua Tangato, he calculated, and they would soon be over the Icewastes. If they ended up there, they would surely die.

'Majesty, we have to get down. How can we lose height?'

'I don't know,' she admitted, 'but there must be a way.' And without another word, she climbed further up, her silks flapping around her.

Raythe followed, each movement making the rope spin dizzyingly. Once his hands slipped, and by the time he had reached Shiazar's former perch, he knew he really was spent. But when he called up to see how she was doing, she'd reached the body of the kite, firmly anchored her feet and was examining it.

The oblong kite was two cubes made from lightweight wooden poles lashed together, with silk covering each face. Someone had painted a dragon's face, fierce and wise, on each side.

'Majesty,' he called, 'try slicing one of those smaller panels, so that the kite catches a little less air. Do you have a blade?'

'I don't need one,' Shiazar replied. Instead she conjured energy on a fingernail and drew a cautious cut on a small left-hand panel. At once the silk parted, then ripped side to side, and the kite lurched to the right and began to slowly spin, losing height . . . too fast.

'Other side, even it up!' Raythe shouted, but she was ahead of him, already reaching around to the other side and slicing through the material.

The spinning evened out, and so too did the speed of their descent as the kite's main sails caught the air properly again. 'It's working,' she called.

'Come back down,' he shouted. 'Let it find equilibrium.'

Shiazar instantly slid down from knot to knot, coming to a halt just above where Raythe was clinging on.

The ground was getting closer at an alarming rate. They plunged towards the dark landscape, which was laced with flashes of light where the planetary rings reflected in waterways and ponds. As they drew closer, he could make out campfires dotted here and there, sparks of orange in the darkness. Then suddenly they were soaring low – too low – over the wooded lower reaches of a hill, headed for a jagged peak.

'Holy Gerda,' he exclaimed, '*brace!*'

Shiazar conjured light and he kicked out his legs before him as the treetops reached up and their trailing tether caught in the upper branches of a pine – then he glimpsed a steep slope barely a second before they smashed into it. He struck feet first and rolled, but the impact was softened by waist-deep grass that cushioned him as he rolled over and over. Finally, he stopped himself and just lay there, his face on the ground, panting in relief. Cognatus, fluttering anxiously inside him, was demanding that he be well.

Shiazar landed with Aldar grace on her feet, dropping to one knee to absorb the fall, an image of elegance compared to his own crash-landing. Her eyes sought his; her face was flushed, but composed and always beautiful, framed by a billowing curtain of black hair.

*Dear Gerda—*He felt dazed.

'Raythe?' she asked. 'Are you all right?'

Get up, he tried to tell himself. *There's more to do.*

But for once, his body wouldn't respond. There had been times in his life he'd thought himself spent before, but this was the real thing. He had absolutely nothing left.

The world faded out.

'Wake up,' a voice rasped.

Onkado was surprised he could.

He'd thought himself an accomplished warrior, but the wraith-like witch was a bone-machine of scything limbs and dark power who'd just ploughed straight through him. When he struck the ground, the impact dashed the world away. That was it. His life was gone.

He didn't want to open his eyes and see who'd spoken, so first, he examined himself. His skin and flesh were cold, but a fire was near, radiating heat onto his right side. His head ached dully and there were stinging scratches on his limbs and bruises all down his spine. His lip was split and his spittle tasted of blood.

In Heaven, there is no pain, the Tangato priests believed. So this wasn't Heaven.

'Wake up,' that maleficent voice came again. 'You're in your room – I knew it from the smell. I thought you'd feel more at home here.'

Something stank of dead matter, of rot and foulness. *Her*, instinct told him. *She's dead.* But she was still animated, still potent. And for some reason, she'd kept him alive. He shuddered and reached for his maho, but it was sealed away so thoroughly he couldn't even sense it in himself, as if it had been amputated.

Reluctantly, he opened his eyes to find himself laid out on his bed, tethered to the bedposts like a sacrificial victim. Oil-lamps on the walls gave off a sickly glow. He tried the ropes, but they were knotted tight, with no give, beyond his ability to break or wriggle free. Lower down, a manacle with markings on it bound one ankle. It was radiating cold and he instinctively knew it was preventing him reaching his powers.

Unwillingly, he turned his face to his captor, braced for the worst.

What confronted him was unexpected, but no less horrific. A woman, not young, but not old, despite the greyish skin and long grey hair. She was clad in an ancient Aldar silk kimono, but what showed of her flesh was torn and scarred, dripping pinkish fluids. She positively stank of rot.

He looked away, fighting to keep himself from retching at the stench.

'My name is Teirhinan,' the woman said. 'Who are you?'

Her accent was similar to Zarelda's – she was a countrywoman, perhaps – so he could understand her without his maho. He considered not replying, but he didn't feel strong enough for a mental battle yet. And her curiosity might be the only thing keeping him alive.

'I am Onkado.'

'And you are an Aldar,' the woman purred. She moved jerkily towards him, then to his horror, she straddled his belly, enveloping him in her stink. For a terrifying moment he thought she intended some kind of sordid seduction, to which he couldn't have responded, even were a knife at his throat. But instead, she bent over him, transfixed him with her violet eyes and said, 'Now you tell me *everything* about this place.'

He tried to resist, but it was hopeless. Her eyes bored through him and her snakelike mind slithered into his, quickly stripping it bare.

How long he hung in her mental grasp, he had no idea. She didn't use pain or pleasure, threat or force; she had no need. She was *everywhere*, and nothing could be locked away. He was only thankful that there was so much he *didn't* know and therefore couldn't tell her.

When she finally rose from him, he felt utterly drained, and utterly humiliated. She knew *everything* about him, from his part in his father's coup against Shiazar to his marriage to Zarelda. She knew his soul.

'What a strange creature you are, to harbour such sentimentality towards a lesser,' she commented. 'The Vyre girl is far beneath you.' She fixed him with predatory, proprietorial eyes. 'But I'm not.' She caressed his chest with her frigid hands. 'I'm going to keep you, and you're going to make me happy.'

Onkado couldn't look away, for fear that she would rip his heart from his chest.

Thankfully, she didn't press him further but turned and stalked awkwardly from the room. The door slammed shut and he heard it lock.

Onkado tested his bonds again, but he'd been right the first time – they were unbreakable. Finally, wrists and ankles bleeding from his efforts, he flopped limply. His strength ebbed, reducing him to little more than a trembling child.

8

Conquerors

Columns of red-coated Otravian infantry were slogging over the muddy plains, enduring sudden southeasterly squalls. The marching redjacks bowed their heads against the weather, while their officers rode draped in oilskins, but no one escaped the misery, not even Mirella Mandaryke, who was bedraggled as a paper doll in a puddle. Her pristine ringlets had collapsed into a tangle, her make-up was running and her dress was sodden.

Zar had no sympathy. Mirella could drown in a mud hole for all she cared.

Had she thought she'd get away with it, Zar would have dug in her spurs and galloped off, but they had an escort hemming them in, young Otravian men who were eying her speculatively. She'd given up glaring back, as it only encouraged them.

Then Nemath Torland cantered in and made a show of gallantly wrapping his own cloak around Mirella's shoulders, while his catamite Sonata posed shamelessly on her side-saddle. Zar knew about them from Jesco – they'd been leading lights in Perasdyne's decadent same-sex community, until they turned on their own, naming names for the Ramkiseri agents to hunt down and destroy, while Luc Mandaryke had protected them every step of the way.

I hope they burn in the Pit for eternity.

She turned away, ignoring them, while Torland prattled on and on to Mirella about how arduous a journey it was, but she wasn't to worry as the city wasn't far now, and a warm fire and comfortable rooms awaited them.

All the while, Zar felt Sonata watching her like an elegant vulture.

But Torland wasn't wrong; Zar had begun to recognise landmarks, and sure enough, when they topped the next rise, Rath Argentium and the floating citadel appeared through the murk. Everyone stopped to stare, then cheered vociferously, waving hats and firing flintlocks into the air.

They think they've discovered it, Zar sneered, *but my people got here first, and the Tangato never left.*

Torland's redjacks milled about excitedly until the officers got them moving towards the Hiriwa village. But Mirella's party headed directly for the city, and as the rain faded away, everyone's mood lifted. The sun made a brief reappearance, just in time to set as they rode between the stone dragon guardians, onto the bridge over the ravine, through the gatehouse and into the city. The bridge district was now teeming with grey-clad Bolgravian cavalrymen, hauling up water from the river and roasting dozens of phorus birds on spits in the square. It made Zar feel ill to see these invaders, who'd poured into Otravia when she was a child, here where she'd hoped, finally, to be safe.

Nemath Torland escorted them all the way up to the crater rim, to the big mansion that they'd dubbed Rim House, their bastion, now festooned with Imperial Orbs and Mandaryke banners. When they dismounted, Mirella sagged, much to Zar's disgust, and the maid had to half-carry her up the steps. Zar followed them, bounding effortlessly up the steps; *she* was a warrior, not a pathetic, overbred hollyhock like her mother. Her waterlogged dress was a hindrance, though, and she thought longingly of her much more sensible Tangato attire, which Mirella had spitefully burned.

Torland and Sonata had another mansion awaiting their pleasure. Zar watched them walk off arm in arm, wishing she could propel daggers through their backs. But all that happened was that her mother took her arm and led her inside.

They were shown into the dining hall to find Luc Mandaryke waiting for them. He greeted Mirella, taking her hand and kissing it with impersonal formality, while her dress dripped into a puddle. 'My poor dear,' he said, 'this has been hard on you.'

Zar wondered how real his sympathy was; he had the manner of someone who only really cared about himself. But then he fixed his eyes on her, like a trader assessing wares in a market, and she felt herself shrink.

'So, this is Zarelda.' He walked around her, as if inspecting her points. 'What are the marks on your chin, girl?' he asked. Evidently he'd been warned of her tattoos, because he didn't look surprised.

'They are marks of status among the Tangato,' she replied stonily.

'We'll have them removed when we return to civilisation.' He gripped her by the jaw and made her look at him. Up close, he exuded strength and presence; his combination of heroic looks, size, athleticism and his imposing self-confidence was thoroughly intimidating. She wondered how her father and this man could ever have been friends.

'I trust you now understand your true bloodline?' he asked.

'I've been informed,' she said.

'How do you feel about it?' he demanded, his steely eyes searching her face.

'Ask her.' She gestured at her mother.

'I'm asking you.'

It would have been sensible to say something calculated, placatory and safe, but she didn't have that in her. 'I'm a Vyre,' she answered, 'she's an adulterous bitch and you're a stinking traitor. You both make me sick.'

Luc's right palm cracked across her face, stinging pain scattered her thoughts and her legs wobbled. Her vision blurred, but she felt her mother step to her side and support to keep her upright.

'Come, Luc, our poor daughter has had four years of that man's poison. She'll see sense. I'll deal with it.'

Zar blinked her eyes clear, ignoring her mother's hands on her shoulders, and glared up at her *supposed* father. She saw *nothing* of him in herself.

Luc stared back, his handsome face hard and fists menacing, but then he sighed theatrically and stepped away. 'Fine, fine,' he fumed. 'I'm told you've gained the praxis, girl?'

'Dispel my bindings and I'll show you.'

'When did it come in?'

'This year – but I'm already better than you.'

'I don't think so,' he sniffed. 'Now, listen to me: you can call me "traitor" all you like – you think I've not heard that shit before? The fact is, Otravia was doomed. We either surrendered on our terms, or we got crushed like our allies. I had the vision to see that; Raythe, in his arrogance, didn't. Otravia still exists, and it is solely because of *me*. You don't beat the Bolgravian Empire in open warfare; you fight from the inside. *I* am the true patriot here. Raythe Vyre is a vainglorious fool who led thousands of good men to quite unnecessary death.'

Zar opened her mouth to voice a denial . . . then shut it again, because this *pompous arsehole* clearly believed his own words so completely that there was no point in arguing. House Mandaryke had been part of the old aristocracy, increasingly irrelevant due to the new democracy that had been sweeping the West – until the Bolgravian invasion. Mandaryke's craven capitulation had allowed his house to re-establish their old dominance.

But they did preserve a degree of self-rule, a nagging voice muttered inside her. *He's the only non-Bolgrav governor in the empire.*

However, no way would she allow him any credit. 'You executed the leaders the people wanted and made yourselves rulers,' she retorted. Her life during the rebellion had been full of campfire politics; she'd learned at the knees of the best how to argue a point. 'You're not fighting from the inside; you're just whoring for a place at the table.'

His face became viciously ugly again and he tapped her nose with his forefinger. 'You'll see.' He walked around her again, while Mirella's hand clamped down on Zar's shoulder, holding her in place. 'Are you still a virgin?'

She coloured. 'None of your business.'

'Must I insist on an inspection by a Mater?'

Even though the Deist religion was administered by women, Zar had no desire to have someone poking her nethers. 'I am chaste. You can take my word on that.'

Although I am married, she didn't add, but that made her think of her husband. *Onkado must still be up in the citadel . . .*

Luc looked at Mirella. 'She's your responsibility,' he snapped, and sauntered away without another word.

Once they were alone, Mirella turned Zar in her surprisingly firm grasp, her face composed, her gaze measuring. Zar glowered back at her, although Mirella didn't look in the least put out by her antipathy.

'This is a man's world, Daughter,' she said. 'One day soon you will be married, and your husband will be your absolute master. Or he'll think he is, at any rate. Use your wits and your wiles and you'll hold the real power, but you'll still need to take a few slaps and do a few things you'd rather not. If you are clever – or at least, smarter than him – you can wrest and keep control. Think about that.'

A few slaps . . . and some things you'd rather not do . . .

Zar touched her throbbing face, picturing the scarlet hand-print that surely adorned it, and shook her head. 'You might put up with that shit, but I won't.'

'There, see? You are my daughter,' Mirella smirked. 'Play the long game, Zarelda.' She walked to the door and called in her pallid little maid. 'Edisha, settle my daughter upstairs and attend to her needs. Place a guard over her rooms: she is to be confined to those quarters until further notice.'

The girl curtseyed. 'Of course, madam. I'll look after her.'

The maid ignored Zar's efforts to converse, but she did her duties diligently.

The long, arduous day ended with her first bath in *days*, and although her door was locked, she had the luxury of a real bed. Her last thoughts as she dropped off were of her own people, Magnian and Tangato, flee-ing into the wilds with no homes at all any more.

Toran Zorne spent a sleepless night in the ruins next to the sphere-gate. The light of the sorcerous machine had gone out, Teirhinan had van-ished again, Raythe Vyre was gone, so too Vidar Vidarsson – although in his case, he'd waded ashore and vanished into the forest, soon after the gate closed. Deeming him unimportant, Zorne had let him go; the bearskin was the least of his worries right now. His mind was fixated on Teirhinan Deathless.

She was beheaded and burned to ashes – but still she rose again. That was clearly impossible: even the mizra shouldn't convey such powers. Per-haps praxis and mizra together could? Before he'd met Teirhinan, he'd have thought even wielding the two together was impossible. Regard-less, she was a monster – but she'd also been personally selected by Luc Mandaryke for this expedition. *I approached him about this place because he is Governor. To have discussed this matter with anyone else would have violated protocol.* But he could not disregard his own rage against Raythe Vyre, triggered by the humiliation of defeat. *Was my judgement clouded because I knew Mandaryke hated Vyre?*

No, he insisted to himself, *I just followed the rules. But how much does he know about Teirhinan's powers? She should be executed, not encouraged.*

Clearly, his next actions had to be carefully considered, because there was so much at stake, perhaps even the security of the empire. *I must watch Luc Mandaryke's every move, least he betray my Emperor.*

It was tempting to judge the man pre-emptively, but he resisted the urge. Mandaryke must be deemed faithful, until proven a traitor, he decided. This was too important to rely on guesswork.

His situation was made more difficult because there was no one else here he could trust: Lisenko was a fool, Torland was in Mandaryke's pocket, Teirhinan was too erratic – even Mirella, ostensibly his superior, appeared to be seduced to Luc's cause. He felt isolated, more alone than he'd ever been.

He found no answers during the sleepless hours of darkness, but he was determined to go on. When the sun finally rose, he tethered Teirhinan's horse to his own, then followed the stream out of the hills. Within the hour he was on the plains and by midday, he was crossing the bridge into Rath Argentium.

What he found there was distinctly troubling: this was now the base for Lisenko's cavalry division, but the gatehouse was undermanned and queues had formed outside the infirmary. Most of the men he passed were trying to suppress great racking coughs and hawking up bile.

'This place is cursed,' a Bolgrav veteran warned fearfully.

'I'm looking for Lord Mandaryke.'

The soldier gave him a doubtful look and pointed to the crater rim. 'Biggest house. He moved hisself up there the moment the sickness started – but he ain't moved us.'

Zorne's skin prickled as he sent his mount trotting up the cobbled road. *Not disease*, he found himself muttering, *please, not that*. He loathed physical contact at the best of times, and the fear of plague had fuelled many of his nightmares. His fears deepened as he passed two corpses, rats already stripping the flesh.

This is how it starts, he remembered, thinking of plague-cities he'd passed through in the past. *Civilisation collapses, sometimes in an eye-blink*.

'Who goes?' challenged the sentry outside the mansion on the crater rim.

'Toran Zorne, Under-Komizar of the Ramkiseri, seeking Lord Mandaryke,' he told the man. He could see the Governor, dressed against the cold in a heavy wool greatcoat and beaver-fur hat, standing at the rim wall, three aides beside him, all gazing up at the underside of the floating fortress.

The sentry knew who he was, of course, but he had a job to do. 'Wait here.'

Zorne watched the sentry report his presence, and was relieved to see that Mandaryke immediately waved aside his aides while gesturing for Zorne to join him.

'Ah, Zorne,' he drawled. 'Report.'

Zorne kept his voice low. 'I found a sphere-gate, Milord, ten miles or so to the southeast.'

'I'm told a beam of light was seen yesterday evening from that quarter.'

'That was the gate, sir.'

'Who used it?'

'Raythe Vyre.'

'Kragging Raythe,' Luc cursed. 'Is even Teirhinan Deathless insufficient to kill that bastard?'

'He may yet be dead. Teirhinan followed him through the gate.'

'Was he alone?'

'The bearskin, Vidarsson, was with him, but he also escaped.'

Luc frowned. '*Both* escaped? From Teirhinan, you and a squad of cavalry?'

Zorne skipped past losing *all* his men. 'During the fight, Teirhinan threw Vidarsson into the lake before following Vyre into the gate, which then closed.'

Luc looked up at the rock floating above. 'So Raythe is up there? And Teirhinan?'

'Yes, Milord.' Zorne hesitated, then added, 'They are both Otravian.'

Luc looked at him, his expression hardening. '*I* am Otravian, Zorne.'

It was a warning, but Zorne went on, 'Milord, Teirhinan uses both praxis and mizra. She's a heretic.'

'She actually told you this?' Luc said sceptically. 'She confided in you, a Ramkiseri?'

'I believe she is lonely,' Zorne said uncomfortably.

Luc barked in amusement, 'Did that dead bitch take a liking to *you*, Zorne?'

'I have not been intimate with her,' Zorne replied, keeping his voice neutral. 'Milord, our duty is clear. She must be eliminated before she becomes a danger – despite her usefulness.'

'Does she frighten you?'

'A Ramkiseri does not fear, Milord. We think only of the empire.'

'She gives me the shits, I'll tell you that for free,' Luc admitted. 'Listen, while she's useful, she's innocent. She's the strongest sorceress I've ever seen – and I'll not have her killed on your say-so.'

His heart sinking, Zorne saluted. 'Aye, sir.'

A cry went up and one of the aides shouted, 'Sir, the citadel!'

A shape was dropping from the bowels of the floating rock: a circular platform, descending into the crater.

Luc Mandaryke clapped a spyglass to his eye, then murmured, 'Well, well.' He handed the spyglass to Zorne.

On the platform stood a woman in grey.

'And there she is,' Luc exclaimed. 'I hope she's taken Raythe's head.'

The five of them mounted up and made their way down into the crater, to find Teirhinan Deathless waiting on the stone disc they'd watched descend from the citadel.

'Lord Mandaryke. This is the gate-stone to Shiro Kamigami, the throne of the Aldar Kings. I have taken the citadel in your name. Will you come up and claim it?'

Luc shot Zorne a glance and murmured, 'See, Zorne? Loyal.'

Aye, to you, Zorne didn't reply.

Luc dismounted and went to climb onto the disc when Teirhinan stepped in his way.

'I have a boon to ask,' she said, smiling like a child.

'What boon?' Luc asked stiffly.

'I have captured an Aldar – the last living male.' When the listening men gasped, she giggled shyly. 'I've taken a fancy to it. I want to keep it.'

'An *Aldar*?' Luc exclaimed. 'Truly? A living, breathing Aldar?'

'Yes, yes. He is mine. Do you agree, Lord Mandaryke?'

Zorne could read Luc well enough to know that he was reconsidering his offer to kill her, but all he said was, 'I'll consider your request, Lady

Teirhinan. There are many issues involved, if he is the only one of his kind.'

The sorceress' ghastly face turned sulky. 'But—'

'What befell Raythe Vyre?' the Governor interrupted. 'I'm told he also went up there?'

Teirhinan *tsked* irritably. 'He flew away on a kite.'

'A *kite*?' Luc repeated. He gave Zorne an exasperated look. 'Then who is now up there?'

'Nobody . . . except *my* Aldar.'

'Is it habitable?' Luc asked, ignoring her petulance.

Teirhinan gave him a sly look. 'Oh, yes, Lord. It is a castle fit for a god.'

Luc puffed up. 'Well, then . . . Lady Teirhinan, we will go up, but I wish my wife and daughter to join us.' He gave instructions to one of his aides, then told the sorceress, 'You have done well, Milady. I am very pleased.'

'And you will grant me my boon?'

'I will . . . consider the matter.'

When the sorceress pirouetted away into a childish dance, Luc drew Zorne aside and dropping his voice, said, 'You're right: she's unstable and I don't trust that in anyone. But take your time, find her weakness. This business of using both praxis and mizra disturbs me.'

Thank Deo you've seen the light, Zorne thought, but all he said was, 'Yes, Lord.'

I'll need some time to work out how it can be done, he thought. *But I'll find a way.*

'Good man.' Luc clapped his shoulder before summoning the sorceress back to his side and quizzing her about the castle above, as if he hadn't just ordered her death.

It was almost an hour before Lady Mirella appeared, the epitome of a noble lady, riding side-saddle in a costly habit, her hair intricately coiled around her head, her expression imperious.

Zarelda, her head drooping, rode behind her. Her left cheek and jaw were one big purplish-yellow bruise and her eyes glowed with sullen hatred. Zorne couldn't help remembering the laughing girl he'd seen on the trek here. Clearly this family reunion didn't agree with her. Then Zarelda saw him and glared, a look he returned with equanimity.

Why does Mandaryke tolerate Vyre's daughter? He should just kill her.

Luc helped the two women dismount, full of courtly chivalry, but Zorne had no doubt it was his hand-print decorating Zarelda's cheek. 'Your dress looks well on our daughter. Your taste is, as always, impeccable,' Luc said to Mirella, before turning to Zorne, and his aides. 'Gentlemen, this is Zarelda. She is the trueborn daughter of my wife – *and me.* Raythe Vyre was inadequate as a husband, as well as a traitor and a fool. I took his part in Milady's bed well before the war. Make no mistake: Zarelda is mine.'

Zorne stared at the governor and the girl, comparing their faces, the lines of jaw and cheekbone. *Deo Alive . . . it could even be true . . .* He smiled to himself. *Our noble Governor has just proclaimed his wife to be an adulteress and his daughter a bastard*, he marvelled, watching the women with interest. *The things the rich and powerful can get away with!*

Mirella was clearly unhappy at this public revelation, and so was Zarelda. But the aides applauded as if Luc had just performed some admirable feat, rather than one of the Great Sins.

Perhaps to them it is a feat, Zorne thought sourly. He was surprised to discover that his sympathy was with Zarelda, shorn of the father she adored and yoked to people she clearly despised. The way she carried herself, pent-up and simmering, reminded him of himself, he realised. *I could make a Ramkiseri of her . . . there's enough anger in her for me to work with.* It was a fascinating thought.

They all climbed onto the platform with varying degrees of nervousness. Zorne joined Teirhinan, who was standing by a plinth which clearly operated the device, wanting to see exactly how it worked, but it was simple enough, not even needing sorcery to operate.

He looked up as they rose towards the underside of the mighty floating rock and despite all his training, he felt a thrill of fear. This was the legendary citadel of the Aldar god-kings – and perhaps the most destructive weapon in history.

I must ensure it becomes the property of my Emperor . . .

Zarelda watched those on the platform with her uneasily. She felt detached, as if this were a nightmare she was dreaming, not her new reality. That was just exhaustion, though: she knew it was all too real.

Her eyes moved from the stolidly loathsome Toran Zorne to the uncanny Teirhinan. Her weird complexion – it looked like slug's skin, pallid and grey – made Zar's skin crawl. *What is she? She's even worse than an Izuvei and I didn't think that was possible. Even those self-mutilating creeps didn't look like the walking dead.* Just watching the sorceress felt perilous, so she averted her gaze and stared blindly at the receding city below.

If I threw myself from this disc, would that be a better fate than this?

But Onkado was up there . . . she owed it to him to fight his corner. And Luc's aides were ignoring the glorious scenery and the miracle of the massive floating rock above; instead, they kept returning to one subject: that Raythe had escaped again.

My father – the only father I need – is still alive.

Their tones were instructive, too: she heard fear, but was that pride, too? That *their* rebel was still on the run? *We're all Otravians here*, Zar reminded herself, *except Zorne. Even that horrible grey creature is Otravian.* Though given how her country had torn itself apart, and the hatred the different factions felt for each other, she knew that they'd still kill Raythe if they saw him, if only to please Luc.

But what if Luc was dead . . .?.

They were briefly enveloped in darkness as they entered the shaft, then they emerged into the lowest chamber of the citadel.

The next hour dragged; for everyone else, the floating citadel was new and incredible, but the miracles of the place were commonplace to her by now. She trailed after them as they marvelled triumphantly over their 'discoveries': the old Aldar armouries, the stockpiles of istariol ingots that made them all just about wet themselves with greed, the eerie servants' quarters, and finally, the grandeur and majesty of the castle itself.

At last they reached the guest level, where Onkado was kept. Zar gathered her courage and said to Luc, 'An Aldar man was being up kept here – in that room there. He was the Queen's prisoner.'

Luc shot a glance at Teirhinan, then asked, 'What had he done?'

'He challenged the Tangato Queen and lost,' Zar told him.

Luc gave her a curious glance. 'What's your interest?'

She looked away, not sure how to answer that, or whether she should. Instead, she said, loudly, 'His name is Onkado –' and headed for the door.

To her surprise, Teirhinan shrieked, 'No! He's mine, Milord! You *promised* him to me!'

Zar whirled, staring at the sorceress, who was suddenly hysterical. *'What?'*

Luc made a silencing gesture at Teirhinan, gave Zar an appraising look and had his guards open the door. Zar darted past them and found Onkado naked and spread-eagled on the bed, tied to the frame by his wrists and ankles. He looked dreadful, unnaturally pale and his gaze was unfocused. She ran towards him – but was suddenly picked up in an unseen grip and thrown across the floor.

'Stay away!' Teirhinan shrilled. *'He's mine! He's my prize!'*

Gasping for breath, Zar saw Teirhinan crooning over Onkado, with Zorne behind her, a flat, dead look on his face. *He's going to kill her,* she realised.

Then Luc demanded, 'What is the meaning of this?'

'He's mine,' Teirhinan shrieked. 'You *promised.*'

'You can't have what's mine already,' Zar shot back. *'He's my husband.'*

Every head in the room swivelled, and her mother blurted out, *'What?* No!'

Luc looked astonished . . . and then calculating. 'Explain,' he said, sounding more intrigued than angry.

'No!' Teirhinan shrieked again. 'You promised him to me!'

'I agreed to consider it. I have now considered it, and giving away my daughter's husband is not reasonable,' Luc replied, stepping between Zar and Teirhinan. 'I will decide this.'

Given the way the sorceress was acting, Zar thought he must be either very brave, or *very* stupid. She watched Teirhinan consider whether to rip them all apart – an option she clearly felt entirely feasible and reasonable – then lapse into a sulk. 'It's not a real marriage,' she whined. 'Deo hasn't blessed it. *It's not fair.*'

Luc looked at Zar, who said firmly, 'We are married under Tangato *and* Aldar law.'

Luc frowned, while an angry Mirella tried to reach her daughter. Luc barred her with his arm. 'Are you content with this arrangement?' he asked curiously.

Zar looked at the listening Onkado. 'Yes, I am.'

Mirella made a distressed sound, no doubt alarmed to see her plans for a society wedding for her daughter disintegrating. 'This is *nonsense –*' she began.

'On the contrary, his is the most valuable bloodline imaginable,' Luc purred. 'Well done, Daughter.'

While Zar was grateful for his support, it also made her skin crawl.

Teirhinan gave a graceless curtsey. 'Congratulations on your nuptials, Princess,' she spat, then gathered her skirts and stalked from the room.

Zorne looked at Luc, who shook his head, and the tension in the air dropped palpably.

Mirella seized Zar's shoulders and snapped, 'What have you done?'

'Peace, Mirella,' Luc snapped. 'I would hear how this came about. Daughter, follow me.'

Luc led Zar out to the balustrade overlooking the main stairwell, Mirella following, her face anxious. Luc turned to her first. 'Wife, you may listen, but don't speak without permission. Understood, *Darling*?'

Mirella nodded sourly, and Luc turned back to Zar. 'Tell me of this "marriage".'

Zar didn't like that Luc was the voice of reason here, but she told them how her marriage to Onkado had come about, including the nuances of Tangato marital customs and law that had had to be considered. She also had to admit that the union was unconsummated.

When she was done, Luc rubbed his chin thoughtfully, for all the world like a horse-breeder weighing up the worth of a stud at the market. 'So you're married to the last male Aldar . . . What is the lore on Aldar-human offspring?'

'I'm told that the Aldar traits completely overpower the human characteristics,' Zar said. 'Any child is wholly Aldar.'

'And how do you *feel* about this marriage?'

Zar shuffled uncomfortably. 'We don't really know each other – we've barely had time to speak. When we first met, he was wearing a mask and I had no idea what he was, but I liked him. I think he protected me for reasons of honour, and I reciprocated out of gratitude . . . an honour debt, you might call it.' She gazed at the door to his cell, still bound. 'The Queen and . . . uh . . . Raythe both wanted the marriage dissolved.'

'Do you wish it to be?' Luc asked.

'Of course she does–' Mirella began.

'Hush,' Luc reproved her. 'I wasn't talking to you.'

Zar thought about the life her mother wanted for her: an advantageous marriage to an Otravian notable, a broodmare for future tyrants. Luc probably wanted the same. *Krag them both*, she thought bitterly. *And what about Onkado? I admit I'm fascinated, intrigued. Of course I empathise with his situation . . . and yes, he is beauty itself. I don't know if all that could become love, mutual wholehearted un-coerced love . . . but maybe it could?*

For a moment she thought of Banno and his heroism when they parted. But that didn't change her heart. Even if he was still alive – and that was a very remote possibility – she knew that her heart would never be his.

'I want to see if it can work,' she declared, her voice husky.

Mirella looked appalled, but Luc smiled crookedly. 'I thought so. You

229

have the Mandaryke spirit of adventure and enquiry. I like that. We'll have to manage it carefully, of course. But I believe I can give you the opportunity.' He tousled her hair, a presumption she resented but didn't react to. 'Obviously, both his and your sorcery must remain bound, and your movements restricted, but within reason, we can accommodate this.'

Zar was stunned. *Does he mean this?*

Mirella thought so: for a moment her face contorted in vengeful fury, but as Luc turned to look at her, she theatrically burst into tears, then fled.

'She wanted to rule over some debutante nonsense at home,' Luc sniffed, turning back to Zar. 'But you're a Mandaryke, and you've already secured the best possible match you could ever make. She'll come round.'

Zar's head was still filled with that snarling look she'd seen on her mother's face. But Luc's approval was something she could use. 'Onkado should be treated with dignity,' she said firmly. 'I must tend to him.'

'Of course,' Luc agreed. He waved in a waiting aide. 'Maveros, ensure the Aldar – Onkado – is confined in comfort. My daughter may have full access to him, but he is restricted to his quarters for now. And arrange for Lisenko and Torland to bring their staff up here this afternoon. I need to update them, make plans. And start moving a garrison up here too – Otravian infantry only, just redjacks; no Bolgravs. Let's take control.'

Maveros saluted and bustled away, leaving Zar alone with Luc again.

'So, an Aldar husband,' Luc mused. 'You're a mature girl, Zarelda. I'm impressed.' He ruffled her hair again – something she *really* wished he'd kragging well stop. 'I see much of myself in you – in the way you crave new experiences. An Aldar in one's bed, eh . . .?'

She cringed inwardly, disgusted by his turn of thought, but feigned gratitude. 'I should . . . uh, tend him.'

'Of course. You do that . . . my daughter.'

She endured his smarmy smile and hurried back towards Onkado's room – only to be intercepted by Toran Zorne, who'd been lurking by the door.

'What do you want?' she blurted, startled when he stepped out in front of her.

'There's something you need to know,' Zorne said stiffly. 'I observed on the journey here that you were fond of Banno Rhamp. He is dead. He fell into a ravine and broke his neck, after firing his gun to warn his comrades of our arrival. I identified his body myself.'

She'd been bracing herself for confirmation, but to hear it like that brought back a torrent of memories, of kisses and beaming smiles, hugging him on that lonely camp where they'd almost but not quite done it, back when this trek had been just an adventure. For a time, she'd been so in love with him . . .

I never got to resolve things with him, and now I never will.

She fought the sudden stinging in her eyes, but they still came, so she fled into the nearest empty room and sobbed until she was exhausted.

'Onkado?' Zar called uncertainly as the guards let her into his new suite. It had taken an hour for her tears to dry up, though her eyes were still red, but she desperately needed company, someone to help lift the burden of grief.

'Zarelda?' she heard him respond. 'I am here.'

She entered through a small lobby into a lounge; the bedroom was behind. She heard the door lock again behind her.

Onkado had clearly been permitted to wash and been given clean clothing by Luc's aides. The Magnian attire looked strange on him. He was sitting on a wooden bench, but rose as she entered. 'Please, sit,' he offered, then, frowning, 'You have been crying?'

'No, I haven't,' she blurted, as ridiculous a lie as she'd ever told. 'It's just . . . um, I . . .' Her rehearsed lines about Luc's decision dried up.

'If this is guilt over our so-called marriage, please, seek its dissolution,' he said. 'Though I thank you for keeping me away from that woman. She belongs in the ground.'

'Teirhinan's terrifying,' Zar agreed. 'But she'll stay away from you now.'

Onkado bowed. 'Having thanked you, I also remind you that if you hadn't interfered, Shiazar would have already executed me and I would be spared this nightmare.'

'My father says that despair is death, and hope is life. Things can always get better.'

'Can they?' he asked. 'Who are these new people?'

That took time; she first had to explain the Bolgravian Empire, Luc Mandaryke and Mirella, Toran Zorne, and all the rest.

'The important thing is that now they're here, they'll take *everything*. Luc wants you alive because he's curious. He might even befriend you so he can use you to get what he wants.'

Onkado's disdainful expression told her what he thought of that. 'What about your mother?' he asked.

'She wants our marriage dissolved so she can sell me off back in Otravia.'

'But what do *you* want, Zarelda?'

'I want our people – mine and yours – to survive this. Keeping you alive serves that.' That was true, but it left a lot unsaid, things she didn't have the courage to voice.

He sat in silence for a while, then said, 'Play along. Wait your chance – then take it.' He moved closer and dropping his voice, showed her a rune-etched manacle on his ankle. 'Can you get this off me?'

Her pulse quickened. 'Perhaps? But I'd need tools – and somehow I'll need to get them past the guards. I'll see what I can do.'

He nodded, then leaned in so their faces were almost touching. 'Listen carefully. My grandmother Jinkatia was the Aldar Archivist. She told me of a place in this citadel that controls it – the weapons, and how to move it.'

Her skin prickled. '*Move it?*'

'Aie: the legends are true. Fortresses like this were built as weapons of war, capable of offence and defence. There's a secret room somewhere: the Heart Chamber. If we find it, we can take control of Shiro Kamigami.'

'What would that get us? Luc's already inside the fortress, and so are his men.'

'Jinkatia said that whoever controls the Heart Chamber controls the fortress. We must try.'

Just having a plan felt exciting, a way to stave off despair. 'Aye, you're right. Anything's worth a try. Where is it?'

'I don't know,' he replied, 'which is just as well, because if I did, that creature – Teirhinan? – would as well. She questioned me,' he admitted, shuddering involuntarily.

'Did she hurt you?'

'She used sorcery to bore into my mind,' he admitted, looking away. 'It was . . . *humiliating.*'

She clutched his arm, outraged. 'If she touches you again, *I'll kill her,*' she snarled.

He looked startled by her fervour. 'You are brave as any warrior,' he said – and then suddenly he kissed her, a brief, mind-paralysing press of his lips.

'Don't do that,' she started – then she realised that it had been far from unpleasant – and in any case, they were supposed to be married. 'I mean, not without permission.'

'May I have permission, then?' he asked, his face close, his eyes spearing her.

No . . . I mean . . . Yes . . . Yes!

But Banno was too recent, her grief and guilt unresolved. 'I'm sorry,' she gulped, 'but I can't.' She dashed for the door, hammered on it until the guard let her out, then fled before she could change her mind.

'Gentlemen,' Luc Mandaryke purred, 'welcome to Shiro Kamigami.'

Hosting this meeting at the third hour after noon had required a scramble, but he'd been determined. His staff had found furniture in the storage rooms and set up in what had most likely been the banquet hall; it was badly scorched from some recent conflict, but still usable.

There was a genuine throne, too, maybe used by Vashtariel Last-King himself – or even Tashvariel the Usurper, his brother.

Luc took it for himself, naturally.

I walk in the footsteps of legends . . . and I will become one myself.

Everyone knew of Shiro Kamigami, but entering it was a profoundly unsettling experience. Romoi Lisenko, the Bolgravian general, radiated superstitious dread; Nemath Torland was awestruck, as were the sorcerers, Tresorov and Drusyn – even Toran Zorne and Teirhinan Deathless were subdued.

'Yes,' he went on, addressing his commanders around the table, 'this is the legendary stronghold of the last Aldar King. We have found it and restored it to the world. Now we must secure these lands, which means defeating and enslaving the Tangato people and bringing Raythe Vyre's fugitives to justice.'

'Aye,' General Torland said, 'let's crush them all.'

General Lisenko wasn't so enthusiastic. 'My men are in no condition to fight,' he protested. 'We're suffering an outbreak of some lung disease – I lost seventeen men overnight, and–'

'How many cases overall, Lisenko?' Luc interrupted.

He conferred with Tresorov, then answered, 'More than two hundred–'

'Out of five thousand men,' Torland Nemath sniffed. 'Hardly a crisis.'

'The case numbers are rising – and we have not yet found a treatment for this ailment.'

'It sounds no worse than an ague,' Luc retorted, unconcerned so long as his Otravians remained untainted. 'Soldiers are lazy by nature and will take any excuse to sit idle. Whip them along, Lisenko.'

'But why the urgency?' the Bolgrav whined. 'We have the city and the fortress – and the mines. We can destroy the natives at our leisure.'

'Is this the feared ruthlessness of Bolgravia?' Luc sniffed. 'When you have an enemy on the run, you don't sit on your hands and allow them to reform and recover. We must crush them whilst they are disorganised.'

'But my men–'

'This is not a debate, General Lisenko. We march tomorrow. Be thankful your forces are primarily cavalry. General Torland's men must march on their own two legs.'

'Torland's men aren't dying in droves from an illness we can't fight,' Lisenko protested. 'Let's see what you think when it spreads to your camp.'

'Gerda willing, that won't happen,' Torland replied complacently. He turned to Luc and changed the subject. 'Lord Mandaryke, is it true there are Aldar here?'

'Indeed,' Luc confirmed. 'Just the one, though, and he's my prisoner. The natives have, my daughter informs me, been ruled by Aldar since the Mizra Wars. The Queen of the Tangato is also an Aldar, but we're still hunting her.'

'*Your daughter?* So it's true that Zarelda is your progeny?' Lisenko asked.

'Very true,' Luc confirmed. 'I am finally able to acknowledge her publicly.'

'You cuckolded Vyre?'

'That's one word for it.' Luc shrugged. 'Regardless, she's my blood, and a sorceress in her own right. We've already reached something of an understanding and in time I am sure she will sit among us and give good counsel. In the meantime, gentlemen, return to your divisions and ready them for the march north.'

'Will you ride with us, Milord?' Torland asked.

'I will join you on the eve of battle. There is still much to be learned up here.'

That hadn't been Luc's initial intention, but the more he walked these halls, the more he felt that letting others unpick whatever secrets were hidden here – especially ambitious, ruthless sorcerers – was to invite treachery.

I must certainly be present when we discover how to use the weapons of this castle, he thought, standing.

As everyone followed suit, he said grandly, 'Well, gentlemen, let's crush these natives and finally put an end to Raythe Vyre.'

9

Secret Heart

Raythe woke to cooking smells and the bustle of camp. Opening his eyes, he saw anxious faces fussing over breakfast around a burgeoning fire. The sun was still low in the east and the dew heavy on the grass; everyone's breath was steaming in the frigid air.

Shiazar sat nearby, wrapped in a blanket and talking to an old Tangato man and his fellow travellers, who bore a strong family resemblance. They were clearly in awe of their unmasked Aldar Queen.

Seeing Raythe was awake, Shiazar excused herself and joined him. 'They found us just after you collapsed. They've been very kind.' She studied his face anxiously. 'I had not realised you were so drained.'

'I'm much better now,' he assured her. 'I just needed rest.'

She indicated their hosts. 'This is a Tanuahi family, travelling to the Puketapu village. It's not far from here.'

'I hope Varahana got my people there,' he replied, then he remembered Vidar. *Is he even alive?* He could only hope. *Who else have we lost?* He suspected the answer to that question was *too many.*

For now, he masked his worries – people needed to see their leaders being positive – and allowed Shiazar to introduce him to the Tanuahi family, then he followed her to the crest of a nearby ridge to get the lie of the land. They were appreciably closer to the Icewastes here: the heights were vivid white, with forested hills and undulating uplands stretching around them. When he turned southwest, he could see a small dark dot low on the horizon: Shiro Kamigami, hanging in the sky above Rath Argentium.

'We'll make the Puketapu village by mid-afternoon,' Shiazar told him.

'And then what?' he wondered. 'We can't fight them, and this land is too small to hide us for ever.'

She frowned. 'Why can we not fight?'

'Well, where to start? We have – what, ten thousand people all up – and they're mostly women and children. Luc Mandaryke will have at least two divisions with five thousand men in each: fully trained and equipped for war.'

'We have guns and powder, aie?' Shiazar countered. 'We had begun training our men in their use. We know the land and how to fight our way, using stealth. And we will be fighting for our lands – our homes – and families.'

'That's true,' he admitted, thinking, *It should be me saying such things.* But he'd fought the empire for years, and he'd been through disasters without end and somewhere along the way he'd lost his optimism, trading it away for a bloody-minded refusal to go quietly.

'We'll find a way to make it hard for them,' he promised.

She looked towards Rath Argentium, while he thought about how she'd fought with skill and tenacity the previous night, against a terrifying foe – and how she'd secured the kite and got them both away, a combination of agility, imagination and courage he'd seldom seen matched.

Dear Gerda, she's magnificent.

And whilst dangling hundreds of feet in the air from that enormous kite, she'd kissed him.

He decided that would be a foolish thing to mention.

'I've not had the opportunity to tell you properly just who we face, Majesty,' he said at last. 'The invasion is led by Luc Mandaryke. He's the man who stole my wife and betrayed my country. As a reward, the invading Bolgravians made him Western Governor.'

'Ah,' she said. 'So this is personal. Why would your empire send him here?'

'Not *my* empire. Perhaps he chose to come himself? I also caught sight of Toran Zorne, a Ramkiseri agent – that's the empire's Secret

Service: men and women who act outside any law, in service of the emperor. They are assassins and spies, every one of them. Zorne infiltrated my people. He reached Rath Argentium with us before his lies were unveiled. I thought him dead, but his body was never found. He probably led Mandaryke here.'

Shiazar grimaced. 'Tell me more of what we face.'

'Imperial law dictates that at least half of any expedition is made up of Bolgravs – I've seen only two different divisional insignias, but that's already ten thousand men. There may be more. It does mean there's at least five thousand Otravians, though – my own countrymen.'

'Is that an opportunity?'

'I doubt it. I've been told that many commoners – and soldiers are mostly commoners – respect my resistance of the invasion. But the ruling class think I'm a dangerous warmonger, and Mandaryke's division fought directly against Colfar and my rebels, so I very much doubt they'd flock to my banner out here.'

'How do Otravians and Bolgravians regard each other?' Shiazar asked.

'With outright hatred, usually. The Bolgravians are invaders and oppressors.'

'Can this Luc Mandaryke contain that resentment?'

'If anyone can, it's him.'

Shiazar looked at him. 'How will he treat Zarelda?'

He hung his head. 'Truly? I don't know. I can only pray he respects Mirella enough to leave her daughter alone.'

'I shall pray to Kiiyan for her also,' Shiazar said, her up-tilted face just inches away, and again he thought of that kiss.

He was also conscious of the family below. 'We'd better get moving,' he said.

'Of course.'

Was that a hint of regret in her voice?

'It's not fair to keep these people waiting,' she added.

He glanced down the slope. 'They'll tell their grandchildren of finding their Queen in the wilds, alone with the notorious *gaikiko* rangatira. Scandalous!'

She gave him a sideways look and said, 'Perhaps them finding us prevented the scandal?'

'Are you teasing me?' he asked seriously. He couldn't read her mood, but felt a clear bond, forged by shared dangers, responsibilities and burdens. 'Sometimes I don't know . . .'

'Good,' she smiled, then gave him a more sober look. 'With my own people, I must be Queen, and everything I do has significance. But you are outside the rules, so I can be my real self. Does that make sense?'

'I think so,' he replied carefully. 'Actually, I quite like this "real self", Majesty.'

'I wish I could be her more often, but we're at war,' she said. At that, she stood, and though she had no mask, the remote expression she assumed had much the same effect. 'Come, we need to rejoin the fray.' And with that, she led the way back down to the camp.

Raythe picked up a young boy and put him on his shoulders, fell in beside Shiazar, and they all headed north.

The fortified village of the thousand-strong Puketapu tribe, tiered slopes of pole-houses divided by wooden palisades, was set on a hilltop in the northeast of the Fenua Tangato. The influx of five thousand refugees of the Hiriwa and Tanuahi had resulted in hundreds of lean-tos and hide tents being erected at the bottom of the hill.

From scouts Raythe and Shiazar's party met en route, they learned that the Magnian contingent had got there safely, and as soon as they arrived, Raythe went to find them. He was dreading having to break the news of Vidar's probable death to Mater Varahana – and he had no chance to compose his words, because Varahana saw him coming and immediately detached herself from the hurly-burly of making camp to come and meet him.

'Raythe, darling,' she called, 'it's good to see you.'

For a moment, overcome with grief, he couldn't speak – then Vidar Vidarsson himself emerged from the bustle, Jesco beside him, shouting, 'Raythe, glad you could make it!'

'Oh, thank Deo!' Raythe exclaimed, hugging both men fiercely. 'Vidar, how did you kragging well beat me here?'

'Four legs are faster than two,' Vidar chuckled. 'I got in just before dawn.'

'He's been telling us you were most likely dead,' Jesco drawled. 'I said he shouldn't worry; you're better at running away than anyone I know.'

Raythe snorted. 'Thanks so much – mind, it was a damn near thing.' Then he dropped his voice and said, 'It's Luc Mandaryke leading the imperial forces.'

'That's old news,' Varahana said, smiling. 'Vidar told us.'

'But that's not all. He's had to bring a half-Otravian, half-Bolgravian combined army. The Otravian division's the Ninth Perasdyne. That's –'

'Nemath Torland's division.' Jesco spat.

Raythe laid a consoling hand on his shoulder. 'I'm sorry.'

Jesco had been drawn to Perasdyne by newly liberalised laws on homosexuality, one of many who seized the chance to truly be themselves, even though it meant migrating. But when the Bolgravian-Mandaryke coalition seized control, those same laws had been the first to go – and Nemath Torland, one of their own community, had been put in charge of the purges. Jesco had been one of the very few to escape.

'I'd be ash if you hadn't smuggled me out,' Jesco reminded Raythe. 'So all our best enemies are here, are they? Good. I've been wanting that slime in my sights for years.'

They shared a long, intent look, an unspoken vow to prevail or die trying.

Then Rima walked up and pressing her nose to Raythe's, said, 'You rescued our Queen. We are in your debt.'

'Gerda alive, don't tell him that,' Varahana advised. 'It's hard enough to keep him humble as it is.'

'I'm told you escaped on a kite,' Rima said, ignoring the banter. 'This is good – you are becoming Tangato.'

'I'm very adaptable. Is there any news about Kemara?'

'Nothing,' Rima said, her face turning bleak. 'But I'm glad you're back. Please excuse me, I must attend on the Queen.' She hurried away.

I suppose Kemara really is dead, then, Raythe thought sadly. But he fixed a smile on his face and went to greet his people. They looked tired, scared and footsore, lost in an alien world, but they visibly brightened when he joined them, shaking hands and making promises about securing food and fuel and dozens of other necessities, while trying to buoy them up for the perils ahead.

It was well after dark before he finally got any rest.

Onkado was perched by the window when Zarelda entered his rooms the following morning, shown in by a leering guard who was probably now peeping through the keyhole, hoping to see something salacious.

'Zarelda?'

Her Aldar husband's face lit up as she joined him.

Staring through the window, her voice low, she said, 'I can't find anything for your manacle yet – they won't let me go into the below ground levels. But I'll find a way. Any ideas about the secret chamber. Where do I start looking?'

'All I know is that it's in the core of the building – somewhere close at hand for the ruler. So it must be on the top level, the banqueting level or this guest level.' Onkado traced a shape with his finger, like a small tablet inside a larger one, joined by a vertical line:

'This is what you should look for – it stands for eternity and the infinite.'

Zar committed it to memory. 'Got it.'

'It may be more complex than just finding this symbol,' Onkado warned. 'There might be a key or some other talisman required too. My mother didn't know for sure.' He hissed in frustration, then asked, 'Is there any news of our friends?'

'Luc's army are moving north to find my father and Shiazar's people,' Zar told him. 'We'll have a week at most before it's too late to help them.'

'We must find a way,' he said, but his voice sounded despairing.

Years of trailing after her father through a losing war had taught Zar that giving up wasn't an option. 'We'll think of something.'

Onkado rewarded her with a quiet, appreciative smile. 'Thank you. Sometimes it's hard to . . . you know.' He looked away shyly. 'Being alone all the time weighs me down. Even when I lived among the Manowai, I had to wear a flesh-mask and pretend to be someone else. I had no real friends – and when I was unveiled, that just made me even more untouchable.' He took her hand in both of his. 'I have never really talked to anyone the way I can with you. You are so different to everyone I have ever met. I know we fell into this marriage in a strange way, but I am not sorry, Zarelda. I just wish we had time to know each other better.'

Zar understood exactly what he was describing, for her own fugitive existence as a rebel had often made her feel exactly the same.

It would be so easy to melt into him . . .

But Luc's smarmy face telling her she was a true Mandaryke because she craved 'experiences' reared up inside her mind, as did all her pent-up sorrow and dread, the terror of the unknown. 'I have to go –'

He tightened his grip on her hand. 'Please stay. We can just talk.'

No . . . that's just desperation speaking. It'll go too far.

'When this is done,' she managed, 'we'll work things out, I promise.'

Then she ripped herself free and fled again.

Life . . . vast, impossibly complex, ever-changing life: the endless seas in motion, the grassy turf teeming with myriad creatures above and below the soil, the crystalline perfection of ice, glittering from horizon to horizon, the radiance of the sun, the liquid flow of water . . . it was all here, complex and infinite.

I want it for myself.

The Dreamer drifted through it, caught up in a stolen vision of another place, full of vibrant, painful, beautiful *life*, so intoxicating that the void in which the Dreamer floated became a prison.

I want that . . .

The persistent thought was troubling, not least because the Dreamer was suddenly, inexplicably, thinking of itself as 'I', and was wondering what that implied. But when it tried to enter that vast infinity of life, when it tried to break in, it found no one to help. Those it once touched were now gone, lost to the past, and the few faces and names were insufficient vessels. Locked in a place outside of life and time, the Dreamer sought an entrance . . .

But when it tried to worm its way in, it broke around it like waves or smoke, unable to enter and become . . .

Despairing, it sank back into its dreams . . . until it realised that perhaps it already possessed what it needed . . .

10

Uphill, into the Guns

As a young man, the army had been just a lark for Raythe. It was what young noblemen did to get ahead, and all his friends were enlisting. His father had wanted him to concentrate on sorcery while his mother thought his time best spent on politics, so in the end he'd done all three. He became a dilettante, chasing every whim and dream – and Mirella, too. Pulled in every direction, he mastered nothing.

Then came the invasion and actual bloody, fatal war. Initial victories were too swiftly followed by betrayal and defeat – and at the hands of the Mandarykes, his *friends*. Families were torn apart and his parents executed, and soon war defined his life.

And now here's another one, he thought morosely. *Probably my last.*

'Here we go again,' said Jesco, who understood his moods better than anyone. 'It never kragging stops.'

The past four days had been spent making tough choices and seeing them through. Abandoning the Puketapu village had been the first: it was defensible, to a point, but too easily surrounded, so they'd retreated into the forested hills, shadowed by Krodeshi clansmen who butchered anyone they caught in the open, men, women and children alike.

Now he and Jesco were crouched on a stony ridge, watching the Bolgravian cavalry arrive. The initial trickle of horsemen had become a river. A few had tried to assail the Tangato position, but the steep slopes defeated their horses, so they made camp to await their commander in the valley, which looked like a canyon, with no way out except through the Bolgravians.

They think we're trapped, Raythe mused. *Gerda's Teats, I hope we've chosen the right place for this.*

The valley was bleak and inhospitable: frost and snow streaked the stony ground, there was no vegetation and the steep slopes on either side were covered with treacherous scree. The Tangato and Magnians had laboured to the top the day before and were now perched behind the ridge, huddled over cooking fires and eating a meagre meal.

When the enemy bugles burst into a fanfare, Raythe trained his spyglass on the newest arrivals: senior ranking officers surrounding a portly man with huge moustaches, his uniform heavy with braid and medals. His puce face and brusque manner suggested he wasn't happy.

'What do you think, Jes?' Raythe asked the Shadran.

'That it's the most half-arsed imperial camp I've ever seen. The horses are picketed anywhere there's space and most of them look spent. Some of the tents are barely standing, I've never seen a sloppier perimeter and the lines to the cesspits are a mile long. No wonder their general looks pissed off.'

'I'd noticed the same thing,' Raythe replied. 'If we had anything like their numbers or weaponry, I'd be tempted to sweep down on them. But . . . *hey ho*, what's just happened?'

He pointed to where one of the sentries, who'd been marching to and fro below them like a good little cadet, had suddenly reeled and collapsed. Someone shouted, but instead of his comrades rushing in to help, they were milling around at a distance, as if scared to get close. When Raythe trained his spyglass on the fallen man, he could see he was vomiting wildly.

After a moment he turned to Jesco. 'Holy Gerda,' he breathed. 'They've got the lung-bile disease in their camp.'

'Give me that.' Jesco snatched the spyglass and peered through, then swore. 'Kragga mor, you're right . . . no wonder they're in such a mess.' He handed the spyglass back and licked his lips. 'Ah . . . I might have forgotten to mention that as we left, Varahana threw all her disease samples into the wells. She said she felt like she'd condemned herself to the Pit.'

Raythe could well believe she felt like that. Varahana had always held herself to a high moral code. He slapped Jesco on the back. 'If she's managed to poison that Bolgie army, believe me, I'll be putting in a good word for her with Deo and Gerda and anyone else who cares to listen!'

He retrieved his spyglass and studied the enemy commander again, now standing with a knot of smartly uniformed aides around him. There was visible consternation, waving hands and chatter, and the general's head was bobbing back and forth indecisively.

Perhaps he needs some help making up his mind, Raythe thought.

'Let's get everyone together and make some plans.'

Half an hour later, Raythe joined the Queen and her advisors. Shiazar looked fierce and glorious in her black lacquered armour, her face unmasked and her hair in a warrior's topknot. With her were some of her rangatiras and a handful of mahotsu-kai, led by Rima. Raythe had brought Jesco, Varahana and Vidar.

They all listened intently as Raythe, speaking Gengo-Magnian, which all present understood, outlined the situation.

'The enemy have the lung disease in their camp,' Raythe reported. 'It's possible, given the speed the illness moves, that as many as half are affected. They'll be weak as children right now.'

Varahana, in her priestess robes with her skull freshly shaven, looked guilty as she told them, 'As we evacuated the city, I threw my samples of the disease into the wells of the bridge district, knowing it might cause suffering and death. I have prayed and begged the forgiveness of Deo and Gerda for that heinous act.'

Her remorse was genuine, Raythe knew, but he saw it as a tactical masterstroke, and clearly, so did all the Tangato, who started slapping their thighs in applause.

'I do understand your feelings, Mater,' Shiazar replied, 'but there are always times when we who lead must choose between evils. I am sure your gods will forgive you.' She turned to her advisors. 'How do we take advantage of this?'

'We attack,' boomed the shoganai Imbataki. 'Let us destroy them as they lie helpless.'

Raythe sounded a note of caution. 'Even if half are incapacitated, the rest can still shoot – and they still outnumber our own fighting men.'

'Are you saying we should do nothing?' Natomo, the Hiriwa rangatira, asked.

'Not at all,' Raythe replied. 'But an attack surrenders the biggest advantage we have: the terrain. We came here so that they must attack us uphill, with poor footing. If we launch the attack, we forfeit that advantage.'

'If we do nothing, it buys them time to find a cure, or bring in reinforcements,' Ihanodo, rangatira of the Puketapu, replied. 'Meanwhile, we are running through our supplies. We must force them to fight.'

'Their general would be mad to do so,' Jesco commented, 'especially when he's dealing with an outbreak of disease.'

'Fooling the enemy is part of our heritage,' Natomo said. 'We will goad them into attacking.'

'I like it,' Raythe told him, 'but those people aren't idiots. They might believe your people to be backward, but they will know that any uphill assault in their condition will mean excessive losses.'

'Then what do you suggest?' Monarohi demanded.

'I'll go and talk to them.'

They all looked at him sceptically, but Varahana said, 'It'll work – he's very annoying.'

There were grunts of amusement at her words, and a few – those who'd come into contact with Raythe before – nodded emphatically.

'There's another factor at play here,' Raythe told them. 'There will be tensions between the Bolgravs and the Otravians. I've parleyed with Bolgravian generals before and I know how they think. I can play whoever it is, I'm sure of it.'

They all looked at Shiazar, who gave her assent.

*

Jesco, waving a pale scarf requisitioned from a Magnian woman, managed to convey the request for a parley to the nearest Bolgrav sentry. Soon after, Raythe and Jesco clambered down the slope, stopping some thirty paces from the portly Bolgravian general.

'I'm Raythe Vyre,' he called.

The grey-clad general, who was guarded by a sharpshooter, stuck out his chest. 'I am Romoi Lisenko.'

'The same Lisenko who was on Dasprovic's staff at Vaskonfeld, where Colfar and I routed an army twice the size of our own?' Raythe asked. 'Clearly Luc handpicked you.'

Lisenko's already flushed face went puce. 'You got lucky, Vyre. We had you—'

'Right up until you didn't.' Raythe chuckled. 'Who commands the Otravian division? No, wait, I bet it's Luc's mate, Nemath Torland. Those two always were thick as thieves.'

'Is there a purpose to this parley, Vyre?' Lisenko asked. 'Or are you here to surrender?'

'Oh, there's an army in dire straits here, but it isn't mine. You've got disease in your camp, while we've got the high ground and an escape route ready. And tomorrow, Nemath Torland's vanguard will be at the foot of the valley, yes? That makes you the one who's trapped. We Otravians always did hate you Bolgies.'

'Ridiculous,' Lisenko scoffed. 'We all serve the empire.'

'Of course you do – but there's *such* competition, isn't there? Over who serves it *best*, don't you think? And glory and plunder are doubled when there are only half the men to distribute it to.'

'Nonsense,' the general snorted, but Raythe could see his words striking home: everyone knew Luc Mandaryke was ambitious, and joint imperial expeditions were always plagued with mistrust.

This kingdom is a prize worth any treachery, and Luc's a past master at backstabbing – Lisenko will know that as well as anyone.

'The fact is, you're in the shit, Lisenko. I'll warrant your men were stationed by the bridge, yes?'

Lisenko went pale. 'Yuz?'

'Bad luck, that . . . well, if you can call it luck. I bet Luc has his Otravians stationed elsewhere.' The scouts had already reported this, so Raythe knew his 'bet' was accurate. 'Likely Luc knew the peril of disease.'

'I will *not* be toyed with,' Lisenko blustered, but the hook was planted. 'Why are you here?'

'To offer you a deal,' Raythe answered. 'I have the remedy my people came up with for the lung disease, enough for all your men. Luc and Torland think you'll be easy pickings, but if you're cured – and you have our local knowledge – you could turn the tables on them.'

'Against your fellow Otravians?' Lisenko sneered.

'They're Luc's men: they are every bit as guilty as him. I'd rather decent military men like you prospered over turncoats like him. And you do know he stole my wife – so think of it as my revenge aligned to your patriotism.'

Lisenko's frown suggested that he was half-convinced and somewhat tempted. 'What would you want in return?'

'An imperial pardon and the pleasure of watching House Mandaryke come crashing down.'

Lisenko glanced skywards, then ran his eyes over the empty slopes above, calculating. Then his lip curled. 'The Bolgravian Empire does not negotiate with traitors, and we do not bargain for things we can take. You've stuck your neck out too far, Vyre. Say your prayers!'

With that he whirled and stomped away.

'Phew,' Jesco breathed. 'For a moment there I thought he was actually going to go for it – and I'm kragged if I'll ever ally myself with a blasted Bolgie.'

Raythe threw him a grin. 'Well, you heard the man. Start praying.'

Below them, the Bolgravian camp came alive again, whistles shrilling, trumpets blaring and soldiers stampeding in all directions – and even from the top of the hill, it was apparent that those men weren't well.

We've set the bait, now let's land the fish.

No sooner had Raythe and Jesco reached the ridge again than drums began to thud in the valley and ragged lines took shape, typical of horsemen forced to fight on foot. Lisenko was wasting no time in hammering home his 'advantage'.

Raythe found his mark, a hundred-yard section on the ridge, where Tangato warriors were rubbing shoulders with some of his hunters and a few frightened Magnian villagers who, believing the Bolgravian army to be invincible, were convinced they were going to die. In contrast, the Tangato men and women were in high spirits, singing, slapping their chests and pulling warlike faces.

This could get bloody ugly if it goes wrong, he thought grimly, but he took heart from the Tangato warriors' self-belief. 'All right,' he said, beckoning to Rima, 'tell them to stay low and to hold fire until I give the signal.'

She relayed his words to the Tangato leaders, then rejoined him. Peering down the slope, she murmured, 'They're coming straight at us. I guess you really are as aggravating as Varahana said.'

'Did you doubt it? How sweet.' He glanced left and right: just a few hundred people along the ridge were in sight of the enemy, but they were facing at least two thousand Bolgravians, with more forming a second wave behind them. Either Lisenko was keeping plenty in reserve – or half his men were already too sick to fight.

Either way, the Bolgravs were advancing, wielding their short-barrelled cavalry flintlocks, trying – and failing, Raythe noticed with a grin – to march to the rhythm of the drumbeats. When they struck the scree slopes a couple of hundred yards below the ridge, several stopped to empty their stomachs, but that was normal; you'd see that on any battlefield. These men weren't sick, and their discipline held.

The famous Bolgravian rolling barrage began. This was the technique that had given them the edge when they'd invaded the West: three banks of infantrymen meant one line was always firing while the other two reloaded; the staggered volleys meant their opponents were continuously under fire.

As the first marksmen readied their weapons, Raythe called, 'Down!'

Rima echoed the command in Tangato and the defenders dropped to the ground as lead shredded the soil on the ridge or zipped past into the skies. Six seconds later came the second volley as the first shooters huddled and started reloading, then the third rank came into play. The shots were almost entirely wasted, but they did succeed in their aim, which was to prevent the defenders from returning fire.

'*Cognatus, praesemino*,' Raythe called amidst the din as Rima readied Mokomoko. Both had supplies of istariol, donated by the Tangato, to increase the potency of their magic.

'*Napadat!*' the Bolgravian officers blared. *Advance.*

Now the soldiers started the climb, pausing every six seconds to shoot, then reloading on the hoof. It took hours and hours of training to make the movements automatic under fire, but it was a highly valuable tactic: the constant rattle and blast could break a defender's nerves, and the toll on massed opponents could be devastating. Late in the conquests, the Otravian army worked out how to deal with these tactics and enjoyed a few victories – until the Mandarykes betrayed their own people and ended the war in capitulation.

The Otravians had realised that you didn't have to stand up to a rolling volley: giving ground or using cover wasn't cowardice, and mobility could defeat a static foe. Raythe was intent on demonstrating that now.

'Hold your fire!' Raythe reminded his section, Rima repeated his words and the rangatiras echoed the commands. 'Archers, get ready!'

There were no archers on the ridgeline, but hundreds had been stationed behind and below, safely out of sight of the Bolgravian soldiers. Tangato archers could shoot every few seconds, and they didn't need line of sight against massed foes.

Raythe risked a look in between volleys and seeing that the Bolgravs were about to hit the first mark he'd prepared, he warned Rima, 'On three. One!'

'*Tahi!*' Rima shouted, as another volley blasted the rocks, sending scree everywhere.

'*OBVINI!*' the Bolgrav officers roared: *Attack!*

'*Two!*'

'*Rua!*'

'*Three!*'

'*Toru!*' she screeched, and Raythe checked back and down, where the archers stood or knelt, aiming up and over the ridge.

'*First volley!*'

'*Tuatahi!*' Rima shouted, and the first rank loosed their shafts in a whirring cloud that arched up into the sky – and then sleeted down into the soldiers floundering on the scree.

Two can play at rolling volleys.

'*Seconds up!*' Raythe ordered.

'*Hekona!*' Rima shouted, and when the next group loosed their shafts, the serried ranks of Bolgravians lost their rhythm, their rolling volley faltered – and so did the advance.

'Volley and cover,' Raythe shouted to those behind the ridgeline, and the gunmen – his Magnians and the Tangato they'd taught how to shoot – darted to the ridge, lined up their shots and fired, then ducked behind the rocky ridge to reload.

Peppered with arrows, then struck by a hail of lead from gunmen who were only fleetingly visible, some of the Bolgravians reeled back, shooting blindly – which was when Raythe and the mahotsu-kai unleashed their istariol-augmented earth-spells, making the slopes ripple and triggering rock slides that swept the Bolgravians off their feet.

As the advance fell apart, the Tangato rangatiras along the rim waved the archers to join them. Now able to see their foes, they loosed further flights of arrows, and the dead and wounded piled up on the hillside, until at last horns blared out the rarely heard notes of the Bolgravian retreat.

Raythe looked for Lisenko through his spyglass and found him berating his aides. His losses weren't immense – a few hundred men would never see a new day – but Raythe understood the psychology of battle. How the Bolgravians responded to this setback would tell him a lot about their true state of mind and body.

Then a fire-arrow shot into the air from across the valley: the signal he'd been awaiting. It was followed by a roar of voices as a thousand Tangato warriors streamed down into the Bolgravian camp from that direction. He'd been striving to keep Lisenko's eye focused on him, while the other half of his forces got into position for a flanking attack.

'*Attack!*' Raythe shouted, and in moments, everyone began a measured advance down the slope, while Lisenko's men, seeing the trap closing, completely lost all semblance of discipline. Few cavalrymen could fight on foot and in retreat, and the front and reserve lines quickly disintegrated as those able to sought their horses – or any mount they could grab – and galloped away, seeking safety.

If Lisenko could have rallied his men, they would still have the advantage, both in firepower and numbers – but he couldn't, and his rage was turning to fear as arrows and shot began to strike his command group. In minutes, they too were scampering away.

Raythe led his contingent forward, Jesco directing the men's fire while Monarohi picked out any pockets of resistance for the archers – but they faced little by way of retaliation and were taking few losses, so they hit the camp as it emptied. It quickly became apparent that the Bolgies were suffering badly from the lung disease, quite unable to form anything like a concerted defence – or even, in many cases, to stand upright.

Within half an hour they'd surrendered, and Raythe braced himself for the horrors of the post-battle rout: the butchering of prisoners, the torture and the rapes – because there were women among the Bolgravs, wives and lovers who'd blagged their way into the army as cooks and servants.

But it never happened.

It wasn't just because Shiazar was quickly among them, urging restraint, but to his surprise, the Tangato showed no inclination to harm anyone who didn't fight back. They disarmed those they captured, then herded them to the edge of the camp and let them flee untouched.

'The Queen doesn't know how a proper war is fought,' Jesco noted.

'Oh, it's not really mercy,' Raythe replied. 'Lisenko's got to feed them all, but he's lost his supplies and munitions. He's out of the game, for a while, anyway. Meanwhile that disease-ridden lot have to be fed. This is a logistical nightmare Luc will have to deal with.'

Jesco smirked. 'Mercy isn't supposed to be that merciless. It's just a shame Torland wasn't here.'

Raythe pulled a face. 'I'm not sorry. I'd rather we didn't face the Otravians just yet.'

'It'll happen sometime. Make sure you're ready when it does.'

'I will be,' Raythe promised.

The Tangato warriors wasted no time claiming the abandoned flintlocks, while Vidar and Jesco took charge of the dozens of barrels of powder and lead.

Raythe found Shiazar in the midst of the camp, watching and occasionally intervening as she made sure the looting was restricted to important items – and that every barrel of Bolgravian spirits was emptied out.

'We can't afford the disruption drunkenness would cause,' she told Raythe.

'I don't disagree. What are our losses?'

'Minimal,' she replied. 'Three dozen dead, thrice as many wounded, some seriously.' She sighed, looking skywards. 'But we are grateful for victory. What now?'

'Ideally, we take everything we can and leave. If we do it right, they'll never work out where we've gone.'

'We have guns now, and lots of food. Can we fight them head to head?'

He shook his head. 'Not immediately. This was a special situation. The Bolgravians were hung out to dry, possibly deliberately. But Luc's army won't be sick, and their sorcerers will have istariol, now that Luc controls the citadel stores.'

'So we just run?'

Raythe gazed away down the valley, wondering. 'Think of it more as a tactical withdrawal, Majesty. Let's slip away and take a few weeks to equip and train. Then, maybe, we'll be in a position to take them on.'

'That sounds good to me, although I might have a job convincing my warleaders: they now think we are invincible.' She unleashed her quiet smile on him. 'Thank you, Raythe. Yet again, we are in your debt.'

For a moment, she was the only thing in the world, which was a wonderful place.

Then reality seeped back in, with urgent matters abounding. She looked away; he bowed and went looking for his people. He found them clustered round a wagon, eating a captured stew and broaching a surreptitiously covered barrel of Bolgravian vodka the Tangato had missed.

'What now, boss?' they greeted him, grinning broadly. 'Shall we just go straight back to Rath Argentium and whip Mandaryke's arse?'

'Not yet,' he chuckled. 'We'll take the high pass out of here and head for the Wakatoa lands. There, we'll regroup, train with our captured weapons and plot the next battle. This isn't over.'

Vidar looked round curiously. 'This is a dead-end valley – how do we get out without another fight?'

'It's thanks to Queen Shiazar for this one.' He pointed towards the highest mountains. 'See the cleft between those peaks? It's a pass onto the Icewastes. The Tangato go there at times. They know the way.'

Within the hour, the Tangato and Magnians had laden the captured horses and mules with their looted packs and greatcoats, guns, balls and powder, and were trudging up and out of the valley, while the mahotsu-kai cast spells to conceal their passing. And by nightfall, they stood, high in the mountains, at the edge of the endless ice.

'What?' Luc Mandaryke demanded. 'What do you mean, *"defeated"*?' He thumped the arm of the Aldar King's throne and shoved the remains of his meal away down the giant banquet table. Mirella and Zarelda, sitting on either side, flinched at his rage, while the hovering aides stopped their small talk, their complacent faces suddenly anxious.

The Otravian courser standing in front of him looked like he wished he'd never come.

Toran Zorne, who'd been bored all morning, edged closer to listen.

Mirella was worried, he noticed, but Zarelda looked maliciously delighted at her father's upset.

'There was a battle yesterday, Milord,' the courser answered. 'General Lisenko was lured into a trap and lost many men. The choking plague has swept over the camp and a great many more of his men are seriously ill. He was forced to retreat in disarray.'

Luc slammed down his goblet of Pelarian claret, then rose to face the cringing messenger. 'Kragging Lisenko! How did he manage to lose? I was told there were just savages with sticks out there?'

'General Torland told me to let you know that General Lisenko complained of treachery, Milord.' The courser flinched, clearly unhappy at the words his general had given him to speak, but Luc seized on them.

'What treachery?' he demanded.

'Lisenko ... er, well, he wrote of poisoned wells and, um, Otravian collusion, Milord ...'

Luc's face became thunderous. 'The man's an embarrassment to his rank! Raythe Vyre is the most wanted man in the empire! If Lisenko truly thinks Torland or me capable of colluding with him, then he's utterly deranged!' The governor glared about him, then barked, 'What were his losses, man?'

'Uh, four or five hundred killed in the fighting; more than a thousand captured ... but the enemy released them – they're all sick anyway, sir. Most of the survivors are now unarmed and without horses. Soon afterwards, another four hundred died of the sickness, Milord. Lisenko's emergency camp ...' His voice cracked. 'It's a hellhole, sir, what with the wounded and the sick ... Half the Krodeshi scouts have deserted. And ... uh ... they've lost their supplies. The general begs we send food–'

'What? They can starve, the kragging imbeciles! And I suppose Vyre's savages now have all their guns and mounts, too? *Damn them! Damn Lisenko to the Pit!*' Luc stormed back to the throne, then turned and asked, 'What was the nature of this so-called "trap"?'

'Sir, I have it from an Otravian scout that the general parleyed with

Vyre, then launched an attack, uphill into the enemy's lines. They were repulsed, then hit from the rear.'

Luc sat up. 'That sounds more like idiocy than subterfuge. Deo's Balls, Lisenko is an ass!'

Zorne noticed Zarelda putting her hand over her mouth to hide a grin, but he returned his attention to Luc. His tantrum looked genuine, but Zorne doubted the governor was completely distraught at Lisenko's humiliation.

Was there collusion? No, I very much doubt it: Luc Mandaryke and Raythe Vyre genuinely hate each other. But it's clear that Lisenko has lost any ability he might have had to curb Mandaryke's greed, should it manifest.

Luc turned to his aides. 'All right, it's time to take control of this situation. Order General Torland to advance on the enemy and—'

The courser coughed, his face sickly. 'Excuse me, sir, there is another thing. The enemy have . . . um . . . vanished.'

'*What?*' Luc spat, and then again, '*WHAT?*'

'General Torland's scouts have lost the native army, Milord.' The messenger cringed. 'They've completely vanished from a dead-end canyon.'

Luc visibly teetered on the edge of violence, then mastered himself. He turned to face Mirella and Zarelda. 'Milady, Daughter, I apologise for this interruption, but I must convene a staff meeting. Please, return to your rooms.'

Zorne watched the two women leave, but he lingered, anxious to keep an eye on Mandaryke. *If he turns against my Emperor, I must be here to deal with him.* So he leaned against the wall, hoping to be overlooked.

No such luck: Luc glanced his way, and called, 'Ah, Zorne, just the man. I have given Lady Teirhinan a special assignment, which I'd like you to oversee. She won't be pleased, but tell her I insist. She will be in the Great Hall.'

'What assignment?' Zorne asked.

'She'll explain,' Luc said impatiently, but then he tapped his nose once, so casually it looked like nothing, but Zorne knew what it mean instantly.

Get close to the witch – then do your duty.

11

Dreams and Memories

'Milady?' Toran Zorne called softly from the door. He'd been waiting for an hour outside the royal chamber, in the shadow of the upright sarcophaguses containing the earthly remains of the Aldar kings that lined the wall. The maid had finally gone, leaving Mirella alone. His sorcerous senses detected no use of magic, but as a Ramkiseri, Mirella had such powers. That she chose not to use them didn't surprise him, however. *Presumably her husband doesn't know what she is.*

He knew from experience that infiltration missions made it difficult to keep one's magical gifts secret, unless one was very discreet. She would still be good at certain types of spells – veils, scrying, perhaps mesmerism – but he doubted she had much chance to practise battle-magic, or large-scale ritual magic.

If she's been corrupted, I can deal with her.

Mirella looked up at his entrance, her eyes narrowing. 'Master Zorne, I choose when we communicate, not you.'

Zorne flinched – acting against the will of a superior offended his very being – but he pulled the door to behind him and asked, 'Milady, what are my orders?'

Mirella stood. 'They are unchanged.'

'Your husband has ordered me to shadow and kill Teirhinan.'

'Lady Deathless . . . a challenging assignment.'

He pictured the sorceress at the sphere-gate, rising from her own pyre to assail Raythe Vyre. 'I don't know how to begin,' he admitted. 'She has no vulnerability that I can detect.'

'Then wait, watch and learn. I cannot aid or protect you. My own mission takes priority.'

Zorne nerved himself to ask his next question: 'Milady, I keep asking myself this: does your husband serve the empire – or himself?'

Mirella met his gaze. 'A question that also plagues me. I tell you solemnly, although I share his bed and his confidence, I don't know the answer. Now go, before someone sees us together.'

Zorne turned, then looked back and asked, 'How do you bear it? Being intimate with someone as a duty?'

Mirella laughed. 'Master Zorne, I enjoy my life. I don't need to pretend to take pleasure in all the good things – lavish gifts, fine food or wine . . . or in having my physical needs met by a handsome, powerful man. But I do not forget my true allegiances.'

But do you love your husband more than your empire? Zorne wondered.

And then a worse thought suddenly occurred: *Is she the real danger, not him?*

Unnerved, he made his face go wooden and backed out, no closer to knowing whether he served two potential traitors, or just one . . . and if so, who was it?

Zarelda was confined to the castle, not permitted outside or below ground level, but she spent what time she could seeking the symbol that Onkado had described. She'd finally realised that the building had a central spine, maybe just fifty feet in diameter, which couldn't be accessed on any floor – there were no doors into it, and it was so skilfully disguised that if she hadn't been actively seeking it, she'd never have suspected it was there.

Over the past few days, she'd gone through every level, seeking in vain for the symbol Onkado had shown her, but until now, there had been no chance to look on the upper floor. *Surely, if it's anywhere, it's up here?* she thought. *Especially as the mark symbolises the eternal and infinite . . . like the gods . . .*

The only likely place she could think of was behind the massive statues of the Aldar gods, and that would mean pretending to the guards at the top of the stairs that she was visiting her mother, then darting out of sight so she could examine each one. She'd have no more than a minute or two, and it was hugely risky – if anyone came, she'd have to hide and pray they didn't see her – and there weren't many hiding places there.

But if it's anywhere, it's there, she told herself. *I have to try.*

After steeling herself in her room for what felt like hours, she picked her moment, towards the end of the afternoon but before the watch changed, when the guards were at their least alert. She sauntered up the stairs, made sure the sentries outside the banquet hall saw her, then entered the hall, darting in behind the first of the giant kneeling statues before the men outside the royal suite at the far end of the hall had a chance to spot her.

From there, she worked her way along the line of gods and goddesses, taking cover at the sound of any passing footfall. Fortunately, the marble floor ensured the noise carried, although once she was almost surprised by Toran Zorne, coming from the royal suite. But he looked distracted as he passed, just a few feet from where she was hiding behind the foot of the kneeling Kagemori.

Then she peered cautiously around to make sure she was once again alone – and froze. There it was, engraved on the heel of the next statue: the God-Emperor Ankazo.

The mark was only the size of a fingernail. She went to touch it, then hesitated, having no idea what might happen – if anything.

I need my maho freed, and Onkado with me. We still don't know what it does . . .

She rose to leave, but as she rounded the statue and headed for the hallway, a pale figure blocked her way.

The reek of rotting meat filled the air. 'Bravo, little one,' Teirhinan Deathless laughed. 'You found it for me.'

No! Zarelda tried to run, but unseen hands gripped her arms and pinned her to the dark wall, while the smirking woman prowled closer, waving an admonishing finger.

'I have been tasked with finding the Heart Chamber, and as I search, I notice you, flitting here, darting there, hunting, hunting, and I think to myself: *she's looking for something too*. What for, I wonder? And then my friend Toran sees you hiding here and tells me . . .'

She clicked her fingers and Toran Zorne appeared behind her, empty-handed but looking poised to act.

He was followed by Luc Mandaryke, who was rolling his eyes theatrically. 'Daughter, Daughter.' He *tsked*. 'I'd be disappointed if you weren't so damned predictable. What is it about Raythe Vyre that he can turn everyone's head so thoroughly?'

Then he placed his finger over the symbol on the god's heel and pressed. Immediately, there was a faint grinding sound and a panel next to where Zar was hanging, pressed against the wall, began to move, opening into a doorway. Luc conjured a light in his hand, then gestured to Zorne and Teirhinan. 'Bring her.'

Teirhinan released her spell and Toran Zorne caught her arm and steadied her. He gave her a warning look as he nudged her in the direction of the door, but she knew better than to resist, instead stumbling passively into the hidden chamber.

Luc's light spell revealed a spherical room with no windows, at most twenty yards across. The space was dominated by a throne in the shape of a giant serpent's head, apparently carved from one massive chunk of crystal. It was set in the very centre, on a circular pedestal, and, chillingly, the seat was inside its open mouth.

'So it's true,' Luc crowed. 'There really is a Heart Chamber – and this is the legendary Serpent Throne.'

Oh Gerda – and I've led them straight to it. Zar crumbled inside.

With a triumphant smile, Luc sat on the throne – which was immediately revealed to be hollow, like blown glass, for it suddenly filled up with a scab-red fluid like unhealthy blood: istariol, glowing dully. As it did, the chamber came alive, light panels in the ceiling glowing with steadily increasing strength, until images appeared in the air around the throne, threads of light and glowing runes, while the walls took on a strange, translucent appearance.

Luc stared, then smiled, like some cruel pagan god. 'Ah, I see. Let's see what this does, shall we . . .?'

Luc Mandaryke had always felt that he had one great advantage over any of his rivals – and in the cut-throat world of Otravian politics, there had been many. They were all like him: educated, smart, usually blessed with both athleticism and sorcery, and oozing self-belief.

But I have a destiny . . .

Doubts were crippling things: they made you question yourself, causing comprised strategies and pulled punches. They engendered fear, hesitation or even paralysis when instant action was needed. But Luc had never doubted that he would one day rule the world. It was simply something he *knew*. Everything revolved around him and always had – his parents had worked to increase their already massive resources for one purpose: to serve him. Taking his place on this fearsome, eerie throne and surrendering to its power, something that would surely have daunted anyone else, was just the next step in his road to complete supremacy.

In those first moments it was as if he'd been swallowed by that giant serpent's head. He lost all awareness of the chamber and everyone in it and instead found himself enveloped by another reality. He was inside the skull of a flying beast, hovering in the skies over Rath Argentium, seeing everything. That beast had its own awareness, its own sentience, and this rock and fortress was just the skin it wore.

It regarded him as he regarded it, taking each other's measure.

In his mind's eye, he was floating before the face of an immense dragon-like creature, staring into amber eyes mere inches away, while teeth long enough to impale him glittered like diamonds. A snake-like tongue emerged and he felt it through his clothing, wet and hot and abrasive, flickering over him, tasting him. Then it coiled about him and he felt like some kind of exchange had taken place.

Luc's familiar squealed in terror, then the massive serpent

inhaled – and swallowed the spirit entirely, a painful *rending* that was ameliorated by an immediate inpouring of energy and succour as the dragon-beast itself took his familiar's place.

The difference was *incredible*.

Is there a sorcerer in the world who exceeds me now? Luc wondered. It surely couldn't be possible.

The next few minutes – or ages – were spent bonding with his new dragon-familiar, who was like a massive child. He started having strange visions – of an explosion that flung the dragon into the skies, where it hung, suspended halfway between earth and heaven, a baby torn from the breast of its mother, condemned to aeons of isolation, gazing down on the world but unable to return to it, or its progenitor.

Istariol, Luc thought, awestruck. *Istariol isn't just a mineral – it's* alive – *alive, fully sentient, and possessed of longings.* The immense creature revealed its past, including the years after the Aldar climbed the rock it was encased in, built their citadel and then took it to war. His first master was the Aldar sorcerer-king who devised this chamber and rode this fortress across the skies, blazing fire at other floating citadels until they exploded and those aboard were incinerated or sent plummeting to their deaths.

We were the mightiest, the creature exulted. *We conquered the skies.*

It had a name, given by the successive Aldar Kings who bonded with it: *Dakaji*, a creature from their own divine mythos, the dragon who ruled the stars beyond the sky. Since the death of Tashvariel, five hundred years ago, Dakaji, the mightiest familiar in Creation, had been trapped here in the skies, lonely and desperate for another master to bond with.

'I'll take care of you,' Luc told the beast, 'and together we shall do great things.'

In response, Dakaji exulted, infusing him with love and hunger, like a warm blanket of crackling power.

Let's see what we can do, Luc thought, opening his eyes as awareness of his body returned. Zorne, Teirhinan and Zarelda were staring at him, their eyes round and expectant, expressions somewhere between awe and anxiety.

Extending his hands, he made a *shaping* gesture and threads of light appeared, running outwards from the palms of his hands. As the serpent-head throne slowly rotated, the walls faded, then so did the entire castle, until they appeared to be on a platform overlooking the floating rock, which looked as if it was made of black glass honeycombed with glowing veins: the activated istariol that kept the rock stable in the air.

'Deo and Gerda—' he heard Zarelda gasp, which confirmed that they could see what he saw.

He followed a node of energy that ran directly to the eight dragon-cannons on the outer walls. They were linked by tubes to the central depository of liquid istariol. *The armaments of the castle*, he thought triumphantly, as Dakaji gave him the muscle-memory of how they were activated and used. He saw the four great chains tethering the floating rock to the ground were also glowing.

'So the old legends were true: this is more than a castle, it's a weapon,' he marvelled aloud. 'Look – I could discharge any one of the dragon-cannons – and here … I could make this whole rock move …' He gestured slightly and when the entire citadel and the rock holding it shivered faintly, the chains emitted a tortured protest.

'Deo on high,' Zorne breathed, clearly shocked. 'Have a care, Milord.'

Zarelda looked terrified, and even Teirhinan's face was alarmed.

'It's so intuitive, so easy to manipulate,' Luc gloated. 'As soon as I sat, the lines of force were as clear to me as any solid thing.' He gestured, and three of the dragon-cannons swivelled about. 'No wonder the Aldar kings thought it right that the gods kneel to them. On this throne, one becomes a god.'

Footfalls heralded the arrival of Mirella, who peered through the doorway, her beautiful face pale. 'Luc?'

'We found it,' he told her, 'and it's everything I dreamed it would be.'

The mastery in Luc's voice had Zar wanting to scream. *He'll destroy every-one in his way . . .*

Even Teirhinan and Zorne were looking uneasy.

'Husband? Is this safe?' Mirella asked, more composed than Zar expected.

'Safe?' Luc said, in a musing voice. 'Aye, but for one weakness,' he said, lowering his hands so that they disengaged from the webs of energy. 'The Aldar king waged war against multitudes from this seat, but a single person could have killed him while his mind was engaged. They had to be utterly sure of the loyalty of everyone with access to this chamber. It must have driven them mad.'

'Mad is certainly how they ended up,' Zorne observed.

Why would Luc tell us that? Zar wondered. *Why admit a weakness?*

'How fortunate I am that I can completely trust those closest to me,' Luc went on, rising from the throne and standing beside it. 'Barring my daughter, of course,' he added, looking at Zar with what felt like amused regret. He walked towards her, full of casual menace, and then suddenly gripped her face and spraying spittle, shouted, *'Understand this: I CANNOT BE THWARTED! Zarelda, do you now understand this?'*

She recoiled, shaking in fright and nodding mutely.

He released her and faced the others. 'Do you know the Bolgravian folk tales about domovoi? They are spirits who inhabit a house. This castle possesses such a thing: a being named Dakaji. I have now bonded with Dakaji, like a sorcerer to his familiar. Its power is immense, and thus, so is mine.'

He whispered something, and the whole fortress quivered again, but in a different way, as if something was moving beneath the stone. Teirhinan and Zorne both looked anxious, as if their sorcerous senses had detected something of genuine menace, but all Zar felt was the vibration rising through the floor, radiating from the throne – and whatever lay beneath it.

'Ye–e–e–sss,' Luc purred. 'Oh, this place . . . from here, one could rule the world.' He faced Zorne and with casual irony declared, 'I place it at the feet of our Emperor, of course.' He spoke as if daring Zorne to disbelieve.

Zorne half-bowed, his pudding face taut. 'Milord.'

Luc turned to Teirhinan. 'What say you, Lady Deathless?'

Teirhinan shuffled from foot to foot like a child caught in the pantry, her eyes focused on something unseen. 'I can *see* it,' she purred. 'I can see your Dakaji. It's *immense . . . beautiful . . .* Might I have a turn?'

Zar sensed that the ghoulish sorceress might turn feral at any moment, and noticed that both Zorne and Mirella took a step backwards . . . but Luc waved languidly at Teirhinan. 'I'll need help with it, of course,' he drawled. 'Please, be my guest.'

Teirhinan's head swivelled between the offered throne and Luc, clearly torn between caution and greed – but greed won. She sidled towards the giant block of crystal, stepped onto the lower jaw and sat, as Luc had done, and once again, the luminous crimson crystal lit up. She raised her hands, as Luc had, and the threads of power began to form . . .

Then the crystal serpent's jaws crunched partly closed, its jutting teeth forming a cage. Her head was forced down into her lap, her spine cracked and she flailed about, trying to escape. Zar saw her gathering energy to strike back, but as fast as she conjured, it was drained away into the throne itself, feeding her captor.

Finally she went limp and wailed, *'Master! Mercy—!'*

Luc gestured and the jaw unclenched.

The serpent's eyes, which looked chillingly *alive*, settled on its new master, while Teirhinan, crushed out of shape and helpless, whimpered like a child in its mouth.

'And this is the lesson,' Luc said, as if lecturing students. 'I have bonded with this place and it will tolerate no one else. *No one.* If *anyone* tries to usurp control, they will be swallowed up by a power that is utterly beyond them. Even your spirit will be devoured, Teirhinan Deathless: you will utterly cease to be. Do you understand? *I know what you are, and I know how to destroy you.'*

Teirhinan, staring down mortality for perhaps the first time in her life, squeaked in a plaintive, girlish whimper, *'Mercy—'*

Even Toran Zorne's usually impassive face was sickly as he

confronted powers beyond anything he had ever believed possible. And Mirella was looking at her husband with something in between horror and adoration – although nothing could be trusted where her mother was concerned, Zar was increasingly sure.

And Zar herself was swallowing back bile, on the verge of vomiting at her own idiocy.

Luc strolled back to the throne. 'A god does *not* share power,' he said, looking down at the trapped, contorted Teirhinan. 'He does not tolerate rivals and he does not permit any to stand higher than he.' He stroked the crystal serpent head and said, 'The throne belongs to me.'

He gestured and the serpent spat Teirhinan across the room, where she slammed into the stone walls. They all heard bones shatter and she flopped to the ground, bloodied and for a minute helpless – although her broken body immediately began rebonding, while she sobbed, gasping like a beached fish.

'Have I made my point?' Luc asked.

Zorne instantly answered, 'Yuz, Milord.'

Teirhinan sobbed her assent.

Zar nodded mutely again.

'You are the master, in all ways,' Mirella told him. 'I am very, very proud.'

'Thank you, my darling,' he replied, then looked around the room again. 'Appreciate this moment: we control the single most powerful artefact of sorcery in Creation. A citadel that can fly, one that can level cities – whole armies. I promise you all – even my faithless, ignorant daughter – will share in my victories, and the rewards.'

He turned to Toran Zorne. 'And you, faithful servant of the Empire. How may I reward you? It is your courage, persistence and vision that brought me here, after all. Ask for anything, and it is yours.'

The Ramkiseri bowed his head. 'Milord is generous. But the only reward I seek is the glorious day when my Emperor is handed control of this citadel. Nothing else matters to me.'

Luc's smile didn't falter, although surely he heard the implicit message: *Only by surrendering this to the empire can you prove your loyalty to it.* 'You are a treasure, Zorne,' the governor said lightly. 'Surely there is a title, a monetary gain . . . Can I not promote you, perhaps?'

'Only my superiors control my station in the Ramkiseri,' Zorne replied.

Luc rolled his eyes, then shrugged. 'As you wish, my friend. If I cannot reward you with plaudits, then let me reward you with more work. I need you to take control of Lisenko's division, as Legate. Do you understand? A Legate is the Governor's personal representative: you will take control and you will rebuild them. And arrest the general – he's a fool; his incompetence allowed Vyre's savages to escape.'

To Zar's surprise, Zorne hesitated. 'Sir, I am Ramkiseri, not army. They will refuse my authority.'

Is Luc hoping that might happen? Zar wondered. *So he'll be rid of him without scandal?* It felt plausible. *I'd not be sad if it happened.*

'Lisenko's men will do as they're damned well told,' Luc snorted. 'Take control, *Legate* Zorne. We must find and destroy the natives. Leave at dawn.'

Zorne had no recourse but to salute. 'Thank you, sir. Will you join the hunt for Vyre?'

Luc stroked the crystal serpent head fondly. 'Once you find Raythe's rabble, I'll come,' he promised. 'I want to see this fortress in action, and there's no better target for my wrath than Raythe Vyre.'

Then he turned to Teirhinan, huddled on the floor in her torn dress, her broken body still rebuilding itself while she wallowed in blood and misery. 'And you, Lady Deathless . . . is the nature of our relationship entirely clear now?'

'Yes, Lord,' she croaked.

'Excellent. I have a task for you. The savages here have their own sorcerers. I am placing a bounty on their heads of one istariol ingot per head. Find and kill them all.'

The Otravian sorceress ducked her head in acquiescence before crawling to the door, leaving a snail's trail of smeared blood.

Zar would have pitied anyone else.

Luc turned to Zorne. 'Escort my daughter back to her rooms. It still remains for me to punish her betrayal.'

Finally, he faced Mirella. 'My darling,' he said, with sudden passion, 'let me show you our new toy.'

The Heart Chamber door slid closed behind her as Zar followed Toran Zorne into the hall. They walked between the giant statues to the stairwell, where they both gazed down the shaft, struck mute by all they'd seen.

Finally Zar found her voice. 'I led him straight to that cursed room,' she blurted miserably.

'Yuz, eto pra,' Zorne agreed. 'You lacked the training for such subterfuge. Though it matters little; Teirhinan and I would have found it regardless. Your father would still be master of this place.'

'He's not my father,' Zar muttered stonily, contemplating the drop before her, imagining the hideous impact – and how it would feel if it *didn't* kill her.

'No, you are Vyre's daughter in any way that matters,' Zorne said unexpectedly. It didn't sound like a compliment, but nor was it a condemnation.

Zar discarded the urge to jump and glanced curiously at the Ramkiseri agent. 'I thought he'd kill you for what you said about handing this citadel over to the empire.'

'I cannot be other than what I am.'

'Ramkiseri lie all the time – it's your job.'

'No, I am a guardian of truth,' Zorne replied flatly. 'We serve without thought of personal gain. The only reward I considered asking for was permission to train you as a Ramkiseri.'

Zar's gut twisted at the thought. '*Me?*'

'You are a young sorceress, resourceful, passionate and idealistic. Such things are easily redirected towards a cause. My cause is *empire*. It should also be yours.'

'I'd rather die.'

'Why? Empire is oneness: it is singularity of purpose, with every person pulling together, achieving what individuals cannot. It gives life meaning, removes all doubt and fear. It is the only truth worth pursuing.'

Holy Gerda, he truly believes that, Zar realised. *With all his soul.*

'I am nothing like you, and I hate your empire,' she replied flatly.

He didn't rise to her anger. 'I too once hated. Krodesh has been at war with the Bolgravian heartland for centuries. I was raised a Krodeshi, but I saw the truth that united our enemy: the putting-aside of difference in a common cause that rendered them unstoppable.'

The passion in his voice, the first time she'd ever heard him speak like that, made her believe that this was the only truth he knew – and that he desperately wanted her to think and feel what he did.

The notion sickened her.

She jabbed a finger at him. 'I've seen what your empire does. When they came to Otravia, they rounded up all the minorities – all the intellectuals and thinkers, all the outsiders, even the disabled – and they worked them to death or burned them.' She shook at the memory of those pyres.

'Unity is only possible when difference is eradicated. Any perversity or sickness must be excised.'

She jabbed a finger at him. 'You see, that's what's really strange, because you're the sickest person I know. You should have been burned first.'

For a moment, he was speechless, blinking at her, stunned.

Unable to stomach him any longer, she fled back to her own room, avoiding the blood trail left by Teirhinan. She shut the door and slid down the wall, tears of sick fear overwhelming her again, this time made all the more unbearable by guilt.

She was still sobbing when the door flew open and Teirhinan Deathless burst in, resembling nothing so much as a half-crushed spider. She swarmed forward, the reek of the corpse-witch enveloping her, as Zar froze in terror, for this was surely the end . . .

Then the witch's violet eyes flashed and bored into hers while her claw-like hands caressed Zar's trembling face. Some viscous grey fluid stinking like rot was seeping from a dozen tears in her grey skin. Zar gagged, unable to breathe.

'Tell me of your native friends,' Teirhinan rasped. 'Which ones have magic? I want their names.'

She doesn't understand, Zorne told himself, watching Zarelda run away. She wasn't yet capable of seeing past the ephemera to what really mattered. Even so, her condemnation stung: *You're the sickest person I know.*

All his life, he'd been the isolated one: the other children laughed at him while he floundered in his inability to understand their irrational cruelty. He was the one who misunderstood, the artless one, the stupid one who always fell for their juvenile tricks and humiliations.

It wasn't until I was found to have the sorcerer's gifts, and the empire called me to her, that life took on meaning. The empire is my mother, but that foolish girl doesn't understand. She never will.

He'd been instructed to escort Zarelda Vyre to her rooms, but he had no desire to be near her, instead following her progress by the sound of her footfalls and the slamming of her door – then he latched onto another sound, the rhythmic, muffled gasps of a woman, emanating from the Heart Chamber. It went on for a long time, rising and falling in intensity and abandon.

Eventually Mirella emerged, hair dishevelled, walking with a dazed languor.

How do you do that? he wondered. *How do you fake love?*

'Milady,' he said, 'are you well?'

'Am I well?' She snickered dreamily. 'Perfectly. Never better.' She stopped before him. 'What do you want, Zorne? To condemn me for whoring on behalf of the empire?'

'No, Milady. We all serve as we are able,' he replied, stepping away, because she reeked of sweat and sex. 'Have you divined your husband's purpose?'

'His purpose?' She snorted. 'His purpose is to rule unchallenged from his new "Serpent Throne" ... until, *of course*, he hands it over to our beloved Emperor,' she concluded drily. 'No man gives up power, Zorne.'

He will betray my Empire ...

'What are my orders?' he whispered.

She pulled herself together at that, dragging her mind from whatever rapture she'd experienced and applied herself to his question.

That it took such effort made him anxious that she'd truly been seduced, that she was no longer playing a role.

'He's in no mood to be disobeyed right now, and I can't yet see a chink in his armour. Go to the Bolgravian division as ordered and await my instructions.'

She glided away, leaving Toran Zorne still wondering how she could bear to live such a false life – or if it was false at all.

Something had happened, a stirring that shook the Dreamer closer to waking. An old presence at the corner of its awareness had burst back into life. It could feel it, sense its presence, but not reach or touch it – but that presence rekindled the Dreamer's longing for completion.

Its thoughts returned to the sacrifice it had found. The vessel was empty now, all the memories that gave it identity swallowed up by the Dreamer, so that it could study and relish them at will. But try as it might, those memories were not enough to permit the Dreamer to wake, to re-enter the Dream, to return to Life.

Finally, it gave in to despair and wailed in the void, still alone, still locked out of Paradise, crying with loss, unable to reason or intuit what to do.

I will never escape what I am ...

Hope gone, it began to fall asleep again, forgetting the impulse that had first woken it, the desire to be *more*. Losing that spark, the Dreamer drifted back towards oblivion ... until it heard a name it knew: the name of the sacrificed one.

Kemara.

PART THREE
The Purity of Sacrifice

1

Breaking the Chains

The Tangato, it emerged, had been flitting in and out of the Icewastes for as long as they could remember. The tribes living on the edge of the vast white expanse were fascinated by it, almost the way Rath Argentium fascinated them all, but the Icewastes weren't forbidden, and indeed, formed an important part of their lives, Raythe was told.

'It is a test all Puketapu youth go through, spending a night alone on the ice,' Ihanoho chuckled as they tramped across the frozen, lifeless landscape. 'It's a rite of passage, a place where we learn our mettle.'

'I must admit, I've always thought of the Icewastes as off-limits,' Raythe admitted. 'It's a clever ploy.'

'There is nothing a Tangato warrior appreciates more than a good trick. We've always valued a cunning victory more than one based on brute strength. We will sing long of outwitting the horsemen yesterday.'

The Puketapu rangatira was in good spirits, after the victory over the Bolgravians, and then escaping the dead-end valley. All his people were strutting and striding through the ice, heads up and chests out. The Magnians were more subdued; they knew the empire would strike back harder, having been thwarted.

So far, their luck was holding. The Icewastes were calm beneath a pale blue sky that stretched on for ever, and so bright that they had to tie thin strips of cloth over their eyes to avoid snow blindness. But there was no wind, and the Tangato hunters knew all the routes in and out.

We're dipping our toes into the sea of ice, Raythe mused. Stratagems began to form in his mind. *We could use this trick over and over.*

The night had been bitterly cold, but the weather had held, as the Tangato mahotsu-kai predicted, and now they were making their way northwest, circling round the edge of the Fenua Tangato towards another pass that would lead them back into the habitable lands. The ice was so solid here that the hazards were few, provided the storms stayed away.

Sunset brought its own wonders: vivid shimmering pools of light that danced about the northern horizon, refracted by the ice into rainbow spears, with the planetary rings glowing above like the coronet on the brow of a goddess of light. It was wondrous.

'This is all the reward I need for this mad trek,' Raythe heard Varahana say. She was staring at the sky with Vidar; their arms were linked like lovers on a promenade in Perasdyne.

'Aye, for me also,' Vidar rumbled, his tone making it clear that he didn't mean the lights.

Raythe decided they didn't need his interruption, and looked around the camp for Rima instead. He found her cooking.

'May I join you?' he asked, then, 'Where will we emerge?'

She pointed towards the sunset. 'See those two peaks? Between them is a pass back to the Fenua Tangato. It leads to a place we call Futobasho, the Boiling Place, for the hot pools there. There are legends of a giant reptile lurking there eating the unwary.' She pulled a face and added, 'This is just a story to keep our young people away.'

'Why do you wish them to stay away?'

'It is dangerous – and sacred to the Kaiju,' Rima replied, her voice troubled.

'I have a theory about your Kaiju,' Raythe said. 'If you'll hear it?'

Rima spooned out two bowls of spicy bird-meat stew and offered him one. 'Aie, I will listen.'

Raythe ate a mouthful, appreciating the warmth as much as the rich flavour, then took a swig from his water bottle before beginning, 'When we found the mines beneath Rath Argentium had been worked out, we were confused: how could the land be free of ice, if there was no istariol at the heart of it, to radiate heat and defeat the snow? But Varahana suggested that the istariol must be outside the city, like the roots of a tree still in the ground despite the tree having been cut down. This is supported by the theory that istariol absorbs water, so that despite all the rain and snowmelt that flows into the Fenua Tangato, it's not inundated. With me so far?'

'Of course – this is not incompatible with our own thinking.'

'Good. It doesn't explain everything, but it's plausible so far as we can prove anything. Now, here's the second thing: your Kaiju. I've never heard of a Guardian Spirit, a spirit tied to a specific region. In Magnia, all spirits are small – nothing like the being I sensed that night.'

'Perhaps your people have lost belief, so your own Guardian Spirits have gone away,' Rima suggested.

'Not far off what I was thinking. Because the other thing that no longer can be found in my world, thanks to being mined so heavily, is large deposits of istariol. So I've begun to wonder if the Kaiju is the *spirit* of the *istariol*. I wonder if we in Magnia – with our limited spectrum of praxis or mizra – could never sense that the istariol was sentient. To us, it was merely a mineral to be dug up and used.'

'You are saying you murdered every Kaiju in your world?'

'Harsh – but yes, that's what I'm saying.'

'But there are *millions* of people in your lands – how could *none of you* hear the Kaiju scream?'

'If you want to blame anyone, blame the ancient Aldar: it was they who split sorcery in two, seeking greater power, then used mizra to destroy the world. By the time their rule was broken, we'd forgotten that sorcery had ever been about anything except praxis or mizra. Only your people preserved the middle way: your maho. Our sorcerers grew up knowing only the praxis, and we forced our familiars to be likewise.'

'It still seems . . . inhuman.'

'I'd like to think we'd have been different, had we only known,' Raythe answered. 'But what do you think? Is it possible that your legend of the Kaiju creating the istariol is the wrong way round, and that it's the istariol that created the Kaiju?'

Rima made a noncommittal gesture, which was more than he'd expected. 'Does it matter?'

'I don't know. But imagine it: a single entity beneath the soil, *everywhere* in the Fenua Tangato. What might it do to protect the land, if it was threatened?'

'Nothing, judging by what you say of Magnia,' Rima said.

'But in Magnia, no one spoke to it, or for it,' Raythe replied. 'Here, it's different: there's you and your fellow mahotsu-kai.'

Rima looked troubled. 'What are you wanting me to do?'

'I don't know, I'm just looking for advantages others don't see. A sorcerer must always have an edge.' He met her eyes. 'And this insight might help you find Kemara . . .'

She looked away. 'I no longer hope to find her alive.'

'We should never lose hope,' he said, rising to his feet. The idea had been planted, which had been his goal. 'Thanks for the meal. I wish you goodnight.'

When Raythe had gone, Rima tried to sleep, but she couldn't stop her mind turning over everything he'd said. Then old Kuia joined her, and they discussed Raythe's theory, and agreed it was blasphemous, heretical and alien . . .

But not necessarily wrong.

'Seek Te Kopu, the Womb; it lies in Futobasho,' Kuia urged her again. 'You've done your duty here.'

'Aie, I will,' Rima conceded. 'But I fear I'll be wasting my time, when others need me.'

Kuia gave her a knowing look. 'No, child: what you fear is failure. Don't let that stop you: we must never give up in the face of fear. Find the Kaiju and *demand* the red woman back. It will listen to you, child, I know this.'

*

Next morning, the camp rose in good spirits, still buoyed by their victory and burdened down with loot from the Bolgravian camp, including flintlocks that many had already been trained to use.

Thanks to my Queen's foresight, Rima reflected.

The descent through the pass took most of the day, but dusk saw the Tangato making camp in the foothills. That evening Rima sat with Shiazar as she conferred with the rangatiras, including Raythe Vyre. The Queen wore blood-red silks and a black, demonic mask as befitting a ruler at war; the clothing had been gifted by the Yokei assigned to the Puketapu tribe. They plotted a circuitous route to the Wakatoa village beside Lake Arasaki in the hope that the enemy had not yet found it and they could use it as a rallying point.

After the meeting, when Shiazar was alone, Rima said, 'Majesty, I hesitate to ask, but I need to go to a sacred place nearby: Te Kopu. I am acting upon a suggestion from Rangatira Raythe,' she added, suspecting that using the Magnian's name would be helpful.

Shiazar's expression was hidden by her mask, giving no clue of her thoughts, but she agreed swiftly. 'Raythe said you would ask,' she said, her voice warm. 'So did Kuia.'

Rima pulled a face. 'Am I that predictable?'

'If by that you mean, is it clear to all that you refuse to give up on your friend, then yes, you are predictable,' the Queen said gently. 'Go with my blessing. But return to us swiftly, dear Rima. We need you, regardless of your success or failure.'

Toran Zorne found himself sharing the stone platform to the ground below the citadel with Teirhinan Deathless. The Otravian sorceress looked dreadful, more corpselike than ever. The damage when she'd been crushed by the Serpent Throne hadn't fully healed: her badly healed limbs were crooked and the wounds in her grey skin wept putrescence.

'Zorne,' she said sourly, as they descended. 'Where are you going?'

'To take control of Lisenko's division,' he replied. 'I've been appointed Legate.'

'Tralaa-tralee,' she mocked. 'He doesn't need us any more, Ramkiseri man. He's sending you off to die, like he is me.' She stared at the ground, seething. 'I gave him this fortress and I tricked that silly bint into showing me the Heart Chamber and what do I get in return? Spat out, then lorded over like I'm a child.'

Her bitter assessment had the uncomfortable feel of truth, as did his own certainty that the moment he tried to displace Lisenko, his men would put a lead ball in his back. But until the moment that happened, it was unproven, so his duty was clear. Obedience was required.

'Where do you go, Lady?' he asked uncomfortably, trying not to inhale her stench.

'I'm bounty-hunting,' Teirhinan snorted, brightening as her mind turned from misery to murderous anticipation. 'Zarelda Vyre told me whom I should seek. I'm starting with the one who tutored her: Rima, she's called.'

'Why would Zarelda tell you anything?'

Teirhinan's mouth twisted into a sneer. 'I asked her nicely. And if she wasn't so precious to his Lordship, I'd have ripped her lungs out.'

She looked like she meant it, but Zorne didn't react. 'Do you think istariol can become sentient?' he asked.

The sorceress licked her grey lips. 'The evidence seems clear.' She peered over the edge as the platform dropped into the crater. 'But if large lumps of activated istariol can become sentient, then there may be more of them in the countryside.'

The thought made him shudder. 'You think that likely?'

'I do,' she said hungrily, but with an edge of worry. 'In truth, that creature up there could have destroyed me . . . and you know hard that is. But power is worth any risk.' After a sideways glance at the man controlling the platform to ensure he wasn't able to hear, she said abruptly, 'Can I trust you, Toran Zorne – in the name of the Empire?'

She knew him well enough to know how to bind him. 'Any who

serve the Emperor faithfully have nothing to fear from me,' he said honestly. *But are you truly such a one?*

She pulled out a necklace, an ugly black lump of igneous rock shaped like a heart – not a stylised heraldic heart, but the fleshy organ that pumped blood. This was the size of a walnut. 'This is a part of what makes me invulnerable,' she told him. 'Three times I have been brought back to life by it . . . But that thing inside the Serpent Throne – the serpent or whatever it is – could have consumed it and me at will. If I am to seek another such creature, I can't be wearing this.' She took a deep breath, then held it out to him. 'Swear on the name of the Emperor you will hold it safe for me.' She looked up at him shyly and added, 'I'm offering you my heart.'

He was struck once again by how like a girl she still was, and how lonely. That gave him faith that she was true to the cause, despite her flaws. He accepted the necklace and said, 'I so swear, on the name of the Khagan, Koreimi the Fourth, and all I hold sacred, to keep it safe.'

She moved closer, so that he had no choice but to inhale her foul breath. 'Can you feel its warmth?' she whispered. 'If it goes cold, place it against the skin of someone living – preferably a woman – and call me, as you would your familiar. I will come, and live again.'

In someone else's body, he thought. *Dear Gerda, if that's not mizra, what is?*

But he bowed solemnly and said, 'I understand.' In token of that, he placed it round his neck, then tucked the ugly rock inside his tunic.

They rode the rest of the way in silence. When the platform landed, their horses were brought forth and in minutes they were riding up out of the crater. They parted at the bridge, where she reached out with sudden, girlish playfulness and poked his nose. 'When I return, I may be stronger than even his Lordship,' she said. 'You've chosen wisely, Ramkiseri man. Take care of my heart and it is yours.'

Already, it felt like a dreadful burden – but it also answered many questions, and gave him some interesting thoughts. As soon as she was out of sight he pulled out the necklace and placed some spells of his own on it.

Every sorcerer needs an edge, Teirhinan. You have yours, and now I have mine.

With that, he rode east, seeking the Bolgravian camp, while she went north, to hunt for the native sorceress.

While the Tangato refugees tramped west, towards Lake Arasaki, Rima called a kikihana bird and rode due east, seeking Te Kopu. She had a small food pouch, an edged stone club laced to the waistband of her flax skirt, a water flask and a feather cloak for warmth.

She saw none of the invaders on her journey and by mid-afternoon, her rump battered by the hard spine of the giant bird, she reached the fringes of Futobasho, the Boiling Place.

After dismissing the bird, she ate some dried meat, refilled her water bottle, suspecting the water inside the volcanic region was tainted, then called Mokomoko into her and entered the steamy mist shrouding the place. As she went deeper, the vegetation died away, steam vented from cracks in the ground and the air took on the stink of rotting eggs. She warmed her feet in a rivulet as she followed it upstream. In a pool, she found the body of a shingar lizard, apparently poisoned by the water.

A carved pole loomed before her, one of the tallest she'd ever seen. Weathered demon and dragon faces with broken teeth and claws leered down at her, while the markings on the base in the ancient Aldar tongue warned her to turn back or risk the wrath of Heaven.

She followed a path that led past steaming water too hot to bathe in and pools of viscous grey-brown mud with a reek so strong she felt faint, until she had to wrap a cloth round her nose and mouth if she was to go on.

Visibility was getting worse, the steam so enveloping that she could barely see more than a few yards of a twisting, indistinct path. It was a maze, made to deceive those who shouldn't be here, but there were clues in small rock carvings that she was able to decipher. Finally, she passed through the veil of secrecy to a place she'd heard tales of: a circle of eight standing stones, tall as a man and carved to resemble the Aldar gods. This was Te Kopu, the Womb.

'Hear me, O Great Kaiju,' she keened, in Tangato. 'I am Rima, your servant. We have communed in the past. I pray you, remember me now.' Then she went around each standing stone, moving from god to goddess, kneeling reverently and praying aloud as she quieted her mind. It didn't help that she had no real understanding of what she wanted; nor of what Raythe Vyre's theories might mean in a practical sense. She began to worry that his strange ideas might actually harm her connection to the Kaiju, if it sensed the blasphemous notions. But there was no better place to reach the Kaiju than here.

Regardless of anything else, whether Raythe was right or not, it was clear that the istariol and the Guardian Spirit were linked – and that if the invaders prevailed, they would destroy it.

How do I make the Kaiju see the danger?

Drawing on memories of Hetaru, her murdered mentor and guide, she stilled her mind, letting go of fear and confusion, until she felt calm and ready. Then she took her stand in the middle of the stones and faced the lake, raising her hands and beginning to chant words she hoped would draw the Kaiju to her.

Istariol . . . Kaiju . . . Kiken Shou – danger – and, just in case, *Kemara . . .*

Istariol . . . Kaiju . . . Kiken Shou . . .

At first, the words were just sounds and the Dreamer could attach no meaning to them. Then the name *Kemara* was repeated, rousing it . . .

Kemara . . .

That sound, that *name*, snapped the Dreamer back to wakefulness.

The sacrifice was named Kemara, it remembered. *It is her memories I have been experiencing.*

Those thoughts coalesced once more and suddenly *she* awoke, in a rush of old remembrances, visions made up of light and sound and emotions, from love to anguish to terror to drudgery, and oceans of loss and sadness that flooded her senses. She almost drowned in the over-whelming flood that filled her consciousness, pouring like water into lungs, but the Dreamer cradled her in safety, and permitted her to regain her sense of self. They became separate entities again.

I am Kemara, the woman realised, her first conscious thought in what felt like a very long time. *I'm not dreaming.*

How do you contain all those thoughts? the Dreamer – visible to her as a vast Eye filling the sky – asked in a voice that resonated through her being.

I have to, she answered. *They are everything I am.*

I want to live as you do, the Dreamer boomed. *But I can't.*

She gaped, floundering for understanding . . . and then realised that this *immense* being had taken her into itself, then pulled out all her memories and experiences, driven not by malice but curiosity, jealousy and hunger. And in doing so, she now knew it for what it was.

It's the istariol, she realised. *This being is the istariol's consciousness – it's alive – like a tree with giant roots extending everywhere, for miles and miles.*

But what am I now? She remembered having a body once, and being swallowed up . . .

You were given to me, a gift, the Dreamer boomed. *A sacrifice.*

That wasn't right, she knew, but it was clearly how the Dreamer understood it. And then she heard that voice again, calling, *KEMARA*.

That's me, she thought. *That's my name.* Her memories supplied a face: a beautiful, vivacious, brown-skinned woman, a voice full of impu-dence and wisdom, someone she admired. And a name came: *Rima*.

She's calling us, she told the Dreamer. *We must answer.*

In Magnia and Bolgravia, the pagan gods of Death were men, all super-seded by the Pitlord of Deist theology. But in many other cultures, Death was a woman. In Ferrea, she was a spectral beauty who rose from waterways to drown the living; in Shadra, a monstrous being with a serpent's tail and a woman's torso dwelling under the earth. And to the Krodeshi, Death was a skeletal woman on a white horse who took the weak and unwary.

Teirhinan Deathless knew the myth, and guessed that many in the Bolgravian division would have a superstitious terror of her. The last Krodeshi patrol she'd encountered had made evil eye gestures, gibbering prayers as she passed.

When I find my own giant spirit to enslave, I'll become Lady Death in truth, she vowed, her hand straying to the place between her breasts where her heart-stone usually lay. That Toran Zorne now had it both terrified and reassured her – but she'd had no choice, and she believed that his unswerving love of the empire meant he'd be true.

If I were more alive, would he care for me? she wondered. She'd given up emotions when she became Deathless, but she had been very young, perhaps too young to understand the wounds she was inflicting on herself. But with each passing year, the loneliness of her existence became harder to bear.

Once I've enslaved one of these guardian spirits and destroyed Luc Mandaryke, I'll find a way of inhabiting a body that doesn't kill it. This body she wore wasn't her first. Every new body ended up the same way, a stinking, decaying mess, forcing her to take another before society turned on her.

Zorne sympathises with the girl, she mused jealously. *Perhaps I'll inhabit her next.*

The changing landscape pulled her back from her reveries: the rolling green was giving way to brown rocky hills and stinking fens. Steam came pouring through breaks in the earth's thin crust and bubbling in the swampy pools.

Darkness was falling, but Teirhinan's exhausted horse obeyed her commands to push on. She'd ridden all night, a shadow among the shadows, and now the east was painted in lurid scarlet smears, lighting up an artist's impression of the Pit. She slowed and sniffed the air, listening with all her senses.

Kemara, she heard – not with her ears, but with her soul. *Kemara*.

That was the name Zorne had mentioned: a mizra-witch who'd been among the fugitives. The voice kindled other images and memories ripped from Zarelda Vyre's mind: a native woman with a cloud of curly hair, a thick-lipped, tattooed face, pretty in an alien way.

Rima: that was the woman she sought, and she was somewhere in these hills. Such a call could be heard for many miles; it was an itch in her mind, luring her on, but she reined in her horse at the edge of a steaming ribbon of water winding out of dreary hills. She closed her eyes, listening to that elusive call, trying to gauge distance and direction.

The horse trembled. It knew she was a predator and longed to flee, but she held its heartstrings. 'Be still,' she whispered, sliding from its back. Shod hooves made sounds that carried, even in these swirling, gaseous clouds. 'Remain here.'

She planted her feet, listened again, and smiled.

Yes, this way . . . into the mists. Far, but not too far.

She tied the pale horse to a bush, contemplated taking her water bottle, then left it behind: this dying body wouldn't require sustenance any more. She absently stroked the place where her heart-stone should be, shivered a little, then advanced into the mists as the eastern horizon lit up pale red-gold, the colours caught on the rising steam.

The pale horse watched her vanish, scared to move until she was gone.

Then, once it was alone, thirsty and exhausted, it shuffled to the pool. The water was warm and bitter, but it drank anyway. Then it staggered and fell, shuddered and went still.

Hours had passed and Rima's throat was hoarse. She'd been calling all night from the stone circle, preserved from the cold by the heat of the steam rising from the lake. A scarlet sunrise soaked the steam in rose and gold, eerily beautiful. Her throat was dry and sore and her heart breaking.

The Kaiju hadn't answered.

I've made a mistake. I'm needed elsewhere, but I followed my own selfish desires here.

Miles to the west, Shiazar was gathering her people as the enemy closed in on them. Very soon, the chieftains would gather to devise their stratagems of battle.

They'll die in glory, and I shall live on in shame.

'Kaiju, why won't you come?' she called. 'Please, hear me and come!'

But the only sounds were the hiss of steam and distant sounds of birds, chittering in annoyance at her voice breaking their slumbers. The warm fog over the lake clogged her lungs and her eyes stung.

'Kaiju, Kaiju,' she cried again, fighting not to sound as forlorn as she felt, 'hear me, I beg you! Give us your aid!' and then one last time, 'Kemara!'

Nothing came, just the mocking silence.

I'm here when I should be with my people.

'Mokomoko,' she called sadly, rising up. 'Come to me.'

Rima's familiar had been off exploring, but it came flashing back into her as she mournfully gathered her cloak around her and turned to go, struggling to deal with the bitterness of failure. It was now light enough to see for a few dozen yards, so she scanned the steaming surface of the pool one last time, then sagged and turned to find the rocky path through the noxious fens again.

Then she stopped as a silhouette formed in the mist, blocking her path.

It was a woman.

'Kemara?' she gasped, her heart thudding with hope.

But the woman who emerged was no one she knew: a grey-haired waif with the complexion of a week-old corpse, clad in a torn and soiled Tangato kimono: a white woman who stank like rotting meat, her reek discernible even amid the fumes of the swamp. Her limbs were crooked and she limped with a weirdly insectoid gait.

'Rima, yes?' she rasped, her violet eyes lighting up. 'You are Rima?'

'Mokomoko,' Rima muttered, sensing that she was the prey here. *'Kaneska o maho, junbi suru.'* Prepare yourself ... Energy flowed in and she shaped her fingers while calling in Gengo-Magnian, 'Who are you?'

'Teirhinan,' the pale figure trilled, her tones girlish. 'I'm looking for something, and a friend of yours gave me your name. Zarelda Vyre – you know her, yes. She is my very good friend.'

You don't look like anyone's friend, Rima thought, her stomach tightening. 'Told you when?'

'Just yesterday,' the woman replied, taking a few steps forward. 'Such a good friend. You and I can be friends too, yes. So much we could share.'

Rima engaged full maho-sight and saw a pale bird familiar on Teirhinan's left shoulder and a dark beast on her right, some kind of leathery winged rodent. Both snarled menacingly when they realised she could see them.

Two familiars? How—?

The woman, clearly a sorceress, bared yellowed, rotting teeth. 'Yield, girl. It'll hurt less.'

Rima took a step back as her skin prickled in response to the energy crackling into being in the woman's hands. Violence became clearly inevitable, even though her own instincts were to avert conflict. But this creature looked like a wakened corpse and meant her ill.

'Mokomoko, junbi suru kazei,' she said. *Ready the wind.* The air swirled around, steam dancing in a spiral as she backed up to give herself space.

'We don't have to do this,' she warned the woman, unhooking the stone *patu* club from her waistband, hooking the loop over her wrist, then conjuring shields.

The grey woman cackled. 'Oh, I think we do,' she said, with relish, then she began mumbling – it sounded like gibberish, though it contained snatches of words Rima knew, as if she were speaking two languages at once. The two creatures on her shoulders shrieked and plunged into her, and her aura went puce.

They both lashed out at once, Rima commanding a blast of air that hammered the stick-like girl backwards ... but then she shrieked as unseen claws shredded her shields and lacerated her belly, four claw-rips with blood welling, a moment before another unseen hand gripped her throat and squeezed.

As she was blacking out, she managed to croak, '*Cuzka joki*—' and jabbed her splayed fingers at the advancing sorceress. Instantly, super-heated poisonous gases streamed in from the pools on either side of them, enveloping Teirhinan in what should have been a deadly cloud.

She emerged laughing, 'Pathetic. Is that all you have, girl?'

A second set of claws ripped at Rima's face, but she threw up a hand as they coalesced before her and instead the skin on her arm was ripped open. The grip round her throat tightened – then she was slammed onto her back, knocking the wind out of her.

Teirhinan landed on her a moment later, settling on her bleeding belly and giggling as she gripped her neck physically while she caressed Rima's face with her right hand. The foulness of her stench made Rima retch, filling her throat with bile.

The sorceress gazed down at her, crooning, 'Come out, little familiar. Come to me.'

Rima felt Mokomoko clinging to her, like a climber on a cliff, grip-ping by his fingertips as gravity tore at his grasp. The sorceress' maw opened, a tunnel of rotting fangs, ready to swallow.

Then Rima pulled all the energy inside her into a pulse of force that hurled the witch up into the air and away – then rolled over, her stom-ach wounds shrieking at the violent movement, her throat burning with acid. Somehow she got to her knees, reeling with nausea, spitting to clear her mouth of the foul taste.

Teirhinan landed like a spider, cackling. 'Strong, girl – and con-trolled. Not praxis or mizra either, but something new. We're going to have such an *interesting* talk ...'

Rima got one foot beneath her, thoughts unscrambling as she tried to rise, fighting through the pain and sucking air down her tortured windpipe. She restored shields and channelled energy from the earth into her stone club, then retreated to the edge of the pool as the sorceress stalked her, clearly in no hurry.

'Two familiars,' Rima croaked, stalling for time. 'Impossible.'

'See? We'll have so much to share.' Teirhinan leered at her. 'I want to know you, inside out.'

She slammed a fist of air at her, but Rima saw this one coming and blocked with the stone patu, hurling herself aside as a dark, scythe-like blade of energy slashed at her. As she landed, her belly tore further and more blood welled out, draining her further.

'Help me, Kagemori,' she whispered.

Teirhinan scuttled sideways, patient and wary. 'Yield, girl,' she urged again. 'All the advantages are mine. You see, one factor limits any sorcerer: their mortality. Exceeding your limits will always kill you. But I have no such limit, for I am dead already.' She giggled. 'Isn't that a wonderful thing? Shall I show you how it's done?'

Rima gave ground, interposing the stone club, primed with energy, trying to read where the next attack would come from.

She can use magic to disable and kill – but can she fight hand-to-hand? she wondered. Not many sorcerers were also skilled warriors.

'I don't think you can show me anything, you stinking carcase.' She wanted to goad her foe into error. 'My only question is this: do blowflies lay eggs in your *puta*?'

Teirhinan's eyes bulged, her body going rigid. '*Nobody* speaks to me like that, girl.'

'Dead already, are you?' Rima drawled, edging to her right. 'I can smell that – not even a vulture would want to eat you.'

The grey sorceress shrieked in anger and sprang . . .

. . . while Rima feinted right before stepping aside and as Teirhinan lurched into her reach, stepped in and crunched her edged club through Teirhinan's shielding, shattering her right arm at the elbow, before spinning away from a counter-sweep of claws. Rima pirouetted, then hammered the stone weapon into the woman's jaw, shattering teeth and bone and hurling her sideways.

Got you!

She planted her feet and went in again, but Teirhinan – who should surely have been unconscious or at least stunned by that blow – scuttled aside with inhuman speed ... but not quite quickly enough to avoid a shattering blow to the left knee-cap. She wailed and collapsed, and Rima dropped to one knee over her torso and crashed the patu down on the woman's head, smashing her skull in.

Teirhinan went into spasm, limbs flailing, even the broken ones, until Rima, gritting her teeth, crashed the club down yet again, this time smashing the skull open like a pumpkin, splattering grey brain tissue everywhere.

The grey sorceress thrashed a moment longer, then finally collapsed and went limp.

Rima stepped back, panting, and gave thanks to her gods.

If she's indicative of the empire, may a plague take them all ...

All of a sudden, she felt utterly *disgusting*. Her skin was crawling at the thought of the other woman's blood and brain tissue all over her, and the wounds in her belly were deep and painful. As the adrenalin ebbed, she felt herself swaying. She went for her water flask to rinse out her mouth and wash the wounds, using her cloak lining to wipe away what she could of the gore.

Then she heard a strange sucking sound, spun – and stared, open-mouthed.

Teirhinan was sitting up, her caved-in skull reforming as Rima gaped, although it was far from perfect, malformed and askew, while her broken limbs popped and snapped back into something approaching straight.

The undead sorceress rose like a puppet being pulled erect by invisible strings, her jaw reforming enough for her to slur, 'Did I mention that I can't be killed?'

Her claws grew an extra six inches, as she advanced again.

Rima called to Mokomoko, trying to rekindle the flow of energy in her limbs, but blood-loss and post-combat shock had set in too deeply.

She backed up, stepping into the warm, oily pool, her legs boneless and her mind unable to face the impossible any longer.

'I don't think we're going to be friends any more,' Teirhinan snarled.

Rima raised her patu defiantly.

Then a vast rush of water behind her erupted and she spun, heart in mouth, to see something massive rising from the steaming pool. A giant serpent, its head as large as a meeting house, black as granite with eyes the colour of blood and a gaping maw, roared. Steaming mud and water cascaded over slime-encrusted teeth as it loomed over her, jaws widening.

2

The Keys to the Kingdom

Zarelda sat in her darkened room, too numbed by horror to think.

It was two days since she'd inadvertently led Luc and his people to the Heart Chamber – two days of utter misery. She was now confined to her tiny suite, a few doors away from Onkado, but unable to visit him. Servants brought meals and cleaned her rooms under the constant supervision of the armed guards. And of course, her powers remained locked away: even in her absence, Teirhinan's binding spell remained.

It left her a lot of time free for bitter reflection and self-recrimination. *I've doomed everyone,* she wailed inside. *I led Luc to that chamber and now who can stop him?*

She buried her head in her hands as the tears flowed yet again, weeping her way into oblivion and wishing she could stay there.

When she next woke, it was to the door being unlocked. She sat up on her bed as it swung open and her mother entered. Mirella shut it in the guards' faces, then stood facing Zar, composed and distant. This was the woman Zar remembered in Perasdyne, the socialite who always had better things to do than take an interest in her daughter.

'Well, Zaza, no one can doubt your allegiances, can they?' She sighed. 'You stupid girl.'

Zar raised her tear-streaked face. 'Krag off.'

Mirella snorted under her breath. 'You need to change your colours, Zaza. I can keep him wrapped round my finger only so long without producing another, but . . .' She *tsked* and admitted, 'My womb betrays me. I've had three miscarriages in a row. He could easily put us both aside – and you give him *nothing* to counterbalance that.'

Zar wiped away her tears. 'So that's your big concern, is it? That megalomaniac has just been given unlimited power, but you're worried about your seat at the table? Gerda on High, you're a selfish bitch!'

'Zaza—'

'*Don't* call me that. I'm not a baby.'

Mirella's face hardened, then she began to pace. 'We have to find a way to get you back in his good books.'

Zar curled her lip. 'What, are you losing your allure?'

Mirella stamped her foot in frustration. 'Why are you like this? Damn Raythe – damn him to the Pit!' Then, in a plaintive voice, she said, 'I'm still your mother, Zaza,' and she opened her arms, offering an embrace.

Zar eyed her coldly, then sighed. 'Yes, you're still my mother,' she said, making a show of relenting and letting herself be hugged.

'I'm doing my best for both of us, dear,' Mirella said in her ear, stroking her cheek, then, stepping back, asked, 'Can't you just do the same? All's not lost, so long as we give Luc something to care about.'

Zar set her jaw, bit back a sarcastic response and instead mumbled, 'I'll try.'

Mirella looked at her, clearly not believing her for an instant. When she left, the door locked behind her.

Alone again, Zar opened her right hand and examined the brooch she'd just stolen from her mother's dress. It had a strong pin, perfect for another skill Raythe had taught her.

'Raythe, we have to move,' Jesco called. 'Those cannon are almost ready to fire.'

'Not yet,' Raythe answered, peering through his spyglass across the stream.

They'd spent two days traversing the Icewastes and spent a day recovering at the edge of the volcanic fens Rima had vanished into. The fourth day had taken them into the rugged back country of the

Wakatoa lands. When they finally reached the tribe's hill-fort, they discovered it was even smaller and less defensible than Puketapu's.

Unfortunately, the enemy scouts located the village soon after their arrival. There'd been a sharp skirmish at the ford south of the village; the only good fortune was that the stream was running high from the winter rains and its towering banks were difficult to climb – and therefore to attack across. All day, their best shots had been trading sporadic fire with Otravian sharpshooters lurking in the bushes on either side of the stream.

Now six horse-drawn Otravian cannon had appeared and were being deployed, out of flintlock range, on a low ridge.

'They're in position,' Jesco fretted. 'I can see them sighting on us right now. We're well within range here, Raythe. It really is time we left.'

'In a moment,' Raythe said. 'Damn it, I hate facing my own people.'

'I hate running away from that prick Torland,' Jesco replied, in a strained voice. 'But mostly I hate artillery bombardments, almost as much as I hate being underground, and you know how I feel about that.'

'Oh, that bad?' Raythe winked. 'All right, let's get out, then.'

Together, they darted towards Sitoko's nearby observation post. A moment later, conch shell horns preserved for centuries as tribal treasures droned softly, so as not to carry to enemy ears, and the snipers they'd deployed began squirming back through the undergrowth, just as the first Otravian cannon boomed. The range-finder fell well short, endangering only their own men.

With any luck they won't realise there's no one here until after the bombardment is over, Raythe thought watching everyone crawl to the rear, then file down the far side of the rise, just as the cannon battery really opened up. At first distant booms resounded through the hills, then the explosions drew closer as the teams got their sights in.

Safely out of sight and range, Raythe's troops formed a ragged column that wound back towards the village. Raythe joined Sitoko as they retreated. The rangatira was in a jovial mood. 'Your enemy commanders are foolish,' he chuckled, 'wasting all that fire and noise on nobody.'

'They gain their rank through money, nepotism and conspiracies,' Raythe replied. 'They're deadly at those, but not so much with actual soldiering.'

Sitoko scratched his head. 'How can such a thing be?'

'Usually imperial victory is assured, so the real battle is over dividing the spoils and taking credit. That's politics, not warfare.'

'Madness.'

'I don't deny it.' He glanced over his shoulder, where the sounds of the bombardment were intensifying. 'They'll keep firing for another twenty minutes, then send infantry forward. We must be long gone by then.'

They caught up with Shiazar's main group in a camp to the north, just in time to look back and see smoke engulfing the village five miles behind them. The Wakatoa wailed in dismay to see their home so defiled, and the sullen red glow was still lighting the eastern horizon as the sun set in the west.

Raythe joined his Magnians, who were preparing a meal. They thronged about him, seeking reassurance, though he had little to give, knowing they couldn't run for ever. He forced a confident air though, saying, 'We eluded the enemy again. We're still in the game.'

'You got any sway with them Otravians, Lor' Vyre?' Jed Vine called. 'Can ye talk 'em round?'

'Those are Mandaryke's men, Jed. You all know what he did.'

'He's guvnor of the west now,' someone murmured fearfully.

'And a backstabbing traitor,' Raythe added. 'There'll be some among them who sympathise with us, Jed, but remember, Otravia's been under imperial sway for five years now. We have no choice but to treat them as enemies.'

'We going to fight here or move on?' Reed Selfert asked.

'Aye, we're out on our feet, Lor' Vyre,' Betta Gorly put in. 'We're needing rest, for sure.'

'That's still to be decided,' Raythe answered. 'I'm off to see Queen Shiazar now. The chiefs will have ideas, and I've a few of my own. We'll work it out. Get some food in you, and a good sleep.'

With that he left them to find the Queen's pavilion. The glorious scarlet sunset prophesised clear skies – or maybe that should have been blood – for the following day. The planetary rings carved a shining arc over the rose-gold canopy, which was broken only by thick cloud on the southern horizon.

An evening for painters and lovers, Raythe recited, a verse from an old song. Humming the tune, he joined the Queen's assembled council of rangatiras and their mahotsu-kai. He was greeted with polite wariness by the other chieftains; the conflict and his perceived competence were slowly breaking down their distrust of him.

There was no actual pavilion, just a circle round a fire, with everyone on mats near Shiazar's throne. She was in her war-gear, as usual; tonight's mask was half black, half white, which apparently signified major decisions. Three options had been suggested: to surrender and accept servitude as the price for preserving their people; to flee the land entirely and seek new territories in Verdessa or beyond; or to fight on, knowing they risked extinction.

Natomo tearfully urged surrender, but Sitoko and others counselled fighting right here, believing it was better to die than to yield and become enslaved.

Brave but suicidal. Raythe respected that, but he argued instead for making a new life in another land. 'If we can just slip down that glacier path, the whole of Verdessa awaits, and from there, the whole of north-west Pelaria opens up: forest land, almost entirely uninhabited. Take it and claim it for your own and build a new kingdom.'

'But it's not ours,' the other chieftains replied stonily. 'This is our land, our Fenua Tangato, the land of our ancestors. How can we face them in the Beyond and say we fled the place where their bones lie?'

The arguments went round in circles, until Shiazar called for silence, and told them her decision. 'We will fight on – but not here. I will not surrender our land and nor will I permit a vainglorious "last stand",' she told her chieftains. 'We do not fight to lose honourably. We fight to win. If that means years of striking from the shadows, so be it. We will make these invaders dread the Fenua Tangato.'

The decision was well-received, and the meeting broke up with a sense of positivity and determination. Raythe was about to leave when a Yokei asked him to attend on the Queen. He found her outside, the decision mask tilted up on her head, gazing at the planetary rings. She looked tired, something he'd not seen before, which was comforting in a way, humanising her. He felt a sense of kinship; he was all too aware of the burdens of leadership.

'Your decision to fight on was a good one,' he told her.

'But not what you counselled,' she noted lightly.

'Majesty, I am not Tangato. I do not share the connection of your people to this land. To me it's just soil, no better nor worse than any other place. But you understand your own people better than I.'

'I might understand them, but you understand the enemy.'

'Aye – and those red-coated men are my own countrymen,' he reminded her.

'Who leads them?' she asked.

'Nemath Torland. They call him "Torch" in Otravia, because he's responsible for so many funeral pyres, particularly among minorities – homosexuals especially, though he's one himself.'

'He sounds vile,' Shiazar commented.

'Aye, that he is. But as Luc's man, he's untouchable.'

'Not out here.'

He smiled slowly, admiring this grim, vengeful side of her. 'Aye, not out here.'

'And what of this Luc Mandaryke?"

'Part of me wants to ride to Rath Argentium and challenge him to a duel or some such nonsense,' he confessed. 'But it also gives me hope that Zar is safe, because she's his wife's daughter.'

'And your former wife is here as well?'

'Apparently,' he said stonily. 'He'd be a fool to leave Mirella behind in Otravia.'

'Is she so faithless?'

'I'm not the one to ask. I thought she was an angel, right up until the moment she left me for Luc. Now I think of her as a Pit-Hag. It's taken me years to stop loving her.'

As he spoke, he realised that those unconscious words were true: he really had stopped loving Mirella. He looked at Shiazar, thinking, *Perhaps that's because I'm falling in love with you.*

She met his gaze, her expression impassive, and then half-bowed. 'Good night, Rangatira Raythe. Rest well. We've another long journey tomorrow.'

Next morning, Raythe assembled his Magnians and told them, 'We're heading southwest into Manowai lands. Apparently they're ideal for hiding out: there are rocky heights and swampy fenlands, a right maze. From there, we'll be using hit-and-run tactics to make Mandaryke wish he'd never come here.'

'That the same Manowai lot who tried to wipe us out a few months ago?' old Unwyn Rosset asked, his dubious voice causing an anxious stir.

'They've had a change of leadership,' Raythe reminded them. He waved forward a diminutive Tangato with a whiskery face and a shaven head, save for a greying mane of hair along the ridge of his skull. 'This is Utaka. He's the Manowai who will be guiding us today. Let's get our vulnerable ones to safety, then we can take the fight to Luc's people.'

The Magnians eyed the newcomer dubiously, but Utaka just grinned and bowed to them, before extending an arm, pointing westwards. 'Is path,' he managed in Gengo-Magnian. 'Now you come.'

Raythe set the example, picking up his pack and striding off, and in minutes everyone else had hefted their remaining possessions and were gingerly making their way down heavily wooded slopes towards the valley where the Potowai River flowed eastwards out of Manowai territory. A heavy bank of fog shrouded the lowlands from view.

It wasn't until mid-afternoon that the wind lifted, the mist broke up . . . and with the Tangato and Magnians strung out along the Potowai valley, the trouble began.

'I don't like this,' Jesco Duretto muttered. 'Where's that blasted guide? What's his name?'

'Utaka,' Vidar rumbled, sniffing the air. 'He's nowhere near here.'

'I thought Raythe told him to stay close,' Jesco fumed. He looked behind him, where about half of their people – a hundred men, women and children – were clustered, watching him anxiously. 'I hate being left in charge. It's much more fun criticising Raythe's decisions. He's still with the Queen, isn't he?'

'He is – but Varahana will be here in about half an hour,' Vidar commented. 'She's just rounding up some stragglers. We'll decide what to do then.'

The way ahead was looking problematic: apart from the trees fringing the river, the valley was exposed grassland – and they'd already seen enemy outriders and columns of red-coated infantry: General Torland, divining their intent, was clearly force-marching his men to try and cut them off.

The only good fortune so far was that the redjacks had stuck to the easier route and not ventured to the river . . . but Jesco's scouts were reporting that a detachment of horsemen had been spotted descending to the valley floor, seeking water, and they were, apparently unknowingly, blocking the way forward.

'Do we go round?' Jesco grumbled 'Do we go back?'

'All I know,' said Vidar, 'is that we can't go forward until this lot move on.'

'What's across the river?'

'Marshland, then hills. But it's not an easy crossing, and the swamp looks dangerous. We need our blasted guide,' Vidar concluded grumpily. 'Bloody Manowai . . .'

Jesco bit his lip, then groaned as another group of cavalry appeared over a distant rise – and this lot were bearing the regimental banner.

Alarmed, he put his spyglass to his eye, because they had the look of a command group – and he was right: the plumes worn by the man in the middle marked him out as the Otravian general.

'Vid, look: it's Nemath Torland himself.'

'That's not good,' Vidar growled. 'He's supposed to be at least a dozen miles behind us.'

'The bastard's guessed our route,' Jesco swore. 'He's got that little snitch Sonata with him, too.'

'Who?'

'See the woman?'

Vidar, his bearskin eyes sharper than even Jesco's spyglass, grunted, 'Aye. A looker.'

'Nice you think so. "She" is a man – Torland's favourite slice of rump.'

Vidar coloured, 'I didn't actually think she ... um, *he* ... was a looker.'

Jesco grinned. 'Uh huh.'

'I was being ironic,' the bearskin muttered. 'Didn't Torland command the Purge in Otravia?'

'Aye, he did – but that didn't mean he changed his tastes, or showed any mercy to his old friends in the midnight flock.' Jesco lowered his spyglass. 'Much though I'd love to take a shot at that bastard, we've got to move. We'll backtrack and look for a ford.'

They placated the worries of the waiting Magnians, then Jesco sought out Gan Corbyn.

'Gan, pick a dozen men for a rearguard. I'll stay with you; Varahana will take everyone else into the trees along the river to find a ford and cross.'

'It's jus' swamp o'er t'way,' the hunter pointed out.

'Aye, but it's just redjacks ahead of us,' Jesco replied. 'If they've already caught Utaka, that might explain why he's not here.'

'Or the shifty mutt's abandoned us,' he grumbled.

'Let's give him the benefit of the doubt, Gan,' Jesco urged. 'Keep your dozen here until we reach the river, then join us, covering our backs.'

He turned to Jami Pick and Rawleston Sorley. 'You lads, find us a crossing.'

The two younger man hurried off just as Mater Varahana escorted the last families in. Once Jesco had briefed her, the three of them got the main body of refugees moving. Worried families hushed scared children, but so far, no one was panicking. Anxious minutes crawled by, everyone dreading the sound of fighting – or worse, a cavalry detachment appearing on their flank – but they reached the trees undetected and quickly got under cover.

Vidar and Jesco stayed at the edge, and were soon joined by the rearguard under Gan Corbyn, retreating at a backwards walk, facing the south in a loose skirmish line.

Just as they were thinking they'd got away with it, the riders they'd seen earlier came pounding over a rise, and drew up, pointing down at them excitedly. Then a signal trumpet blared.

Jesco looked back, estimating the distance, but it was too far: they were a good hundred yards or more short of the trees; and the Bolgravs outnumbered them two to one. The horsemen began whipping out pistols and sabres as they advanced.

The Magnians were readying their own flintlocks and drawing bows with practised hands.

'Gunmen, archers, fan out,' Jesco ordered. 'Pick your targets, but hold your fire.'

As the Otravian horsemen trotted forward, Jesco saw to the priming of his own long-barrelled flintlock, then at sixty yards, a comfortable range for such weapons, shouted 'Aim . . . and . . . fire!'

The lead riders reeled at the ragged volley and several went down, although it was mostly the horses hit – but instead of continuing the advance, the rest wheeled sideways in either direction, cracking off pistol shots. A lead ball screamed by Jesco's ear, another kicked up the turf between his feet and two of his men shrieked, clutching their stomachs.

Once their second defensive volley had scattered the horsemen, Jesco got his men moving again, friends supporting the wounded.

'To the river, fast as you can, but stay together,' he called. 'Vid and I will catch you up.'

Gan's men soon vanished into the trees, while Jesco and Vidar watched the Otravian outriders milling about, waiting for orders. They could see an officer speaking to a bugler; signals sounded and after a moment, distant responses could be heard. The ground was rumbling now, so more enemy were approaching, out of sight but numerous.

You're in the wrong place, Raythe, Jesco fretted. *Get here, now. This is about to get messy.*

Some of the biggest battles of the Bolgravian Conquests had begun by accident, when armies who had no idea the other was near had just blundered into each other. This was beginning to feel very much that way.

'C'mon,' Jesco muttered, as he and Vidar fell back beneath the willows shrouding the sunlight. 'Let's find the river.'

When they reached the near bank they discovered they were standing on the higher bank, looking down on a sluggish, murky flow of water; the current was almost at standstill, thanks to the fenlands on the far side. There was no trace of Varahana's civilians or Gan's scouts; Jesco hoped that meant they'd already found a ford nearby.

Vidar found footprints and gestured west, upstream. 'They all went that way.'

As they began to jog, a shot rang out and a lead ball hit the tree right next to Jesco. He took cover, and soon spotted a green-coated sharpshooter peering through the gloom, and another one taking aim. He jerked aside as the second shot whistled past.

Damn, too close.

But they weren't quite alone: their own men returned fire from just ahead: two of Elgus Rhamp's former mercenaries, led by Falgram and Aramak. The blond Norgans were reloading smoking flintlocks with the look of men enjoying themselves. Jesco and Vidar, racing to join them, topped a low wooded ridge and found the main body of Magnians standing by a ford of sorts. The women and children were already hip-deep in the water.

303

'There's more of them ahead of us, sweeping the woods,' Falgram told Vidar, pointing southeast. 'We cross here, or nowhere.'

'We have to protect the crossing until Vara's people are away,' Jesco said, looking round until he spotted Gan Corbyn. 'Gan, take your group west, form a cordon, will you? Vidar, round up a dozen more to help us here.'

Vidar selected men and women armed with long flintlocks and positioned them in overlapping perimeters, one facing southeast, the other looking west.

Redjacks began to appear amid the trees, guided in by the sharp-shooters. Shouting to each other, they all hovered just out of reliable range, respectful of the marksmanship they'd encountered. But within a few minutes, hundreds of red-coated men could be seen in the distance, forming up lines several waves deep, facing the ford.

'They're goin' to try us, Jes,' Gan Corbyn shouted, a moment before the bugles rang out the charge. With a great cry, the Otravians came marching forward.

'Hold fire – hold your fire . . . aim . . .' Jesco called, and as the redjacks came into range, he yelled, *'Fire!'*

With a staccato rattle the guns belched smoke, punching holes in the scarlet ranks – but there were too many to slow them down this time and the second rank came on, stepping over their dead compatriots, blasting back at the defenders before stowing pistols and baring sabres, ready to seek enemies who were little more that shadows and muzzle-flashes.

Had Jesco's men panicked and run, things could have gone very badly, but anchored by the war-trained mercenaries, they held to their cover and protected by tree trunks and boulders, remained virtually untouched, despite the hail of lead that came their way.

The exposed Otravians were definitely getting the worse of it, until those who'd come through unscathed hit the Magnian cordon, and Jesco's tiny force started fighting for their lives. His sword flashing, he deflected a sabre, gutted the attacker. Spinning away, he danced beneath another pair of blades while thrusting up under the ribs of one, then turning on the other, shouted, 'Ira Shadra, ira Shadra!' as battle fury ignited in him. For a few moments all he saw was steel and blood, then a counter-rush led by Vidar and the mercenaries broke up the attack and the redjacks fell back.

A big arm grabbed Jesco from behind as he went to pursue. 'Easy, Jes,' Vidar said.

The familiar voice calmed him. 'E dueno,' Jesco murmured. 'I'm good.'

'Thought it was supposed to be me who lost it in a fight,' the bearskin chuckled.

'I was always in control,' Jesco panted. 'Can we cross now?'

Vidar pointed through the trees, where another wave of Otravian redjacks were already stamping into the gloom of the trees. 'We go now and they'll be shooting us in the back as we cross. We've got to hold this next wave.' He lifted his voice. 'Reload, lads! Second wave coming!'

They saw to their own weapons and prepared those pilfered from fallen enemies as the edge of the woods filled up with redjacks. The bugles sounded the advance – then another fanfare heralded the arrival of the command group, visible, but too far off for reliable shooting. He saw Nemath Torland and 'Lady' Sonata directing the advance, and Otravian soldiers cheering as if the fight was already won.

Join the attack, Nemath, Jesco muttered. *Give me one shot at you and I'll die happy.*

The drums began – *rat-a-tat-tat, rat-a-tat-tat* – and the redjack lines began to move forward . . .

'Where are the Tangato?' Aramak, reloading behind the next willow, muttered to Jesco.

Jesco had no answer to that, and didn't bother to try. 'Pick your targets,' he shouted. 'Make every shot count. This'll get messy, so hearken to my voice – and may Deo and Gerda be with us all.'

It's not Deo or Gerda we need, he thought grimly. *We need Raythe or*

Shiazar or whoever to realise that we're in deep shit and get their arses here, right now . . .

The fighting – too brief and sporadic to label it a 'battle' but too deadly to dismiss as a skirmish – had set Nemath Torland's nerves on edge. This wasn't war as he liked it, with galloping cavalry and valorous charges; it was more a disorganised muddle with shots coming from all directions from a foe they could barely see. It was all absolute confusion, and a thorough disappointment.

His useless scouts insisted there were no more than a dozen men, women and children in the narrow strip of trees, but the fire that had poured out of the woods as his men advanced had left him certain that they had stumbled upon far more than that. His soldiers – who despised him for what he was – were losing heart, sick and tired from being blasted from hiding by foes who then melted away.

I have to take charge, he kept telling himself. *I have to gain control. I wish I could see the whole battlefield – it's impossible to coordinate the attacks properly.* But the combination of mist and black powder smoke made that impossible.

He couldn't bear the humiliation of reporting this to Luc Mandaryke if it didn't end well, but he knew better than to expose himself. Heroes ended up dead, and his plumes made him a prime target for the enemy. So he stayed under cover and sent his aides off to pass on his orders. He kept trying to persuade Sonata to go the rear, but her blood was up and she wanted to be in at the kill – especially as someone had reported seeing Jesco Duretto somewhere amongst the trees.

'I want that bastard – I am going to personally castrate him!' she kept insisting.

'Did he jilt you or something?' he asked thoughtlessly.

Sonata bared her teeth. '*No one* gets to jilt me,' she snarled, which didn't really answer the question.

But his favourite regiment had arrived, lifting his spirits. The Gosstram Guard, the notorious 'Blackjacks', had helped him clean up the degenerates of Perasdyne. Colonel Bladyn led them into the clearing, stepping perfectly in time with the pulsing drumbeats. Torland was pleased to see the craggy-visaged officer had not given up his giant moustaches.

'Gosstram, form up!' Bladyn barked, then he snapped a salute at Torland. 'Orders, sir?'

'Duretto's here, holding the near side of a ford,' the general said curtly. 'We need to punch through and mop 'em up, Bladyn. Send them to the Pit.'

The colonel's iron face remained unchanged, but his eyes glinted. 'I'll bring you his body, sir,' he promised, saluting again, then he stomped away, bellowing orders. 'Blackjacks high!' he concluded. 'Blood and steel!'

The drums pounded and the black-jacketed men marched off into the trees.

Sonata nudged her horse to Torland's, leaned across and brushed his lips with hers. 'Let's follow,' she purred. 'I want to watch the annihilation of Jesco Duretto.'

Shit, it's the Blackjacks, Jesco realised as the next wave closed in. As the distance narrowed between his thin line of hunters and farmers and the ranks of highly trained and coordinated black-jacketed men, Jesco felt the hyperawareness of combat engulf him: he was aware of everything – the darting movements of the snipers, the blurring hands as they reloaded, the look of breathless relief every time a shot was discharged and the shooter pressed their back to their guardian tree or rock, praying. Each moment of continued survival was a triumph, a miracle and a gift.

They unleashed two volleys at the advancing lines of Blackjacks, then cowered as the Otravians returned rolling volleys which went smashing into trees and rocks and shredded the undergrowth. Despite the ferocity of the fire, there weren't too many casualties – but Gan Corbyn was shouting an order when the side of his head exploded.

Aramak and Hadric were caught trying to retreat, tumbling to the ground without a sound, and young Liddy Toll, who'd turned out to be a natural with the musket, was caught in the eye by a ricochet while she was reloading.

Then the blackjacks fixed bayonets and hefting their flintlocks like spears, came screaming forward.

Jesco's men fired one last deadly volley, and more of the soldiers fell bleeding or dead to the ground, then the bloodthirsty Blackjacks burst into their cordon – and Jesco exploded from cover to meet them.

He felt a shot graze his shoulder, but he was committed to his first blows, slashing his target's belly open, smashing his hilt into the jaw as he doubled over, then a straight thrust into the next man's ribs, kicking him off the blade as he fell – then, instinctively, he jerked aside just as an officer's pistol cracked, splintering the branch beside his face . . .

Beside him, Tawyn Fulter, who'd lost his brother Lew only months ago, was stabbed in the back by another blackjack; Jesco slashed the man's throat, then leaped between two boulders and found Falgram fighting for his life against two grinning soldiers. He gutted the nearest, leaving Falgram to swing his old-fashioned broadsword to hack down the other.

Then the man who'd shot at him reappeared, and Jesco spun, ducked under a slashing sabre and rammed his curved blade into the man's groin. When he ripped it sideways, the officer dropped to his knees, howling, bloody intestines bursting from his belly.

'Get to the ford,' Jesco shouted to Falgram. 'I've got your back.'

Falgram threw him a grateful look and took off – but as Jesco went to follow, something punched him in the thigh and he gasped as his leg gave way in a burst of white-hot agony. He collapsed and somehow managed to roll beneath a bush as men thudded past him, pursuing Falgram. With a monumental effort, Jesco wormed his way deeper into the thicket just before another squad thumped past, swearing loudly at the carnage he'd left in the clearing behind him.

'The ford's close by,' he heard someone say. 'Tell Blaydon to press on.'

By the Pit, Jesco realised, *that's Nemath Torland's voice!*

He pressed himself into the sodden ground, wincing at the pain in his thigh, as a rush of vivid memories overwhelmed him: wild parties, fountains of wine and tangled bodies, and a giddy feeling of freedom in giving voice to his true nature, hidden until he had reached Perasdyne and could be free.

Torland threw the best parties . . . and Sonata was everyone's muse . . .

Then he heard her voice and his heart thudded.

'I'm sure I saw Duretto,' she said softly. 'Just a glimpse, but I know how he moves.'

Aye, you do – and I know how you move, too, Jesco remembered. *I was so in love . . .*

But that was a long time ago, and a very different world. The faces of old friends and lovers floated before him, ghosts raised by her voice, and if he could, Jesco would have risen up and charged. But his gun was lost and his leg was useless.

Swallowing his pride and anger, he went to creep away . . .

. . . when someone touched his shoulder.

His head jerked, eyes bulging, as he saw a man looming over him. *Utaka –?*

The ugly little Manowai hunter, his face glistening with sweat, grinned at him and whispered, 'Utaka find. Manowai men, here now.'

Jesco felt his heart thud. *Deo does work in mysterious ways,* he thought dazedly.

But in the clearing, Sonata was saying, 'He must be close.'

A pistol cocked, and hooves thumped on the soft ground just a few yards away.

Then he heard Nemath Torland exclaim, 'Look – there!'

Guns cracked and lead tore through the undergrowth around him as Utaka, who threw himself on top of Jesco, gasped as his body jerked and went limp . . .

Nemath Torland caught sight of his prey lying in the mud under a small, brown-skinned man with an ugly, bulgy-eyed face.

Sonata fired—

—and the trees around them erupted with natives – *armed with Bolgravian guns.*

A hail of lead raked him and his escorts, who were shouting in alarm, but unlike the little native who had shielded Jesco, there was no one there to protect him. His horse was shot in the head and chest and the world lurched when it collapsed sideways, trapping his left leg in a quite horrendous blaze of pain. He howled in agony, pawing the earth for the blade he'd dropped, wondering if he could scrabble free, even though he'd felt his bones cracking under the dead weight of his horse.

'Help me!' Torland shrieked, looking round frantically. His aides had all been taken down, but there was Sonata, swaying in her saddle. '*Sonata!*' he shrilled, trying to move, but it hurt too much. '*Help me!*'

She looked down at him, her big, beautiful eyes round with horror – and only then did he see that she had her hands cradled in her lap, and blood was pumping through them.

'*No! Sonata—*'

She fell from her horse, face-down in the mud, and lay there, her body contorted and unmoving.

No—!

Then dark shapes loomed over him and something came down on his head . . .

Varahana felt like a shepherdess, herding her flock to safety – but the landscape across the river offered little promise of refuge. The fenland was a pathless morass of stagnant pools, muddy rivulets and lush, treacherous glades. Dozens of shingar lizards were stalking them; they had taken to beating the water, trying to keep them away. And all the while, the flintlocks rattled in the forest behind them.

Did I tell Vidar how I feel? she wondered. *Did I actually say the words?*

She couldn't remember, and now he was somewhere behind, lost in the fighting.

'*Gerda, please,*' she whispered, but here was another group of stragglers, Radia Woodburn's family, so she put her calm face back on and urged them to keep moving. Then the nearest armed man, bald, grey-bearded Pad Geldermark, his placid face taut with anxiety, raised a hand. 'Listen!'

The shooting was now sporadic, but they could hear lots of splashing, as if an entire regiment of men were running through the fens towards them. They had no chance of outrunning them; most of her charges were old men or women burdened with infants.

'Hide,' she told them urgently, 'anywhere you can.'

They scattered as dark shapes pelted out of the woods – then she squeaked in relief: the first few were their men, led by Falgram, the Norgan former mercenary, who was bloody and muddy but moving freely.

She rose and waved to attract his attention and as he squelched towards her, he called, 'We 'ad to fall back, Mater – they sent in the Blackjacks an' it were too much. Aramak's down, an' a few others, but most got out.'

'Jesco?' she asked hoarsely. 'Vidar?'

'They was behind me. Didn't see Vid, but Jes sent me on, said he'd be right behind me.' He looked back over his shoulder, his face downcast. 'Don' reckon he made it.'

Varahana's eyes stung – and they all heard the shooting across the river reaching a crescendo, and then going silent. Her heart felt like it really was in her mouth, like the poets liked to say, and her gorge rose. *Jesco,* she wailed inwardly, *and my Vidar . . .*

Distant bugles blared and her skin prickled with fear and hope as she recognised the order.

'That's the retreat,' Pad Geldermark blurted, wide-eyed. 'That's the Otravian army's retreat signal.'

It probably wasn't sensible, but they all stayed where they were. The stragglers who were still arriving were hugged by whoever was nearest, then they too joined in the breathless vigil. But none of them were Jesco or Vidar . . . and then they stopped coming.

Varahana turned away, surreptitiously wiping at her stinging eyes . . .

. . . and then someone exclaimed, 'Deo's Balls – it's Lor' Vyre hisself–'

She spun and stared as a mass of mostly Tangato emerged from the trees, and Raythe Vyre really was with them, waving as he saw her, his anxious face cracking into a smile.

Queen Shiazar was nearby, carried on a palanquin by four burly warriors who were clearly struggling to keep it level as they slid through the mud. Abruptly, the Queen lost patience with the whole affair and jumped free, just as the bearers slipped and went splashing down into the noxious water.

Varahana would have loved to see her face behind the red demon mask as she rose. As it was, the four warriors, looking utterly mortified, at once dropped to their knees, even though the water came up to their chests. As one, they pulled out bone-handled bronze daggers and placed them against their own throats.

Shiazar berated them in their own tongue – not for dropping her, Varahana quickly realised, but for offering suicide in recompense – and the men sheepishly put the daggers away again, although they still looked appalled at themselves. Shiazar, hands on hips like a Magnian goodwife berating a tradesman, switched to Gengo-Magnian, snapping, 'Get up, you fools!' Then she stomped towards Raythe, streaming water and fen-slime. 'I told them it couldn't be done, and I have two perfectly good legs.'

Unable to suppress her grin, Varahana went to meet them. 'Raythe – thank Gerda you've found us!'

He was already striding through the knee-deep muck to her. 'Mater, it's good to see you,' he exclaimed, hugging her. 'Where is everyone?'

'Ahead of us,' she panted. 'What happened back at the river? How are you here?'

'We realised that Torland's men had got ahead of us – he'd obviously guessed our route and was trying to cut us off – so we picked up our pace. It's all thanks to the Tangato runners that we got the advance guard to turn back. It got messy, but we managed to catch Torland's men in a pincer movement at the ford. It was just a skirmish, but we had the best of it and they've drawn off for the moment.'

'Thank Gerda! Um . . . is Vidar . . . uh . . .?' She felt herself colouring.

'Vidar's fine.' He patted her shoulder. 'Jesco took a ball in the thigh, but I've cleaned and bandaged him. He's being stretchered to the rear – Vidar's with him. Right now, we need to put some distance between us and the redjacks while we still can.'

Varahana hugged him again in sheer relief, then cleared her expression as the Queen stalked by, still muttering as muddy water trickled through the joints of her armour.

'I suppose we're not meant to laugh,' she whispered, but Raythe chuckled softly.

'She's not the sort to hold a grudge.' Then he winked and added, 'And she's right, she has two perfectly good legs.'

'Careful,' Varahana warned, trying and failing to stop her immediate thought. *Oh dear, he's not tilting at impossible women again, is he?*

The jauntiness in his step told her he absolutely was.

There was no more fighting that day. The Otravians were, Raythe hoped, in confusion at the loss of their commander, and apart from some scouts across the river, they'd pulled their camp back to the plains.

With Varahana's help, they rounded up the Magnians and set up camp on the first dry land they found, a small hill overlooking the swamps.

Then he and Shiazar, washed and wearing her plainest silk robes while her armour was cleaned and dried, went up to the highest nearby peak to plot their route westwards. It was going to be a slow journey through the treacherous fens, and even once they reached the hills, although it would be dryer, it was not going to be much easier.

'I thought we'd lose everything today,' he admitted, as they surveyed the darkening lands. Shiazar had removed her mask and it was hard to keep his eyes on the landscape, but he didn't wish to risk their relationship by some foolish over-familiarity.

'But we didn't lose,' she answered, 'because our two peoples never gave up on each other. Even the Manowai came to your aid, despite all that lies between us. We are one people now.' She smiled at him, her serene expression lit up by the setting sun. 'We work well together, Raythe,' she added.

Oh, dear Gerda, he thought helplessly. *I've not been this entranced since I first met Mirella.*

Finding himself thinking of Mirella when he was here alone with the Queen annoyed him. *That's over now*, he reminded himself. *She's no longer the yardstick for my feelings.*

Somewhat overwhelmed, he turned away – and something in the far distance caught his eye: a flash of forked lightning in the clear sky. He stopped and stared, and it came again, then again, and a dozen times more, before abruptly stopping. He felt vaguely uneasy, although he couldn't say why. When he glanced at Shiazar, she too was frowning.

'A lightning storm, perhaps?' she suggested, but she didn't sound convinced.

Maybe, he thought, *but why was there no thunder?*

3

Helpless

Luc Mandaryke had been immersing himself in the Serpent Throne, spending every moment he could spare with his body and mind locked to the spirit controlling the fortress. *Dakaji: my new, unrivalled familiar.* He was exhausted, but his mind was clear. He was currently exploring all the mental and hand-eye coordination required to prepare and discharge the dragon-cannons, and how to move the floating rock whilst maintaining stability.

He didn't begrudge a moment of the task; indeed, he resented having to stop to deal with worldly matters. The campaign to destroy Raythe Vyre and his savages was ongoing, but this mattered far more.

It's here that my fate will be decided.

It was three days before he deemed himself ready: three days in which his forces were left entirely in the hands of their commanders. He and Dakaji had become a shared identity, fusing sorcery and manmade machinery into a devastating weapon. He dreamed of it when he slept and lived it when he woke; all other matters faded to irrelevance.

When I guide this monstrosity over the skies of Reka-Dovoi and the Emperor quakes below me, I must be able to see every threat and use every weapon. It must be completely intuitive.

He was making new gains every day, including mastering the ocular and aural properties of the Serpent Throne. He could see not only what lay below in intricate detail and for several miles, but could also view any part of the fortress he concentrated on. What was needed now was practise disconnecting the giant chains and flying this great rock.

Before doing so, he called his aides into the banquet hall for the breakfast meeting and told them what he'd achieved. Some were stunned, but some of the brighter men had guessed already, and they were all excited as he explained the possibilities, although there was a certain nervousness about being on the rock if it went horribly wrong.

Luc met that fear head-on. 'Any man who wishes to disembark may do so,' he announced, knowing full well that not one would risk being seen as a coward by doing so. Sure enough, no one asked to leave.

He left them with orders to make sure the guards and servants knew what was going to happen, so there'd be no panic, then went to see Mirella. He found her in the royal suite, perfect as a porcelain doll, clad in deep blue velvet with her hair piled artfully and her stunning creamy cleavage on display.

Deo on high, barren or not, she's an addiction any man would crave. Child of Otravia's richest family, intelligent and beautiful – and so much more. She really was his most prized trophy. But he needed a legitimate son. There were women in Perasdyne he'd fathered bastards on, who he could legitimise at a stroke. But the notion of putting Mirella aside rankled – and it came with too many other risks.

I really need two wives, he thought. *Mirella for all she brings, and a brood-mare for sons.*

Then he smirked at the thought that once he'd positioned this fortress over Perasdyne and forced the occupying Bolgravians to surrender, he'd make his own rules, form his own religion if need be, so that he could have who and what he wanted.

Who will be able to deny me anything then?

'You look perfect, Wife,' he praised her. 'Have you chastised our daughter?'

'I have reprimanded her, but punishment is your right, Husband.'

It was the right response. 'I shall consider.' He stepped before her and cupped her cheek. 'I know her recalcitrance pains you, but believe me, she will appreciate us when we've taken complete control. Her stupidity can and will be corrected, one way or the other.'

She met his gaze. 'Do not spare the rod if it's required.'

'And you accept her Aldar marriage?' he asked.

'Yes,' she sighed. 'You are right about that.'

'And your Ramkiseri allegiances?'

Raythe Vyre had never seen that side of his trophy wife, but he'd discovered it years ago. When he'd confronted her, they'd made their own treaty: that what was good for them was good for the Empire.

'They'll never know the danger until it's too late,' Mirella reassured him. 'Zorne thinks I still serve his precious emperor, and once he's out of the way, there'll be no one to warn them.'

'You are Ramkiseri: you feel no inner conflict?'

She wrapped her arms around him. 'Darling, we'll be strengthening the Empire by assuming leadership and moving the centre of power from that Bolgravian backwater to old Magnia. We'll be making it stronger by deposing that old barbarian Koreimi. Magnians should rule the world, not Bolgravs – they're only a hair's-breadth away from the nomadic savages they're descended from.' She smiled triumphantly. 'So you see, there's absolutely no conflict whatsoever with my vows. What's good for us really is good for the Empire.'

'I love you when you're scheming,' he told her, bending his lips to hers.

'And I love you forever,' she replied, letting him kiss her. She began to unlace her bodice. 'One day, we'll make love on the Imperial Throne.'

She was so tempting – but right now, the one thing he wanted was to renew his bond with Dakaji and unleash this fortress on the world.

'Later, my love,' he told her. 'Right now, I have miracles to perform.'

She pouted a little, as she should, but she knew to relinquish him after another kiss.

Feeling like an opium addict, always craving more, he forced himself to leave and returned to his den. He locked the chamber and sat in the Serpent Throne, exulting as it came alive, the walls fading and the energy threads linking him to the dragon-cannons. The chains and the forces that controlled movement crackled back to life.

317

Time to see if I've learned aright . . .

He gathered in the four strands of energy required, then with a deft gesture activated them – and on the ground far below, metal jaws holding the chains sprang open. The metal chains, moving like immense tentacles, retracted a little way into the rock, which lurched very slightly. Luc held his breath, but there was no sudden rising nor tilting, nor falling masonry or screaming.

He did hear some muffled cries of alarm from the guards outside, but he blanked those and concentrated on controlling his new kingdom. As he'd been instructed by Dakaji, he reached out to unseen energy currents and linked the castle to them so they'd draw the fortress into motion . . .

With another lurch, the rock began to move through the air, or a north-northeast heading. Unconsciously grinning, he fused his praxis with the energy of the superstructure and began drawing up clouds from the south to encase the citadel in fog and rain. His enemies wouldn't know he was coming until he was right above.

I'm doing it! he exulted. *I'm the first man to wield these forces in five centuries . . . In fact, I am probably the first non-Aldar ever! Damned right those Aldar gods out there should kneel to me!*

Toran Zorne had tried to warn Luc Mandaryke that the regular army hated the Ramkiseri and would want nothing to do with him, and so it proved. Despite the botched skirmish against Vyre and the Tangato, when Zorne presented his credentials as Legate and demanded command of the division, the Bolgravian regimental commanders rallied round General Lisenko, with all the misplaced loyalty of children for an unsuitable nanny.

'We will never submit to a Ramkiseri stealing command of us,' a blusterer named Isarov thundered, while Lisenko just hung his head. 'Take your legateship and ram it up your arse.'

To be legally in the right but unable to enforce it wasn't an unusual situation for Zorne, and he didn't want this role anyway. *I should be watching Mandaryke's back – in case I must put a knife in it.* So he didn't renew the demand, though he mentally marked Isarov for retribution.

'I shall return to Governor Mandaryke and inform him of your response,' he told the dazed-looking Lisenko, turning his back and walking away, as if daring them to cut him down.

Offering such encouragement wasn't his intent, but showing fear would have invited death. Sometimes only bravado could get you out of a tight spot alive. Nevertheless, he was holding his breath all the way out of the tent and across the parade ground, watched uneasily by those few healthy soldiers who were neither wounded nor dying from the lung disease.

He was just as unsettled, for a different reason: Lisenko's division had been mauled by Vyre's savages, but it was the disease that was slaughtering them. No one appeared to be immune: half the officers were now showing symptoms – and he'd just shared a tent with some of them.

Gerda, watch over me, he muttered. *I don't want to die like that.*

He reached his horse without being shot. He was two days' ride from Rath Argentium and a no-doubt chilly reception when he explained how he'd failed to take control. *Will Mandaryke use it as an excuse to order my death?* It felt like a very real possibility.

It would be sensible to stay here tonight, as dusk was drawing in, and set out tomorrow morning – but as that would probably see him lynched at midnight, he resolved to ride for a few hours and shake off any pursuers before making camp somewhere well-hidden.

Depressingly, the sky was filling up with menacing cloud, rolling in from the southwest. No doubt it would rain soon, making his trek all the more miserable.

Men are born to suffer, he reminded himself. *Paradise must be earned.*

No one bade him farewell, although many marked his departure with narrowed, hostile eyes. Not long after leaving the suffering division behind, he found himself riding towards a rolling wall of drizzle and fog. When it folded around him, he felt like the only man left alive in a world that was dissolving into chaos – then he found a clear patch, looked up – and gasped in shock.

Shiro Kamigami was almost directly overhead. Its four mighty chains were dangling beneath, but they must be partially retracted, as they weren't touching the ground. It was at roughly its usual altitude, half a mile above ground, but it was visibly moving across the sky – towards Lisenko's division.

Zorne could feel Luc Mandaryke's presence as clearly as if his triumphal face was superimposed over the sky.

Why would he bring the castle here?

The answer was terrifyingly obvious.

He turned and galloped back towards the Bolgravian camp.

It's time.

All day, Luc Mandaryke had been growing increasingly tense. This was a real breaking point for Mirella and him. He could have been content to be the trailblazer for the Bolgravian Empire, the hero who conquered these lands in the name of Khagan Koreimi the Fourth, then meekly hand it over to the Emperor. His future, already rosy, would have been for ever secure, for no man could have given the Emperor a greater gift.

But from then on, I'd be an inconvenience to His Imperial Majesty. Powerful men find it intolerable to be indebted to another, and Khagan Koreimi IV is a paranoid old man with sons to protect.

And in truth, Luc's position was already tenuous: the Emperor had honoured their deal, giving him the Governorship of the Western Empire and his father the rule of Otravia, but his courtiers had always resented that – and half of Otravia wanted him dead as well. Assassination was a regular hazard.

The only way to secure myself fully is to keep ascending the ladder of power, and that means destroying the Emperor himself – then I'll be the hero of Otravia and the West – and ironically, I'll have achieved what Raythe and Colfar failed to do.

His doubts assuaged, he turned his mind to the task ahead. The dragon-cannons were fully armed and ready and he'd been testing them as they flew steadily northeast towards Lisenko's disease-ridden camp. The results had been pleasing: each blast had destroyed a large patch of ground, leaving just charred rocks and smouldering tree stumps. The rate of fire was the same as an ordinary cannon, but he could control it all from up here, and there was enough liquid istariol in the tanks for thousands of discharges.

And now, just as evening fell, here was Lisenko's camp below him.

If I do this, I'm a rebel, like Raythe . . . except that I can actually win.

Accepting the challenge, he readied the dragon-cannons – only the front four had a decent line of fire, but they would suffice. Calling on his bond with Dakaji, he inhaled pure intoxicating energy, sharpened his view through the ocular and focused on the command tent, where the commanders would be gathered, hopefully now under the direct control of Toran Zorne.

Zorne was still half a mile short of the camp when he saw it come alive, the sentries gawking up at the flying fortress, wondering what it portended.

Then a livid blast of scarlet light bloomed on the citadel walls and lanced downwards into the centre of the camp – right where Lisenko had his tent. A searing blast of fire erupted, hurling debris everywhere, and for a moment, time seemed to freeze as those outside the blast range went rigid with shock. A moment later, three more bursts hammered home, huge flashes that dazzled in the twilight gloom. The citadel flowed forward, and a minute later, its dragon-cannons fired again, this time working out from the centre as the survivors finally reacted, trying to flee.

Zorne reined in his terrified horse and watched aghast as a division of his beloved empire's army was destroyed. Men, horses and equipment were immolated and disintegrated in vast, impersonal explosions, each more destructive than any massed artillery barrage. As the smoke cleared, he could see nothing left but burnt bodies, anything living reduced to charred bones, and smouldering wreckage.

He fell from his horse, dropped to his knees and screamed at the skies.

'I brought him here,' he whispered. 'My choices led to this treachery.' He cocked the pistol in his hand, feeling the trigger beneath his quivering finger, and pressed the muzzle to his own temple.

I deserve this, he thought. *I've failed my empire.*

He went to fire –

– then lowered the gun, panting hard.

Suicide was an Eternal Sin, a vanity for guilty souls too craven to seek redemption – or a weakness of the degenerate. He was neither: he had to put this right – and perhaps he was the only one who could.

You are a Ramkiseri, trained to eliminate threats to the empire, he snarled at himself. *You do not despair, and you never surrender.*

So he fought for and found something like dispassion, analysing the fortress as it moved ponderously onwards, systematically raking the medical tents where thousands were dying anyway, then slaughtering the groups of fleeing horsemen. He noted the rates of fire and the extent of each blast until, finally, the dragon-cannons stopped – and without so much as slowing down, it changed course and headed northwest, towards where Raythe Vyre's natives and rebels had fled – and where Mandaryke's Otravian division was currently massed: five thousand men who could easily be accommodated in the bowels of the floating fortress.

'I see your mind, Luc Mandaryke,' Zorne shouted aloud. 'I see your blackened soul. You have rebelled against Deo's throne, so I must cast you into the Pit, and save my Empire.'

4

Deo's Throne

It was a red morning. Dark clouds poured in after dawn, blocking the planetary rings from view and shrouding the Fenua Tangato. Guides led the Magnians and Tangato southwest, deeper into the maze of hills bordering Manowai territory, all carrying their lives on their backs, into an uncertain future.

By midday, the murk was worsening, thick rolling clouds rushing in from the southeast, where they'd seen those strange flashes the previous evening. When they reached an abandoned Manowai hill-fort, Raythe found a good vantage point – but the views were not encouraging.

Whoever now commanded the Otravians hadn't backed off, despite the setbacks of the previous day. The Otravians had once again anticipated their line of march: he could see at least one regiment directly in their path, while the rest were coming up fast on the trail behind them. Worse, the hills to the north looked completely impassable.

Whether he wanted it or not, a battle was shaping up to be fought right here.

'This feels like a trap,' Raythe muttered to himself, contemplating their shrinking options.

'Why?' an unexpected voice asked.

He turned to see Shiazar, once again in her leather armour, climbing the slope to join him. Her bare face looked almost predatory as she surveyed the enemy ahead and behind.

'Your Majesty. I was just wondering if there's a path out of this place.' He indicated the soldiers. 'Because if not, we're cornered. We'll have no choice but to fight our way out.'

'There are paths, but they are hard, the guides tell me,' she replied. 'They're often blocked at this time of year. I've sent scouts to see if they are usable.'

'Then we may come under attack before we can leave,' he said, peering about him at the dilapidated remains of fortifications. 'It won't be easy to hold this hill, but it's the best we've got.' He lowered his voice. 'We'll need a rearguard to cover our withdrawal – but those warriors will be sacrificing themselves to save others.' When she flinched, he added, 'It's a hard command to give. My advice is, don't pretend it's anything but what it is.'

'I shall ask for volunteers,' she said miserably. 'I wish Rima was here. We could use her high spirits.'

'It would be good to see her,' Raythe agreed, watching the clouds swirling towards them – and his jaw dropped as they suddenly parted.

Shiro Kamigami hoved into view above the Otravian columns, its chains swaying beneath the rock like gigantic tentacles, a monstrous beast replete with menace.

Luc's actually managed to untether it, Raythe thought numbly. All his hopes, all his plans and intentions, crumbled before that awesome, awful sight. *Those lights I saw last night . . . Dear Gerda, what has he done?*

The Queen stared, all expression falling from her face. Below, their people had also begun to notice. A few wailed in despair, but most just gaped. No one moved, or even thought to run. This was *doom.*

The Tangato rangatiras gathered behind their Queen. Natomo looked stunned, and even the normally irrepressible Sitoko was speechless. When he looked for Varahana and Vidar and all his people behind them, they were looking hopelessly at the end of all their dreams.

Then Shiazar shouted aloud in the Tangato tongue, while Cognatus murmured the translation in Raythe's mind.

In a high, carrying voice, she cried, *'Behold, my people! These thieves take that which is ours: our lands, our Fenua Tangato – our Shiro Kamigami! This cannot be! I will not be enslaved. I will not yield our land unfought. Better to die than to bend the knee!'* Then she fell into a fighting crouch, smacking her hands against her thighs, her teeth bared as she pounded the rhythm on her body, shrieking in High Aldar, 'E na'a kagiga! Tangato-hai! E na'aka toa mai!'

Raythe never heard the translation, because every Tangato in hearing, from the very old to the young, was repeating her chant in an ear-splitting howl, over and over, defying heaven and earth, history and logic.

Kragga mor, he thought, and then, *Well, what better way to face death?* and joined in.

As the shingar lizard – it must have been the size of a building – reared up from the pool, Rima thought it was some demon summoned by the grey-haired witch. She shot sideways, but the massive creature wasn't interested in her. It roared in affronted fury at Teirhinan – and then Rima realised that it wasn't a beast at all: its body was formed from the earth: shifting mud and stone made a body of convenience for a spirit who needed one.

The Kaiju . . .

The grey sorceress, shrieking imprecations to her mismatched familiars, began to conjure . . .

But the Kaiju struck before she could unleash her spells: the giant jaws flew open and it shot forward, engulfing the witch as she stood, her arms spread wide as if in offering. The young hag dissolved into black smoke that rose into the air – then turned like a striking snake and flowed into the Kaiju's wide mouth.

The Kaiju faltered, its eyes bulged and then turned a dirty violet colour. *The colour of the Magnian witch's eyes.*

Even as Rima grasped this, the giant lizard crashed to the ground before her in a hot, wet squelching crunch – and came apart.

She stared, appalled . . . and then dragged herself backwards as the mud began to reform into a crudely human body, which lisped, '*Ahh, this form gives me so much more . . .*'

Rima stared, shocked. All she could think of was to call to the only one who might prevent this . . .

The galling limitation to Teirhinan's power had always been physical. Her successive bodies were just dying traps housing her soul; the ugly, hateful flesh disintegrated all too quickly, crushing her with its weakness, preventing her from achieving the true immortality she craved.

But now she had found this: a spirit more powerful than any familiar she'd ever experienced, even Dakaji inside the floating citadel: for this creature was to Dakaji as a giant to a dwarf, a mountain to a sand hill – a mother to a child.

When Dakaji broke away from the earth, this is who it broke from . . .

And now it had swallowed her, drawn her in . . . For a moment she'd faced what she'd feared when Dakaji held her: *obliteration*. That was, after all, why she had given her heart-stone to Toran Zorne.

But this new creature didn't appear to be able to destroy her. Perhaps life and death was just one process to it: a means of converting one form to another in an endlessly renewing cycle. So she turned being swallowed into an invasion, and now it belonged to her.

She bored inwards, taking it pore by pore, thought by thought, feeling its panic as it realised it had no barrier against her, nothing with which to fight back. She shrieked in glee as it fled, pursuing it back to its nexus to seize full control.

I shall surpass even Luc Mandaryke on his heavenly throne.

I will become a goddess—

She burst into the centre of the spirit's massive mind . . . and found someone already there.

'KEMARA!' the Dreamer heard, and she was jolted from slumber and hurled back to awareness. Where she was, she had no idea. It was as if she'd been sucked into a giant's heart. Fleshy scarlet walls thudded in time to the steady beat of a massive drum as light gushed in, then out, filling the chamber. Filling her.

KEMARA, the voice called again, *SAVE US!*

Kemara? she wondered, and then: *I am Kemara.*

She had no time to ask, *From what?* before she saw a hole torn open in the flesh walls, and a shadowy figure ripping its way in, a scrabbling thing like a new-born, born ancient, shrieking in triumph – and then convulsing in shock as it saw Kemara.

'No! This place is *mine*,' the figure rasped, at once girlish and ferocious. It burst into motion again, a writhing knot of claws and teeth, that launched itself at her.

If Kemara had never fought for her life before, she wouldn't have survived the next moment – but she had been a mizra-witch with the Aldar spirit Buramanaka inside her, and it was those instincts which had armour forming on her body even as she lashed out with the blade taking shape in her hand. She swung it through the tangled knots of toothed tentacles and scything claws, power coursing through her and into the blade.

'*Get out!*' she roared, slicing and hacking, and for a moment, she thought she'd prevailed. The ghastly knot of ever-changing flesh wasn't able to keep her out; it was fighting on other levels at the same time, shrieking out spells and gesturing towards someone or something that Kemara couldn't see.

Then it focused on her, lashing out with a dozen tentacles at once. Kemara let muscle memory guide her, back-flipping out of reach, then hacking her way forward, crunching through bone and severing tentacles – but as fast she cut, no matter how deep she sank her conjured blade, the shapeshifting hag just reformed faster – and then, with a gleeful shriek, she sent a dozen tentacles right through Kemara's ribs and belly, transfixing her.

Agony numbing her, Kemara lost control of her limbs and the conjured blade disintegrated.

The ghastly, girlish face loomed before her as she fell onto her back, paralysed.

'I'm done with my body now,' she announced. 'I think I'll take yours.'

*

327

For a few strange moments, Rima was sure someone else was present, because this girl-hag of mud and stone kept lashing out in another direction. But whenever Rima struck at her, she was battered back by unseen bursts of force that left her stunned.

But she kept trying, possessed by the mad idea that the unseen presence was Kemara, and that she needed all the help Rima could give. She enchanted her stone patu and charged, was smashed backwards again – and then stopped.

This was futile – and she'd suddenly remembered one of Hetaru's lessons: the three-tiered ritual of *oiharau* to exorcise those malign spirits, especially ghosts, who tried to steal a new life.

Rima called to Mokomoko for power, then began, '*Kaneska, taki saru!*' She shouted the opening invocation.

The stone hag, now kneeling as if over a fallen body, looked at her with contempt–

–that became a sudden rush of fear as pieces of her body crumbled.

'*No!*' she screamed, reaching–

'*Mata, kaneska taki saru!*' Rima shouted, the second invocation, and watched the energies shudder through the sorceress.

Teirhinan rose, her violet eyes blazing, a nimbus of dark and light forming round her hands–

–'*Kaneska, taki saru – saishu!*' Rima concluded, the third command, and unleashed the spell with all the force she could muster.

The pale witch screamed, her body collapsing, and smoke pouring from her mouth that streamed towards Rima; who gestured and shouted a banishing – and the black smoke went dissipating away through the air, and was gone . . .

Rima panted, staring after it, not trusting that she might yet be safe, until a glutinous sound drew her attention back to the glade. The stone and mud, all the remained of the Kaiju's body, was flowing away, back into the pool.

She watched it, feeling such loss . . . but no – this wasn't the end, for something was appearing from the muddy pool: a head, followed by shoulders and a torso: a naked woman with long red hair plastered to her skin, rising from the steaming water like the avatar of some primaeval goddess. Her eyes were like liquid fire, her skin burnished gold.

'Kemara,' Rima breathed, unable to comprehend. *'Kemara?'*

One by one, memories returned, dropping into her soul and taking shape. *I am Kemara. I'm a woman.*

She remembered her mother . . . then she had a vague image of her father, and a childhood of beatings and trauma, things she'd rather have not recalled, and then . . . *Oh Deo* . . .

She remembered Ionia again, not just those last traumatic moments, but the good times, too – maybe not love, exactly, but something they had both needed.

Then she focused on a brown-skinned woman staring at her in awe. Her face told her that her being here was miraculous, and so it felt.

I have a body again, she marvelled. *I'm back.*

'Rima,' she said, as the name dropped back into her head.

For a moment, struck dumb, they just stared into each other's eyes.

Then Rima asked breathlessly, 'What happened to the Kaiju?'

Kemara thought about that question. 'I *am* the Kaiju,' she answered, but no, that wasn't the entirety, so she added, 'Or I'm a part of it. But I'm still me, too. I'm still Kemara.'

Then, because words weren't enough, she went to Rima and crushed her in an embrace that said everything she couldn't, careless of her nakedness and her wet skin, just wanting to hold her, to breathe in her scent, to try to freeze the moment for ever . . .

But images began to flash through her head: of the Tangato singing on a hilltop, of red-coated men advancing in lines . . . and a massive rock in the sky, soaring above them with a mind of cold steel within. Through the Kaiju, she knew where, too: not far, if one could fly . . .

Holy Deo, it's happening now – *that's where we have to be. But first—*

Kemara kissed Rima with all the strength in her heart, tasting her life and fire – and then started to recoil as she realised she didn't even know if Rima liked her, let alone *this*.

But Rima was responding in kind, a hungry devouring kiss that had no end. It was glorious, a joyous awakening – but *right now*, Life was fighting Death in the skies above them.

'Rima, stop,' Kemara blurted, pulling her face away. 'I want this – *so much* – but *everything* is happening *right now*. We have to go.'

The Tangato girl's face went from rapt to confused. 'Where?'

'West, not far – Shiro Kamigami is there, and so are our people, and they're all going to die unless we reach them.' *Perhaps even if we do . . .*

She reached inside for her newfound power, for now she knew what the Kaiju knew: that bodies are fleeting, and there were so many different ways the particles could form, and now Kemara knew them too: bird or beast, tree or flower, fish or eel, and everything in between, flora, fauna or even mineral. The one she chose now was akin to the Kaiju itself, a magical creature from a Ferrean myth she'd adored as a child. She drew into herself the water and the leaves, the soil and stone, sucking them in to her in one massive rush, while Rima, gaping, backed away to give her space.

When she was done, a few agonisingly painful minutes later, she beat the air with webbed wings, lifting her body, big as a house. Her mouth could barely frame words, but somehow she roared, '*COME – CLIMB UP!*'

Rima obeyed, leaping onto her foreleg and pulling herself onto Kemara's back. When she had settled herself between the spinal plates, Kemara twisted her long neck, checking she was secure, then, trumpeting a warning, began to run, beating at the air with her wings – *I HAVE WINGS!* – until she could feel them gaining purchase on the air. She leapt, and as they rose, she caught the wind, skimming the fens, swooping upwards, away from the clinging steamy mists, seeing the foggy landscape all round penetrated by low hills, the Icewastes a distant gleam. Then she banked towards the west and shot across the skies, scared she was already too late.

Miles from where the Kaiju rode the wind, Toran Zorne felt the heart-shaped stone hanging round his neck go cold. It took a moment to realise what it meant: that Teirhinan Deathless had finally found an opponent who was beyond her.

So now I am supposed to put it against the skin of a living person and say her name. He thought about the mad sorceress, one of the few beings who truly terrified him. But she had served the empire, in her own way. And he'd made a solemn vow to call her back.

Yes, I will fulfil that vow, he told the piece of stone. *But I never promised when . . .*

He took it off and put it into his belt pouch, safely away from his own skin, before he nudged his horse back into motion. He could see his destination, and there was no time to lose.

The citadel ploughed through the murk Luc had conjured up, so other than the occasional glimpse of plains or forests or the glint of water, there was little for Mirella to look at from her perch on one of the forward-facing watchtowers. But her mind wasn't on the landscape; she was pondering the events of recent days, remembering the incredible power she'd felt, even by proxy, as she watched Luc's dragon-cannons annihilate the Bolgravian division. She longed to see it destroy Raythe's natives as well.

But someone's got to work the mines, so we'll give them the chance to surrender.

Not Raythe, though. He'd get the noose.

At first, betraying him had been a game: she'd been young, newly recruited as a Ramkiseri and determined to reach the top by any means. Raythe, an incurable Liberali and the man everyone *knew* would be a future leader, was her obvious target. He was clever, but hamstrung by his ethics.

It had been fun – cuckolding him with Luc, feeding names to her handlers – until things became dangerous; she was always afraid that someone would unmask her. Even victory didn't bring her closure, because Raythe escaped.

And he stole my daughter. That was when she began to hate him.

When he was dead, her little Zaza would finally be free of his baleful influence. She'd be restored, take her rightful place in high society, the position decreed for her by her blood. Mirella knew her own body: she would never bear another child. Zaza would be her only tangible bond with Luc, and that frightened her.

For now we have passion, she reminded herself, *but I have witnessed passion die many a time.*

'Milady?' a voice called, and two of Luc's aides, Jiani Maveros and Vorn Sherard, joined her in the cupola.

'The Otravian regiment is almost below us,' Sherard announced. 'Milord Mandaryke requests that you descend to negotiate the enemy's surrender.'

Mirella frowned. 'I thought General Torland would handle that?'

Sherard pulled an unconvincingly sad face. 'General Torland is dead, Milady.'

'*Dead?* How?'

'Our scouts say he was shot.' Maveros sniffed. 'His body was found last night.'

She processed that, reminding herself that Raythe's uncanny ability to surprise should never be underestimated. But Torland was no loss: she'd never liked him, or his undue influence on Luc. 'Was that nasty little guttersnipe he carted round with him killed as well?'

Sherard smirked. 'Shot in the belly and bled out.'

'What a *shame*. Very well, I shall take charge down below. Who's been appointed to replace Torland?'

'I have,' Maveros replied. 'My first command.'

Of course, the golden boy, Mirella thought, noting how peeved Sherard looked. 'Congratulations.'

Maveros smiled. 'One man's misfortune can be another's benison.'

'Seize the moment,' she advised him. 'My husband despises indecision.'

He nodded thanks for the advice and led the way down through the fortress to the loading platform. They dropped down the exit shaft, emerging into a freezing wind. The grey-green landscape below was streaked with ground mist, and the Otravian division, positioned facing a distant hillside, was little more than a dirty smear. Knowing that Raythe was there gave her a tangible sense that all her life's threads were knotting together in this alien place.

Let's take a knife to a few, she thought coolly.

Their destination was a patch of clear ground near the Otravian divisional command's tent, where Torland's former aides would be waiting to learn who their new commander was to be. Vorn Sherard was still eyeing Maveros sourly, but she doubted Maveros had even noticed.

The redjacks watched them land, clearly as scared as they were excited by the floating citadel. By now, they'd probably heard rumours about the Bolgravians, which would be deepening their unease.

With Maveros and Sherard at her heels, Mirella strode through the ranks to meet the colonels. They were greeted apprehensively, and when Maveros read aloud his appointment letter from Luc, the officers saluted woodenly. With the fortress hanging over them, this was not the time for objections or personal agendas.

Maveros ordered horses and an escort for Mirella, for the parley. 'I'll accompany you myself, if you wish?' he offered.

There were things Raythe might say that she'd prefer went unheard by others, so she said, 'Thank you, General Maveros, but you will have a great many calls on your time now. I'll manage this small duty by myself.'

It took more than an hour for the parley to be arranged. 'There were thousands of 'em up there, ma'am – men an' wimmin an' childer too,' the envoy, a scout from some rural backwater, reported on his return. 'Their Queen wore a mask, but the fellahs are sayin' she's a real live Aldar.'

'That is the rumour,' Mirella said lightly. 'Did you see Lord Vyre?'

'Aye, ma'am,' the scout said, sounding a shade too impressed about it. 'He says he'll meet ye. An' he asked after 'is daughter?'

'*My* daughter, not his,' Mirella sniffed. 'What did you tell him?'

'That I din' know.'

'Good answer.'

She took a squad of sharpshooters, all loyal Mandaryke men, who marched alongside her. The parley would take place on patch of flat ground beneath a terraced hill that was swarming with natives. She heard them singing as she approached, a primitive, belligerent song full of bellowing and thigh-slapping.

'You've grown savage, Raythe,' she murmured, scanning the scene.

About a hundred yards above, she saw a figure in a red mask and black armour, seated on a wooden throne. *The mysterious Aldar Queen,* she supposed. *I imagine she'll look like a female Onkado.* There were thousands of warriors swarming around her, men and women too, in leather cuirasses and helms, brandishing flintlocks or primitive clubs.

We don't even need the fortress to slaughter this rabble, she thought dismissively, before it occurred to her that Nemath Torland had likely thought the same thing. It was always foolish to underestimate Raythe.

And then, suddenly, there he was, appearing round the hillside just a hundred feet away. He stopped – doubtless to assess her and her escort – then advanced to the other side of the clearing. He had only one person with him, a shaggy man with Norgan features who reeked of violence.

'Your safety is guaranteed,' she called to Raythe.

'As is yours,' he replied.

She left her escort and advanced to the centre of the space to meet him.

She was struck by how much older he looked. It was five years since he'd stolen Zarelda and fled. Back then, he'd been a Liberali firebrand, full of idealism and passion, his dark hair wild and his quicksilver tongue brutal in condemnation of the Mandarykes.

Now his forehead was lined, crows' feet were etched into the sides of his eyes and grey streaked his hair: the effect of three years of war culminating in bitter defeat, then two on the run, until somehow he'd ended up here, off the edge of the map, indeed, the very world. He looked worn as an old sword hilt.

She compared him to Luc, who was still youthful and vibrant. There was a lot to be said for winning.

'Well,' she said, 'here we are. How do you wish to die? In battle with everyone you care about, or alone on the gallows?'

Seeing Mirella brought so much back. For five years, Raythe had carried her seraphic face with him: his wife of twelve years, the 'Angel of Perasdyne', the woman everyone said he'd never win. She was a paragon of all things aristocratic: that, and the mother of his beloved daughter – and his soulmate, or so he'd believed.

Mirella had been at his side during every meeting, rallying people to fight the increasing alignment of the old aristos with the Bolgravians. They'd routed the Mandarykes in the elections, won the initial battles when the Bolgies first invaded, even worked out how to defeat those infamous rolling volleys.

But then she defected to Luc, and all his Liberali friends and allies began to be picked off, even those the Mandaryke autocrats and their Bolgravian allies shouldn't have known about. Spies were blamed, but they'd never found out who was betraying them so effectively.

It was always obvious, though. I just wouldn't admit it to myself.

'It was you, wasn't it?' he said, searching her face. 'Who gave the Ramkiseri our old friends' names?'

'Your friends, not mine.' She shrugged. 'That's old history. I have no desire to discuss the past, other than to say that it was hard for me to be

335

tied to a losing cause when the whole world could see the inevitability of Bolgravian victory. And to drag my daughter into that carnage – I'll never forgive you for that.'

She really doesn't care, he reflected. *She never gave a shit.*

It wasn't a revelation but confirmation that Mirella had *never* been the woman he'd believed her to be. Even if their love had ever been real, it was truly ashes now.

Deo, why don't you age her? Shouldn't the ugliness inside be visible to all?

He straightened, putting the past aside, at least for now. 'My Queen commands me to s–'

'"My Queen"?' she snorted. 'You, the arch-Liberali democrat, acting as mouthpiece for a Queen? How ironic. Do any of your principles remain, or did they die with the thousands of people you lured into rebellion?'

'My Queen,' he resumed calmly, 'is the ruler of this land. She commands that you and your men return whence you came and leave her people in peace.'

Mirella barked with laughter, an ugly, contemptuous sound. 'Well, that's not happening, Raythe. This is the Game of Nations, and winner takes all.' She pointed up at the floating citadel. 'We've already destroyed the Bolgravian division. Our next step will be to mine this place of every last fleck of istariol, then return to Otravia and claim it for ourselves – and yes, Luc and I will achieve what you failed to do. We will be the undisputed rulers of the world. As for your "Queen", as the last Aldar woman, we'll certainly keep her alive. She will join our Aldar male in our menagerie and we will breed her.'

Her gloating certainty silenced him, even as his heart thudded with rage he could barely contain. *I should kill her*, he thought, *right now – and damn the rules of parley.*

Why he didn't, he had no idea.

But Mirella, unaware of how close she was to death, was still talking. 'Tell me, Raythe: how does it feel to lose *everything*? You lost me, your daughter, your country – and now this backwards place. You're a failure, Raythe, as usual, caught up in something too big for you. It takes a colossus to rule this world, and you were never such a man.'

He exhaled slowly, carefully, as his fiery rage turned to ice.

I will destroy everything she and Luc build, no matter how long it takes, he vowed silently.

'Tell "your Queen" to yield,' Mirella went on airily. 'If she surrenders herself to us, we may let her people live. Refuse, and we'll annihilate every single person. Those are our terms. But either way, Raythe, *you* are dead. I advise you to take the coward's way out to avoid the humiliation of a trial and execution.'

'There'll be no surrender,' he replied flatly. Unable to look at her vain, glorious face any longer, he turned away.

'What, no final message for Zaza?' she sneered. 'She's not even yours,' she added cruelly. 'Luc's her real father.'

For a moment, his whole body convulsed with the need to lash out. *Zar*, his brain screamed, *Zar, my beloved child, you are* mine! – but it was only for a moment, before the discipline so deeply instilled in him reasserted itself. He went utterly still, wrapped stone around his heart and breathed.

Vidar put a restraining hand on his arm and snarled, 'Get out of here – take your lying words and leave.'

Mirella just smirked as she turned and sauntered away. She raised her hand once, in a casual salute, as if dismissing him from her mind for ever. Then her redjacks closed around her and they left.

'She lied, Raythe,' Vidar was saying. 'You know what she's like – she's just playing with you. Don't give her the satisfaction.'

But they aren't lies, Raythe thought in despair, all the fight draining from him. It was horribly plausible. He remembered everything she'd said at the time to explain Zar's early arrival: that she'd been conceived when he'd been home from leave, later than the midwives originally calculated. *The simplest explanation for Zar's birth date was the one I refused to consider: she was conceived when I was away* . . .

'Zar's not my daughter,' he blurted, his voice broken.

'Oh yes she is,' Vidar growled. 'Rebellious, independent, annoying as a fleabite? She's yours, and not a person would ever doubt it. *Nurture* wins, even over nature, Raythe. She's yours, through and through.' He grabbed Raythe's shoulders. 'So, we fight on, yes?'

Feeling like a child in the big man's grasp, Raythe looked up the slope to where Shiazar sat on her carved throne. He pictured the defiant fury with which she'd led her people – and him – in song, when the citadel appeared.

My Queen.

'Aye, he said, 'we fight on.'

But with the citadel looming overhead, he could see no way of getting everyone out of here. The scouts had returned with news that the northern passes were clear of snow, but enabling the main body to retreat required a delaying action here. Whoever was left to hold the rearguard was going to die.

If that includes me, so be it.

Mirella wore a languid smile as she rode back to the Otravian officers waiting beneath the floating citadel. The memory of Raythe crumpling as he realised the truth was a delight; a more fitting punishment for stealing her daughter, she could not imagine – well, until the moment Luc's cannon obliterated him and his savages.

'Milady? Are we to attack?' Maveros wanted to know as he came to greet her.

'They've refused terms. Let Luc know I'm on my way back to share the moment he rains fire down on them. The sooner he does it, the more he'll catch in the open.'

Maveros' face lit up – he was clearly eager to see the fortress in action again. He kissed her proffered hand, then walked her to the platform, where Vorn Sherard made a point of helping her up. She rather enjoyed the two of them competing for her favour like boys at a debutantes' ball.

'Return us to Milord's citadel,' Sherard told the sorcerer at the controls, and they all braced for the ascent – until a grey-coated man emerged from the press and advanced on the platform. Guards shouted warnings as he threw up his hands and shouted, 'Message for Lord Mandaryke.'

Mirella caught her breath: Toran Zorne was unshaven and smeared in ash, but nonetheless unmistakable.

'Zorne?' Maveros exclaimed. 'What are you doing here?'

'Message for the Governor,' the man repeated doggedly.

'You ... you're dead,' Sherard stammered uncertainly. 'Er ... I mean – we heard ...'

Mirella stared, trying to read the Ramkiseri agent's face, but it was expressionless. 'Report,' she ordered, wondering how he'd survived. *Surely he must know we sent him to die? So what's he doing here?*

'I arrived to find General Lisenko's division destroyed,' Zorne said flatly. 'I presume judgement was passed upon him and his men. I have a message for the Governor, from the Emperor, Khagan Koreimi himself.'

'That's impossible,' Sherard snapped, looking to Mirella for guidance.

Unlikely is the more apt word, she worried. 'What message?'

'It's in my head,' Zorne told her flatly, making a gesture in sign-cant: *I am loyal.*

Aye, to your empire, Mirella thought, but she replied, *Obey me, subordinate.* She snapped her fingers at a sergeant. 'You there – choose six men for prisoner escort – and disarm him.'

Zorne made no move as his pockets were emptied and his belt, sword, pistol and dagger were removed, as well has his pouches. Then the two biggest men pushed him onto the platform. The sergeant walked behind Zorne and placed his pistol to the Ramkiseri's head, growling, 'Don't even breathe.'

Mirella nudged Zorne's possessions and told Sherard, 'Bring these. They may have value.' The aide took up the weapons belt gingerly, mounted the platform, then turned to offer her his arm. She ascended gracefully, while Zorne was manhandled aboard and they prepared to ascend to the skies again.

Mirella ordered the sorcerer at the controls to cast a binding spell over Zorne's praxis. The assassin's face was stony, but his eyes were flickering about, taking in everything, before he let his face lapse into glazed, sullen defeat.

Mirella kept her eyes fixed on him as the overloaded platform rose slowly towards the citadel, her good mood tarnished by this unexpected development.

But it wouldn't be for long. *Once we're up there, I'll have him shot.*

Luc's dirty laundry wasn't for the public eye.

Sometimes life hung on the skills you'd picked up, even the odd things you'd never thought you'd need to know.

After Colfar's final defeat, Zarelda and Raythe had fled west, sheltering in root cellars and lofts belonging to rebel sympathisers. It had been a terrifying time, hunted by the invaders and their treacherous allies, but her father knew a lot of strange things for a nobleman and he'd taught Zar a range of unusual survival skills – not just how to ride, to fight with a knife or her fists or run like an athlete, but other, darker skills. His lessons had been a lifeline for her, something to focus on instead of fear, and they'd regained the bond they'd shared when she was younger, before the Bolgravian crisis took him away.

One of those skills was lock-picking.

There was a guard outside, but the guest rooms all had windows opening onto the tiled gable roof. Until she had somewhere to go, though, there was no point escaping – and in any case, she had to get Onkado out too.

She'd been intending to slip out in the night, rescue Onkado, then make for the platform, until she'd felt the fortress come alive and begin to move. Not knowing precisely where they were had forced her to bide her time. She ate the meals the guards brought without complaint and feigned remorse whenever her mother visited.

Then she sensed the massive energy discharges, saw the dragon-cannons firing from her window and glimpsed the devastation they wrought. She overheard the guards saying the Bolgravians had been destroyed – which puzzled her – and that 'Vyre's savages' would be next, which didn't.

It's all coming to a head. I have to do something. She had no idea what that might be, but felt with growing certainty that if she waited any longer, there would be no point to anything at all. Even if she just cast herself from this floating rock in protest, the time was now.

The moment they cleared away her breakfast dishes, she set to work. In a few seconds she was out of the window and clambering along the narrow mossy gutter around the jutting buttresses, trying to picture the citadel's layout.

From a turret on the roof, she could see her mother sitting in a cupola, watching the Otravian army appearing through the mist – and then tiny figures moved on the distant hill: the Tangato, she was sure. Her mother was joined by two men and as they all went below, the fortress came to a stately halt.

By now she knew how these things worked: there'd be a parley, a demand for surrender, and then – because she absolutely could not imagine the proud Queen Shiazar yielding to *anyone* – there would be carnage.

What she could do about any of it, she had no idea, but she had to try.

She came to a section where she had to cling to a narrow ledge a finger's-width wide, then drop onto a tiny catwalk which she guessed must have been used by builders to effect repairs, until she finally reached Onkado's window. She peered in and saw him sitting cross-legged on the floor, his majestic features impassive, meditating away the hours of captivity.

She tapped on the window.

He looked up, first in alarm, then in amazement when he realised who it was. He rose and shot to the window, where she was examining the lock. It wasn't sophisticated, but it was inside, with nothing for her to work with from the outside. But the window itself was very basic, with simple pin-hinges on the outside, so all she had to do was work the two pins out, then she could pull the window out of its frame, despite the lock.

She placed it carefully in the guttering so that it couldn't slide, then she slid in backwards, until she felt Onkado's hands on her waist. He lowered her carefully to the floor, and when she turned to face him, his face was rewardingly impressed.

'You're amazing,' he breathed.

'I know,' she whispered, looking up at him and forgetting to breathe. 'Fancy getting out of here?'

'I'll just pack,' he said drily, then he pecked her on the lips. 'There, I'm ready.'

She blushed scarlet, feeling a tingling all over her skin, and it felt so kragging good. She grinned at him and mouthed, 'Let's go!'

This time he went first: she boosted him up and out so he could use his strength to pull her up. They picked their way down the outside of the castle, avoiding the large windows and keeping out of sight of the watchmen on the outer walls below, although they were all completely focused on what was happening on the ground.

They found a balcony with an open door on the second level and slipped back inside, where they took to the least used corridors, grateful that the castle was so sparsely populated. Two floors below took them to the service corridors encircling the underground levels. They paused only to slip into the ancient armouries to arm themselves with curved Aldar swords and daggers. They tried to force Onkado's sorcery-binding manacle off, but it obviously required both sorcery and metal-working tools to do so. Frustrated, they moved on, heading for the lowest chamber and the floating platform that would afford them an escape.

But when they arrived they stopped, confounded, because the platform was gone.

'Damn!' Zar swore, looking down the shaft at the distant circle of light. Far, far below, she could make out a grassy field, dotted with men in red uniforms: Luc's Otravian division – who were rapidly being blotted out by the platform, which was rising towards her, packed with people.

Just then, a bell far above in the fortress began to hammer out an alarm. Moments later, they heard shouting from much closer at hand.

'I think we've been missed,' she told Onkado, looking round for hiding places. This lower chamber was circular, with the shaft in the middle ringed by a low safety wall, but it had some storage nooks, presumably for supplies being offloaded.

'If we go back up, there are more places to hide,' Onkado suggested.

'Aye, but if we hide here, we can jump onto the platform as soon as the room clears,' Zar replied, thinking aloud. 'But there's an army down there . . . No, let's hide on the next floor up.'

But before they could move, a squad of men burst into the chamber, giving them barely time to throw themselves down on the far side of the safety wall, directly opposite the doors. If the soldiers fanned out to search, they'd be spotted in seconds. Once more she bitterly cursed the bindings on their maho.

But their luck held.

'No one's here,' said the sergeant leading them. 'Let's try the next level – shut these doors, lads.'

A few seconds later, they were gone. Zar and Onkado cautiously got to their feet – and she felt the change in the air rising from the shaft as it was blocked by the platform.

If we run now, those soldiers who just left may see us . . .

'Stay down,' she hissed. 'We'll move when whoever's on the platform is gone.'

Onkado gave her a nod and once more they pressed low to the back wall, holding their breath and waiting. Their eyes met, and Onkado's hand closed on hers – and then he squeezed in shock as a series of shots rang out, echoing up the shaft.

The men holding Toran Zorne's arms bent them back harder, but still he showed no reaction. The gun muzzle pressed to the back of his skull had him pinned in place and the other soldiers had their flintlocks primed and ready, even with his praxis bound. Clearly the tales of a Ramkiseri's deadly skills had taken root among them, because they all looked petrified, even the sorcerer controlling the platform.

But Mirella Mandaryke was watching him like a hungry vulture. He could read the look in her eyes plainly: he'd be dead already if he'd not made sure to present himself in public – but as soon as he was out of sight, she'd order his death.

'We were worried for you,' she said, for appearance's sake.

Contemptible lie. Zorne framed a reply, then thought, *Why bother?*

The floating rock above grew ever larger as they rose between the massive, swaying chains. Then the platform entered the shaft – and the sound of a tolling bell echoed all around them as they plunged into darkness . . .

And Zorne moved.

First he flopped in the arms of the two men holding him, dropping his head below the muzzle and using their support to swing his legs round. He brought the man on his right crashing down, a split-second before the sergeant reacted by pulling the trigger. The blast seared an image onto his retinas: of Vorn Sherard's face, contorted in premonition, an instant before the shot shattered his head.

The sound jolted the one still holding him: he held on – which enabled Zorne to use him as leverage to swing round. He dipped his hand, coming out with the man's dagger, and in almost the same movement, severed the man's jugular. As the lamplight from the chamber above started to penetrate the pitch-black of the shaft, he punched the dagger into the sergeant's back as he stood there gaping at the aide he'd just murdered. Catching the sergeant, he pulled him round, using his body as a shield, in time for the two remaining soldiers to fire their long-barrelled flintlocks into the sergeant's gut. The soldiers gaped witlessly as they realised what they'd done, but Zorne had already dropped the body. He kicked one in the face, spun and slashed open the other's throat.

Momentum took him to the side of the sorcerer, who'd managed to summon his familiar and was shouting a spell, but Zorne's chop to the throat choked off the words. He took a moment to finish off the man he'd kicked in the face, smashing his boot heel down on the neck, then he faced Mirella, the only other person remaining upright.

The noblewoman had gone deathly pale, her lips moving as she conjured. A bird familiar appeared on her shoulder and plunged into her aura. He went at her before they could complete the connection, backhanding her savagely, cutting off the spell and sending her to the ground, her nose and lip bleeding. When she tried again, he smashed a fist into her jaw, knocking her senseless.

I'll deal with you in a minute, he promised her silently as he turned back to the sorcerer. Placing his stolen dagger to the man's throat, he said, 'Free my power and you live.' Faced with death, men did foolish things, in his experience.

The sorcerer released the binding, then looked at him beseechingly. He was a scholarly sort, better suited to university halls than a military campaign.

'My thanks,' he said, and drove the dagger into his heart.

No true patriot would surrender an advantage to an enemy. No wonder Otravia is a conquered nation.

The platform had docked, although it was not yet locked in place.

'Praesemino, Ruscht,' he called, and his familiar joyously flooded back into him. He conjured wards, recovered his weapons belt and saw to the priming of his pistol. He picked up another, primed it and rammed it through his belt for good measure. He checked the pouches to ensure nothing had been lost before rising and surveying the carnage.

Mirella groaned and stirred. He straddled her body and slapped her back to consciousness. 'My Lady,' he said coolly, studying her, seeing the way the blood and snot from her broken nose marred the perfection, breaking her enchantment.

It was tempting to slash her throat, but he might need her as a hostage to get close enough to Luc, so he tied her hands with the sergeant's boot laces and hauled her to her feet. Then he cast a binding that would prevent her familiar from entering her. He felt the fluttering of unseen wings and heard a shriek as it fled.

'The Holy Bolgravian Empire will always prevail,' he told the groggy woman. 'Take me to your husband and I will give you the chance to redeem yourself in the eyes of your Emperor.'

He hauled her off the disc and locked it in place, then shoved her towards the doors, whilst his familiar extended his senses, heightening his awareness . . . and he realised that they weren't alone. 'Stand up,' he told the shadows. 'Show yourself, or I'll torch you where you hide.'

He saw the silhouette waver, then someone stood.

For once, even he was taken aback.

Zarelda Vyre . . . unarmed and alone . . . Deo does give the strangest gifts.

He aimed his pistol. 'Come forward and join your mother.'

5

Live Through This

The signal had been given – *Vyre refuses to yield* – and a few moments ago, thanks to Dakaji's senses, Luc had felt the flying platform dock below. Mirella was back, which meant his floating fortress was free to move again. With growing excitement, he spread his arms, grasped anew the threads of energy about him and Shiro Kamigami shuddered into motion again.

We ride to war . . . Or rather, to slaughter, because *no one* could touch him.

As they lurched into motion, he focused his ocular vision on the hill five miles to the north and the tiny figure of Raythe Vyre, surrounded by his primitive friends.

Yes, he thought, *there you are.* He'd spent five years fantasising about destroying his old rival – that Raythe still lived had been a constant itch, despite all the power and glory he'd enjoyed. *It's time to end this and move on to worthier foes.*

He focused on the foremost dragon-cannon, ensured it was armed and trained it on the hill. It was still three miles away, currently beyond his range, but they would traverse that distance in minutes. He gestured, Dakaji responded and the citadel picked up speed as it gained momentum. As they flowed forward, Dakaji shared its memories of an ancient sky battle in which the God-King Yasterion II destroyed a floating citadel wielded by a rival Aldar lord from Shadra. The last of the rival citadels to fall, it had been blasted apart so that rocks and bodies rained down from heaven.

When I invade the skies over Reka-Dovoi and overthrow the Emperor of Bolgravia, all Creation will beg for mercy.

With that glorious thought in mind, Luc flexed his fingers and adjusted the ocular instruments, focusing it on the hill as the range shortened.

Raythe, old friend, he smirked, *time to finish this.*

Raythe remembered the sickening moment when Colfar's centre was breached at Burstenstad and they'd realised that this was the end. The next half an hour, galloping through the rout seeking his daughter among those fleeing headlong, was the most terrifying of his life. But seeing Shiro Kamigami flowing towards the hilltop came a very close second. Even the Tangato had stopped their defiant songs and just stared.

The lightning we saw flashing in the skies last night was the citadel, he realised.

He opened his mouth to bellow an order when an incredible sound boomed out: perfectly formed words, rolling like thunder across the plains.

Luc Mandaryke was calling his name.

'RAYTHE!' he boomed triumphantly. '*I SEE YOU!*'

He turned to Shiazar. 'Majesty, we have to go. Scatter and run! Remember your plan! '

Her perfect face was set in fury; the whole hillside of Tangato had been building themselves up for some last stand, their intentions to mount guerrilla warfare forgotten in the shock of seeing Shiro Kamigami deployed against them. For a moment he wondered if she and her people were too far gone into battle fury to see reason.

But Shiazar's face cleared and with a visible effort she mastered herself, turning to her chieftains and snapping off orders to retreat: to scatter and seek the Manowai lands. 'We will fight on,' she shouted, 'but not here.'

Raythe ran to his own people, making for Varahana, ashen-faced, who was praying over her flock of Magnians. 'Vara!' he shouted, 'get everyone out – run like the wind. North or east, it doesn't matter – just scatter and run!'

The priestess had seen her share of victories and defeats; she reacted instantly, berating every Magnian in sight, shrieking at them to *'Move, move, MOVE!'* Vidar and Jesco and the Tangato chieftains were doing likewise, and in seconds, the entire tribe was scattering.

But the citadel was looming ever closer, moving faster than a galloping horse now, coming straight for him.

He really can see me, Raythe realised, *maybe even hear me – and we can't outrun him.*

Abandoning his people to Varahana, he drew his sword and strode back to the front of the hill, the only man not fleeing for his life. In seconds he was alone.

Then the Queen appeared, running like a cat. She caught his arm and pulled him back with surprising strength. Her eyes gigantic, she cried, 'Raythe, we must go!'

'No, it's me he's after. Get everyone out – I'll draw his eyes away.'

Her expression was stricken. *'No! Come with me! That is a command!'*

'I respectfully refuse, your Majesty. Please, *go*.'

She gaped at him, all colour draining from her face. 'No. I need you.'

Everything that could have been swelled up in her face, and in his heart. Cursing Fate, he thrust her away, pleading. 'Go! Please, Shia – remember duty – *go!*'

Then he strode forward to meet the advancing castle, shouting, 'Can you hear me, Luc? Come on, you kragging coward! You want to have this out, then come down here and fight like a man!'

'I'M NO MERE MAN!' Luc's voice boomed. *'I AM A GOD!'*

The shadow of the fortress fell over him. The dragon-cannons kindled on the walls, half a mile above and deadlier than lightning bolts. He glanced back, saw Shiazar still on the hillside above him, her expression torn, her limbs frozen.

'*Go!*' he shouted to her. *'Please, just go!'*

349

Then he faced the cannons again, remembering Mirella on their wedding day, how much he'd been in love, and Zar's red-faced rage at being born, and the last words of his father on the executioner's block – and his first sight of Shiazar's true face when she lifted her mask and tore his heart in two.

Above, something screamed like an enraged eagle, and the cannons twinkled with blue fire . . .

. . . as a giant claw engulfed him, almost breaking his spine as it snatched him from the ground and bore him away at blinding speed, just feet above the ground.

Behind him, the air went incandescent, livid light and heat blasting the turf where he'd been standing seconds before.

'*Raythe!*' Rima's voice shouted from somewhere above, as the thing holding him banked savagely, evading another energy bolt that shot past and exploded on the ground below. Then the Tangato girl shouted, 'Now the Queen – go, Kemara, go!'

Kemara?

If the Ferrean healer had returned – well, that was wonderful, but right now all that mattered to him was Shiazar. He twisted in the grip of the beast and saw the Queen a hundred yards below, sprinting around the hillside. The flying creature – *a dragon?* – banked and swung towards her, dodging the bolts of fire flashing left and right, for Luc was trying to anticipate their flight path. They swooped in, the ground a blur – and Shiazar spread her arms and *leapt.*

The beast caught her in its fore-claws, then swept onwards, roaring in triumph.

'Raythe, Shiazar, are you all right? Rima shouted. 'If you can, climb up!'

Raythe slapped at the claw that held him, which loosened enough for him to painfully wriggle free. He grasped the knee – the dragon's hide resembled scaled leather, red and gold, slippery to the touch – and pulled himself up, trying to ignore the ground flashing past below. Now he could see Rima, perched between the wings. He discovered the spine was a lumpy ridge of bone, but between the spikes were softer spaces. As he settled in one, Shiazar made it up behind him.

He threw her an amazed look, reached back and squeezed her hand in wonder.

'Subarashi!' she shouted – *Wonderful!* – as the dragon soared out and away. The blasts from Shiro Kamigami became more erratic, but the fortress was still a threat to them. 'Which way now?'

Raythe looked below. The Tangato were melting into the forests, but the Otravians were still in their lines, scared to advance into a fire-storm. The citadel had stopped moving again, and he could almost taste Luc's frustrated rage.

So who's up there with him? he wondered. *Zar, that's who . . .*

'Luc Mandaryke will never rest until every single one of us is dead. Up there, he thought himself untouchable – I warrant he has only a small garrison. This could be our one chance . . . and Zar's up there, Onkado too. Majesty, we must attack!'

Rima turned, looking astounded. 'Those dragon-cannons need only hit us once,' she reminded them. 'The risk is too great!'

Shiazar raised her hand, asking for silence as she thought. Her bare face always had a masklike quality, but he knew her well enough to see the agony of decision-making behind her eyes. She had to be so tempted to just fly away . . .

But then her face hardened. 'Aie, we have a chance, and may never have another. Rima, take us in. We must attack now, or we never will.'

Raythe looked round, but couldn't see the Ferrean anywhere. 'You keep calling to Kemara – where is she?'

'You are riding her,' Rima called back. 'Hold on tight!'

Raythe gaped as the dragon banked and then went hurtling back towards the flying fortress, weaving and spinning as it went. The dragon-cannons opened up again and a storm of livid energy tore across the skies, straight at them.

Clinging on for dear life, Raythe shielded his eyes and prayed as the blasts ripped the air around them, as the dragon – *Kemara, if that could be true!* – zigzagged across the sky, and the distant fortress grew to fill their sight.

How do we do this? Raythe wondered. Then it came to him. 'Kemara,' he shouted above the roaring winds and sizzling bolts of energy, 'take us underneath!'

For the first time, doubt intruded on Luc's thoughts. His ocular vision was linked to the dragon-cannons, but he couldn't shift their aim swiftly enough to bring the giant winged beast down. As it spun and wheeled away from another storm of fire, he suddenly realised that he had only seconds before the damned beast reached the fortress and maybe landed.

Suddenly, he felt mortal again.

Snarling at the fear besetting him, he engaged the aural mechanism and blared, *'ATTENTION ALL GUARDS. PREPARE FOR AN ATTACK UPON THE KEEP. FIRST COMPANY SECURE THE TOP LEVEL. SECOND COMPANY, SEEK OUT ANY INTRUDERS AND KILL THEM. THIRD COM-PANY TO THE LOADING PLATFORM – YOU WILL ESCORT LADY MIRELLA TO ME.'*

He commanded Dakaji to seal the Heart Chamber, as the dragon-cannons recharged, then he fired again, and again, but the dragon spun away from his volley and vanished somewhere beneath the rock.

Damn them! He slammed his fist into his hand, fear chilling him. He had three companies up here, but would sixty men be enough against sorcerers? His own praxis-wielders were with the army below, and in any case, they were mostly apprentices. Teirhinan was away hunting enemy sorcerers and the Bolgravians were all dead. Suddenly – unexpectedly – he felt vulnerable.

Where's Mirella? he wondered. She should have been on the platform when it docked ten minutes ago – surely she was almost here? He focused the ocular on the main stairs, and when he couldn't find her, he worked down and down with growing unease . . .

Then he saw the platform and swallowed. The stone disc was in place, but it was covered with bodies. It took him a moment to identify them: there were six soldiers, a junior sorcerer and Vorn Sherard, lying in pools of coagulating blood.

Thankfully, there was no sign of Mirella, which begged the question: who did the killing?

Deo, has she turned on me too? No . . . no, not Mirella.

The pistol in Toran Zorne's hand moved from Zarelda to her mother and back as the Ramkiseri agent forced them up through the levels of the floating rock, taking the very same back corridors she and Onkado had used. In his left hand he held the rope halters he'd tied round their necks and linked together. Her mother's nose and mouth were bleeding and she looked dazed, not really aware of what was happening.

Sometimes Zar sensed that Zorne's attention wasn't wholly upon her, but she knew better than to risk anything; the carnage she'd seen on the platform kept her subdued for now. But the Ramkiseri wasn't infallible: he'd missed Onkado. Deo willing, he could use the now unguarded platform to escape.

Comforted by that, she turned her thoughts to her own predicament. They'd heard Luc's voice booming through the citadel and knew that there were at least three companies above them. That made the chances of reaching the top undetected minimal, but as yet, no one had come their way. Every level below ground was like a wagon wheel, with eight halls extending outwards from the central stairwell, linked by concentric circular corridors. They were making their way to the outer corridor, where there were stairs going up and down.

They'd reached the third of the ten levels below ground before finally they heard soldiers approaching. Zorne forced them into a storage room and made them both kneel in a corner, while he guarded the door. Mirella's eyes were still glazed and unfocused, so she was of no use to

Zar, busy seeking options, the way her father would. She even considered trying to alert the guards – but it was looking very much like Toran Zorne intended to kill Luc, and that was just fine with her.

The patrol was coming closer, searching room to room.

Zar felt Zorne summon his familiar and wished she had Adefar back with her. He conjured an image of the bare back wall in front of them, so when the door opened a moment later, the two men silhouetted in the doorway faced what was apparently just another empty room.

They didn't leave immediately, shining a lantern around, but the illusion held.

'Nothing,' the lantern-holder sighed.

'Whoever we're hunting is probably a kragging sorcerer,' his companion grumbled. 'Raythe Vyre, like as not. Deo, I hope we don't find 'em.'

'Me too,' the lantern-holder said fervently. 'C'mon.'

They vanished and were quickly out of earshot, working with all the cursory attention to detail of underpaid snake-catchers, Zar thought scathingly.

Zorne kept the room dark until they were out of earshot, then lit a sorcerous light in his hands and rechecked their bonds.

Mirella was finally regaining focus. 'Zorne,' she mumbled, 'I can explain–'

'I don't want your explanations,' Zorne retorted. 'You betrayed your vows.'

Zar watched them intently, because this wasn't her whining, vapid mother – and it didn't sound like Zorne meant her wedding vows.

'No, I haven't,' Mirella replied. 'I had to let him destroy Lisenko's division to retain his trust. I knew you wouldn't get caught in the attack.'

Zorne gave Mirella a hard look. 'I find that implausible, given your training. You share the man's bed.'

'*Training?*' Zar asked, looking at her mother again. *She's been trained in etiquette and fashion and bugger-all else, as far as I can see.* 'What training?'

Mirella scowled, then said, 'Before I met Raythe, I was recruited by the Ramkiseri.'

That was so unexpected that Zar let out a derisive snort. Then she thought about it, and her skin began to crawl. 'Truly?'

'Truly,' Mirella said. 'Bolgravia had conquered Magnia and was turning on the former vassal-kingdoms, including Otravia, but there was a peace treaty – everyone was pretending the next wave of invasions wouldn't happen and that the Emperor had no desire for more war.'

'The False Peace,' Zorne murmured. 'Only the gullible believed it would last.'

'Indeed,' Mirella said. 'I'd never reached my full potential in the praxis – my loving family needed a well-trained *marriageable* daughter more than they needed a sorceress – but the Bolgravians recognised what I could be. They made the approach, and my father somewhat grudgingly arranged a place in a Magnian finishing school that was really a Ramkiseri training camp. When I graduated, I was both eminently marriageable and an excellent secret agent. I pursued Raythe Vyre on the instructions of my handlers. I also played a double game with Luc – and that got complicated.' She glanced at Zar. 'Especially when I had you. But it worked out well in the end.'

Zar's mouth filled with bile. '*Worked out well?* You gave away our country and tens of thousands died! And now Bolgravians and turncoats rule. Gerda on high, I didn't think I could ever hate you more than I did, but guess what, *Mother . . .*'

She turned away, shaking with rage and disgust.

Mirella turned back to Zorne. 'You must believe me: I have done all I could. But my sorcery has perforce atrophied, so I can't overpower Luc, and now he spends all his waking hours in the Heart Chamber, where I can't reach him. I'm not your enemy, Zorne.'

'You are unbelievable,' Zar spat out. 'You cannot be my kragging mother.'

'I very much am,' she retorted, not shifting her eyes from Zorne. 'I have been the Emperor's eyes in Luc's household for two decades. I have sacrificed everything for my mission – including losing my daughter. Let me complete it.'

Zorne considered her words, his face remained as impassive as ever.

Mirella's eyes hardened. 'Have you never wondered why you've never been promoted beyond fieldwork, *Under*-Komizar?' Her voice was glacial. 'It is because you lack the emotional intelligence to read complex human relationships – this you know from your own handlers. But you have been trained to trust in hierarchy: that is the Empire's way. So I say to you again: *trust it now.*'

Zar, staring at Zorne's face, saw a very faint frown and guessed that Mirella's assessment was both accurate and painful to him. And she also suspected this new, ruthless incarnation of her mother would destroy him the instant his guard lapsed.

She thought about her options – and chose a side.

'Zorne,' Zar warned him, 'she will knife you in the back. She's with Luc on this: they're out to rule the whole kragging Empire . . . but you know that I want Luc dead as much as you do.'

'That's Raythe Vyre speaking through her,' Mirella sneered. 'Hark at his little pet revolutionary. You can disregard every lying word from her lips, Toran. Every syllable is calculated to breed dissent.'

'Shut up, both of you,' Zorne snarled. 'I will learn the truth when I confront Governor Mandaryke.' He indicated the door. 'We go on.'

'Fool,' Mirella started, but she shut up when Zorne jammed the pistol into her temple.

'Silence,' he ordered, and this time Mirella obeyed, but the venomous look she shot Zar promised a world of punishment once she regained control.

They took the next flight of stairs upwards, until they heard movement above and returned to the outer corridor, seeking an alternate staircase. This was the level with the vats of liquid istariol, visible through open doors as they passed.

Zorne paused and pointed to the giant glass tanks gurgling as the liquid flowed out. 'This is why he must be stopped. Only the Emperor can be permitted to wield such a power.'

'I am pledged to give him exactly that,' Mirella muttered.

'Tell that to General Lisenko's ghost,' Zorne retorted. 'Now, be silent or die.'

They found another stairway and climbed up to the ground floor, where they found the massive kitchens had servants' stairs leading up into the citadel. They saw no one: all Luc's men must be either waiting above or searching fruitlessly below.

But we heard Luc ordering a whole company to the top level, Zar thought. *However good Zorne is, he can't possibly take on twenty men by himself.*

As they reached the next level, she glanced back at Zorne. 'Let me help you,' she pleaded. 'You must believe I want Luc Mandaryke dead with every fibre of my being.'

Zorne shook his head, his eyes stony. 'Mother and daughter: I see no difference. It's the same serpent blood.'

Zar bowed her head, not in defeat but to hide her expression – because as he spoke she'd seen movement at the bottom of the stairs. There was a figure ghosting along in their wake.

It's Onkado – he stayed!

Toran Zorne had a nagging feeling he was being followed, but he forced it from his mind. There was too much ahead to be concerned about what lay behind. He urged the two women on, up the servants' stairs into the fortress itself, although they went no further than the third floor: the ancient Aldar god-kings had been paranoid, permitting no one to approach the upper floors except in plain sight.

Zorne ushered his hostages into an empty corridor that led to the central staircase. From here on, they had no choice but to move in the open.

He knew his own limit. With no way of approaching unseen, and two hostages to protect and manage, twenty armed men was beyond him. Even the praxis could do only so much.

But he did have a plan. Reluctantly, he pulled Teirhinan's heart-stone from his belt-pouch and placed it around Mirella's neck. The noblewoman looked worried; her daughter just watched with a puzzled expression.

He put his mouth to Mirella's ear and whispered, 'Teirhinan.'

Mirella gave him a sharp look. 'What did y–?' Her eyes flew wide and she clutched at her head.

Zorne clapped his left hand over her mouth and pressed her against the wall, trying to keep her silent.

Zarelda took an involuntary step back, and he swung his pistol in her direction.

'Stay,' he told the girl, then turned back and watched Mirella's eyes. He saw panic – then terror as she began to fight–

–until her eyes flashed violet.

'Toran,' Teirhinan Deathless mumbled into his hand. 'I knew I could trust you.'

Zarelda was staring at her mother's transformation in utter horror. *'What have you done?'* she whispered.

He ignored her, too busy checking Teirhinan/Mirella with a sorcer-er's eye, sensing her familiars streaming in, one mizra and one praxis. Mirella's own familiar, fluttering impotently at a distance, shrieked and vanished. Her skin grew paler as her aura intensified – as did the look of gloating pleasure on her face as she pirouetted, looking down at Mirella's lush body with amazement.

'And you gave me *her* ... oh, what a gift!' She gave him an awk-wardly coquettish smile. 'Maybe I'll reward you later.' Then she beamed at Zarelda. 'Hello, *Daughter*,' she giggled. 'Oh, this is going to be *such* fun!'

As she settled into Mirella's body, the hair went from blonde to iron grey.

Zarelda took an involuntary step back, making her halter jerk, and Zorne levelled his gun at the girl. 'Stand still,' he reminded her. 'In case I decide I no longer need you.'

She went rigid.

Zorne put aside his revulsion and touched the woman's shoulder, bringing her attention back to him. 'Teirhinan, we're inside the fort-ress. Luc Mandaryke has declared his true purpose: to bring down the empire. You – as Mirella – are my hostage against him, but he has soldiers outside the Heart Chamber. I need you to deal with them, then help me with him.'

A rational being would have needed time to process the shock of being in a different body; they'd have had a thousand questions, wanted a million reassurances. But Zorne had embroidered the heart-stone's core spells with a few of his own, giving him an unseen edge over the sorceress. Instead of doubt, she grinned enthusiastically and asked, 'Where?'

'I'll show you.' He removed her halter, but left Zarelda Vyre's in place. 'Let's go.'

Luc sat sweating on the Serpent Throne, locked into its ocular senses. Scanning the halls and stairs, he saw no threat, but he was still blind to Raythe's dragon. Mirella hadn't appeared, either, and the doubt and the mounting tension were making his stomach roil. He wanted his enemies before him: he wanted to torch them and cleave them and batter them ... but instead he squirmed impotently, imagining the worst. Even with his First Company standing guard outside this chamber, he didn't feel safe.

Raythe's out there somewhere, I'm sure of it ... Damn it, must I do every-thing *myself?*

Then he reminded himself that in here, with Dakaji's might behind him, he was all but untouchable.

'Let them come,' he snarled. 'I'll kill them all!' He activated the aural instruments and blared, '*SECOND AND THIRD COMPANIES, TO THE TOP FLOOR! NOW!*'

The ocular showed them cowering on the lowest levels, but to his relief they began to break cover and gather in the halls, rallying to his call. They were still far below him when he felt a surge in sorcerous energy, a conflagration right outside the doors to the Heart Chamber. Voices were shouting, shots ringing out, but everything was muffled by the walls and he couldn't work out what was happening. He grasped the ocular's controls frantically, desperate to find out what was happening, right outside his door . . .

'Take us up under the fortress,' Raythe shouted again as the dragon-cannons seared the air behind them, blasting a crater amongst the Otravian lines and causing panic among the surviving soldiers. 'If we go in underneath, he shouldn't be able to reach us.'

The winged beast was already responding, banking into a spiralling climb up into the rock.

'What are we going to do?' Rima shouted over her shoulder.

'I'm thinking we go straight for the throat.'

'How do you mean?'

'Those dragon-cannons fire out and down, so if we just skim the edge of the rock we'll be out of range. I reckon we head for the biggest windows – that'll be the Great Hall.'

'Luc Mandaryke will surely have soldiers there,' Shiazar warned.

'That can't be helped,' Raythe replied. 'We've got to get inside and find Luc – and get to Zar and Onkado – as quickly as we can. Whether he's got a regiment of guards or just a company, our choice must be the same.'

Shiazar nodded in acceptance and gripped her sword hilt. 'You and I again, my hitoshii. This is Destiny.'

'No such thing,' he retorted, although right now, he wished there was. Having her with him made him feel invincible. *I would die for you*, he realised, *but I'd rather live.*

'Are you ready?' Rima called, as the dragon manoeuvred close to the floating rock.

'Aye,' Raythe called. 'Let's go.'

Zarelda watched with sick fear, tension boiling in her gut, as the grey-haired parody of her mother flounced down the corridor. The revelations about Mirella and the feeling of unreality she'd felt since her escape began to be overtaken by the knowledge that chaos was about to be unleashed in Shiro Kamigami, and she began to look for chances to break away and run, regardless of the risk. *Just survive*, she told herself. *Live through this.*

Onkado was near, but neither of them had their sorcery unlocked and she was terrified of what Zorne might do if he saw the Aldar. But no opportunities for escape arose, and they reached the main stairs, where Teirhinan/Mirella conjured shields, then bounded up, almost skipping, with glee written all over her face.

Zorne tugged on Zar's halter. 'Wait here,' he ordered. 'We're not needed.'

A sentry above shouted, 'Halt!' in a cracked, fearful voice, and in answer, Mirella's voice cackled with mad laughter. Flintlocks blasted into life, followed by hideous shrieks and panicky orders.

More shots came, and screams, and the sound of running.

It was over inside a minute and they heard the sorceress sigh in disappointment. 'All gone,' she announced.

Zorne tugged on the halter, and Zar followed him upwards, into a smoky nightmare. The smouldering remains of more than a dozen men were scattered amid pools of steaming blood. There were more soldiers – the rest of the company, Zar assumed – piled in pathetic heaps along the corridor. Teirhinan/Mirella, humming a child's song, was standing outside the doors to the Heart Chamber.

'That creature is in there,' she said hesitantly.

She's scared of Dakaji – really, actually, scared. Zar wasn't sure if that was a good thing or not.

'That's all right,' Zorne said. He murmured something, and Teirhinan suddenly looked stricken.

'Zorne?' Her talons curled, she lurched towards him, snarling out a spell . . .

... and Mirella's body suddenly seemed to empty, the stone round her neck pulsing as she fell to her knees.

Zorne pulled Zar along with him as he walked over to Mirella. He reached down, removed the cord from round her neck, studying the heart-shaped stone briefly, before tucking it back into his belt-pouch.

'Milady?' he said quietly, holding his pistol to Mirella's head.

Mirella gave him a shaky look, still dazed and disoriented. 'What—?' Then she saw the carnage and gasped. 'Zorne, what—?'

Zorne's got that dreadful Teirhinan on a leash too, Zar realised. *But why did he put her back into that artefact?* After a moment, she realised Zorne trusted the madwoman no more than he trusted Mirella. *If she killed Luc, she'd just take his place . . .*

If she could have curled into a ball and closed her eyes now, she would have, because she could see no way to get out of this alive. She was a mouse in a den of lions.

Zorne turned to face the concealed door to the Heart Chamber, implacable in defence of his precious empire. '*Luc Mandaryke! Hear me! I have your wife and daughter. Come out, or they die.*'

The familiar voice repeated, 'Come out, or your wife and daughter die.'

Toran Zorne. Luc went rigid. *He's supposed to be dead – he was in Lisenko's command tent, surely?*

'*OPEN UP!*' Zorne called again.

His heart thudding, Luc turned the Serpent Throne to face the door. Through the ocular, he saw Zorne holding a pistol to Mirella's head. After a moment he realised both women had rope nooses around their necks, and the ropes were in Zorne's other hand. Behind them he saw the remains of his First Company looking like the aftermath of an explosion in an abattoir.

Inside him, Dakaji snarled in fury, and that steadied him. *I'm invincible,* Luc reminded himself. *The one thing that* won't *happen is my death.*

'I have your wife and your daughter,' Zorne called for the third time. 'Surrender the throne, or they die.'

Luc trained the ocular on first Mirella, then Zarelda. *My darling wife . . . who is barren, and cannot give me the son I need. And my disloyal, brainwashed daughter.* Both were expendable – but still, they were worth saving if he could. *Mirella is extremely valuable to me, and Zarelda will come around. Breeding will out in the end.*

He let go the lines of force and rose from the Serpent Throne. This was a risk – but he'd never been afraid of a wager: confidence in one's own powers was vital to any sorcerer. Doubt was for losers. He drew his sword, then gestured and the chamber's door slid open, revealing the Ramkiseri and his prisoners in the flesh.

'Well, Master Zorne,' he said coolly. 'You appear to have the advantage.'

Still snarling inside his skull, Dakaji fed him energy. *The moment he gives me clear sight*, he silently promised, *we'll tear him apart.*

With that, he walked through the doors, sword held casually, knowing only that in the next few seconds, Zorne was going to die. Who else did was largely irrelevant.

Zorne began, 'That's far enou–'

His words faltered as something smashed into the fortress, shaking the entire castle and setting stone cracking apart, wood splintering and shattering glass tinkling down. Then a giant beast's roar echoed up the stairwell.

Raythe braced himself as the dragon flashed over the rim of the floating rock, right past one of those deadly cannon muzzles, but it neither moved nor belched fire. They passed over the outer walls and circled the citadel once to get their bearings, then headed straight for the huge wall of banked windows that marked the Great Hall.

The three riders buried their heads just before the massive body hammered through, bringing windows and frames down in an almighty crash. Flying glass and splintered wood filled the air, ricocheting off shields and raking the beast's leathery skin – then they hit the vast marble floor and skidded. Dragon-Kemara was howling in pain and fright, scrambling in vain at the smooth stone, until a pillar stopped their progress, cracking in half and bringing them to a sudden, painful halt.

For a moment Raythe was sure the whole edifice would collapse on them. He rolled off the dragon's back, landed gracelessly and sprawled at Rima's feet, in time to see Shiazar land on her feet with agility and elegance.

Feeling like a clumsy child, Raythe scrambled to his feet. He scanned the massive hall, stopping at the great double doors opening to the lower levels. A number of red-coated soldiers were standing there, gaping at them.

He scrambled to his feet, yelling, 'Oi, you lot! Where's my daughter?'

'It's Vyre!' one shouted – a little redundantly, Raythe thought – and they drew their flintlocks to their shoulders, took aim and fired.

So much for the brotherhood of Otravia, Raythe thought, conjuring shields, but before the powder had even ignited, the dragon had found its feet and with a deafening roar, interposed its body between the soldiers and Raythe, Shiazar and Rima.

The lead balls pinged harmlessly off its flanks, at which the redjacks squawked and ran for their lives. Raythe went after them, but they were already vanishing down the spiral stairs.

Damn. Now how am I going to find out where Zar is? His instincts told him up. *She's Mirella's daughter; they wouldn't keep her below-ground.*

He was slamming shut the giant doors when the dragon made a keening sound, then a more human groan, and its body collapsed into a sludge of rocks and mud from which a naked Kemara Solus stumbled to her feet. He had a moment to notice that her body was somehow perfected, with not an ounce of fat and the musculature of a warrior – or a predator – before she conjured leathery armour like Shiazar's. Her scarlet hair was lustrous, her skin like alabaster. She could have been an Aldar – and he doubted that was coincidence.

Kemara took Rima's hand and brushed her lips across her cheek before facing Raythe.

'Lord Vyre,' she drawled, in the sardonic voice she reserved for him, 'It's good to see you're still popular with your countrymen.'

'Welcome back, Kemara,' he replied, matching her tone. 'What do I need to know?'

Rima spoke first. 'You were right – the guardian spirit, the Kaiju – is in the istariol.'

'It *is* the istariol,' Kemara clarified, 'and it's my familiar now. Or I'm its familiar. Something like that.'

Shiazar's eyes went wide. '*Ah*,' she said, in a profoundly awestruck voice.

Holy Deo! Raythe thought.

'But I'm still me,' Kemara insisted, looking at Rima. 'I'm just . . . other things as well.'

But all that would have to wait, because somewhere above them they heard angry voices, followed by two shots. Raythe looked up –

– and Shiazar yanked him back as a dark shape plummeted down in a shower of broken stonework that shattered into smaller fragments while the body bounced and went limp.

'What was that?' Zarelda gasped, as the whole citadel shuddered at the impact of whatever had struck the building. Her mother, beside her, was visibly quaking and even Torne Zorne had flinched – but Luc just kept walking towards them, sword held casually off-guard.

'Oh, I imagine that's Raythe making an entrance,' he said casually. 'Kragging show-off.'

Zar's heart thudded. *Father!*

From below came a mighty roar, and a volley of shots rang out, but Zorne's attention had already flashed back to the immediate threat. He shifted his aim to Luc's chest and snapped, 'That's close enough, Mandaryke. On your knees.'

Mandaryke smiled, stopped and spread his arms, as if greeting a close friend. Zar tensed for movement, even though with her neck in a halter and her hands and sorcery bound, she felt as helpless as a kitten.

Why's Luc so kragging confident? she wondered, sensing that Zorne was doing the same. *Away from that cursed throne, he should be severed from Dakaji . . .*

'Zorne, you're making a mistake,' Luc remarked. 'I still serve the empire – and so does my wife: your superior.' He looked at Mirella. 'What's he done to your hair, darling?'

Mirella blinked, then tossed her head. Her long tresses flicked onto one shoulder and when she saw the state of it, grey and tangled, she gave a small shriek.

Luc began to walk forward again, sword still pointed at the floor.

'Halt, I said!' Zorne snarled. 'Stop right there!'

'Or what? You'll kill a Ramkiseri komizar? Or maybe my completely superfluous daughter?' Luc smiled and levelled his sword at Zorne. 'If this were a card game, you'd be folding your hand and cashing out.'

Zorne thumbed the hammer back. '*I said to stop.*'

Smirking, Luc took another step . . .

. . . and Zorne fired, the ball punching into Luc's chest, making him stagger.

Mirella screamed as he clutched his chest and glared at the blood welling between his fingers.

Zar was too stunned to know how to react, just stared—

—until Luc looked up, gave a fiendish grin and raised his sword. 'Have you not worked this out yet, *Under-Komizar*? I am beyond such weapons. What else have you got?'

Zar saw Zorne's composure crack, just for a fragment of a moment, and realised that he'd gambled everything on luring Luc out of the Heart Chamber, believing he'd be vulnerable. But his mask of implacability reformed instantly and his hand flashed to the pouch where Teirhinan's heart-stone lay.

Luc, though, was faster, flashing forward and ramming three feet of steel into Zorne's midriff, thrusting the Ramkiseri backwards into the charred balustrade, which broke with a crack, sending him plummeting into the darkness, pulling free of Luc's blade as he fell.

With a shriek, half throttled by their leashes, Mirella and Zar were dragged after Zorne, who was still clutching the ropes. They slammed into the balustrade, just as the ropes were ripped from Zorne's limp hand and he fell away . . .

For a moment Zar lay there, her throat cruelly sore and bloody from where the rope had nearly hanged her. Her mother was thrashing beside her as Luc cut her bonds, a look of grim triumph on his face. The wound on his chest was still bleeding, but he was oblivious to what should have been a mortal injury.

He looked into his wife's eyes and smiled triumphantly. 'Well,' he breathed, 'shall I attend to our other guests?'

Dear Gerda, Father doesn't stand a chance, Zar wailed inside.

All the same, she opened her mouth and tried to shout, '*Father – we're up here!*'

Nothing came out but a croak, but even so, Luc pushed Mirella aside and was bunching his fist, about to swing for her – when Onkado blurred out of the shadows between two of the giant statues, leading with a pistol shot to the forehead which felled the nobleman, following it up by thrusting his Aldar blade into Luc's chest.

Luc slid noiselessly to the ground with a stunned look on his face.

Onkado turned to Zar. 'Are you well?'

Behind him, Mirella's eyes had contorted in horror and hate . . .

The body that had fallen from above was Toran Zorne, and he was still alive – but not for long. There was a gaping sword wound in his chest and he was already grey and twitching towards oblivion.

Raythe grabbed the man's bloody shirt, and hissed, 'Zorne!'

The Ramkiseri looked up him, glassy-eyed, tried to speak and failed.

Shiazar pulled on his sleeve. 'Raythe, he's gone. We need to find Zar.'

She was right – but Toran Zorne had hunted him for the last four years, so watching his face empty was like watching the moon set over a desert: emptiness turning to entropy.

'Go to the Pit and burn,' he snarled, before gripping Shiazar's offered hand and letting her draw him up.

Looking up, Raythe could see where Zorne had fallen from, a broken balustrade at the top of the sweeping spiral staircase.

'Top floor,' he told Kemara and Rima, who were brandishing their weapons expectantly. 'We have to hurry.'

Together, they took to the stairs.

Luc knew he should be dying: both the pistol shot and the sword blow would have been fatal on their own, but together, and with the shock of the unexpected wounds, he was barely clinging on. His body went limp as he stared down at his riven torso, pierced by the shining steel, and then up at the golden fury of the Aldar's face.

Then Mirella moved as if possessed by a Pit-beast. With a throaty croak, she gripped Onkado's sword-arm with her left hand, while backhanding him across the face with her right. Only she and Luc knew about the tiny needle hidden in the huge diamond ring he had gifted her on their wedding day, and it did its job: blood was already welling up on the Aldar's cheek from a deep scratch.

The Aldar spun to face her, sword raised – until the venom hit him and he reeled drunkenly.

Zar, gasping painfully, reached for him, but Mirella wasn't done: she battered her fist into Onkado's jaw with the full force of honed muscles and Ramkiseri skill, snapping his head back and stretching him out on the floor, then she wrenched out Luc's dagger, glaring as her daughter tried to shield the stricken Aldar.

Luc's vision was starting to fade; for a moment, he felt like he was floating inside his own body. Dakaji had pinned him to life when he should have been swept away: to the spirit beast, the wounds were just holes, the blood loss nothing worth attention and his pain not even a distraction. He clung to that link as his body began to reknit itself, popping out the hot lead ball in his skull, which rolled harmlessly across the marble floor.

Mirella gripped his face, giving him the most intense look of admiration and desire he'd ever seen: a moment that transcended pain and pleasure alike.

'Husband,' she whispered hoarsely, as if in the throes of pleasure, 'you are *everything*.'

She was dishevelled, grey and pallid, like a vision of her future old age, and yet he had never loved her more. He broke Zorne's binding on her sorcery, then hugged her with all his strength.

'We're going to krag them *all*, Mirella,' he told her. 'You and me, together.'

Boots echoed on the stairs: Raythe was on his way and right now neither of them were in any shape to deal with his old foe and his dragon-riding comrades. He looked down at his daughter, crouched over the body of this Aldar youth when she should have been aiding her *parents*.

For an instant, he wanted to kill her . . .

Instead, he gestured, conjuring force to rip her from the Aldar's prone body. He hurled her bodily into the Heart Chamber, then peered over the balustrade. At first the stairs looked empty, then he saw shadows on the outside edge, just out of direct sight. At the bottom of the shaft he could see Toran Zorne, lying unmoving in a pool of blood. *Good riddance, you stubborn bastard*, he thought.

'Do I kill this one?' Mirella was standing over Onkado, his Aldar blade in her hand.

Luc shook his head. 'We may yet need him once we've finished slaughtering Raythe and his interfering friends, for our menagerie.'

His body was still regenerating, the pain a distraction, but moving was getting easier by the second, so he helped Mirella to stagger back into the Heart Chamber, then slammed the door shut. With a gesture, he swept Zar off the floor and pinned her against the far wall, before lurching painfully to the throne and sitting.

'Mirella, my love, ward the door,' he said, surrendering himself to Dakaji. 'I can handle Raythe's cronies if I'm in this throne. We're going to end this, right now.'

Dakaji cleaved to him fully and he felt its body shifting inside the stone walls – for this was no serpent, or any kind of creature, but the activated istariol within the stone and it could be whatever shape it wished. Its energy thrilled through him, and he embraced and guided it, an exquisite symbiosis.

Through the ocular he could see shadowy figures ghosting along outside the chamber, closing in: Raythe, and three others. One, a woman, darted to the prone body of Onkado and knelt over it, then rose and returned to the shadows again.

He drew on Dakaji, bringing more of its fluid form up into the walls around this chamber. It took only moments to make the chamber a death trap. 'Stay behind the throne,' he told Mirella. 'This will get messy.'

'You know what Raythe's like,' she croaked. 'Don't give him a chance.'

Sound advice. 'As soon as they're all in reach, they die,' he promised. He conjured his shields and readied himself for the carnage to come.

A few seconds later, a counter-spell broke Mirella's wards, the doors slid open and a lead ball bounced impotently off his shields.

A moment later Raythe himself appeared, smoking gun in his hand.

'You don't get to do it the easy way, Raythe,' Luc told him.

'I never do,' he sighed, tossing the gun away and shifting his sword to his right hand.

Raythe entered the room, followed, somewhat to Luc's surprise, by three stunning women who fanned out around him: a flame-haired Ferrean, a native woman and the Aldar Queen. Each radiated sorcerous power, whatever familiars they used inside them and primed. But they moved with the wariness of climbers on an unknown rockface.

What fun I'll have with you all, Luc thought. *If there's anything left of you when this fight's over.*

He was poised to strike, but Dakaji had tensed at the sight of the red-head, so he withheld his planned blow, instead letting them absorb the sight of Mirella behind him, and the helpless Zarelda, pinned to the wall behind him.

Dakaji? he asked. *What is it?*

He got no reply, but sensed a quiver of anticipation, anxiety, hatred . . . and a touch of fear, which suggested the outcome of this day was not, after all, a foregone conclusion. This could yet go badly . . .

Masking his uncertainty, he called, 'How is it you lose every battle and yet still you survive, Raythe? It is truly an incredible skill. But I'm glad you're here, strangely. It will be so much more satisfying to kill you in person. Taking you down from a mile away with a cannon was too impersonal for such a very *personal* feud.'

'We'll see,' Raythe said, sounding oddly calm.

He looked worn-out but resolute, Luc thought, and he was shielding the Aldar woman, which suggested yet another of his famously mismatched romances.

'Let Zarelda go,' Raythe said, 'so you and I can settle this.'

'I don't think so,' Luc sniffed. 'You see, I think you value her more than I do – so maybe you should just yield now, or I'll dismember her.'

He sensed Mirella stiffen at that, but he'd explain later: *Just a bluff,* he'd tell her, although it wasn't.

He looked at the Aldar Queen. 'I'm planning to breed a new line of Aldar. I'll be sure to include you.'

Her eyes hardened, but she too made no move, instead visibly weighing up her surroundings like a seasoned fighter, with no sign of fear.

Luc's eyes trailed across the other two as Dakaji filled his mind with images and words – they had all walked the corridors up here, and it knew who they were. 'Kemara Solus . . . and Rima. Well, no promises for either of you, except to assure you that I will be sure to enjoy your last moments.'

'Are you done talking?' Kemara growled.

Inside Luc, Dakaji shivered at her voice, as if the Ferrean woman represented some massive opportunity that it desperately craved ... but also the greatest risk.

Life is risk, he thought. *So let's roll the dice.*

Kemara had felt it the moment she entered the castle: it was deep in the stone, a lurking presence that had been asleep when she was last here, lulled by centuries of stasis. But it was awake now, and here in this chamber it was totally present, bound up in the eerie crystal serpent-shaped throne.

She understood it, too, for it was, in a sense, a child of the Kaiju, whose spirit now infused her. This rival spirit had been the central node of the istariol veins lying beneath what was now the Fenua Tangato. When it broke away from the ground, taking with it the rock that encased it, it floated upwards and then just remained there, a barren lump hanging above the broken crater, while the earth below seethed with life. Alone and forlorn, for it was sentient, and aware of what it had lost, it was trapped in the sky until the Aldar came. Their sorcery enabled them to reach the floating rock and claim it for their own, turning it into the fortress Shiro Kamigami, while beneath them, a city grew. Then the Aldar King Tariel discovered the presence within the istariol and bonded with it, naming it Dakaji or Fire Serpent. Dakaji gave Tariel strength, and in return lived vicariously through the king and his heirs.

Then came the wars, rival kingdoms fighting with floating citadels. Dakaji was untethered and went to battle, blasting away using weapons devised by the Aldar until the rival cities fell, one after the other – each victory meaning the death of other entities just like itself.

War changed the fire serpent: he had been infected by the Aldar kings' destructive sorcery, which had left a scar it couldn't even perceive. It started to revel in the destruction, identifying itself strongly with the god-kings, even beginning to conceive of itself as male.

Eventually, Dakaji was the last one left.

But those glory days ended suddenly. Finally there was just him and Tashvariel the Usurper, a being so insane that even Dakaji recognised it and shut himself away, refusing to serve. Without Dakaji, Tashvariel could no longer defend the citadel, so he triggered a mizra storm – then he and his acolytes vanished from Dakaji's perceptions.

Dakaji was dimly aware that his Mother still existed far below, shielding a handful of humans and Aldar from the freezing of the world, but they couldn't reach each other, and with his proto-emotions shaped by mizra, war and hate, he feared her too much to try. The subsequent five centuries crawled by, with him raging in his loneliness, mourning all he'd lost.

Finally, new life beckoned: Luc Mandaryke had awakened him and he'd bonded with his new god and master. He refused to let this chance slip.

All this, the Kaiju – and through her, Kemara – sensed, along with the realisation that Dakaji was terrified of her. But up here, with the Kaiju within her but separated from the land below, Dakaji had the edge.

He lashed out with all his pent-up might.

She had a moment's warning as the walls of the chamber turned opaque and she caught sight of the entity behind them: a writhing mass of istariol threads wriggling through the stone. Then Luc roared aloud, his face red with fury, a true Pit Fiend – and dozens of thick tendrils of istariol smashed through the stonework and burst into the chamber.

Kemara glimpsed Rima, Raythe and Shiazar trying to escape as almost every flailing limb came for her. Behind him, his wife was gaping, but not in triumph – she looked shocked, as if she'd finally realised that her husband had gone far beyond any power to contain him.

The writhing istariol tentacles had clamped around Kemara before she could defend herself, a mouth opened up in its body and she was pulled into that gaping maw, the tentacles tearing into her body . . .

Walking into the lair of your worst enemy wasn't a great plan, but it was the only one available – and Luc looked so cocky that perhaps he might let something slip. His body and the spells he'd readied were balanced between fight and flight, and Shiazar and Rima mirrored his movements, poised but uncommitted. *Something* was about to happen, that was clear, but only Luc knew what.

Then the stone walls burst inwards on all sides and things like giant red tree-roots erupted through. Before they could react, most of those appendages had converged on Kemara, taking her down in a hideous spray of blood – and she was pulled into a giant maw that opened in one wall, a teeth-laden throat that snapped shut on her before they could move an inch. Even Mirella looked shocked – but Luc was roaring in triumph.

Kemara! he thought, reeling in shock – but there was no time to process what had happened, for the lesser threads had turned their attention on the other intruders.

Raythe darted backwards, shouting to Cognatus to shield him as he slashed at the tendrils. His blade lopped through two or three at a time, sending liquid istariol spurting across the chamber . . .

Enraged, Luc unleashed a wave of force, throwing Raythe, Rima and Shiazar against the walls, despite their shielding. Those wardings flashed on impact as Rima flew through the door behind them, smashed into one of the statues and went limp. Bones audibly broke when Shiazar's shoulder hit the doorframe; reeling, she slid to the ground. More istariol tentacles were exploding from the floor, mouths opening in the tips like giant worms, reaching for Raythe, the only one still standing.

Too dazed to think straight, he shouted to Cognatus, '*Ignis istarios!*' – surely the most reckless spell he'd ever assayed – and hurled himself towards the door.

Mirella and Zar were shielded by the giant crystal throne, but Luc was facing Raythe as the liquid istariol jetting through the chamber burst into flame and imploded in a great flash. Luc, trapped in the throne, lit up like a torch, while Raythe was hurled outwards, past Shiazar and Rima and into the broken balustrade.

The burning tentacles themselves were trying to thrash their way back into the walls, most of them falling to ash as they fled. Bricks started crashing down around the holes they left as they slithered back out of sight, and a ghastly shrieking filled the air: Luc, still linked to Dakaji, was screaming in agony as his skin blackened and his hair blazed, but still he managed to howl out a dousing spell, his voice resonating through the entire citadel through some attribute of the throne.

The realisation that his spell could have disintegrated the entire fortress almost paralysed Raythe, as did the knowledge that only her position behind the throne had saved Zar. But he threw off the shock and staggered back into the maelstrom, sword in hand . . .

Luc saw him coming.

When the spells and counter-spells the two men snapped out at each other fell apart, Raythe guessed that Luc's powers were tied to this chamber, and were either drained or thrown into turmoil, because his spells, earlier so potent, now had no more heft than anyone else's.

Encouraged, he closed the gap at the run, as Luc, his body still smoking, snatched up his blade and met him head-on.

For a few seconds Raythe attacked, each blow potentially lethal, desperate to end this, but Luc, apparently impervious to his hideously seared body, kept turning his blows aside.

Then he began to counter and Raythe lost momentum. *I've never beaten Luc in a straight-up fight*, he couldn't forget, and as doubt began to infect him, he fell for the same old trick Luc always pulled. Lured into a lunge, he thrust, over-extended and saw the end coming as Luc ghosted sideways, parried and riposted.

Caught off-balance, Raythe twisted desperately, taking the blade in his hip. He roared in pain, feeling the steel ripping through muscle and gouging into bone. Giving ground, defending desperately, his back hit the curved wall, next to where Zar was sprawled. A moment later Luc slashed open Raythe's left forearm; he tried to recover but slipped in blood and liquid istariol and fell.

His enemy loomed over him.

Behind him, Raythe glimpsed a dishevelled, grey-haired Mirella, looking more sickly than he'd ever seen her. Her dark eyes were fixed on him, but there was neither love nor remorse. She'd pulled a tiny purse-pistol from somewhere and was training it on him, but she couldn't fire yet, for fear of hitting Luc. It looked like she wouldn't need to, anyway: he was lost.

'Loser,' Luc snarled, as once again, his tortured flesh slowly began to reform, ash flaking from his skin. 'Politics, love and war – I've whipped you at *everything*.' He bared his teeth in a rictus grin. 'Thanks for coming.'

Then he thrust, unerringly, for Raythe's heart . . .

Kemara died in seconds as giant spikes burst from the tentacled horror gripping her, spearing her torso and skull, then she was pulled apart and swallowed by Dakaji.

This wasn't death, though, but transfiguration: her body was one with the Kaiju, and the Kaiju and Dakaji were kin. When Dakaji took her in, she entered not as food, but as a disease. His blood began to boil and he went mad, fleeing inside himself, trying to deal with physical agony, a sensation he'd never before felt.

But Kemara knew all about it, and she rode the wave into Dakaji's core. This was the reverse of her own fight with Teirhinan Deathless for the soul of the Kaiju: this time she was the aggressor, and there was no one to cast her out. Dakaji couldn't fight, for she was already inside. Finally, in despair, he turned at bay, scared of losing himself and terrified of her. He lashed out, remembering that here, he was the giant, and *she* was the interloper.

That struggle might have destroyed them both, but the Kaiju reached through Kemara and spoke to her lost child.

I am your mother, Kemara heard, deep inside herself. *Come to me, my child . . .*

It dimly occurred to Zar that she was alive, groggy but unrestrained, lying on the floor of the Heart Chamber. The searingly hot air was filled with smoke, the walls were in ruins, punctured from behind, with broken bricks and masonry fallen everywhere. Some kind of blast of energy had changed everything, including releasing the forces that had bound her to the wall. She could barely fill her lungs, but her sight was clearing, enough to see her mother, a pistol in her hand, sitting on the floor just a couple of yards away, watching Luc and Raythe fighting.

Then a dagger clattered to the ground, Raythe faltered and fell, and Luc loomed over him, his own blade poised for the kill.

She grabbed the knife, rolled and *stabbed*.

Luc's leg buckled as Zar thrust Raythe's dagger into his right calf. Roaring in outrage, his leg gave way, his blade gouged the floor beside Raythe's shoulder, he fell forward – to find Raythe meeting him with a head-butt, crunching his forehead into Luc's face.

Luc felt a cheekbone break – then they were going for each other's throats. Luc was bigger and stronger and on top; he quickly took control, his scalded face mottled with hate.

Zar reared up, bloody knife in hand, and tried to stab again, but she'd forgotten to keep an eye on her mother.

Mirella backhanded her away, then trained her pistol on her daughter. 'You will stay out of this,' she snarled.

'*Ignus!*' Luc shouted, snatching up his sword, which burst into flame.

Dakaji wavered, torn between the fear and rage of this lonely existence and the longing to return to the bosom of the earth, where life teemed and bloomed, never silent, never still. Remembering what had been, all desire to fight vanished. Like a river seeking the sea, all Dakaji wanted was to go *home*. Dakaji surrendered and became one with his Mother the earth, and Kemara found herself wrapped up inside that embrace, inextricably part of it.

Mother, Dakaji cried, broken and seeking a new mould.

Hush, child, the Kaiju answered. *You're safe now.*

Kemara reached in and quietly bound both entities to her, severing the cord that tied Luc Mandaryke to his monstrous familiar.

The flames licking Luc's blade winked out. He reeled, unbalanced, with no idea what the krag had happened. Dakaji had vanished from his awareness; suddenly, he was hollowed out.

In that instant of hesitation, Raythe snatched up his own sword and plunged the blade into Luc's chest from the left side, skewering the heart.

Luc gasped, staring down at him in shock . . . then his eyes went blind and his body flopped to the ground.

Mirella screamed hoarsely as her husband sagged sideways, his sword clanging to the floor. She fell on him, shrieking at him to get up, then she swung round, brandishing her little pistol, staring along the barrel at Raythe.

There was nothing he could do to stop her—

Zar interposed herself, facing her mother defiantly.

Mirella's finger twitched . . . then she lowered the pistol, rolled onto her side and curled up in a foetal position, sobbing.

Raythe struggled up, threw his arms round his daughter and thanked every god there ever was.

6

Some Kind of Peace

At first, there was bliss; the embrace of his daughter, who'd saved his life, anchored Raythe to the moment. But then he let her go to Onkado while he sought Shiazar and Rima, propping each other up outside the chamber. Shiazar's collarbone was broken, and so was Rima's shin. He answered their dazed questions while he helped them get comfortable: *yes, Luc was dead. Maybe they were safe.* He didn't really know.

Kemara's gone again, he thought numbly. *Something happened.*

'We need splints,' Shiazar said, breaking his train of thought. 'Raythe? Rima needs a splint for her leg.'

Nodding vacantly, he limped to the broken balustrade. As he was breaking off a piece of wood, he glanced down . . .

His heart thudded and he went from grieving to icy dread.

Toran Zorne's body was gone, leaving just a smeared puddle of blood.

Holy Gerda . . .

He hurried back to Shiazar, trying not to show his fear, because everyone was hurt and there was nothing she could do. Handing over the short wooden pole, he said, 'I'll see what else I can find.' He hoped she'd think it was pain making the sweat bead on his forehead.

He scooped up his sword, hobbled to the door and found his pistol, reloaded and primed it, then took the stairs as fast as he could, though his hip was bleeding and each step was agony. He solved that by riding the bannister, sliding down level after level until he landed in the Great Hall.

Zorne's blood trail led to the double doors and the stairwell leading down.

He followed, fear growing in his heart.

The Ramkiseri were trained to prioritise goals and devise fall-back plans. Toran Zorne had always been an exemplary agent and he knew what he had to do. When he came up here, he'd intended to seize control of the fortress himself, kill everyone else and then fly it home to Reka-Dovoi. His Emperor would expect nothing less: the ultimate weapon belonged by right to the ultimate ruler, the Khagan himself.

When Luc Mandaryke bested him – and not just bested him, but made him see that he was so outmatched that to even try had been a monumental error – his goal changed.

This thing cannot be permitted to remain in the hands of these traitors.

He'd been fading into unconsciousness when Raythe Vyre knelt over him, so he'd played one last, desperate trick: he'd feigned death, although in truth, he was barely pretending. Any other man with those injuries would have died, but he was a sorcerer with a familiar. Not for the first time, Ruscht sustained him, keeping body and soul united, soaking up pain and lending energy.

If you can't run, you walk, and if you can't do that, you crawl. For your empire, you give your all.

He did give his all, dragging himself across that massive hall, too weak and delirious to conceal the snail-trail of blood marking his passing. Even with Ruscht labouring inside him, he was in danger of bleeding out.

Then came the torture of the stairs, each step a new trial, knowing a slip would rip open his wounds once again. He slithered like a dying animal into the darkness below.

But his thoughts were shining and bright, because salvation lay in martyrdom. *My Emperor will know I saved him. Deo will whisper it in his ear. Gerda will sing of me.*

Such thoughts sustained him down the stairs, to the level where the deadly liquid istariol was stored in giant glass vats.

'All the Empire asks of you is everything,' the Ramkiseri Autarch told my class on graduation. *'Will you give it?'*

'Ya dou!' we all thundered. I shall. And I will.

He crawled along the darkened corridor, his lifeblood pumping out despite everything Ruscht could do, knowing that ahead of him was an open door, where the pale red glow of the liquid istariol would light his way to salvation.

'Remember this, my shadow warriors: it is through you that oneness shall be achieved: a world with no war, because there will be no enemies. A world with no poverty, for all are equal in servitude to our Emperor.'

He heard boots on the stairs: someone was coming for him, and they were running.

With a silent scream, he hauled himself to his feet and tried to do likewise.

Someone shouted his name . . .

His shoulder burning, his hip screaming, the blood soaking his clothing eroding his strength, Raythe threw all he had left into movement, following the scarlet smear down the stairs, along a hallway and towards the rooms containing the liquid istariol.

No one impeded him as he ran – any soldiers still below hadn't come to check out the racket; they might have already used the platform to escape. With teeth gritted against the arrows of pain trying to bring him down, he pressed on until he finally caught a glimpse of someone lurching towards an open door emanating pale red light.

'ZORNE!' he shouted, but the Ramkiseri had already vanished inside.

Terror lent Raythe wings as he pelted along the corridor, ignoring the agony of every footfall. He tore through the door, pistol extended and sword ready.

Steel flashed, but he was already throwing himself headlong, passing beneath a scything blow that would have taken off his head, rolling and coming up with pistol ready.

Zorne, looking as implacable as ever, was muttering praxis commands as he aimed his own pistol – at the nearest vat of liquid istariol. Inside the gun barrel where light was glimmering, Raythe read the spell's effect: Zorne had enchanted the lead ball so that it would ignite the istariol.

'No!' Raythe gasped. 'Gerda's Teats, man, you'll kill everyone in this valley.'

'Rebels and savages. This fortress cannot fall into such hands.' Zorne's face was a sickly grey, he was bleeding profusely and swaying, but his gun hand was steady and his eyes intent. 'Mandaryke wished to destroy the Empire, the only unifying force this world has. Those are your own goals. I will not permit it.'

'I renounced any return to Magnia,' Raythe said. 'This is my home now.'

'Liar. You've never given up your rebel dreams.'

'No! The istariol belongs to the Tangato – I don't want it.' It was the absolute truth, and he tried to put every ounce of his conviction into expressing it, but he already knew that Zorne would not believe him.

Zorne's finger tightened – but another voice rang out. *'Under-Komizar, stand down!'*

He looked past Raythe at Mirella, grey-haired, battered and bloodied, standing at the door with her little purse-gun aimed at Zorne's head.

He frowned. 'Komizar? Pokem dol ya?'

Raythe knew enough Bolgravian to translate: *Komizar, why must I?*

'Komizar?' he blurted incredulously, looking at Mirella in shock.

'Yuz, etu moi raan,' she drawled, her eyes locked on Zorne. *Yes, that is my rank.*

Ramkiseri . . . I was married *to one of them . . .*

For a moment Raythe thought his heart would give out.

'I must complete my mission,' Zorne replied. 'For my Empire.'

His trigger finger tightened again – and a shot rang out.

It was not from Zorne's gun.

Mirella's shot was true, punching a hole in Zorne's temple. His head snapped back, his body convulsed, the pistol he held discharged as his hand jerked in spasm.

Raythe held his breath in rigid terror – as the ball smacked into the wall, the spell on it causing a flash of sorcerous energy that would have ignited the istariol and destroyed the fortress and all around it.

As the Ramkiseri crumpled, Raythe twisted and trained his pistol on Mirella. 'This is loaded. Yours isn't.'

She gave him a world-weary, contemptuous look. 'Point that damn thing elsewhere. You know you won't use it.'

To prove herself right, she moved forward, bent over Zorne and closed his eyes. 'Possibly the saddest man I've ever met: someone so unable to comprehend humanity that he had to make it orderly by eliminating anyone who didn't conform to his concept of *life as duty*.'

Raythe kept his gun raised. 'Unlike yourself and all the "good" Ramkiseri that just murder for good old-fashioned reasons like patriotism and greed?'

She faced him haughtily. 'Grow up, Raythe. Otravia had spies, we Ramkiseri had better ones. Your stupid idealism dragged tens of thousands of men and women into an utterly hopeless rebellion. You've got far more blood on your hands than I will ever have.'

'So freedom's not worth fighting for?' he snapped back.

'Freedom is an illusion.' She bent to pick up Zorne's pistol, but Raythe put his foot on it. Hissing in frustration, she returned to Zorne's body. From his belt-pouch she pulled out a leather cord holding an ugly stone pendant that looked like a small, calcified heart. She dropped it to the floor and kicked it over to him. 'Feed this into a furnace,' she advised, 'and whatever you do, don't touch the stone. It contains the soul of Teirhinan Deathless.'

Raythe's skin crawled, but he picked it up by the cord, peered at it, whirled it around – and smashed it into a pillar. It shattered with a faint wailing sound that quickly vanished into the air.

'Or do that.' Mirella sniffed. 'Good kragging riddance.'

Raythe rose painfully to his feet, knowing he was reaching the edge of endurance. Willpower driving him on, he crunched the shards of stone to powder, then retrained his pistol on his former wife, and said 'Walk.'

There's an army below us, and soldiers up here. If I falter, she could turn on me. This isn't over yet . . .

Mirella gave him a hard, assessing look, and he knew she was thinking exactly the same. However, grimacing, she complied wordlessly with his command and they hobbled back to the stairwell.

Cognatus was fluttering about inside him, keeping him on his feet, and he guessed Mirella's familiar was doing the same for her.

Glancing down the stairwell, he could see soldiers far below, cowering in fear of dragons and sorcerers and the madness of the world. They would need to be dealt with later, but they could wait for now; he had to ensure Mirella didn't take command of them. He lifted his pistol. 'Upstairs.'

Mirella measured his intent . . . he tightened his finger on the trigger . . .

Then she bowed her head and started up the steps, and he followed, exhaling in guarded relief.

When they entered the Great Hall, Mirella drifted toward the ancient imperial throne in the middle of the giant space. Fingering her tangled grey hair morosely, she turned to face Raythe.

'Well,' she said, gesturing as if in ownership, 'here we are. We could take this citadel back and free our homeland, then all of Magnia. My family are still the biggest powerbrokers in Otravia – with our money and this fortress, you could finally become the hero you always thought you were.'

'What about your Ramkiseri duties?'

'I don't give a krag about Bolgravia. I want power. That's what Luc wanted too. His death doesn't change the equation overly.' She lowered her lashes in in a languid, come-hither look. 'Who knows, maybe we could even rediscover that passion we once had?'

The callous changing of her skin utterly repulsed him. Shaking his head, he said, 'It doesn't belong to you or me,' he replied. 'It belongs to Queen Shiazar.'

'It's the property of anyone strong enough to control it.'

'Then it still belongs to the Queen.' *Or Kemara*, he reflected, *not that she likely wants it.* 'We've built lives here, Mirella – or we were trying to, until you showed up. We're not going back – and nor are you.'

She scowled disgustedly. 'The Raythe Vyre *I* knew had ambition. He would have razed cities to *win*. The only difference between you and Luc was that he backed the right side.'

'No, whatever my family was, I was always Liberali. That's a whole world of difference.'

'It's all just labels.'

'You're wrong, Mirella. A Liberali believes in the rule of the people, for the people. I fight for the *whole* community, for minorities and misfits, not just the elite and their sycophants. It's not a faction, it's a cause.'

'Says the noble-born Lord Vyre,' she sneered. 'Maybe your idealism is why you always lose.'

'Actually, today we won,' he snapped back, already sick of her cynicism. 'And here's what's going to happen. You'll be locked away. The Otravian soldiers will be offered the same choice that my people were: to remain and serve the Queen – for ever – or die.'

'You speak for her, do you?' Mirella sneered. 'Are you bedding her?'

'That's none of your business. Oh, and I'd advise you to be more conciliatory with Queen Shiazar: when you stand trial, she'll be the one sitting in judgment. You are aware treason carries the death penalty, I assume.'

She went pale. 'You wouldn't let that happen.'

'I'll be leading the prosecution.'

With arrogant defiance, she spat, 'I *despise* you. A real man would take this weapon and conquer the world with it – and one day, one will come: he'll take it, and he'll take down you and your pathetic Queen and–'

He'd had enough of her posturing and theatrics. 'Mirella Mandaryke, you are hereby arrested and–'

'Krag off,' she shrieked, stamping her foot. 'You can't touch me.'

'– charged with high treason, espionage and conspiracy to murder.'

'You are scum! Let me see my daughter –'

'She's right here,' Zar said, stepping gingerly from behind a nearby pillar. She looked a bit better than the last time he'd seen her, and she had her familiar back, the little fox Adefar.

'Zaza!' Mirella reached out her arms in embrace. 'You'll stand by me, yes, yes – you'll protect me from this madman and his –'

Zar slapped her hands away. 'I hope I see you hanged.'

After securing Mirella's praxis, disarming her and locking his very-much-ex-wife in a guest room – one that didn't look out onto a roof, balcony or anything climbable – Raythe went looking for Shiazar and Rima. That didn't take long: Shiazar had put Rima to bed in a room a few doors down.

Raythe knocked softly, entering when there was no response– and stopped abruptly. Kemara was sitting at Rima's side, watching over the sleeping woman.

'Holy Gerda,' he exclaimed.

Kemara snorted. 'Was nowt to do with her. Pleased to see you too.'

He took a deep breath, heart thumping, and admitted, 'Oh, I'm beyond pleased. I just thought I was seeing a ghost.'

Kemara's face softened. 'Fair enough – but I'm not sure I *can* die any more.' She bent over Rima and stroking her hair, added, 'Nor do I want to. I've got a lot to live for . . . and that's a phrase I never thought I'd ever say.'

Raythe took a seat. 'How is she?'

'I've given her something to make her sleep. She'll be fine as long as she stays where she is for long enough to let the bones knit properly.'

'That's good news.' Raythe studied the healer, noting subtle changes with some unease: she was still recognisably Kemara, but Kemara *perfected*. Indeed, she looked more Aldar than human. 'What happened in that chamber?'

'There's a sentient istariol-spirit up here – the Aldar named him

Dakaji,' Kemara replied. 'He was part of the Kaiju – that's the land-based guardian spirit – but when this floating rock was formed, it broke away and became a separate entity. That happened long before human-kind dwelt here, maybe before we existed, who knows? The Aldar poisoned it with mizra, but when it ... when Dakaji *ate* me' – she couldn't repress her shudder – 'the Kaiju got inside and healed him.'

Raythe whistled softly. 'Did you know that would happen?'

'No,' she admitted. 'I had to adapt.'

A memory struck him and he grinned slyly. 'So what you're saying is that you had no real plan and relied on wits and luck to pull you through?'

She broke into a genuine laugh. 'The fact that you can give my own words back to me shows you do listen.' Then, changing the subject, her face serious again, she said, 'The army down below is Otravian, Lord Vyre. Will they surrender to you, or do we have to kill them?'

'I *really* hope it won't come to that,' Raythe replied. 'But we can't let anyone go home. We have to protect this land. And that reminds me: we'll need to send out search parties to make sure there aren't already deserters trying to head back to the empire.'

Kemara surprised him with a sympathetic look. 'Why don't you let me look after that? I can be at the glacier pass in under an hour, and no one will get past me. Actually, I think I can make the glacier impassable while I'm at it.'

He didn't doubt that she could. Here in the Fenua Tangato, she prob-ably had no meaningful limits at all. 'That would be appreciated,' he replied. 'So, you and Rima . . . not that it's my business.'

'You have a problem?'

He looked surprised. 'Why on earth would I have a problem? I hope you're happy together. It might make you less of a pain in the arse.'

'No chance,' she chuckled. 'So, Lord Vyre, another victory pulled from defeat's jaws.'

'My specialty. But in truth, it's not my victory: *everyone* played a part, up here and down below. We needed every single person – those who fought, those who tended the sick, those who pushed themselves to stay ahead of the pursuit and buy us all time . . .'

'You always said that community was our only strength.'

'Well, the fact that you can give my own words back to me shows you listen, I guess,' he drawled.

Kemara snorted softly, then gave him a piercing look. 'Are you really able to just forget that Otravia is under Bolgravian rule?'

He set his jaw. 'I'll be completely honest with you, if no one else. It will haunt me to my dying day. But sometimes you have to sacrifice your dreams. If that's the price I have to pay for us being here and free, I'll pay it. I can't and won't force Shiazar to fight my battles. And sometimes you just have to accept that not all dreams come true.'

'And the fact that you're drooling over her like a swooning squire is neither here nor there, I presume?'

'Swooning? I think not . . .'

'Well, I suppose you've earned some happiness. Hope you know what to do with it.'

'I'm sure it'll be fleeting,' he sighed. 'You can save the world all you like, but if the day after you fail to sort out some ruckus over Magga Kern's chickens or deal with Relf Turner's latest gripe, your name is mud.'

They both rose, and because it felt natural, they hugged with genuine respect and warmth – and then Kemara pressed a finger to his lips. 'I know what you're like after a fight: try kissing me and I'll punch you.'

Raythe grinned and headed for the door, just as Rima woke. He paused, watching the way her face lit up as she saw Kemara. That look told him everything he needed to know.

Then he slipped away unnoticed, smiling wistfully.

An hour later, he stood on the battlements of Shiro Kamigami, thinking of all the things that had to be done. They had to persuade the soldiers hiding in the lower levels to surrender; and the rest of their division below, too. They had to work out how to control this fortress, and see to the dead and clean up. And somehow, they had to feed everyone and get them back to Rath Argentium . . . Oh, and *then* reorganise this whole society to integrate the Otravians . . .

And then there was Zarelda to check in on, and Onkado. She'd insisted on tending to him herself, and as the look of obsessive adoration on her face hadn't changed in days, he was keeping well out of the way.

'A ruler's work is never done,' Shiazar commented, startling him as she appeared at his side. Her unmasked face was bruised and scabbed, but she smiled fondly. Despite the superficial signs, her sorcery had largely healed her wounds; she was showing no discomfort when she moved.

'I was just thinking that very thought,' he sighed. 'We can never rest.'

'I know,' she said, looking at him impassively. 'I've come to tell you that I no longer require your people to remain here. With Shiro Kamigami now in our command, we can deal with any future invaders, so I no longer fear your people returning to their world. Although they are welcome to stay, of course.'

He swallowed, strangely unsettled by her offer – and its implicit rejection. 'I swore loyalty to you,' he replied. 'My place is here now.'

'But your rival is dead and your wife is free. I am aware you still harbour feelings for her.'

'No,' he said bluntly. 'No feelings at all.'

Shiazar blinked. Was she *maybe* supressing a smile? 'But what of freeing your country?' she asked. 'Was that not always your dream?'

'Otravia is no longer mine. I wish to stay here and serve you, Majesty.'

He would have sworn her face took on a subtle glow – or perhaps that was just what he hoped to see.

'Thank you, Raythe, but I don't want your service.'

'But–'

'Hear me out. Since the Mizra Wars, my people have been ruled by Queens, because we feared male rulers. That fear remains. But perhaps a male and female, ruling as partners, could bridge the gap between past and present, our world and the outside, Aldar and human . . .' Her voice trailed off and she looked at him questioningly.

He stared, trying to read words that could be interpreted a lot of ways.

'My Queen, what are you saying, *exactly*?'

'I am asking you to marry me, Raythe Vyre. Is that not clear?'

Staring into her brilliant eyes, he felt a moment of fright that he might be hallucinating. But the stone beneath his feet felt real, and so did the hand she placed in his, her face upturned and hopeful.

'Yes,' he stammered. 'Yes, of course I will.'

She stepped in and kissed him, not a stolen peck this time, nor a hot devouring, but a soft, deep kiss, open-eyed and staring into each other's souls.

If time stopped right now, Raythe thought, *eternity would be perfect.*

But it didn't, and that was perfect too.

Zarelda had a lump in her throat as she stared through the window at the two figures standing on the wall below: Shiazar, her copper face and black hair burnished by the sun, and her father, dour in his usual grey. They were kissing with that blend of passion and restraint that only two people who were always conscious of being scrutinised could pull off.

Here we go again, she thought, remembering her father's past romantic failures. But this one did feel different: anyone could see that he and Shiazar were alike in temperament and thought. *They suit each other, like silk and leather – and the fact they're from different races and cultures makes them stronger, not weaker*, she decided.

She glanced back at the sleeping Onkado and smiled. *Like father, like daughter.*

She shivered at the memory of the past hour. She'd found Onkado awake and slid in beside him, full of trepidation and need. He was battered but unbroken, and as tender with her as if she'd been made of gossamer. His taste lingered on her lips, his scent on her skin.

She gave her father an unseen wave, then rejoined her husband in bed, to be there when he woke again.

Epilogue

Ceremony

Mater Varahana faced Kuia, the Tangato priestess, and offered the sacred chalice. The old woman accepted and raised it, and the massed people below, dark faces and pale ones intermingled, stared back up at them, excited and grateful, for this ritual signified that the crisis of the invasion was truly over.

The Tangato and Raythe's Magnians were gathered on the plains south of Rath Argentium. Above the city floated Shiro Kamigami, the citadel once again tethered by its four great chains. Watching it move back into position had left everyone awestruck, a demonstration by Kemara of her mastery over the fortress and a silent reminder to the watching Otravian soldiers that whilst Shiazar and Raythe offered reconciliation, there was an iron fist in the silken glove.

Those soldiers weren't far away: they'd been disarmed and were now encamped south of the city. They were gradually coming to terms with their fate; although many were still sullen and resentful, a growing number saw a bright side to their sentence. Permanent exile in a land that was small but bountiful, with no taxes, no press gangs or forced servitude offered a better life than most could ever have aspired to at home.

'Let other men fight imperial wars – it's not *our* empire,' Varahana had heard some of them say.

The ritual of reconciliation and thanksgiving was presided over by the newly wed and crowned King and Queen of the Fenua Tangato, who sat enthroned nearby, draped in silk and splendour.

Raythe, you rogue, Varahana thought fondly, *how is it you always land on your feet?*

She let her eyes drift over the congregation, picking out faces. Kemara, glowing from within, Rima by her side. Zarelda Vyre, hand in hand with Onkado, her husband, both dressed in Tangato silks. Although there was no bulge in Zara's belly yet, it would not be long, she guessed. *An Aldar child*, as if there weren't enough wonders in the world. Jesco Duretto, cradling his fiddle, watched the couples with wistful happiness.

Her imagination conjured absent faces as well: Cal Foaley, Lew Fulter, Sheena Grigg, Norrin Harper and many others. She even missed that snake Elgus Rhamp and his poor son Banno. Then her eyes found Vidar Vidarsson, solid and real as stone, gazing back at her with frank admiration. *Soon*, she thought. *Soon.*

Once the ritual was completed, Varahana and Kuia presented the new joint rulers with goblets of summer ale from Gravis Tavernier's latest batch – the innkeeper had been one of a handful of prisoners found alive, if in very sorry condition, on their return to Rath Argentium.

And finally, formalities ended, food and drink were brought out by the Tangato and the festivities could begin. The air resounded with cheering.

Varahana walked over to the cluster of Magnians, the remainder of their original caravan, and called out, 'The formal ceremonies are over, my friends – but before we celebrate, I have an announcement.'

She paused, feeling a strange sense of dislocation, as if she wasn't really here but dreaming it. During those harrowing months on the road and their time in this impossible, magical place, she'd come to know these people intimately: the Turners and the Borgers, the Griggs and the Fulters, Woodburns and Geldermarks and all the rest. Her little flock: villagers, farmers, tradesmen and hunters – and some of Rhamp's mercenaries, who'd crept into her morning services, even though they'd been forbidden from doing so. In the last days, a couple of the new men,